John Inglesant
A Romance
Vol. II

by
John Henry Shorthouse

John Inglesant
A Romance
Vol. II
by John Henry Shorthouse

Copyright © 2024

All Rights reserved.

No part of this publication may be reproduced, stored in a retrieval system, or transmitted in any form or by any means, electronic, mechanical, photocopying or Otherwise, without the written permission of the publisher.
The author/editor asserts the moral right to be identified as the author/editor of this work.

ISBN: 978-93-62768-79-7

Published by
DOUBLE 9 BOOKS
2/13-B, Ansari Road
Daryaganj, New Delhi – 110002
info@double9books.com
www.double9books.com
Tel. 011-40042856

This book is under public domain

ABOUT THE AUTHOR

Joseph Henry Shorthouse was an English novelist. His debut work, John Inglesant, was praised as a "philosophical romance". It is about a theological intrigue in the English 17th century. Shorthouse was born on September 9, 1834, in Birmingham's Great Charles Street, the eldest of three sons to Joseph Shorthouse (1797-1880) and his wife, Mary Ann, née Hawker. He grew raised on Calthorpe Street in Edgbaston. His father inherited a family chemical factory that manufactured vitriol, and his mother's father established Birmingham's first glasshouse. Both family were Quaker. He received his education both at home and at Grove House School in Tottenham, and went on to become a chemical maker. On August 19, 1857, in the Friends meeting house in Warwick, he married a boyhood friend, Sarah Scott (1832-1909), the eldest daughter of John and Elizabeth Scott. Two significant events occurred. He and his wife joined the Church of England in 1861, and he suffered the first of numerous epileptic seizures in January 1862. Shorthouse later identified as a member of "the new Oxford school of High Churchmen," although he preferred the Anglican church's independence and reason to Roman Catholicism's rule over individual judgment.

CONTENTS

CHAPTER I 7
CHAPTER II 32
CHAPTER III 45
CHAPTER IV 52
CHAPTER V 59
CHAPTER VI 81
CHAPTER VII 93
CHAPTER VIII 107
CHAPTER IX 113
CHAPTER X 122
CHAPTER XI 131
CHAPTER XII 142
CHAPTER XIII 151
CHAPTER XIV 158
CHAPTER XV 169
CHAPTER XVI 180
CHAPTER XVII 187
CHAPTER XVIII 200
CHAPTER XIX 209

CHAPTER I

Inglesant travelled to Marseilles, and by packet boat to Genoa. The beauty of the approach by sea to this city, and the lovely gardens and the country around gave him the greatest delight. The magnificent streets of palaces, mostly of marble, and the thronged public places, the galleries of paintings, and the museums, filled his mind with astonishment; and the entrance into Italy, wonderful as he had expected it to be, surpassed his anticipation. He stayed some time in Genoa, to one or more of the Jesuit fathers in which city he had letters. Under the guidance of these cultivated men he commenced an education in art, such as in these days can be scarcely understood. From his coming into Italy a new life had dawned upon him in the music of that country. Fascinated as he had always been with the Church music at London and Oxford, for several years he had been cut off from all such enjoyment, and, at its best, it was but the prelude to what he heard now. For whole hours he would remain on his knees at mass, lost and wandering in that strange world of infinite variety, the mass music—so various in its phases, yet with a monotone of pathos through it all. The musical parties were also a great pleasure. He played the violin a little in England, and rapidly improved by the excellent tuition he met with here. He became, however, a proficient in what the Italians called the viola d'amore, a treble viol, strung with wire, which attracted him by its soft and sweet tone. Amid a concord of sweet sounds, within hearing of the splash of fountains, and surrounded by the rich colours of an Italian interior, the young Englishman found himself in a new world of delight. As the very soul of music, at one moment merry and the next mad with passion and delightful pain, uttered itself in the long-continued tremor of the violins, it took possession in all its power of Inglesant's spirit. The whole of life is recited upon the plaintive strings, and by their mysterious effect upon the brain fibres, men are brought into sympathy with life in all its forms, from the gay promise of its morning sunrise to the silence of its gloomy night.

From Genoa he went to Sienna, where he stayed some time—the dialect here being held to be very pure, and fit for foreigners to accustom themselves to. He spoke Italian before with sufficient ease, and associating with several of the religious in this city he soon acquired the language perfectly. There can be nothing more delightful than the first few days of life in Italy in the company of polished and congenial men. Inglesant enjoyed life at Sienna very much; the beautiful clean town, all marble and polished brick, the shining walls and pavement softened and shaded by gardens and creeping vines, the piazza and fountains, the cool retired walks with distant prospects, the Duomo, within and without of polished marble inexpressibly beautiful, with its exceeding sweet music and well-tuned organs, the libraries full of objects of the greatest interest, the statues and antiquities everywhere interspersed.

The summer and winter passed over, and he was still in Sienna, and seemed loth to leave. He associated mostly with the ecclesiastics to whom he had brought letters of introduction, for he was more anxious at first to become acquainted with the country and its treasures of art and literature than to make many acquaintances. He kept himself so close and studious that he met with no adventures such as most travellers, especially those who abandon themselves to the dissolute courses of the country, meet with, — courses which were said at that time to be able to make a devil out of a saint. He saw nothing of the religious system but what was excellent and delightful, seeing everything through the medium of his friends. He read all the Italian literature that was considered necessary for a gentleman to be acquainted with; and though the learning of the Fathers was not what it had been a century ago, he still found several to whom he could talk of his favourite Lucretius and of the divine lessons of Plato.

When he had spent some time in this way in Italy, and considered himself fitted to associate with the inhabitants generally, the Benedictines took Inglesant to visit the family of Cardinal Chigi, who was afterwards Pope, and who was a native of Sienna. The cardinal himself was in Rome, but his brother, Don Mario, received Inglesant politely, and introduced him to his son, Don Flavio, and to two of his nephews. With one of these, Don Agostino di Chigi, Inglesant became very intimate, and spent much of his time at his house. In this family he learnt much of the state of parties in Rome, and was advised in what way to comport himself when he should come there. The Cardinal Panzirollo, who with the Cardinal-Patron (Pamphilio), had lately been in great esteem, had just died, having weakened his health by his continued application to business, and the Pope had appointed Cardinal Chigi his successor as first Secretary of State. The Pope's sister-in-law, Donna Olympia Maldachini, was supposed to be banished, but many thought this was only a political retreat, and that she still directed the affairs of the Papacy. At any rate she soon returned to Rome and to power. This extraordinary woman, whose loves and intrigues were enacted on the stage in Protestant countries, was the sister-in-law of the Pope, and was said to live with him in criminal correspondence, and to have charmed him by some secret incantation—the incantation of a strong woman over a weak and criminal man. For a long time she had abused her authority in the most scandalous manner, and exerted her unbounded ascendency over the Pope to gratify her avarice and ambition, which were as unbounded as her power. She disposed of all benefices, which she kept vacant till she was fully informed of their value; she exacted a third of the entire value of all offices, receiving twelve years' value for an office for life. She gave audience upon public affairs, enacted new laws, abrogated those of former Popes, and sat in council with the Pope with bundles of memorials in her hands. Severe satires were daily pasted on the statue of Pasquin at Rome; yet it seemed so incredible that Cardinal Panzirollo, backed though he was by the Cardinal-Nephew, should be able to overthrow the power of this woman by a representation he was said to have made to the Pope, that when Innocent at length, with great reluctance banished Olympia, most persons supposed it was only a temporary piece of policy.

The Chigi were at this time living in Sienna, in great simplicity, at their house in the Strada Romana, and in one or two small villas in the neighbourhood; but they were of an ancient and noble family of this place, and were held in great esteem, and were all of them men of refinement and carefully educated. They had made considerable figure in Rome during the Pontificate of Julius II.; but afterwards meeting with misfortunes, were obliged to return to Sienna, where they had continued to reside ever since. At this time there was no idea that the Cardinal of this house would be the next Pope, and though well acquainted with the politics of Rome, the family occupied themselves mostly with other and more innocent amusements—in the arrangement of their gardens and estates, in the duties of hospitality, and in artistic, literary, and antiquarian pursuits. The University and College of Sienna had produced many excellent scholars and several Popes, and the city itself was full of remains of antique art, and was adorned with many modern works of great beauty—the productions of that school which takes its name from the town. Among such scenes as these, and with such companions, Inglesant's time passed so pleasantly that he was in no hurry to go on to Rome.

The country about the city was celebrated for hunting, and the wild boar and the stag afforded excellent and exciting, if sometimes dangerous sport. Amid the beautiful valleys, rich with vineyards, and overlooked by rocky hills and castled summits, were scenes fitted both for pleasure and sport; and the hunting gave place, often and in a moment, to *al fresco* banquets, and conversations and pleasant dalliance with the ladies, by the cool shade near some fountain, or under some over-arching rock. Under the influence of these occupations, so various and so attractive both to the mind and body, and thanks to so many novel objects and continual change of scene, Inglesant's health rapidly improved, and his mind recovered much of the calm and cheerfulness which were natural to it. He thought little of the Italian, and the terrible thoughts with which he had connected him were for the time almost forgotten, though, from time to time, when any accident recalled the circumstances to his recollection, they returned upon his spirits with a melancholy effect.

The first time that these gloomy thoughts overpowered him since his arrival at Sienna was on the following occasion. He had been hunting with a party of friends in the valley of Montalcino one day in early autumn. The weather previously had been wet, and the rising sun had drawn upward masses of white vapour, which wreathed the green foliage and the vine slopes, where the vintage was going on, and concealed from sight the hills on every side. A pale golden light pervaded every place, and gave mystery and beauty to the meanest cottages and farm-sheds. The party, having missed the stag, stopped at a small osteria at the foot of a sloping hill, and Inglesant and another gentleman wandered up into the vineyard that sloped upwards behind the house. As they went up, the vines became gradually visible out of the silvery mist, and figures of peasant men and women moved about—vague and half-hidden until they were close to them; pigeons and doves flew in and out. Inglesant's friend stopped to speak to some of the peasant girls; but Inglesant himself, tempted by the pleasing mystery that the mountain slope—apparently full of hidden and beautiful life—presented, wandered on, gradually climbing higher and higher, till he had left the vintage far below him, and heard no sound but that of the grasshoppers among the grass and the olive trees, and the distant laugh of the villagers, or now and then the music of a hunting horn, which one of the party below was blowing for his own amusement. The mist was now so thick that he could see nothing, and it was by chance that he even kept the ascending path. The hill was rocky here and there, but for the most part was covered with short grass, cropped by the goats which Inglesant startled as he came unexpectedly upon them in the mist. Suddenly, after some quarter of an hour's climbing, he came out of the mist in a moment, and stood under a perfectly clear sky upon the summit of the hill. The blue vault stretched above him without a cloud, all alight with the morning sun; at his feet the grassy hill-top sparkling in dew, not yet dried up, and vocal with grasshoppers, not yet silenced by the heat. Nothing could be seen but wreaths of cloud. The hill-top rose like an island out of a sea of vapour, seething and rolling round in misty waves, and lighted with prismatic colours of every hue. Out of this sea, here and there, other hill-tops, on which goats were browsing, lay beneath the serene heaven; and rocky points and summits, far higher than these, reflected back the sun. He would have seemed to stand above all human conversation and walks of men, if every now and then some break in the mist had not taken place, opening glimpses of landscapes and villages far below; and also the sound of bells, and the music of the horn, came up fitfully through the mist. Why, he did not know, but as he gazed on this, the most wonderful and beautiful sight he had ever seen, the recollection of Serenus de Cressy returned upon his mind with intense vividness; and the contrast between the life he was leading in Italy, amid every delight of mind and sense, and the life the Benedictine had offered him in vain, smote upon his conscience with terrible force. Upon the lonely mountain top, beneath the serene silence, he threw himself upon the turf, and, overwhelmed with a sudden passion, repented that he had been born. Amid the extraordinary loveliness, the most gloomy thoughts took possession of him, and the fiend seemed to stand upon the smiling mount and claim him for himself. So palpably did the consciousness of his choice, worldly as he thought it, cause the presence of evil to appear, that in that heavenly solitude he looked round for the murderer of his brother. The moment appeared to him, for the instant, to be the one appointed for the consummation of his guilt. The horn below sounding the recall drew his mind out of this terrible reverie, and he came down the hill (from which the mist was gradually clearing) as in a dream. He rejoined his company, who remarked the wild expression of his face.

His old disease, in fact, never entirely left him; he walked often as in a dream, and when the fit was upon him could never discern the real and the unreal. He knew that terrible feeling when the world and all its objects are slipping away, when the brain reels, and seems only to be kept fixed and steady by a violent exertion of the will; and the mind is confused and perplexed with thoughts which it cannot grasp, and is full of fancies of vague duties and acts which it cannot perform, though it is convinced that they are all important to be done.

The Chigi family knew of Inglesant's past life, and of his acquaintance with the Archbishop of Fermo, the Pope's Nuncio, and they advised him to make the acquaintance of his brother, the Cardinal Rinuccini, before going to Rome.

"If you go to Rome in his train, or have him for a patron on your arrival, you will start in a much better position than if you enter the city an entire stranger,—and the present is not a very favourable time for going to Rome. The Pope is not expected to live very long. Donna Olympia and the Pamphili, or pretended Pamphili (for the Cardinal-Nephew is not a Pamphili at all), are securing what they can, using every moment to enrich themselves while they have the power. The moment the Pope dies they fall, and with them all who have been connected with them. It is therefore useless to go to Rome at present, except as a private person to see the city, and this you can do better in the suite of the Cardinal than in any other way. You may wonder that we do not offer to introduce you to our uncle the Cardinal Chigi; but we had rather that you should come to Rome at first under the patronage of another. You will understand more of our reasons before long; meanwhile, we will write to our uncle respecting you, and you may be sure that he will promote your interests as much as is in his power."

The Cardinal Rinuccini was at that time believed to be at his own villa, situated in a village some distance from Florence to the north, and Don Agostino offered to accompany Inglesant so far on his journey.

This ride, though a short one, was very pleasant, and endeared the two men to each other more than ever. They travelled simply, with a very small train, and did not hurry themselves on the route. Indeed, they travelled so leisurely that they were very nearly being too late for their purpose. On their arrival at the last stage before reaching Florence, they stopped for the night at a small osteria, and had no sooner taken up their quarters than a large train arrived at the inn, and on their inquiry they were informed it was the Cardinal Rinuccini himself on his way to Rome. They immediately sent their names to his Eminence, saying they had been coming to pay their respects to him, and offering to resign their apartment, which was the best in the house. The Cardinal, who travelled in great state, with his four-post bed and furniture of all kinds with him, returned a message that he could not disturb them in their room; that he remembered Mr. Inglesant's name in some letters from his brother; and that he should be honoured by their company to supper.

The best that the village could afford was placed on the Cardinal's table, and their host entertained the two young men with great courtesy.

He was descended from a noble family in Florence, which boasted among its members Octavio Rinuccini the poet, who came to Paris in the suite of Marie de Medicis, and is said by some to have been the inventor of the Opera. Besides the Pope's Legate another brother of the Cardinal's, Thomas Battista Rinuccini, was Great Chamberlain to the Grand Duke of Tuscany. All the brothers had been carefully educated, and were men of literary tastes; but while the Archbishop had devoted himself mostly to politics, the Cardinal had confined himself almost entirely to literary pursuits. He owed his Cardinal's hat to the Grand Duke, who was extremely partial to him, and promoted his interests in every way. He was a man of profound learning, and an enthusiastic admirer of antiquity, but was also an acute logician and theologian, and perfectly well-read in Church history, and in the controversy of the century, both in theology and philosophy. Before the end of supper Inglesant found that he was acquainted with the writings of Hobbes, whom he had met in Italy, and of whom he inquired with interest, as soon as he found Inglesant had been acquainted with him.

The following morning the Cardinal expressed his sorrow that the business which took him to Rome was of so important a nature that it obliged him to proceed without delay. He approved of the advice that Inglesant had already received, and recommended him to proceed to Florence with Don Agostino, as he was so near; so that he might not have his journey for nothing, and might see the city under very favourable circumstances. Inglesant was the more ready to agree to this as he wished to see as much of Italy as he could, unshackled by the company of the great, which, in the uncertain state of health both of his body and mind, was inexpressibly burdensome to him. He had already seen in this last journey a great deal of the distress and bad government which prevailed everywhere; and he wished to make himself acquainted, in some measure, with the causes of this distress before going to Rome. As he rode through the beautiful plains he had been astonished at the few inhabitants, and at the wretchedness of the few. Italy had suffered greatly in her commerce by the introduction of Indian silks into Europe. Some of her most flourishing cities had been depopulated, their nobles ruined; and long streets of neglected palaces, deserted and left in magnificent decay, presented a melancholy though romantic spectacle. But bad government, and the oppression and waste caused by the accumulated wealth and idleness of the innumerable religious orders, had more to do in ruining the prosperity of the country than any commercial changes; and proofs of this fact met the traveller's eye on every hand.

It seemed to Inglesant that it was very necessary that he should satisfy himself upon some of these points before becoming involved in any political action in the country; and he shrank from entering Rome at present, and from attaching himself to any great man or any party. In a country where the least false step is fatal, and may plunge a man in irretrievable ruin, or consign him to the dungeons of the Holy Office, it is certainly prudent in a stranger to be wary of his first steps. Having communicated these resolutions to his friend, the two young men, on their arrival at Florence, took lodgings privately in the Piazza del Spirito Santo; and occupied their time for some days in viewing the city, and visiting the churches and museums, as though they had been simply travellers from curiosity.

Inglesant believed the Italian to be in Rome, which was a further reason for delaying his journey there. He believed that he was going to engage in some terrible conflict, and he wished to prepare himself by an acquaintance with every form of life in this strange country. The singular scenes that strike a stranger in Italy—the religious processions, the character and habits of the poorer classes, their ideas of moral obligation, their ecclesiastical and legal government—all appeared to him of importance to his future fate.

As he was perfectly unacquainted with the person of his enemy, there was a sort of vague expectation—not to say dread—always present to his mind; for, though he fancied that it would be in Rome that he should find the Italian, yet it was not at all impossible that at any moment—it might be in Florence, or in the open country—he might be the object of a murderous attack. His person was doubtless known to the murderer of his brother, and he thus walked everywhere in the full light, while his enemy was hidden in the dark.

These ideas were seldom absent from his mind, and the image of the murderer was almost constantly before his eyes. Often, as some marked figure crossed his path, he started and watched the retreating form, wondering whether the object of his morbid dread was before him. Often, as the uncovered corpse was borne along the streets, the thought struck him that perhaps his fear and his search were alike needless, and that before him on the bier, harmless and strewn with flowers, lay his terrible foe. These thoughts naturally prevented his engaging unrestrainedly in the pursuits of his age and rank, and he often let Don Agostino go alone into the gay society which was open to them in Florence.

In pursuit of his intention Inglesant took every opportunity, without incurring remark, of associating with the lower orders, and learning their habits, traditions, and tone of thought. He chose streets which led through the poorer parts of the town in passing from one part to another, and in this way, and in the course of his visits to different churches and religious houses, he was able to converse with the common people without attracting attention. In excursions into the country, whether on parties of pleasure or for sport, he was also able to throw himself in the same way among the peasantry. Under the pretence of shooting quails he passed several days in more than one country village, and had become acquainted with several of the curés, from whom he gained much information respecting the habits of the people, and of their ideas of crime and of lawful revenge.

One of these curés—a man of penetration and intellect—strongly advised him to see Venice before he went to Rome.

"Venice," he said to him, "is the sink of all wickedness, and as such it is desirable that you should see the people there, and mix with them; besides, as such, it is not at all unlikely that the man you seek may be found there."

"What is the cause of this wickedness?" asked Inglesant.

"There are several causes," replied the priest. "One is that the Holy Office there is under the control of the State, and is therefore almost powerless. Wickedness and license of all kinds are therefore unrestrained."

Inglesant mentioned this advice to Don Agostino, and his desire to proceed to Venice; but as the other was unwilling to leave Florence till the termination of the Carnival, which was now approaching, he was obliged to postpone his intention for some weeks.

On one of the opening days of the Carnival, Inglesant had accompanied Don Agostino to a magnificent supper given by the Grand Duke at his villa and gardens at the Poggia Imperiale, some distance outside the Romana gate.

Inglesant had succeeded in throwing off for a time his gloomy thoughts, and had taken his share in the gaiety of the festival; but the effort and the excitement had produced a reaction, and towards morning he had succeeded in detaching himself from the company, many of whom—the banquet being over—were strolling in the lovely gardens in the cool air which preceded the dawn, and he returned alone to the city. As this was his frequent custom, his absence did not surprise Don Agostino, who scarcely noticed his friend's eccentricities.

When Inglesant reached Florence, the sun had scarcely risen, and in the miraculously clear and solemn light the countless pinnacles and marble fronts of the wonderful city rose with sharp colour and outline into the sky. It lay with the country round it studded with the lines of cypress and encompassed by the massy hills—silent as the grave, and lovely as paradise; and ever and anon, as it lay in the morning light, a breeze from the mountains passed over it, rustling against the marble façades and through the belfries of its towers, like the whisper of a God. Now and again, clear and sharp in the liquid air, the musical bells of the Campanili rang out the time. The cool expanse of the gardens, the country walk, the pure air, and the silent city, seemed to him to chide and reprove the license and gaiety of the night. Excited by the events of the Carnival, his mind and imagination were in that state in which, from the inward fancy, phantoms are projected upon the real stage of life, and, playing their fantastic parts, react upon the excited sense, producing conduct which in turn is real in its result.

As Inglesant entered the city and turned into one of the narrow streets leading up from the Arno, the market people were already entering by the gates, and thronging up with their wares to the Piazze and the markets. Carpenters were already at work on the scaffolds and other preparations for the concluding festivals of the Carnival; but all these people, and all their actions, and even the sounds that they produced, wore that unreal and unsubstantial aspect which the very early morning light casts upon everything.

As Inglesant ascended the narrow street, between the white stone houses which set off the brilliant blue above, several porters and countrywomen, carrying huge baskets and heaps of country produce, ascended with him, or passed him as he loitered along, and other more idle and equivocal persons, who were just awake, looked out upon him from doorways and corners as he passed. He had on a gala dress of silk, somewhat disordered by the night and by his walk, and must have appeared a suitable object for the lawless attempts of the ladroni of a great city; but his appearance was probably not sufficiently helpless to encourage attack.

Half-way up the street, at the corner of a house, stood an image of the Virgin, round which the villagers stopped for a moment, as much to rest as to pay their devotions. As Inglesant stopped also, he noticed an old man of a wretched and abject demeanour, leaning against the wall of the house as though scarcely able to stand, and looking eagerly at some of the provisions which were carried past him. True to his custom, Inglesant—when he had given him some small coin as an alms—began to speak to him.

"You have carried many such loads as these, father, I doubt not, in your time, though it must be a light one now."

"I am past carrying even myself," said the other, in a weak and whining voice; "but I have not carried loads all my life. I have kept a shop on the Goldsmith's Bridge, and have lived at my ease. Now I have nothing left me but the sun—the sun and the cool shade."

"Yours is a hard fate."

"It is a hard and miserable world, and yet I love it. It has done me nothing but evil, and yet I watch it and seek out what it does, and listen to what goes on, just as if I thought to hear of any good fortune likely to come to me. Foolish old man that I am! What is it to me what people say or do, or who dies, or who is married? and why should I come out here to see the market people pass, and climb this street to hear of the murder that was done here last night, and look at the body that lies in the room above?"

"What murder?" said Inglesant. "Who was murdered, and by whom?"

"He is a foreigner; they say an Inglese—a traveller here merely. Who murdered him I know not, though they do say that too."

"Where is the body?" said Inglesant. "Let us go up." And he gave the old man another small coin.

The old man looked at him for a moment with a peculiar expression.

"Better not, Signore," he said; "better go home."

"Do not fear for me," said Inglesant; "I bear a charmed life; no steel can touch me, nor any bullet hurt me, till my hour comes; and my hour is not yet."

The old man led the way to an open door, carved with tracery and foliaged work, and they ascended a flight of stairs. It was one of those houses, so common in Italian towns, whose plain and massive exterior, pierced with few and narrow windows, gives no idea of the size and splendour of the rooms within. When they reached the top of the stairs, Inglesant saw that the house had once, and probably not long before, been the residence of some person of wealth. They passed through several rooms with carved chimney-pieces and cornices, and here and there even some massive piece of furniture still remained. From the windows that opened on the inner side Inglesant could see the tall cypresses of a garden, and hear the splash of fountains. But the house had fallen from its high estate, and was now evidently used for the vilest purposes. After passing two or three rooms, they reached an upper hall or dining-room of considerable length, and painted in fresco apparently of some merit. A row of windows on the left opened on the garden, from which the sound of voices and laughter came up.

The room was bare of furniture, except towards the upper end, where was a small and shattered table, upon which the body of the murdered man was laid. Inglesant went up and stood by its side.

There was no doubt whose countryman he had been. The fair English boy, scarcely bordering upon manhood—the heir, probably, of bright hopes—travelling with a careless or incompetent tutor, lay upon the small table, his long hair glistening in the sunlight, his face peaceful and smiling as in sleep. The fatal rapier thrust, marked by the stain upon the clothes, was the sole sign that his mother—waking up probably at that moment in distant England, with his image in her heart—was bereaved for ever of her boy. Inglesant stood silent a few moments, looking sadly down; that other terrible figure, upon the white hearthstone, was so constantly in his mind, that this one, so like it, scarcely could be said to recall the image of his murdered brother; but the whole scene certainly strengthened his morbid fancy, and it seemed to him that he was on the footsteps of the murderer, and that his fate was drawing near.

"His steps are still in blood," he said aloud; "and it is warm; he cannot be far off."

He turned, as he spoke, to look for the old man, but he was gone, and in his place a ghastly figure met Inglesant's glance.

Standing about three feet from the table, a little behind Inglesant, and also looking fixedly at the murdered boy, was the figure of a corpse. The face was thin and fearfully white, and the whole figure was wrapped and swathed in grave-clothes, somewhat disordered and loosened, so as to give play to the limbs. This form took no notice of the other's presence, but continued to gaze at the body with its pallid ghastly face.

Inglesant scarcely started. Nothing could seem more strange and unreal to him than what was passing on every side. That the dead should return and stand by him seemed to him not more fearful and unreal than all the rest.

Suddenly the corpse turned its eyes upon Inglesant, and regarded him with a fixed and piercing glance.

"You spoke of the author of this deed as though you knew him," it said.

"I am on the track of a murderer, and my fate is urging me on. It seems to me that I see his bloody steps."

"This was no murder," said the corpse, in an irritated and impatient voice. "It was a chance melée, and an unfortunate and unhappy thrust; we do not even know the name of the man who lies there. Are you the avenger of blood, that you see murder at every step?"

"I am in truth the avenger of blood," said Inglesant in a low and melancholy voice; "would I were not."

The corpse continued to look at Inglesant fixedly, and would have spoken, but the voices which had been heard in the garden now seemed to come nearer, and hurried steps approached the room. The laughter that Inglesant had heard was stilled, and deep and solemn voices strove together, and one above the rest said, "Bring up the murderer."

The corpse turned round impatiently, and the next moment from a small door, which opened on a covered balcony and outside staircase to the garden, there came hurriedly in a troop of the most strange and fantastic figures that the eye could rest upon. Angels and demons, and savage men in lions' skins, and men with the heads of beasts and birds, swarmed tumultuously in, dragging with them an unfortunate being in his night-clothes, and apparently just out of bed, whom they urged on with blows. This man, who was only half-awake, was evidently in the extremity of terror, and looked upon himself as already in the place of eternal torment. He addressed now one and now another of his tormentors, as well as he could find breath, in the most abject terms, endeavouring, in the most ludicrous manner, to choose the titles and epithets to address them most in accordance with the individual appearance that the spectre he entreated wore to his dazzled eyes—whether a demon or an angel, a savage or a manbeast. When he saw the murdered man, and the terrible figure that stood by Inglesant, he nearly fainted with terror; but, on many voices demanding loudly that he should be brought in contact with the body of his victim, he recovered a little, and recognizing in Inglesant, at least, a being of an earthly sphere, and by his dress a man of rank, he burst from his tormentors, and throwing himself at his feet, he entreated his protection, assuring him that he had been guilty of no murder, having just been dragged from a sound sleep, and being even ignorant that a murder had been committed.

Inglesant took little notice of him, but the corpse interposed between the man and the fantastic crew. It was still apparently in a very bad humour, especially with Inglesant, and said imperiously,—"We have enough and too much of this foolery. Have not some of you done enough mischief for one night? This gentleman says he is on the track of a murderer, and will have it that he sees his traces in this unfortunate affair."

At these words the masquers crowded round Inglesant with wild and threatening gestures, apparently half earnest and half the result of wine, and as many of them were armed with great clubs, the consequences might have seemed doubtful to one whose feelings were less excited than Inglesant's were.

He, however, as though the proceeding were a matter of course, merely took off his hat, and addressed the others in explanation.

"I am indeed in pursuit of a murderer, the murderer of my brother—a gallant and noble gentleman who was slain foully in cold blood. The murderer was an Italian, his name Malvolti. Do any of you, signori, happen to have heard of such a man?"

There was a pause after this singular address, but the next moment a demon of terrific aspect forced his way to the front, saying in a tone of drunken consequence,—

"I knew him formerly at Lucca; he was well born and my friend."

"He was, and is, a scelerat and a coward," said Inglesant fiercely. "It would be well to be more careful of your company, sir."

"Have I not said he was my friend, sir?" cried the demon, furious with passion. "Who will lend me a rapier?"

A silent and melancholy person, with the head of an owl, who had several under his arm, immediately tendered him one with a low bow, and the masquers fell back in a circle, while the demon, drawing his weapon, threw himself into an attitude and attacked Inglesant, who, after looking at him for a moment, also drew his rapier and stood upon his guard. It soon appeared that the demon was a very moderate fencer; in less than a minute his guard was entered by Inglesant's irresistible tierce, and he would have been infallibly run through the body had he not saved himself by rolling ignominiously on the ground.

This incident appeared to restore the corpse to good humour; it laughed, and turning to the masquers said,—

"Gentlemen, let me beg of you to disperse as quickly as possible before the day is any farther advanced. You know of the rendezvous at one o'clock. I will see the authorities as to this unhappy affair. Sir," he continued, turning to Inglesant, "you are, I believe, the friend of Don Agostino di Chigi, whom he has been introducing into Florentine society; if it will amuse you to see a frolic of the Carnival carried out, of which this is only the somewhat unfortunate rehearsal, and will meet me this afternoon at two o'clock, at the Great Church in the Via Larga, I shall be happy to do my best to entertain you; a simple domino will suffice. I am the Count Capece."

Inglesant gave his name in return. He apologized for not accepting the Count's courtesy, on the plea of ill-health, but assured him he would take advantage of his offer to cultivate his acquaintance. They left the house together, the Count covering himself with a cloak, and Inglesant accompanied him to the office of police, from whence he went to his lodging and to his bed.

He arose early in the afternoon, and remembering the invitation he had received, he went out into the Via Larga. The streets formed a strange contrast to the stillness and calm of the cool morning. The afternoon was hot, and the city crowded with people of every class and rank. The balconies and windows of the principal streets were full of ladies and children; trophies and embroideries hung from the houses and crossed the street. Strings of carriages and country carts, dressed with flowers and branches of trees, paraded the streets. Every variety of fantastic and grotesque costume, and every shade of colour, filled and confused the eye. Music, laughter, and loud talking filled the ear. Inglesant, from his simple costume and grave demeanour, became the butt of several noisy parties; but used as he was to great crowds, and to the confused revelries of Courts, he was able to disentangle himself with mutual good-humour. He recognized his friends of the morning, who were performing a kind of comedy on a country cart, arched with boughs, in imitation of the oldest form of the itinerant theatre. He was recognized by them also, for, in a pause of the performance, as he was moving down a bye-street, he was accosted by one of the company, enveloped in a large cloak. He had no difficulty in recognizing beneath this concealment his antagonist of the morning, who still supported his character of demon.

"I offer you my apologies for the occurrences of this morning, signore," he said, "having been informed by my friends more closely concerning them than I can myself recollect. I am also deeply interested in the person of whom you spoke, who formerly was a friend of mine; and I must also have been acquainted with the signore, your brother, of which I am the more certain as your appearance every moment recalls him more and more to my mind. I should esteem it a great favour to be allowed to speak at large with you on these matters. If you will allow me to pay my respects at your lodgings, I will conduct you to my father's house, il Conte Pericon di Visalvo, where I can show you many things which may be of interest to you respecting the man whom I understand you seek."

Inglesant replied that he should gladly avail himself of his society, and offered to come to the Count's house early the next day.

He found the house, a sombre plain one, in a quiet street, with a tall front pierced with few windows. At the low door hung a wine-flask, as a sign that wine was sold within; for the sale of wine by retail was confined to the gentry, the common people being only allowed to sell wholesale. The Count was the fortunate possessor of a very fine vineyard, which made his wine much in request, and Inglesant found the whole ground-floor of his house devoted to this retail traffic. Having inquired for the Count, he was led up the staircase into a vestibule, and from thence into the Count's own room. This was a large apartment with windows looking on to the court, with a suite of rooms opening beyond it. It was handsomely furnished, with several cages full of singing birds in the windows. Outside, the walls of the houses forming the courtyard were covered with vines and creeping jessamine and other plants, and a fountain splashed in the centre of the court, which was covered with a coloured awning.

The old Count received Inglesant politely. He was a tall, spare old man, with a reserved and dignified manner, more like that of a Spaniard than of an Italian. Rather to Inglesant's surprise he introduced him to his daughter, on whom, as she sat near one of the windows, Inglesant's eyes had been fixed from the moment he had entered the room. The Italians were so careful of the ladies of their families, and it was so unusual to allow strangers to see them, that his surprise was not unnatural, especially as the young lady before him was remarkably beautiful. She was apparently very young, tall and dark-eyed, with a haughty and indifferent manner, which concentrated itself entirely upon her father.

The Count noticed Inglesant's surprise at the cordiality of his reception, and seemed to speak as if in explanation.

"You are no stranger to us, signore," he said; "my son has not only commended you to me, but your intimacy with Count Agostino has endeared you already to us who admire and love him."

As Agostino had told him the evening before that he knew little of these people, though he believed the old Count to be respectable, this rather increased Inglesant's surprise; but he merely said that he was fortunate in possessing a friend whose favour procured him such advantages.

"My son's affairs," continued the old man, "unavoidably took him abroad this morning, but I wait his return every moment."

Inglesant suspected that the Cavaliere, who appeared to him to be a complete debauchée, had not been at home at all that night; but if that were the case, when he entered the room a few moments afterwards, his manner was completely self-possessed and quiet, and showed no signs of a night of revelry.

As soon as they were seated the Cavaliere began to explain to Inglesant that both his father and himself were anxious to see him, to confer respecting the unfortunate circumstances which, as they imagined, had brought him to Italy upon a mission which they assured him was madly imprudent.

"Our nation, signore," said the Cavaliere, "is notorious for two passions—jealousy and revenge. Both of these, combined with self-interest, induced Malvolti to commit the foul deed which he perpetrated upon your brother. While in Italy your brother crossed him in some of his amours, and also resented some indiscretions, which the manners of our nation regard with tolerance, but which your discreeter countrymen resent with unappeasable disgust. Our people never forgive injuries; nay, they entail them on their posterity. We ourselves left our native city, Lucca, on account of one of these feuds, which made it unsafe for us to remain; and I could show you a gentleman's house in Lucca whose master has never set foot out of doors for nine years, nay, scarcely looked out of window, for fear of being shot by an antagonist who has several times planted ambushes to take away his life. It is considered a disgrace to a family that one of its members has forgiven an injury; and a mother will keep the bloody clothes of her murdered husband, to incite her young sons to acts of vengeance. You will see, signore, the evil which such ideas as these winds about our lives; and how unwise it must be in a stranger to involve himself needlessly in such an intrigue, in a foreign country, unknown and comparatively without friends. Italy swarms with bravos hired to do the work of vengeance; merchants are assaulted in their warehouses in open day; in the public streets the highest personages in the land are not safe. What will be the fate then of a stranger whose death is necessary to the safety of an Italian?"

"I understand you, signore," said Inglesant, "and I thank you for your good-will, but you are somewhat mistaken. I am not seeking the man of whom we speak, though, I confess, I came to Italy partly with the expectation of meeting him, when it is the will of God, or the will of the Devil whom He permits to influence the affairs of men, that this man and I should meet. I shall not attempt to avoid the interview; it would be useless if I did. The result of that meeting who can tell! But as I said yesterday to the Count Capece, till my hour comes I bear a charmed life that cannot be taken, and any result I regard with supreme indifference, if so be I may, by any means, escape in the end the snares of the Devil, who seeks to take me captive at his will."

The two gentlemen regarded Inglesant with profound astonishment as he uttered these words; and the young lady in the window raised her eyes towards him as he was speaking (he spoke very pure Italian) with some appearance of interest.

After a pause Inglesant went on, "I also venture to think, signore," he said, "that you are unaware of the position of this man, and of the condition to which his crimes have brought him. I am well informed from sure sources that he is without friends, and that his crimes have raised him more enemies in this country even than elsewhere; so that he is afraid to appear openly, lest he fall a victim to his own countrymen. He is also in abject poverty, and is therefore to a great extent powerless to do evil."

The Cavaliere smiled. "You do not altogether know this country, signore," he said; "there are always so many different factions and interests at work that a daring useful man is never without patrons, who will support and further his private interests in return for the service he may render them; and (though you may not be fully aware of it) it is because it is notorious that you are yourself supported and protected by a most powerful and widely spread faction, that your position in this country is as assured and safe as it is."

His words certainly struck Inglesant. The idea that he was already a known and marked man in this wonderful country, and playing an acknowledged part in its fantastic drama, was new to him, and he remained silent.

"From all ordinary antagonists," continued the Cavaliere, "this knowledge is sufficient to secure you; no man would wish, unless ruined and desperate, to draw on his head the swift and certain punishment which a hand raised against your life would be sure to invoke. But a reckless despairing man stops at nothing; and should you, by your presence even, endanger this man's standing in the favour of some new-found patron, or impede the success of some freshly planned scheme—perhaps the last hope of his ruined life—I would not buy your safety at an hour's rate."

While the Cavaliere was speaking it was evident that his sister was listening with great attention. The interest that she manifested, and the singular attraction that Inglesant felt towards her, so occupied his thoughts that he could scarcely attend to what the other was saying, though he continued speaking for some time. It is possible that the Cavaliere noticed this, for Inglesant was suddenly conscious that he was regarding him fixedly and with a peculiar expression. He apologized for his inattention on the ground of ill-health, and soon after took his leave, having invited the Cavaliere to visit him at his lodgings.

As Inglesant walked back through the streets of the city, he was perplexed at his own sensations, which appeared so different from any he had previously known. The attraction he experienced towards the lady he had just seen was quite different from the affection he had felt for Mary Collet. That was a sentiment which commended itself to his reason and his highest feelings. In her company he felt himself soothed, elevated above himself, safe from danger and from temptation. In this latter attraction he was conscious of a half-formed fear, of a sense of glamour and peril, and of an alluring force independent of his own free-will. The opinion he had formed of her brother's character may have had something to do with these feelings, and the sense of perpetual danger and insecurity with which he walked this land of mystery and intrigue no doubt increased it. He half resolved not to visit the old nobleman again; but even while forming the resolution he knew that he should break it.

The circumstances in which he was placed, indeed, almost precluded such a course. The very remarkable beauty of the young lady, and the extraordinary unreserve with which he had been introduced to her—unreserve so unusual in Italy—while it might increase the misgiving he felt, made it very difficult for him to decline the acquaintance. The girl's beauty was of a kind unusual in Italy, though not unknown there, her hair being of a light brown, contrasting with her magnificent eyes, which were of the true Italian splendour and brilliancy. She had doubtless been kept in the strictest seclusion, and Inglesant could only wonder what could have induced the old Count to depart from his usual caution.

The next day, being Ash Wednesday, Inglesant was present at the Duomo at the ceremony of the day, when the vast congregation received the emblematic ashes upon their foreheads. The Cavaliere was also present with his sister, whose name Inglesant discovered to be Lauretta. Don Agostino, to whom Inglesant had related the adventure, and the acquaintance to which it had led, was inclined to suspect these people of some evil purpose, and made what inquiries he could concerning them; but he could discover nothing to their discredit, further than that the Cavaliere was a well-known debauchée, and that he had been involved in some intrigue, in connection with some of the present Papal family, which had not proved successful. He was in consequence then in disgrace with Donna Olympia and her faction,—a disappointment which it was said had rendered his fortunes very desperate, as he was very deeply involved in debts of all kinds. Don Agostino, the Carnival being over, was desirous of returning to Sienna, unless Inglesant made up his mind to go at once to Venice, in which case he offered to accompany him. His friend, however, did not appear at all desirous of quitting Florence, at any rate hastily, and Don Agostino left him and returned home, the two friends agreeing to meet again before proceeding to Venice.

His companion gone, Inglesant employed himself in frequenting all those churches to which Lauretta was in the habit of resorting during the Holy Season; and as every facility appeared to be given him by her friends, he became very intimate with her, and she on her part testified no disinclination to his society. It will probably occur to the reader that this conduct was not consistent with the cautious demeanour which Inglesant had resolved upon; but such resolutions have before now proved ineffectual under similar circumstances, and doubtless the like will occur again. Lauretta looked round as a matter of course, as she came out of the particular church she had that day chosen, for the handsome cavalier who was certain to be ready to offer the drop of holy water; and more than one rival whom the beautiful devotee had attracted to the service, noticed with envy the kindly look of the masked eyes which acknowledged the courtesy; and, indeed, it is not often that ladies' eyes have rested upon a lover more attractive to a girl of a refined nature than did Lauretta's, when, in the dawn of the March mornings, she saw John Inglesant waiting for her on the marble steps. It is true that she thought the Cavaliere Inglese somewhat melancholy and sad, but her own disposition was reserved and pensive; and in her presence Inglesant's melancholy was so far charmed away that it became only an added grace of sweetness of manner, and of tender deference and protection. The servant of the polished King of England, the companion of Falkland and of Caernarvon, the French Princess's favourite page, trained in every art that makes life attractive, that makes life itself the finest art, with a memory and intellect stored with the poetry and learning of the antique world,—it would have been strange if, where once his fancy was touched, Inglesant had not made a finished and attractive lover.

The familiar streets of Florence, the bridges, or the walks by the Arno, assumed a new charm to the young girl, when she saw them in company with her pleasant and courteous friend; and whether in the early morning it was a few spring flowers that he brought her, or a brilliant jewel that he placed upon her finger as he parted in the soft Italian night, it was the giver, and the grace with which the gift was made, that won the romantic fancy of the daughter of the south. Their talk was not of the kind that lovers often use. He would indeed begin with relating stories of the English Court, in the bright fleeting days before the war, of the courtly refined revels, of the stately dances and plays, and of the boating parties on the wooded Thames; but most often the narrative changed its tone instinctively, and went on to speak of sadder and higher things; of self-denial and devotion of ladies and children, who suffered for their King without complaint; of the Ferrars and their holy life; of the martyred Archbishop and of the King's death; and sometimes perhaps of some sight of battle and suffering the narrator himself had seen, as when the evening sun was shining upon the glassy slope of Newbury, and he knelt beside the dying Caernarvon, unmindful of the bullets that fell around.

"You have deserved well of the King," he whispered: "have you no request that I may make to him, nothing for your children, or your wife?"

And with his eyes fixed upon the western horizon the Earl replied,—

"No, I will go hence with no request upon my lips but to the King of kings."

How all this pleasant dalliance would have terminated, had it continued, we have no means of knowing, for a sudden and unexpected end was put to it, at any rate for a time.

Easter was over, and the Cavaliere had invited Inglesant to join in a small party to spend a day or two at his vineyard and country house among the Apennines, assuring him that at that time of the year the valleys and hill-slopes were very delightful.

The evening before the day on which the little company was to start, Inglesant had an engagement at one of the theatres in Florence, where a comedy or pantomime was being performed. The comedies in Italy at this time were paltry in character in everything except the music, which was very good. Inglesant accompanied a Signore Gabriotto, a violin player, who was engaged at the theatre, and of whom Inglesant had taken lessons, and with whom he had become intimate. This man was not only an admirable performer on the violin, but was a man of cultivation and taste. He had given much study to the music of the ancients, and especially to their musical instruments, as they are to be seen in the hands of the Apollos, muses, fauns, satyrs, bacchanals, and shepherds of the classic sculptors. As they walked through the streets in the evening sunlight, he favoured his companion, whom he greatly admired as an excellent listener, with a long discourse on this subject, showing how useful such an inquiry was, not only to obtain a right notion of the ancient music, but also to help us to obtain pleasanter instruments if possible than those at present in use.

"Not, signore," he said, "that I think we have much to learn from the ancients; for if we are to judge their instruments by the appearance they make in marble, there is not one that is comparable to our violins; for they seem, as far as I can make out, all to have been played on either by the bare fingers or the plectrum, so that they could not add length to their notes, nor could they vary them by that insensible swelling and dying away of sound upon the same string which gives so wonderful a sweetness to our modern music. And as far as I can see, their stringed instruments must have had very low and feeble voices from the small proportion of wood used (though it is difficult to judge of this, seeing that all our examples are represented in marble), which would prevent the instruments containing sufficient air to render the strokes full or sonorous. Now my violin," continued the Italian with enthusiasm, "does not speak only with the strings, it speaks all over, as though it were a living creature that was all voice, or, as is really the case, as though it were full of sound."

"You have a wonderful advantage," said Inglesant, "you Italians, that is, in the cultivation of the art of life; for you have the unbroken tradition, and habit and tone of mind, from the old world of pleasure and art—a world that took the pleasures of life boldly, and had no conscience to prevent its cultivating and enjoying them to the full. But I must say that you have not, to my mind, improved during the lapse of centuries, nor is the comedy we shall see to-night what might be expected of a people who are the descendants of the old Italians who applauded Terence."

"The comedy to-night," said the Italian, "would be nothing without the music, the acting is a mere pretence."

"The comedy itself," said Inglesant, "would be intolerable but for the buffoons, and the people show their sense in demanding that place shall be found in every piece for these worthies. The play itself is stilted and unreal, but there is always something of irony and wit in these characters, which men have found full of satire and humour for four thousand years: Harlequin the reckless fantastic youth, Pantaleone the poor old worn-out

'Senex,' and Corviello the rogue. In their absurd impertinences, in their impossible combinations, in their mistakes and tumbles, in their falling over queens and running up against monarchs, men have always seemed to see some careless, light-hearted, half-indifferent sarcasm and satire upon their own existence."

When they reached the theatre, the slant rays of the setting sun were shining between the lofty houses, and many people were standing about the doors. Inglesant accompanied the violinist to the door of the playhouse, and took his place near the orchestra, at either end of which were steps leading up on to the stage. The evening sunlight penetrated into the house through Venetian blinds, lighting up the fittings and the audience with a sort of mystic haze. The sides of the stage were crowded with gentlemen, some standing, others sitting on small stools. Many of the audience were standing, the rest seated on benches. The part occupied in modern theatres by the boxes was furnished with raised seats, on which ladies and people of distinction were accommodated. There was no gallery.

As the first bars of the overture struck upon Inglesant's ear, with a long-drawn tremor of the bass viols and a shrill plaintive note of the treble violins, an irresistible sense of loneliness and desolation and a strange awe crept over him and weighed down his spirits. As the fantastic music continued, in which gaiety and sadness were mysteriously mingled, the reverberation seemed to excite each moment a clearer perception of those paths of intrigue and of danger in which he seemed to walk. The uneasy sentiment which accompanied, he knew not why, his attachment to Lauretta, and the insidious friendship of the Cavaliere, the sense of insecurity which followed his footsteps in this land of dark and sinful deeds, passed before his mind. It seemed to his excited fancy at that moment that the end was drawing very near, and amid the fascination of the lovely music he seemed to await the note of the huntsman's horn which would announce that the toils were set, and that the chase was up. From the kind of trance in which he stood he was aroused by hearing a voice, distinct to his ear and perfectly audible, though apparently at some considerable distance, say—

"Who is that man by the curtain, in black satin, with the Point de Venice lace?"

And another voice, equally clear, answered, "His name is Inglesant, an agent of the Society of the Gesu."

Inglesant turned; but, amid the crowd of faces behind him, he could discern nothing that indicated the speakers, nor did any one else seem to have noticed anything unusual. The next moment the music ceased, and with a scream of laughter Harlequin bounded on the stage, followed by

Pantaleone in an eager and tottering step, and after them a wild rout of figures, of all orders and classes, who flitted across the stage amid the applause of the people, and suddenly disappeared; while Harlequin and Pantaleone as suddenly reappearing, began a lively dialogue, accompanied by a quick movement of the violins. As Inglesant took his eyes off the stage for a moment, they fell on the figure of a man standing on the flight of steps at the farther end of the orchestra, who regarded him with a fixed and scrutinizing gaze. It was a tall and dark man, whose expression would have been concealed from Inglesant but for the fiery brilliancy of his eyes. Inglesant's glance met his as in a dream, and remained fixed as though fascinated, at which the gaze of the other became, if possible, more intense, as though he too were spell-bound and unable to turn away. At this moment the dialogue on the stage ceased, and a girl advanced to the footlights with a song, accompanied by the band in an air adapted from the overture, and containing a repetition of the opening bars. The association of sound broke the spell, and Inglesant turned his eyes upon the singer; when he looked again his strange examiner was gone.

The girl who was singing was a Roman, reputed the best treble singer then in Italy. The sun by this time was set, and the short twilight over. The theatre was sparsely lighted by candles, nearly the whole of the available light being concentrated upon the stage. This arrangement produced striking effects of light and shade, more pleasing than are the brilliantly lighted theatres of modern days. The figures on the stage came forward into full and clear view, and faded again into obscurity in a mysterious way very favourable to romantic illusion, and the theatrical arrangements were not seen too clearly. The house itself was shadowy, and the audience unreal and unsubstantial; the whole scene wore an aspect of glamour and romance wanting at the present day.

When the girl's song was over there was a movement among the gentlemen on the stage, several coming down into the house. Inglesant took advantage of this, and went up on the stage, from which he might hope to see something of the stranger who had been watching him so closely, if he were still in the theatre.

Several of the actors who were waiting for their turn mingled with the gentlemen, talking to their acquaintance. The strange light thrown on the centre of the stage in which two or three figures were standing, the multitude of dark forms in the surrounding shadow, the dim recesses of the theatre itself full of figures, the exquisite music, now soft and plaintive, anon gay and dance-like, then solemn and melancholy, formed a singular and attractive whole. Lauretta had declined to come that night, but Inglesant thought it was not improbable that the Cavaliere would be there, and he was curious to see whether he could detect him in company with the mysterious stranger. From the moment that he had heard the distant voice inquiring his name, the familiar idea had again occurred to his mind that this could be none other than the murderer of his brother, of whom he was in search; but this thought had occurred so often, and in connection with so many persons, that had it not been for the fixed and peculiar glance with which the stranger had regarded him, he would have thought little of it. He was, however, unable to distinguish either of the persons of whom he was in search from the crowd that filled the theatre; and his attention was so much diverted by the constantly changing scene before him that he soon ceased to attempt to do so. At that moment the opening movement of the overture was again repeated by the band, and was made the theme of an elaborate variation, in which the melancholy idea of the music was rendered in every variety of shade by the plaintive violins. Every phase of sorrow, every form and semblance of grief that Inglesant had ever known, seemed to float through his mind, in sympathy with the sounds which, inarticulate to the ear, possessed a power stronger than that of language to the mental sense. The anticipation of coming evil naturally connected itself with the person of Lauretta, and he seemed to see her lying dead before him upon the lighted stage, or standing in an attitude of grief, looking at him with wistful eyes. This last image was so strongly presented to his imagination that it partook almost of the character of an apparition; and before it the crowded theatre, the gaily dressed forms upon the stage, the fantastic actors, seemed to fade, and alone on the deserted boards the figure of Lauretta, as he had last seen it, slight and girl-like, yet of noble bearing, stood gazing at him with wild and apprehensive eyes. Curiously too, as his fancy dwelt upon this figure, it saw in her hand a sealed letter fastened with a peculiarly twisted cord.

The burden of sorrow and of anticipated evil became at last too heavy to be borne, and Inglesant left the theatre and returned to his lodgings. But here he could not rest. Though he had no reason to visit the Count that night, and though it was scarcely seemly, indeed, that he should do so, yet, impelled by a restless discomfort which he sought to quiet, he wandered again into the streets, and found himself not unnaturally before the old nobleman's dwelling. Once here, the impulse was too strong to be denied, and he knocked at the low sunken door. The house seemed strangely quiet and deserted, and it was some time before an old servant who belonged to the lower part of the establishment, devoted to the sale of the wine, appeared at the wicket, and, on being assured whom it was who knocked at that unseasonable hour, opened the door.

The house was empty, he averred. The family had suddenly departed, whither he knew not. If the signore was pleased to go upstairs, he believed he would find some letters for him left by the Cavaliere.

Inglesant followed the old man, who carried a common brass lamp, which cast an uncertain and flickering glare, the sense of evil growing stronger at every step he took. His guide led him into the room in which he had first seen Lauretta, which appeared bare and deserted, but showed no sign of hasty departure. Upon a marble table inlaid with coloured stones were two letters, both directed to Inglesant. The one was from the Cavaliere, excusing their departure on the ground of sudden business of the highest political importance, the other from Lauretta, written in a hasty trembling hand. It contained but a few lines—"that she was obliged to follow her father;" but Inglesant hesitated a moment before he broke the seal, for it was tied round with a curiously twisted cord of blue and yellow silk, as he had seen in the vision his fancy had created.

CHAPTER II

Lauretta's letter had informed Inglesant that she would endeavour to let him know where she was; and with that hope he was obliged to be content, as by no effort he could make could he discover any trace of the fugitive's route. Florence, however, became distasteful to him, and he would have left it sooner but for an attack of fever which prostrated him for some time. Few foreigners were long in Italy, in those days, without suffering from the climate and the miasmas and unhealthy vapours, which, especially at night, were so hurtful even to those accustomed to the country. In his illness Inglesant was carefully nursed by some of the Jesuit fathers, and those whom they recommended; and it is possible that they took care that he should not be left too much to the care of the physicians, whose attentions, at that period at any rate, were so often fatal to their patients. In the course of a few weeks he was sufficiently recovered to think of leaving Florence, and he despatched a messenger to Don Agostino, begging him to meet him at Lucca, where they might decide either to visit Venice or go on straight to Rome. It was not without some lingering hope that he might find Lauretta in the town of her birth, that he set out for Lucca, but misfortune followed his path. It was reported that the plague had broken out in Florence, and travellers who were known to have come from thence were regarded with great suspicion. Inglesant's appearance, recently recovered from sickness, was not in his favour; and at Fucecchio, a small town on the road to Lucca, he was arrested by the authorities, and confined by them in the pest-house for forty days. It was a building which had formerly been a gentleman's house, and possessed a small garden surrounded by a high wall. In this dreary abode Inglesant passed many solitary days, the other inmates being three or four unfortunates like himself,—travellers on business through the country,—who, their affairs being injured by their detention, were melancholy and despondent. He was short of money, and for some time was unable to communicate with any of his friends either in Florence or Sienna. With nothing but his own misfortunes to brood upon, and with the apprehension of the future, which almost amounted to religious melancholy, frequently before his mind, it is surprising that he kept his reason. To add to his misfortunes, when the greater portion of the time fixed for his detention was expired, one of the inmates of the pest-house suddenly died; and although the physicians pronounced his disease not to be the plague, yet the authorities decreed that all should remain another forty days within its dreary walls. The death of this person greatly affected Inglesant, as he was the only one of the inmates with whom he had contracted any intimacy.

During the first part of his sojourn here, there was brought to the house, as an inmate, a wandering minstrel, who, the first evening of his stay, attracted the whole of the gloomy society around him by his playing. He played upon a small and curiously shaped instrument called a vielle, somewhat like a child's toy, with four strings, and a kind of small wheel instead of a bow. It was commonly used by blind men and beggars in the streets, and was considered a contemptible instrument, though some of these itinerant performers attained to such skill upon it that they could make their hearers laugh and dance, and it was said even weep, as they stood around them in the crowded streets. Inglesant soon perceived that the man was no contemptible musician, and after his performance was over he entered into conversation with him, asking him why he, who could play so well, was content with so poor an instrument. The man, who appeared to have a great deal of intelligence and humour, said that he was addicted to a wandering and unsettled life, among the poorer and disorderly classes in the low quarters of cities, in mountain villages, and in remote hostelries and forest inns; that the possession of a valuable viol, or other instrument, even if he should practice sufficient self-denial to enable him to save money to purchase such a one, would be a constant anxiety to him, and a source of danger among the wild companions with whom he often associated. "Besides, signore," he said, "I am attached to this poor little friend of mine, who will speak to me though to none else. I have learnt the secrets of its heart, and by what means it may be made to discourse eloquently of human life. You may despise my instrument, but I can assure you it is far superior to the guitar, though that is so high bred and genteel a gentleman, found in all romances and ladies' bowers. For any music that depends upon the touch of a string, and is limited in the duration of the distinct sounds, is far inferior to this little fellow's voice."

"You seemed trained to the profession of music," said Inglesant.

"I was serving-lad to an old musician in Rome, who not only played on several instruments, but gave a great deal of time to the study of the science of harmony, and of the mysteries of music. He was fond of me, and taught me the viol, as I was apt to learn."

"I have heard of musicians," said Inglesant, "who have written on the philosophy of sound. He was doubtless one of them."

"There are things concerning musical instruments," said the man, "very wonderful; such as the laws concerning the octaves of flutes, which, make them how you will, you can never alter, and which show how the principles of harmony prevail in the dead things of the world, which we think so blockish and stupid; and what is more wonderful still, the passions of men's souls, which are so wild and untamable, are all ruled and kept in a strict measure and mean, for they are all concerned in and wrought upon by music. And what can be more wonderful than that a maestro in the art can take delight in sound, though he does not hear it; and when he looks at some black marks upon paper, he hears intellectually, and by the power of the soul alone?"

"You speak so well of these things," said Inglesant, "that I wonder you are content to wander about the world at village fairs and country weddings, and do not rather establish yourself in some great town, where you might follow your genius and earn a competence and fame."

"I have already told you," replied the man, "that I am wedded to this kind of life; and if you could accompany me for some months, with your viol d'amore, across the mountains, and through the deep valleys, and into the old towns where no travellers ever come, and where all stands still from century to century, you would never leave it, any more than I shall. I could tell you of many strange sights I have witnessed, and if we stay long in this place, perhaps you will be glad to hear some tales to while away the time."

"You spoke but now," said Inglesant, "of the power that music has over the passions of men. I should like to hear somewhat more of this."

"I will tell you a curious tale of that also," said the man.

THE VIELLE-PLAYER'S STORY

"Some twenty-five years ago there lived in Rome two friends, who were both musicians, and greatly attached to each other. The elder, whose name was Giacomo Andria, was maestro di capella of one of the churches, the other was an accomplished lutinist and singer. The elder was a cavaliere and a man of rank; the younger of respectable parentage, of the name of Vanneo. The style of music in which each was engaged was sufficiently different to allow of much friendly contention; and many lively debates took place as to the respective merits of 'Sonate da Chiesa' and 'Sonate da Camera.' Their respective instruments also afforded ground for friendly dispute. Vanneo was very desirous that his friend should introduce viols and other instruments into the service, in concert with the voices, in the Church in which Vanneo himself sang in the choir; but the Cavaliere, who considered this a practice derived from the theatre, refused to avail himself of any instrument save the organ. Vanneo was more successful in inducing his friend to practice upon his favourite instrument the lute, though Andria pretended at first to despise it as a ladies' toy, and liable to injure the shape of the performer. His friend, however, though devoted to secular music, brought to the performance and composition of it so much taste and correct feeling, that Andria was ravished in spite of himself, and of his preference to the solemn music of the Church. Vanneo excelled in contrasting melancholy and pensive music with bright and lively cords, mingling weeping and laughter in some of the sweetest melodies that imagination ever suggested. He accompanied his own voice on the lute, or he composed pieces for a single voice with accompaniment for violins. In a word, he won his friend over to this grave chamber music, in some respects more pathetic and serious than the more monotonous masses and sonatas of the Church composers. Vanneo composed expressly for this purpose fantasies on the chamber organ, interposed, now and then, with stately and sweet dance music, such as Pavins (so named from the walk of a peacock) Allemaines, and other delightful airs, upon the violins and lute. In these fancies he blended, as it were, pathetic stories, gay festivities, and sublime and subtle ideas, all appealing to the secret and intellectual faculties, so that the music became not only an exponent of life but a divine influence. After these delightful meetings had continued for several years, circumstances obliged Vanneo to accompany a patron to France, and from thence he went over into England, to the great King of that nation, as one of his private musicians; for the Queen of England was a French Princess, and was fond of the lute. His departure was a great grief to the Cavaliere, who devoted himself more than ever to Church music and to the offices of religion. He was a man of very devout temper, and was distinguished for his benevolent disposition, and especially for his compassion for the poor, whom he daily relieved in crowds at his own door, and in the prisons of Rome, which he daily visited. From time to time he heard from his friend, to whom he continued strongly attached."

"I was brought up at the English Court," said Inglesant, "and have been trying to recall such a man, but cannot recollect the name you mention, though I remember several lutinists and Italians."

"I tell the story as I heard it," replied the other. "The man may have changed his name in a foreign country. One day the Cavaliere had received a letter from his friend, brought to him by some English gentleman travelling to Rome. Having read it, and spent some time with the recollections that its perusal suggested to his mind, he set himself to the work in which he was engaged—the composition of a motet for some approaching festival of the Church; but although he attempted to fix his mind upon his occupation, and was very anxious to finish his work, he found himself unable to do so. The remembrance of his friend took complete possession of his mind;

and his imagination, instead of dwelling on the solemn music of the motet, wandered perversely into the alluring world of phantasied melody which Vanneo had composed. Those sad and pensive adagios, passing imperceptibly into the light gaiety of a festival, never seemed so delightful as at that moment. He rose from time to time, and walked to and fro in his chamber, and as he did so he involuntarily took up a lute which Vanneo had left with him as a parting gift, and which always lay within reach. As he carelessly touched the strings, something of his friend's spirit seemed to have inspired him, and the lute breathed again with something of the old familiar charm. Each time that he took it up, the notes formed themselves again under his hand into the same melody, and at last he took up a sheet of paper, intended for the motet, and scored down the air he had involuntarily composed. His fancy being pleased with the occurrence, he elaborated it into a lesson, and showed it to several of his associates. He gave it the name of 'gli amici,' and it became very popular among the masters in Rome as a lesson for their pupils on the lute. Among those who thus learnt it was a youth who afterwards became page to a Florentine gentleman, one Bernard Guasconi, who went into England and took service under the King of that country, who, as you doubtless know better than I do, was at war with his people."

"I know the Cavaliere Guasconi," said Inglesant, "and saw him lately in Florence, where he is training running horses for the Grand Duke."

"This war," continued the man, "appears to have been the ruin of Vanneo; for the English people, besides hating their King, took to hating all kinds of music, and all churches and choristers. Vanneo lost his place as one of the King's musicians, and not being able to earn his living by teaching music where so few cared to learn, he was forced to enlist as a soldier in one of the King's armies, and was several times near losing his life. He escaped these dangers, however; but the army in which he served being defeated and dispersed, he wandered about the country, wounded, and suffering from sickness and want of food. He supported himself miserably, partly by charity, especially among the Loyalist families, and partly by giving singing lessons to such as desired them. He was without friends, or any means of procuring money to enable him to return to Italy. As he was walking in this manner one day in the streets of London, without any hope, and with scarcely any life, he heard the sound of music. It was long since the melody of a lute, once so familiar, had fallen on his ear; and as he stopped to listen, the notes came to him through the thick moist air like an angelic and divine murmur from another world. The music seemed to come from a small room on the ground-floor of a poor inn, and Vanneo opened the door and went in. He found a young man, plainly dressed, playing on a double-necked theorbo-lute, which, from the number of its strings, enables, as you know, the skilful lutinist to play part music, with all the varieties of fugues and other graces and ornaments of the Italian manner. The piece which the young man was playing consisted of an allegro and yet sweet movement on the tenor strings, with a sustained harmony in thorough bass. The melody, being carefully distributed through the parts, spoke to Vanneo of gaiety and cheerfulness, as of his old Italian life, strangely combined at the same time with a soothing and pathetic melancholy, like a corpse carried through the streets of a gay city, strewn with flowers and accompanied with tapers and singing of boys. The whole piece finished with a pastorale, or strain of low and sweet notes. As Vanneo listened he was transported out of himself. It was not alone the beauty of the music which ravished him, but he was conscious that a mysterious presence, as of his friend the Cavaliere, was with him, and that at last the perfect sympathy which he had sought so long was established; and that in the music he had heard a common existence and sphere of life was at last created, in which they both lived, not any longer separate from each other, but enjoying as it were one common being of melody and ecstatic life of sound. When the music ceased Vanneo accosted the lutinist, and inquired the name of the composer; but this the young man could not tell him. He only knew it was a favourite lesson for skilful pupils among the music-masters in Rome, and as such he had learnt it. Vanneo was confident the piece had been written by Andria, and by none other, and told the young man so. By this time they had discovered that they were fellow-countrymen, and the lutinist sent for refreshments, of which Vanneo stood very much in need. He also told him that his name was Scacchi, and that he was page to the Signore Bernard Guasconi, who was then in arms for the King, and was besieged in some town of which I have forgotten the English name."

"It was Colchester," said Inglesant; "I was in prison at the time of the siege; but I know the history of it and its sad ending."

"Becoming very familiar with Vanneo, he advised him to accompany him to Colchester. His master, he said, would doubtless be set at liberty immediately as a foreigner and a friend of the Grand Duke's, and he could accompany him home to Italy as a domestic. As no better prospect was open to Vanneo of returning to his native country, he gladly accepted the page's offer, and agreed to accompany him next day. The besiegers of the town which you call Colchester were engaging persons from all parts of the country to work their trenches, and the town not being far from London, many persons went from that place to earn the wages offered. Many of the Loyalists also took advantage of this pretext, intending to join the besieged if a favourable opportunity offered. To one of these parties

Vanneo and the page joined themselves. You may wonder that I know so much of these matters, but I have heard the story several times repeated by the page himself. The weather was very cold and wet, and the companions underwent much hardship on their march. They travelled through a flat and marshy country, full of woods and groves of trees, and crossed with dykes and streams. Vanneo, however, who had endured so much privation and suffering, began to sink under his fatigues. After travelling for more than two days they arrived at the leaguer. They were told that the besieged were expected every day to surrender at discretion; but they were sent into the trenches with several other volunteers to relieve those already there, many of whom were exhausted with the work, and were deserting. As they arrived at the extreme limit of the lines the besiegers had planted four great pieces of battering cannon against the town, and fired great shot all the forenoon, without, however, doing much damage. The Royalists mustered all their troops upon the line, intending, as it afterwards appeared, to break out at night and force their way through the leaguer. The lines were so close that the soldiers could throw stones at each other as they lay in the trenches; and Vanneo and the page could see the King's officers plainly upon the city walls. The Royalists did not fire, being short of ammunition, and in the night a mutiny took place among some of the foot-soldiers, which prevented the project of cutting their way out from taking effect. The soldiers of both armies were now already mixed on many places upon the line, and no fire was given on either side, as though the Royalists were already prisoners. The page left Vanneo, who was worn-out and ill, and easily made his way into the town, where he found his master. When he returned to the trenches he found Vanneo very ill, and a physician with him, a doctor of the town, named Gibson, as I remember, who told the page that he thought his companion was dying. Vanneo, in fact, appeared to be insensible, his eyes were closed, and he was perfectly pale. He lay in a small house, just within the lines, which had been deserted by its inhabitants, who were weavers. The gentlemen were under arrest in the town, and it was reported that several were to be immediately shot, of whom it was whispered the Signore Guasconi was to be one. About two in the afternoon the general of the besieging army entered the town, and a great rabble of the soldiers with him. The latter broke into many houses to search for plunder, and among them into that in which Vanneo was lying. As they came into the room and saw the dying man, they stopped and began to question the page as to who he was. Before he could reply Vanneo opened his eyes with a smile, raised himself suddenly from the straw on which he lay, and, stretching out his hand eagerly as one who welcomes a friend, exclaimed in Italian, 'Cavaliere, the consonance is complete;' and having said this he fell back upon the straw again, and, the smile still upon his face, he died."

The musician stopped a moment, and then glancing at Inglesant with a curious look said, "It is confidently said that about that very moment the Cavaliere Andria died at Rome; at any rate when the page returned to Italy and inquired for him at Rome, he was dead. He caught a fever in one of his visits to the prisons, and died in a few days."

"Did the page tell you of the two gentlemen who were shot at Colchester?" said Inglesant.

"Yes, he told me that Guasconi stood by with his doublet off expecting his turn; but when the others were shot he was taken back to his prison. They only found out he was an Italian by his asking leave to write to the Grand Duke."

"I have been told," he continued, "that this poor King was a great lover of music, and played the bass viol himself."

"He was a great admirer of Church music," said Inglesant; "I have often seen him appoint the service and anthems himself."

As the conversation of this man was a great entertainment to Inglesant, so his sudden and unexpected death was a great shock to him. The physician could give no clear explanation of his decease, and the general opinion was that he died of the plague, though it was, of course, the interest of every one in the pest-house that this should not be acknowledged.

A few days after the burial two of the Jesuit Fathers arrived from Florence, accompanied by Don Agostino, who, having in vain waited for his friend at Lucca, had sought him at Florence, and finally traced him to his dreary prison. By their influence Inglesant was allowed to depart; and actuated still by his desire to see Venice, set out, accompanied by Don Agostino, in the hope of reaching that city. They crossed the Apennines, and journeyed by Modena, Mantua, Verona, and Padua. These places, which at other times would have excited in Inglesant the liveliest interest, were passed by him now as in a dream. The listless indifference which grew day by day, developed at Padua into absolute illness; and Agostino took lodgings for his friend in one of the deserted palaces of which the city was full. A few days' rest from travel, and from the excitement produced by novel scenes and by the scorching plains, had a soothing and beneficent effect; but Venice being reported to be at that time peculiarly unhealthy, and Inglesant becoming sensible that he was physically unable to prosecute any inquiries there, the friends resolved to abandon their journey in that direction, and to return towards Rome. At this juncture Don Agostino received letters which compelled him to return hastily to Sienna, and after spending a few days with his friend, he left, promising to return shortly and accompany Inglesant to Rome, when he was sufficiently recruited by a few weeks' repose.

The failure of the silk trade, owing to the importation of silk from India into Europe, had destroyed the prosperity of many parts of Italy; and in Padua long streets of deserted mansions attested by their beauty the wealth and taste of the nobility, whom the loss of the rents of their mulberry groves had reduced to ruin. Many houses being empty, rents were exceedingly cheap, and the country being very plentiful in produce, and the air very good, a little money went a long way in Padua. There was something about the quiet gloomy town, with its silent narrow streets and its long and dim arcades,—by which you might go from one end of the city to the other under a shady covert,—that soothed Inglesant's weary senses and excited brain.

His was that sad condition in which the body and the mind, being equally, like the several strings of an ill-kept lute, out of tune, jarred upon each other, the pains of the body causing phantasms and delusions of the mind. His disappointment and illness at Florence, his long confinement in the pest-house, and the sudden death of his friend the poor musician, preyed upon his spirits and followed him even in his dreams; and his body being weakened by suffering, and his mind depressed by these gloomy events and images, the old spiritual terrors returned with augmented force. Nature herself, in times of health and happiness so alluring and kind, turns against the wretch thus deprived of other comfort. The common sights and events of life, at one time so full of interest, became hateful to him; and amid the solemn twilights and gorgeous sunsets of Italy, his imagination was oppressed by an intolerable presentiment of coming evil. Finally, he despaired of himself, his past life became hateful to him, and nothing in the future promised a hope of greater success. He saw himself the mere tool of a political faction, and to his disordered fancy as little better than a hireling bravo and mercenary. The rustling of leaves, the falling of water, the summer breeze, uttered a pensive and melancholy voice, which was not soothing, but was like the distant moaning of sad spirits foreboding disaster and disgrace. On his first arrival in Padua Don Agostino had introduced him to two or three ecclesiastics, whose character and conversation he thought would please his friend; but Inglesant made little effort to cultivate their acquaintance. His principal associate was the Prior of the Benedictine monastery, a mile or two beyond the Ferrara Gate, who, becoming at last distressed at his condition, advised him to consult a famous physician named Signore Jovanni Zecca.

This man had the reputation of a wit, maintained chiefly by a constant study of Boccalini's "Parnassus," with quotations from which work he constantly adorned his discourse. He found Inglesant prostrate on a couch in his apartment, with the Prior by his side. The room had been the state reception room of the former possessor, and the windows, which were open, looked upon the wide space within one of the gates. It was the most busy part of the city, and for that reason the rooms had been chosen by Don Agostino, as commanding the most agreeable and lively prospect.

The Prior having explained to the physician the nature of Inglesant's malady, as far as he was acquainted with it, inquired whether the situation of the rooms seemed suitable to the doctor, or whether it would be well to remove to some country house. The scene from the windows indeed was very lively, and might be considered too distracting for an invalid. The prospect commanded the greater part of the Piazza, or Place d'Armes, the gate and drawbridges and the glacis outside, with a stretch of country road beyond, lined with poplars. This extensive stage was occupied by ever-varying groups,—soldiers on guard in stiff and picturesque uniform, men carrying burdens, pack-horses, oxen, now and then a carriage with a string of horses and with running footmen, peasant women, priests, children, and beggars, with sometimes a puppet-show, or a conjuror with apes, and side by side with these last, in strange incongruity, the procession of the Host.

"From what I know of this gentleman's malady and disposition," said the physician, "I should suppose that these sights and sounds, though perhaps hurtful to his physical nature, are so dear to his moral nature that to speak against them were useless. These sounds, though physically unpleasant, contain to the philosophic mind such moral beauty as to be attractive in the highest degree, and to such a nature as this my patient possesses offer a fascination which it would be unwise to contend against."

"If," said the Prior to Inglesant with a smile, "your case requires philosophic treatment, you are fortunate in having secured the advice of Signore Zecca, who has the reputation of a philosopher and wit, as well as that of a most skilful physician."

"With respect to my calling as a physician, I may make some claim certainly," said the doctor, "if descent has any title to confer excellence, for my great-grandfather was that celebrated Jovanni Zecca, after whom I am named, the Physician of Bologna, whom you will find mentioned in the most witty 'Ragguagli' of Messere Tragano Boccalini; therefore, if I fail in my profession, it is not for want of generations of experience and precept; but as regards my proficiency as a philosopher, I have no one to depend upon but myself, and my proficiency is indeed but small."

"You are pleased to say so, Signore Fisico," said Inglesant languidly, "with the modesty usual with great minds; nevertheless the remark which you have just made shows you to be familiar with the deepest of all philosophy, that of human life. It is my misfortune that I am too deeply impressed already with the importance of this philosophy, and it is my inadequate following of its teaching which is killing me."

"It is a subject of curious study," said the physician, "for perplexity perhaps, certainly for much satire, but scarcely, I should think, for martyrdom. The noblest things in life are mixed with the most ignoble, great pretence with infinite substance, vain-glory with solidness. The fool of one moment, the martyr of the next: as in the case of that Spaniard mentioned by Messere Boccalini, whose work doubtless you know, signore, but if not, I should recommend its perusal as certain to do much to work your cure. This man—the Spaniard, I mean—dying most gallantly upon the field of honour, entreated his friend to see him buried without unclothing him; and with these words died. His body, being afterwards examined, it was found that he who was so sprucely dressed, and who had a ruff about his neck so curiously wrought as to be of great value, had never a shirt on his back. This discovery caused great laughter among the vulgar sort of mankind; but by order of Apollo, the great ruler of learning and philosophy, this Spaniard was given a public and splendid funeral, equal to a Roman triumph; and an oration was pronounced over him, who was so happy that, in his great calamity, he was careful of his reputation before his life. His noble funeral seems to me rather to proclaim the fact that our worst meannesses cannot deprive us of the dignity of that pity which is due to human nature standing by the brink of an open grave. A man has mistaken the secret of human life who does not look for greatness in the midst of folly, for sparks of nobility in the midst of meanness; and the well-poised mind distributes with impartiality the praise and the blame."

"It is my misfortune," replied Inglesant, "that my mind is incapable of this well-poised impartiality, but is worn out by the unworthy conflict which the spirit within us wages with the meannesses of life. As the Psalmist says, 'The very abjects make mouths at me, and cease not.'"

"You are like those people, signore," said the physician, "mentioned by Messere Boccalini, whom the greatest physicians failed to cure, but who were immediately restored to active health by the simple and common remedies of a quack. You seek for remedies among the stars and the eternal verities of creation, whereas your ailment of mind arises doubtless from some physical derangement, which perchance a learner in healing might overcome."

"The fatal confusion of human life," said Inglesant, "is surely too obvious a fact to be accounted for by the delusions of physical disease."

The physician looked at Inglesant for a moment and said,—

"Some time, signore, I will tell you a story, not out of Boccalini, which perchance will convince you that, strange as it may seem, the realities of life and the delusions of disease are not so dissimilar as you think."

"If it be so," said Inglesant, "your prescription is more terrible than my complaint."

"I do not see that," replied the other. "I have said nothing but what should show you how unwise you will be, if you overlook the bodily ailment in searching into the diseases of the soul."

"I am well aware," replied Inglesant, "that my ailment is one of the body as well as of the mind; but were my body made perfectly whole and sound, my cure could scarcely be said to be begun."

"I hold that most of the sorrows and perplexities of the mind are to be traced to a diseased body," replied the physician, not paying much attention to what his patient said; "the passion of the heart, heavy and dull spirits, vain imaginations, the vision of spectres and phantoms, grief and sorrow without manifest cause,—all these things may be cured by purging away melancholy humours from the body, especially as I conceive from the meseraic veins; and the heart will then be comforted, in the taking away the material cause of sorrow, which is not to be looked for in the world of spirits, nor in any providential government of God, nor even in outward circumstances and perplexities, but in the mechanism of the body itself."

"What cures do you propound that may be hoped to work such happy results?" said the Prior, for Inglesant did not speak.

"We have many such cures in physics—physics studied by the light of the heavenly science," said the physician; "such as the Saturica Sancti Juliani, which grows plentifully on the rough cliffs of the Tyrrhenian Sea, as the old Greek chronographers called it, called St. Julian's Rock; the Epithymum, or thyme, which is under Saturn, and therefore very fitted for melancholy men; the Febrifuga, or, in our Italian tongue, Artemisia Tenuifolia, good for such as be melancholy, sad, pensive, and without power of speech; the distilled water of the Fraga, or Strawberry, drunk with white wine reviveth the spirits, and as the holy Psalmist says, 'Lætificat cor hominis;' and the herb Panax, which grows on the top of the Apennine, and is cherished in all the gardens of Italy for its wonderful healing qualities; but the liquor of it, which you may buy in Venice, is not distilled in Italy, but is brought from Alexandria, a city of Egypt."

"You do not speak of the chemical medicines," said Inglesant, "which were much thought of in England when I was in Oxford; and many wonderful cures were worked by them, though I remember hearing that the young doctor who first introduced them, and wrought some great cures, died himself soon after."

"I have indeed no faith in the new doctrine of chemical compositions and receipts," said the physician, "which from mere empirics must needs be very dangerous, but from a man that is well grounded in the old way may do strange things. The works of God are freely given to man. His medicines are common and cheap; it is the medicines of the new physicians that are so dear and scarce to find."

Signore Zecca soon after took his leave, promising to send Inglesant a cordial, the ingredients of which he said were gathered on "a Friday in the hour of Jupiter," and which would be sufficient to give sleep, pleasant dreams, and quiet rest to the most melancholy man in the world. For, as he sensibly observed, "waking is a symptom which much tortures melancholy men, and must therefore be speedily helped, and sleep by all means procured. To such as you especially, who have what I call the temperament of sensibility, are fearful of pain, covet music and sleep, and delight in poetry and romance, sleep alone is often a sufficient remedy."

The doctor frequently visited Inglesant, who found his humour and curious learning entertaining; and on one occasion, when they were alone together, he reminded him of his promise to relate a story which would prove his assertion that the ills of the soul were occasioned by those of the body.

NOTE.—The MSS. are here imperfect.

CHAPTER III

In spite, however, of the reasonings and prescriptions of the physician, the oppression upon Inglesant's brain became more intolerable. Every new object seemed burnt into it by the sultry outward heat, and by his own fiery thoughts. The livid scorched plains, with the dark foliage, the hot piazzas and highways, seemed to him thronged with ghastly phantoms, all occupied more or less in some evil or fruitless work. As to his physical sense all objects seemed distorted and awry, so to his mental perception the most ordinary events bore in them the germs, however slight, of that terrible act of murderous terror that had marred and ruined his own life. In some form or other, in the passionate look, in the gambler's gesture, in the lover's glance, in the juggler's grimace, in the passion of the little child, he saw the stealthy trail of the Italian murderer, before whose cowardly blow his brother fell. The cool neglected courts of Padua afforded no relief to his racked brain, no solace to his fevered fancy. He frequented the shadowed churches and the solemn masses daily without comfort; for his conscience was once more weighted with the remembrance of Serenus de Cressy, and of his own rejection of the narrow path of the Holy Cross. A sense of oppression and confusion rested upon him mentally and physically, so that he could see no objects steadily and clearly; but without was a phantasmagoria of terrible bright colours, and within a mental chaos and disorder without a clue. A constant longing filled his mind to accept De Cressy's offer, and he would have returned to France but for the utter impossibility of making the journey in his condition of health. He withdrew himself more and more from society, and at last, without informing his friends of his intention, he retired to a small monastery without the city, about a mile from the Traviso Gate, and requested to be admitted as a novice. The result of this step at the outset was beneficial; for the perfect seclusion, and the dim light of the cells and shaded garden, relieved the brain, and restored the disordered sense of vision.

It was some time before Don Agostino received intelligence, through the Prior, of this step of his friend's. He immediately came to Padua, and had several interviews with Inglesant, but apparently failed to produce any impression upon him. He then returned to Florence, and induced the Cardinal Rinuccini, from whose influence upon Inglesant he hoped much, to accompany him to Padua.

The Cardinal was a striking-looking and singularly handsome man, his countenance resembling the reputed portraits of Molière, whose bust might be taken for that of a pagan god. There was the same open free expression, as of a man who confined his actions by no bounds, who tasted freely of that tree of good and evil, which, it is reported, transforms a man into a god, and of that other tree which, since the flaming sword of the cherubim kept the way to the true, has passed in the world for the tree of life; who had no prejudices nor partialities, but included all mankind, and all the opinions of men, within the wide range of perfect tolerance and lofty indifference. He found Inglesant in his novice's dress, walking in the small walled-in garden of the monastery, beneath the mulberry trees, his breviary in his hand. After the first greeting the Cardinal inquired touching his health.

"You are familiar with English, Eminence," replied Inglesant, "and remember Hamlet; and you will therefore understand the state of a man for whom the world is too strong."

"It is only the weak," replied the Cardinal, "for whom the world is too strong. You know what Terence says, 'Ita vita est hominum quasi cum ludas tesseris,' or, as we should rather say, 'Life is like a game of cards;' you cannot control the cards, but of such as turn up you must make the most."

"Illud quod cecidit forte, id arte ut corrigas."

"The freewill, the reason, and the power of self-command, struggle perpetually with an array of chance incidents, of mechanical forces, of material causes, beyond foresight or control, but not beyond skilful management. This gives a delicate zest and point to life, which it would surely want if we had the power to frame it as we would. We did not make the world, and are not responsible for its state; but we can make life a fine art, and, taking things as we find them, like wise men, mould them as may best serve our own ends."

"We are not all wise, your Eminence, and the ends that some of us make our aim are far beyond our reach."

"I was ever moderate in my desires," said the Cardinal with a smile; "I shoot at none of these high-flying game. I am content to live from day to day, and leave the future to the gods; in the meantime sweetening life as I can with some pleasing toys, here and there, to relish it."

"You have read Don Quixote, Eminence," said Inglesant; "and no doubt hold him to have been mad."

"He was mad, doubtless," replied the Cardinal smiling.

"I am mad, like him," replied the other.

"I understand you," said the Cardinal; "it is a noble madness, from which we inferior natures are free; nevertheless, it may be advisable for a time to consult some worldly physician, that by his help this nobleness may be preserved a little longer upon earth and among men."

"No worldly physician knows the disease, much less the cure," said Inglesant. "Don Quixote died in his bed at last, talked down by petty common-place, acknowledging his madness, and calling his noble life a mistake; how much more shall I, whose life has been the more ignoble for some transient gleams of splendour which have crossed its path in vain! The world is too strong for me, and heaven and its solution of life's enigma too far off."

"There is no solution, believe me," said the Cardinal, "no solution of life's enigma worth the reading. But suppose there be, you are more likely to find it at Rome than here. Put off that monk's dress, and come with me to Rome. What solution can you hope to find, brooding on your own heart, on this narrow plot of grass, shut in by lofty walls? You, and natures like yours, make this great error; you are moralizing and speculating upon what life ought to be, instead of taking it as it is; and in the meantime it slips by you, and you are nothing, and life is gone. I have heard, and you doubtless, in a fine concert of viols, extemporary descant upon a thorough bass in the Italian manner, when each performer in turn plays such variety of descant, in concordance to the bass, as his skill and present invention may suggest to him. In this manner of play the consonances invariably fall true upon a given note, and every succeeding note of the ground is met, now in the unison or octave, now in the concords, preserving the melody throughout by the laws of motion and sound. I have thought that this is life. To a solemn bass of mystery and of the unseen, each man plays his own descant as his taste or fate suggests; but this manner of play is so governed and controlled by what seems a fatal necessity, that all melts into a species of harmony; and even the very discords and dissonances, the wild passions and deeds of men, are so attempered and adjusted that without them the entire piece would be incomplete. In this way I look upon life as a spectacle, 'in theatro ludus.' Have you sat so long that you are tired already of the play?"

"I have read in some book,"[#] said Inglesant, "that it is not the play— only the rehearsal. The play itself is not given till the next life. But for the rest your Eminence is but too right. There is no solution within my own heart, and no help within these walls."

> [#] What this book is I do not know. The remark was made by Jean Paul, in Hesperus, some hundred years after Inglesant's day.

There can be little doubt that had Inglesant remained much longer in the monastery, he would have sunk into a settled melancholy. The quiet and calm, while it soothed his brain, and relieved it of the phantoms that distracted it, allowed the mind to dwell exclusively upon those depressing thoughts and ideas which were exhausting his spirit and reducing him well-nigh to despair. However undesirable at other times the Cardinal's philosophic paganism might be, no doubt, at this moment, his society was highly beneficial to Inglesant, to whom, indeed, his conversation possessed a peculiar charm. It could, indeed, scarcely fail to attract one who himself sympathized with that philosophy of tolerance of, and attraction to, the multiform aspects of life which Paganism and the Cardinal equally followed. On the other hand, Rinuccini had from the first been personally strongly attracted towards Inglesant, and, as a matter of policy, attached just importance to securing his services, both on account of what he had learnt from his brother, and from the report of the Jesuits.

After some further conversation the Cardinal returned to Padua in triumph, bringing Inglesant with him, whom he loaded with kindness and attention. A suite of apartments was placed at his disposal, certain of the Cardinal's servants were ordered to attend him, and the finest horses were devoted to his use on the approaching journey. After waiting in Padua some days, to make preparations which were necessary in the neglected state of Inglesant's affairs, they set out for Rome. Don Agostino was still in Florence, the politics of his family not suffering him to visit the papal city at present.

Their first day's journey took them, through the fertile and well-cultivated Venetian States, to Rovigo, where they crossed the Po, dividing the territory of the Republic from the Ferrarese, which State had lately been acquired by the Pope.

This country, which, while it possessed princes of its own, had been one of the happiest and most beautiful parts of Italy, was now abandoned and uncultivated to such an extent that the grass was left unmown on the meadows. At Ferrara, a vast city which appeared to Inglesant like a city of the dead as he walked through streets of stately houses without an inhabitant, the chief concourse of people was the crowd of beggars who thronged round the Cardinal's coach. After dinner Inglesant left his companion, who liked to linger over his wine, and walked out into the quiet streets. The long, deserted vistas of this vast city, sleeping in the light and shadow of the afternoon sun, disturbed now and then only by a solitary footstep, pleased his singular fancies as Padua had done. He entered several of the Churches, which were mean and poorly adorned, and spoke to several of the priests and loiterers. Everywhere he heard complaints of the poverty of the place, of the misery of the people, of the bad unwholesome air, caused by the dearth of inhabitants to cultivate the land. When he came to inquire into the causes of this, most held their peace; but one or two idlers, bolder or more reckless than the rest, seeing that he was a foreigner, and ignorant that he was riding in the train of a Cardinal, whispered to him something of the severity of the Papal government, and of the heavy taxes and frequent confiscations by which the nephews of several Popes had enriched themselves, and devoured many of the principal families of the city, and driven away many more. "They talk of the bad air," said one of these men to Inglesant; "the air was the same a century ago, when this city was flourishing under its own princes—princes of so eminent a virtue, and of so heroical a nobleness, that they were really the Fathers of their country. Nothing," he continued with a mute gesture of the hands, "can be imagined more changed than this is now."

"But Bologna is under the Pope, also," said Inglesant, "and is flourishing enough."

"Bologna," he answered, "delivered itself up to the Popedom upon a capitulation, by which there are many privileges reserved to it. Crimes there are only punished in the persons of those who commit them. There are no confiscations of estates; and the good result of these privileges is evident, for, though Bologna is neither on a navigable river nor the centre of a sovereignty where a Court is kept, yet its happiness and wealth amaze a stranger; while we, once equally fortunate, are like a city in a dream."

Inglesant returned to the inn to the Cardinal, and related what he had heard; to all which dismal stories the Prelate only replied by significant gesture.

The next morning, however, as he was entering his carriage followed by his friend, he seemed to take particular notice of the crowd of beggars that surrounded the inn. In Inglesant's eyes they only formed part (together with the strange, quiet streets, the shaded gardens, and the ever-changing scenes of their journey) in that shifting phantasm of form and colour, meaningless to him, except as it might suddenly, and in some unexpected way, become a part and scene of the fatal drama that had seized upon and crippled his life. But to the Cardinal, who had the training of a politician, though he subordinated politics to enjoyment, these swarms of beggars and these decaying states had at times a deeper interest.

"These people," he said, as the carriage moved on, "certainly seem very miserable, as you told me last night. To those whose tastes lay that way it would not be a useless business to inquire into these matters, and to try to set them right. Some day, probably far distant, some of us, or those like us who clothe in scarlet and fine linen, will have to pay a reckoning for these things."

"They are less unhappy than I am," said Inglesant. "As to the luxurious persons of whom you speak, it has been my fate to be of their party all my life, and to serve them for very poor reward; and I doubt not that, when their damnation, of which your Eminence speaks, arrives, I shall share it with them. But it might seem to one who knows little of such things that some such attempt might be looked for from a sworn soldier and prince of the Church."

The Cardinal smiled. The freedom with which Inglesant's sarcastic humour showed itself at times, when the melancholy fit was upon him, was one of the sources of attraction which attached the young Englishman to his person.

"Life is short," he said, "and the future very uncertain; martyrs have died, nay, still harder fate, have lived long lives of such devotion as that which you wish me to attempt, and we see very little result. Christianity is not of much use apparently to many of the nations of the earth. Now, on my side, as I pass my life, I certainly enjoy this world, and I as certainly have cultivated my mind to sustain, as far as I can foresee the probable, the demand and strain that will be put upon it, both in the exit from this life, and in the entrance upon another. Why then should I renounce these two positive goods, and embrace a life of restless annoyance and discomfort, of antagonism to existing systems and order, of certain failure, disappointment, and the peevish protestation of a prophet to whom the world will not listen?"

"There is no reason why, certainly," said Inglesant, "for a sane man like your Eminence. I see clearly it must only have been madmen who in all ages have been driven into the fire and upon the sword's point in pursuit of an idea which they fancied was worth the pain, but which, as they never realized it, they could never put to the test."

"I perceive your irony," said the Cardinal, "and I recognize your wit. What astonishes me is the interest you take in these old myths and dreary services. The charm of novelty must have worn itself out by this time."

"Christ is real to many men," said Inglesant, "and the world seems to manifest within itself a remedial power such as may be supposed to be His."

"I do not dispute such a power," replied the Cardinal; "I only wonder at the attachment to these old myths which profess to expound it."

"The world has now been satisfied with them for some centuries," said Inglesant; "and for my own part, even in the blaze of a purer Mythos, I cannot help thinking that some of us will look back with longing to 'one of the days of the Son of man.' I do not perceive either that your Eminence attempts to improve matters."

"I can afford to wait," replied the Cardinal, with lofty indifference; "the myths of the world are slow to change."

"This one certainly," replied Inglesant, with a smile, "has been slow to change, perhaps because men found in it something that reminded them of their daily life. It speaks of suffering and of sin. The cross of Christ is composed of many other crosses—is the centre, the type, the essence of all crosses. We must *suffer* with Christ whether we *believe* in Him or not. We must suffer for the sin of others as for our own; and in this suffering we find a healing and purifying power and element. That is what gives to Christianity, in its simplest and most unlettered form, its force and life. Sin and suffering for sin: a sacrifice, itself mysterious, offered mysteriously to the Divine Nemesis or Law of Sin,—dread, undefined, unknown, yet sure and irresistible, with the iron necessity of law. This the intellectual Christ, the Platonic-Socrates, did not offer: hence his failure, and the success of the Nazarene. Vicisti Galilæe."

CHAPTER IV

Among the letters of introduction to persons in Rome which Inglesant carried with him, was one from Father St. Clare to the Rector of the English College, a Jesuit. The Cardinal had invited him to remain an inmate of his family, but there were several reasons which induced Inglesant to decline the offer. He was desirous of observing the situation and habits of the great city in a more unfettered way than he would probably be able to do if attached to the household of a great man. This reason alone would probably have decided him, but it was not the only one. In proportion as his mind recovered its natural tone, and was able to throw off the depression which had so long troubled him, another source of perplexity had taken its place. Most men, in those days, with the exception of very determined Puritans, approached Rome with feelings of veneration and awe. Inglesant's training and temperament inclined him to entertain these feelings as strongly perhaps as any man of the day; but since he had been in Italy, his eyes and ears had not been closed, and it had been impossible for him to resist a growing impression, scarcely perhaps amounting to conviction, that the nearer he approached the Papal capital the more wretched and worse governed did the country appear on every side. In the muttered complaints which reached his ear these evils were charged partly upon the abuses of the Papal chair itself, but principally upon the tyranny and oppression of the society of the Jesuits. Inglesant made these observations mostly in the taverns or cafés in the evenings when those who were present, perceiving him to be a foreigner, were more disposed to be communicative than they otherwise would have been. But the Cardinal was known to associate rather with the Fathers of the Oratory than with the Jesuits; and men did not hesitate therefore to speak somewhat freely on these matters to his familiar companion. These accusations did not destroy Inglesant's faith in the Society, but they made him anxious to hear the other side, and to see, if possible from within, the working of this great and powerful organization, and to understand the motives which prompted those actions which were so much blamed, and which were apparently productive of such questionable fruits. If this were to be done, it must be done at once. He came to Rome recommended to the Jesuits' College, almost an accredited agent. He would be received without suspicion, and would probably be enabled to obtain an insight into much of their policy. But if at the outset he associated himself with persons and interests hostile, or at least indifferent, to those of the party to which he belonged, and which he wished to understand, this opportunity would doubtless soon be lost to him. Acting upon these considerations, he parted from the Cardinal, to whom he confided his motives, and made his way to the English College or house, which was situated in the street leading to St. Peter's and the Vatican, and not far from the Bridge and Castle of St. Angelo.

The College was a large and fair house, standing in several courts and gardens. Inglesant was received with courtesy by the rector, who said that he remembered seeing him in London, and that he had also been at his father's house in Wiltshire. He named to him several Priests who had also been there; but so many Papists had been constantly coming and going at Westacre, during the time that Father St. Clare had resided there, that Inglesant could not recall them to mind. The rector, however, mentioned one whom he remembered, the gentleman who had given him St. Theresa's Life. He advised Inglesant to remain some days at the College, as the usual and natural resort of all Englishmen connected in any way with the Court and Church of Rome, promising him pleasant rooms. He showed him his apartment, a small but handsome guest-chamber, looking upon a garden, with a sort of oratory or closet adjoining, with an altar and crucifix. The bell rang for supper, but the rector had that meal laid for himself and his guest in his private room. The students, and those who took their meals at the common table, had but one good meal in the day, that being a most excellent one. Their supper consisted of a glass of wine and a manchet of bread.

The rector and Inglesant had much talk together, and after the latter had satisfied his host, as best he could, upon all those points—and they were many—connected with the state of affairs in England upon which he desired information, the rector began in his turn to give his guest a description of affairs in Rome, and of those things which he should see, and how best to see them.

"I will not trouble you now," he said, "with any policy or State affairs. You will no doubt wish to spend the next few days in seeing the wonderful sights of this place, and in becoming familiar with its situation, so that you may study them more closely afterwards. A man must indeed be ill-endowed by nature who does not find in Rome delight in every branch of learning and of art. The libraries are open, and the students have access to the rarest books; in the Churches the most exquisite voices are daily heard, the palaces are crowded with pictures and with statues, ancient and modern. You have, besides, the stately streets and noble buildings of every age, the presence of strangers from every part of the world, villas covered with 'bassi relievi,' and the enjoyment of nature in enchanting gardens. To a man who loves the practices of devotion I need not mention the life-long employment among the Churches, relics, and processions. It is this last that gives the unique completeness of the Roman life within itself. To the abundance of its earthly wealth, to the delights of its intellectual gratifications, is added a feeling of unequalled security and satisfaction, kept alive, in a pious mind, by the incessant contemplation of the objects of its reverence. I do not know if you are by taste more of a scholar than of a religious, but both tastes are worthy of cultivation, nor is all spiritual learning necessarily confined to the last. There is much that is very instructive in the lessons which the silent stones and shattered monuments of the fallen cities over which we walk teach us. It has been well observed that everything that has been dug out of the ruins of ancient Rome has been found mutilated, either by the barbarians, fanaticism, or time; and one of our poets, Janus Vitalis, seeing all the massive buildings mouldered or mouldering away, and the ever-changing Tiber only remaining the same, composed this ingenious and pleasing verse—

'Disce hinc quid possit fortuna; immota labascunt;

Et quæ perpetuo sunt fluitura, manent.'

You will find that the Italian humour delights much in such thoughts as these, which make the French and other nations accuse us of melancholy. The Italian has a strong fancy, yet a strong judgment, and this makes him delight in such things as please the fancy, while at the same time they are in accordance with judgment and with reason. He delights in music, medals, statues, and pictures, as things which either divert his melancholy or humour it; and even the common people, such as shoemakers, have formed curious collections of medals of gold, silver, and brass, such as would have become the cabinet of a prince. Do you wish to begin with the Churches or with the antiquities?"

Inglesant said he wished to see the Churches first of all.

"You will, no doubt," said the rector, "find a great satisfaction in such a choice. You will be overcome with the beauty and solemnity of these sacred places, and the sweetness of the organs and of the singing will melt your heart. At the same time, I should wish to point out to you, to whom I wish to speak without the least reserve, that you will no doubt see some things which will surprise you, nay, which may even appear to you to be, to say the least, of questionable advantage. You must understand once for all, and constantly bear in mind, that this city is like none other, and that many things are natural and proper here which would be strange and ill-fitted elsewhere. Rome is the visible symbol and representation of the Christian truth, and we live here in a perpetual masque or holy interlude of the life of the Saviour. As in other countries and cities, outward representations are placed before the people of the awful facts and incidents on which their salvation rests, so here this is carried still farther, as indeed was natural and almost inevitable. It was a very small step from the representation of the flagellation of Christ to the very pillar on which He leant. Indeed, where these representations were enacted, the simple country people readily and naturally conceived them to have taken place. Hence, when you are shown the three doors of Pilate's house in which Jesus passed and repassed to and from judgment, the steps up which He walked, the rock on which He promised to build His Church, the stone on which the cock stood and crowed when Peter denied Him, part of His coat and of His blood, and several of the nails of His cross,—more possibly than were originally used, over which the heretics have not failed to make themselves very merry;—when you see all these things, I say, and if you feel, as I do not say you will feel—but if you feel any hesitancy or even some repulsion, as though these miraculous things were to you matters more of doubt than worship, you will not fail at once to see the true nature and bearing of these things, nor to apply to them the solution which your philosophy has doubtless given already to many difficult questions of this life. These things are true to each of us according as we see them; they are, in fact, but shadows and likenesses of the absolute truth that reveals itself to men in different ways, but always imperfectly and as in a glass. To the simple-hearted peasant that pavement upon which in his mind's eye he sees Jesus walking, is verily and indeed pressed by the Divine feet; to him this pillar, the sight of which makes the stinging whips creep along his flesh, is the pillar to which the Lord was tied. Our people, both peasant and noble, are of the nature of children—children who are naughty one moment and sincerely penitent the next. They are now wildly dissolute, the next day prostrate before the cross; and as such, much that is true and beautiful in their lives seems otherwise to the cold and world-taught heart. But our Lord honoured the childlike heart, and will not send away our poor peasants when they come to Him with their little offerings, even though they lay them at the feet of a Bambino doll."

"But do you not find," said Inglesant, "that this devotion, which is so ephemeral, is rather given to the sensible object than to the unseen Christ?"

"It may be so," said the rector; "there is no good but what has its alloy; but it is a real devotion, and it reaches after Christ. Granted that it is dark, no doubt in the darkness it finds Him, though it cannot see His form."

"Doubtless," said Inglesant, who saw that the rector did not wish to dwell on this part of the subject, "as we say in our service in England, we are the sheep of His pasture, and we are all branded with the mark which He puts upon His sheep—the innate knowledge of God in the soul. I remember hearing of a man who believed that he had a guardian spirit who awoke him every morning with the audible words, 'Who gets up first to pray?' If this man was deluded, it could not have been by Satan."

In the morning, when Inglesant awoke, he saw from his window, over the city wall, the Monte Mario, with its pine woods, and the windows of its scattered houses, lighted by the rising sun. The air was soft and balmy, and he remained at the open window, letting his mind grow certain of the fact that he was in Rome. In the clear atmosphere of the Papal city there was a strange shimmer of light upon the distant hills, and on the green tufts and hillocks of the waste ground beyond the walls. The warm air fanned his temples, and in the stillness of the early morning a delicious sense of a wonderful and unknown land, into the mysteries of which he was about to enter, filled his mind.

It was indeed a strange world which lay before him, and resembled nothing so much as that to which the rector had aptly compared it the night before, a sacred interlude full of wild and fantastic sights; Churches more sublime than the dreams of fancy painted, across whose marble pavements saints and angels moved familiarly with men; pagan sepulchres and banqueting chambers, where the phantoms flickered as in Tartarus itself; vaults and Christian catacombs, where the cry of martyrs mingled with the chanting of masses sung beneath the sod, and where the torch-light flashed on passing forms of horror, quelled everywhere by the figure of the Crucified, that at every turn kept the place; midnight processions and singing, startling the darkness and scaring the doers of darkness, mortal and immortal, that lurked among the secret places, where the crimes of centuries stood like ghastly corpses at every step; and above all and through all the life of Jesus, enacted and re-enacted year after year and day by day continually, not in dumb show or memorial only, but in deed and fact before the eyes of men, as if, in that haunt of demons and possessed, in that sink of past and present crime, nothing but the eternal presence and power of Jesus could keep the fiends in check.

The rector took Inglesant over the College, and showed him the life and condition of the inmates under its most pleasing aspect. As he then saw it it reminded him of a poem he had heard Mr. Crashaw read at Little Gidding, describing a religious house and condition of life, and he quoted part of it to the rector:—

> "No cruel guard of diligent cares, that keep
> Crowned woes awake, as things too wise for sleep:
> But reverend discipline, and religious fear,
> And soft obedience, find sweet biding here;
> Silence and sacred rest, peace and pure joys."

When they had seen the College the rector said,—

"We will go this morning to St. Peter's. It is better that you should see it at once, though the first sight is nothing. Then at three o'clock we will attend vespers at the Capello del Coro, where there is fine music every day in the presence of a cardinal; afterwards, as Rome is very full, there will be a great confluence of carriages in the Piazza of the Farnese Palace, which is a favourite resort. There I can show you many of the great ones, whom it is well you should know by sight, and hear something of, before you are presented to them."

As they passed out into the street of the city the rector began a disquisition on the discovery of antiquities in Rome. He advised Inglesant to study the cabinets of medals which he would meet with in the museums and palaces, as they would throw great light upon the statues and other curiosities.

"A man takes a great deal more pleasure," he said, "in surveying the ancient statues, who compares them with medals, than it is possible for him to do without some such knowledge, for the two arts illustrate each other. The coins throw a great light upon many points of ancient history, and enable us to distinguish the kings and consuls, emperors and empresses, the deities and virtues, with their ensigns and trophies, and a thousand other attributes and images not to be learnt or understood in any other way. I have a few coins myself, which I shall be glad to show you, and a few gems, among which is an Antinous cut in a carnelian which I value very highly. It represents him in the habit of a Mercury, and is the finest Intaglio I ever saw. I obtained it by accident from a peasant, who found it while digging in his vineyard."

Inglesant was too much occupied watching the passers-by in the thronged streets to pay much attention to what he said. The crowded pavements of Rome offered to his eyes a spectacle such as he had never seen, and to his imagination a fanciful pageant such as he had never pictured even in his dreams. The splendid equipages with their metal work of massive silver, the strange variety of the clerical costumes, the fantastic dresses of the attendants and papal soldiers, the peasants and pilgrims from all countries, even the most remote, crossed his vision in an entangled maze.

As they crossed the bridge of St. Angelo, the rector informed him of the invaluable treasures of antique art which were supposed to lie beneath the muddy waters of the river. They passed beneath the castle, and a few moments more brought them to the piazza in front of the Church.

The colonnade was not finished, one side of it being then in course of completion; but in all its brilliant freshness, with the innumerable statues, white from the sculptor's hand, it had an imposing and stately effect. The great obelisk, or Guglia, as the Italians called it, had been raised to its position some seventy years before, but only one of the great fountains was complete. Crossing the square, which was full of carriages, and of priests and laymen on foot, the rector and Inglesant ascended the marble stairs which had formed part of the old Basilica, and up which Charlemagne was said to have mounted on his knees, and passing through the gigantic porch, with its enormous pillars and gilt roof, the rector pushed back the canvas-lined curtain that closed the doorway, and they entered the Church.

The masons were at work completing the marble covering of the massive square pillars of the nave; but though the work was unfinished, it was sufficient to produce an effect of inexpressible richness and splendour. The vast extent of the pavement, prepared as for the heavenly host with inlaying of colours of polished stone, agate, serpentine, porphyry, and chalcedon; the shining walls, veined with the richest marbles, and studded with gems; the roof of the nave, carved with foliage and roses overlaid with gold; the distant walls and chambers of imagery, dim with incense, through which shone out, scarcely veiled, the statues and tombs, the paintings and crucifixes and altars, with their glimmering lights;—all settled down, so to speak, upon Inglesant's soul with a perception of subdued splendour, which hushed the spirit into a silent feeling which was partly rest and partly awe.

But when, having traversed the length of the nave without uttering a word, he passed from under the gilded roofs, and the spacious dome, lofty as a firmament, expanded itself above him in the sky, covered with tracery of the celestial glories and brilliant with mosaic and stars of gold; when, opening on all sides to the wide transepts, the limitless pavement stretched away beyond the reach of sense; when, beneath this vast work and finished effort of man's devotion, he saw the high altar, brilliant with lights, surmounted and enthroned by its panoply of clustering columns and towering cross; when, all around him, he was conscious of the hush and calmness of worship, and felt in his inmost being the sense of vastness, of splendour, and of awe;—he may be pardoned if, kneeling upon the polished floor, he conceived for the moment that this was the house of God, and that the gate of heaven was here.

CHAPTER V

"It is almost impossible for a man to form in his imagination," said the rector to Inglesant, as they left the Church, "such beautiful and glorious scenes as are to be met with in the Roman Churches and Chapels. The profusion of the ancient marble found within the city itself, and the many fine quarries in the neighbourhood, have made this result possible; and notwithstanding the incredible sums of money which have been already laid out in this way, the same work is still going forward in other parts of Rome; the last effort still endeavouring to outshine those that went before it."

Inglesant found this assertion to be true. As he entered Church after Church, during the first few days of his sojourn in Rome, he found the same marble walls, the same inlaid tombs, the same coloured pavements. In the sombre autumn afternoons this splendour was toned down and veiled, till it produced an effect which was inexpressibly noble,—a dim brilliance, a subdued and restrained glory, which accorded well with the enervating perfume and the strains of romantic music that stole along the aisles. In these Churches, and in the monasteries adjoining, Inglesant was introduced to many priests and ecclesiastics, among whom he might study most of the varieties of devout feeling, and of religious life in all its forms. To many of these he was not drawn by any feeling of sympathy; many were only priests and monks in outward form, being in reality men of the world, men of pleasure, or antiquarians and artists. But, introduced to the society of Rome in the first place as a "devoto," he became acquainted naturally with many who aspired to, and who were considered to possess, exceptional piety. Among these he was greatly attracted by report towards a man who was then beginning to attract attention in Rome, and to exert that influence over the highest and most religious natures, which, during a period of twenty years, became so overpowering as at one time to threaten to work a complete revolution in the system and policy of Rome. This was Michael de Molinos, a Spanish monk, who, coming to Rome some years before, began to inculcate a method of mystical devotion which he had no doubt gathered from the followers of St. Theresa, who were regarded with great veneration in Spain, where the contemplative devotion which they taught was held in high esteem. On his first coming to Rome Molinos refused all ecclesiastical advancement, and declined to practise those austerities which were so much admired. He associated with men of the most powerful minds and of the most elevated thoughts, and being acknowledged at once to be a man of learning and of good sense, his influence soon became perceptible. To all who came to him for spiritual comfort and advice he insisted on the importance of mental devotion, of daily communion, and of an inward application of the soul to Jesus Christ and to His death. So attractive were his personal qualities, and so alluring his doctrine to minds which had grown weary of the more formal ceremonies and acts of bodily penance and devotion, that thousands thronged his apartments, and "the method of Molinos" became not only a divine message to many, but even the fashionable religion of Rome.

It spoke to men of an act of devotion, which it called the contemplative state, in which the will is so united to God and overcome by that union that it adores and loves and resigns itself up to Him, and, not exposed to the wavering of the mere fancy, nor wearied by a succession of formal acts of a dry religion, it enters into the life of God, into the heavenly places of Jesus Christ, with an indescribable and secret joy. It taught that this rapture and acquiescence in the Divine Will, while it is the highest state and privilege of devotion, is within the reach of every man, being the fruit of nothing more than the silent and humble adoration of God that arises out of a pure and quiet mind; and it offered to every man the prospect of this communion—a prospect to which the very novelty and vagueness gave a hitherto unknown delight—in exchange for the common methods of devotion which long use and constant repetition had caused to appear to many but as dead and lifeless forms. Those who followed this method generally laid aside the use of the rosary, the daily repeating of the breviary, together with the common devotion of the saints, and applied themselves to preserve their minds in an inward calm and quiet, that they might in silence perform simple acts of faith, and feel those inward motions and directions which they believed would follow upon such acts.

To such a doctrine as this, taught by such a man, it is not surprising that Inglesant was soon attracted, and he visited Molinos's rooms several times. On one of these occasions he met in the anteroom a gentleman he had seen more than once before, but had never spoken to. He was therefore somewhat surprised when he accosted him, and seemed desirous of some private conference. Inglesant knew that he was the Count Vespiriani, and had heard him described as of a noble and refined nature, and a hearty follower of Molinos. They left the house together, and driving to the gardens of the Borghese Palace, they walked for some time.

The Count began by expressing his pleasure that at so early a period of his residence in Rome Inglesant had formed the acquaintance of Molinos.

"You are perhaps," he said, "not aware of the importance of the movement, nor of the extent to which some of us are not without hope that it may ultimately reach. Few persons are aware of the numbers already devoted to it, including men of every rank in the Church and among the nobility, and of every variety of opinion and of principle. It cannot be supposed that all these persons act thus under the influence of any extraordinary elevation of piety or devotion. To what then can their conduct be ascribed? It cannot have escaped your notice, since you have been in Italy, that there is much that is rotten in the state of government, and to be deplored in the condition of the people. I do not know in what way you may have accounted for this lamentable condition of affairs in your own mind; but among ourselves (those among us at any rate who are men of intelligence and of experience of the life of other countries, and especially Protestant ones) there is but one solution—the share that priests have in the government, not only in the Pope's territory, but in all the other courts of Italy where they have the rule. This does not so much arise from any individual errors or misdoing as from the necessary unfitness of ecclesiastics to interfere in civil affairs. They have not souls large enough nor tender enough for government; they are trained in an inflexible code of morals and of conduct from which they cannot swerve. To this code all human needs must bow. They are cut off from sympathy with their fellows on most points; and their natural inclinations, which cannot be wholly suppressed, are driven into unworthy and mean channels; and they acquire a narrowness of spirit and a sourness of mind, together with a bias to one side only of life, which does not agree with the principles of human society. All kinds of incidental evils arise from these sources, in stating which I do not wish to accuse those ecclesiastics of unusual moral turpitude. Among them is the fact that, having individually so short and uncertain a time for governing, they think only of the present, and of serving their own ends, or satisfying their own conceptions, regardless of the ultimate happiness or misery which must be the consequence of what they do. Whatever advances the present interests of the Church or of themselves, for no man is free altogether from selfish motives—whatever enriches the Church or their own families, for no man can help interesting himself in those of his own house,—is preferred to all wise, great, or generous counsels. You will perhaps wonder what the mystic spiritual religion of Molinos has to do with all this, but a moment's explanation will, I think, make it very clear to you. The hold which the priests have upon the civil government is maintained solely by the tyranny which they exercise over the spiritual life of men. It is the opinion of Molinos that this function is misdirected, and that in the place of a tyrant there should appear a guide. He is about to publish a book called 'Il Guida Spirituale,' which will appear with several approbations before it,—one by the general of the Franciscans, who is a Qualificator of the Inquisition, and another by a member of the society to which you are attached, Father Martin de Esparsa, also one of the Qualificators. This book, so authorized and recommended, cannot fail not only to escape censure, but to exert a powerful influence, and will doubtless be highly esteemed. Now the importance of Molinos's doctrine lies in this, that he presses the point of frequent communion, and asserts that freedom from mortal sin is the only necessary qualification. At the same time he guards himself from the charge of innovation by the very title and the whole scope of his book, which is to insist upon the necessity of a spiritual director and guide. You will see at once what an important step is here gained; for the doctrine being once admitted that mortal sin only is a disqualification for receiving the sacrament, and the necessity of confession before communion being not expressed, the obligation of coming always to the priest, as the minister of the sacrament of penance, before every communion, cannot long be insisted upon. Indeed, it will become a rule by which all spiritual persons who adhere to Molinos's method will conduct their penitents, that they may come to the sacrament when they find themselves out of the state of mortal sin, without going at every time to confession; and it is beginning to be observed already in Rome that those who, under the influence of this method, are becoming more strict in their lives, more retired and serious in their mental devotions, are become less zealous in their whole deportment as to the exterior parts of religion. They are not so assiduous at mass, nor in procuring masses for their friends, nor are they so frequent at confession or processions. I cannot tell you what a blessing I anticipate for mankind should this method be once allowed; what a freedom, what a force, what a reality religion would obtain! The time is ripe for it, and the world is prepared. The best men are giving their adherence; I entreat you to lend your aid. The Jesuits are wavering; they have not yet decided whether the new method will prevail or not. The least matter will turn the scale. You may think that it is of little importance which side you take, but if so, you are mistaken. You are not perhaps aware of the high estimation in which the reports and letters which have preceded you have caused you to be held at the Jesuits' College. You are supposed to have great influence with the English Catholics and Protestant Episcopalians, and the idea of promoting Catholic progress in England is the dearest to the mind of the Roman Ecclesiastic."

Inglesant listened to the Count attentively, and did not immediately reply. At last he said,—

"What you have told me is of the greatest interest, and commends itself to my conscience more than you know. As to the present state and government of Italy I am not competent to speak. One of the things which

I hoped to learn in Rome was the answer to some complaints which I have heard in other parts of Italy. I fear also that you may be too sanguine as to the result of such freedom as you desire. This age is witness of the state to which too much freedom has brought England, my own country, a land which a few years ago was the happiest and wealthiest of all countries, now utterly ruined and laid waste. The freedom which you desire, and the position of the clergy which you approve, is somewhat the same as that which existed in the Protestant Episcopal Church of England; but the influence they possessed was not sufficient to resist the innovations and wild excesses of the Sectaries. The freedom which I desire for myself I am willing to renounce when I see the evil which the possession of it works among others and in the State. What you attempt, however, is an experiment in which I am not unwilling to be interested; and I shall be very curious to observe the result. The main point of your method, the freedom of the blessed sacrament, is a taking piece of doctrine, for the holding of which I have always been attracted to the Episcopal Church of England. It is, as you say, a point of immense importance, upon which in fact the whole system of the Church depends. I have been long seeking for some solution of the mysterious difficulties of the religious life. It may be that I shall find it in your society, which I perceive already to consist of men of the highest and most select natures, with whom, come what may, it is an honour to be allied. You may count on my adherence; and though I may seem a half-hearted follower, I shall not be found wanting when the time of action comes. I should wish to see more of Molinos."

"I am not at all surprised," said the Count, "that you do not at once perceive the full force of what I have said. It requires to be an Italian, and to have grown to manhood in Italy, to estimate justly the pernicious influence of the clergy upon all ranks of society. I have travelled abroad, and when I have seen such a country as Holland, a land divided between land and sea, upon which the sun rarely shines, with a cold and stagnant air, and liable to be destroyed by inundations; when I see this country rich and flourishing, full of people, happy and contented, with every mark of plenty, and none at all of want; when I see all this, and then think of my own beautiful land, its long and happy summers, its rich and fruitful soil, and see it ruined and depopulated, its few inhabitants miserable and in rags, the scorn and contempt instead of the envy of the world; when I think of what she was an age or two ago, and reflect upon the means by which such a fall, such a dispeopling, and such a poverty, has befallen a nation and a climate like this;—I dare not trust myself to speak the words which arise to my lips. Those with whom you associate will doubtless endeavour to prevent these melancholy truths from being perceived by you, but they are too evident to be concealed. Before long you will have painful experience of their existence."

"You say," said Inglesant, "that one or two ages ago Italy was much more prosperous than at present; were not the priests as powerful then as now?"

"I do not deny," replied the Count, "that there have been other causes which have tended to impoverish the country, but under a different government many of these might have been averted or at any rate mitigated. When the commerce of the country was flourishing the power of the wealthy merchants and the trading princes was equal or superior to that of the priests, especially in the leading States. As their influence and wealth declined, the authority of the clergy increased. A wiser policy might have discovered other sources of wealth and of occupation for the people; they only thought of establishing the authority of the Church, of adorning the altars, of filling the Papal coffers."

Inglesant may have thought that he perceived a weak point in this explanation, but he made no reply, and the Count supposed he was satisfied.

A few days afterwards he had the opportunity of a long and private conversation with Molinos.

The Spaniard was a man of tall and graceful exterior, with a smile and manner which were indescribably alluring and sweet. Inglesant confided to him something of his past history, and much of his mental troubles and perplexities. He spoke of De Cressy and of the remorse which had followed his rejection of the life of self-denial which the Benedictine had offered him. Molinos's counsel was gentle and kindly.

"It was said to me long ago," said Inglesant, "that 'there are some men born into the world with such happy dispositions that the cross for a long time seems very light, if not altogether unfelt. The strait path runs side by side with the broad and pleasant way of man's desires; so close are they that the two cannot be discerned apart. So the man goes on, the favourite seemingly both of God and his fellows; but let him not think that he shall always escape the common doom. God is preparing some great test for him, some great temptation, all the more terrible for being so long delayed. Let him beware lest his spiritual nature be enervated by so much sunshine, so that when the trial comes, he may be unable to meet it. His conscience is easier than other men's; what are sins to them are not so to him. But the trial that is prepared for him will be no common one; it will be so fitted to his condition that he cannot palter with it nor pass it by; he must either deny his God or himself.' This was said to me by one who knew me not; but it was said with something of a prophetic instinct, and I see in these words some traces of my own fate. For a long time it seemed to me that I could serve both the world and God, that I could be a courtier in kings' houses and in the house of God, that I could follow the earthly learning and at the same time the learning that is from above. But suddenly the chasm opened beneath my feet; two ways lay before me, and I chose the broad and easy path; the cross was offered to me, and I drew back my hand; the winnowing fan passed over the floor, and I was swept away with the chaff."

"I should prefer to say," replied the Spaniard,—and as he spoke, his expression was wonderfully compassionate and urbane,—"I should prefer to say that there are some men whom God is determined to win by love. Terrors and chastisements are fit for others, but these are the select natures, or, as you have yourself termed them, the courtiers of the household of God. Believe me, God does not lay traps for any, nor is He mistaken in His estimate. If He lavishes favour upon any man, it is because he knows that that man's nature will respond to love. It is the habit of kings to assemble in their houses such men as will delight them by their conversation and companionship, 'amor ac deliciæ generis humani,' whose memory is fresh and sweet ages after, when they be dead. Something like this it seems to me God is wont to do, that He may win these natures for the good of mankind and for His own delight. It is true that such privilege calls for a return; but what will ensure a return sooner than the consideration of such favour as this? You say you have been unworthy of such favour, and have forfeited it for ever. You cannot have forfeited it, for it was never deserved. It is the kingly grace of God, bestowed on whom He will. If I am not mistaken in your case, God will win you, and He will win you by determined and uninterrupted acts of love. It may be that in some other place God would have found for you other work; you have failed in attaining to that place; serve Him where you are. If you fall still lower, or imagine that you fall lower, still serve Him in the lowest room of all. Wherever you may find yourself, in Courts or pleasure-houses or gardens of delight, still serve Him, and you will bid defiance to imaginations and powers of evil, that strive to work upon a sensitive and excited nature, and to urge it to despair. Many of these thoughts which we look upon as temptations of God are but the accidents of our bodily temperaments. How can you, nursed in Courts, delicately reared and bred, trained in pleasure, your ear and eye and sense habituated to music and soft sounds, to colour and to beauty of form, your brain developed by intellectual effort and made sensitive to the slightest touch—how can religious questions bear the same aspect to you as to a man brought up in want of the necessaries of life, hardened by toil and exposure, unenlightened by learning and the arts, unconscious of the existence even of what is agony or delight to you? Yet God is equally with both of these;

in His different ways He will lead both of them, would they but follow, through that maze of accident and casualty in which they are involved, and out of the tumult of which coil they complain to the Deity of what is truly the result of their own temperaments, ancestry, and the besetments of life. I tell you this because I have no fear that it will exalt you, but to keep you from unduly depreciating yourself, and from that terrible blasphemy that represents God as laying snares for men in the guise of pretended kindness. God is with all, with the coarse and dull as with the refined and pure, but He draws them by different means,—those by terror, these by love."

Inglesant said little in answer to these words, but they made a deep impression upon him. They lifted a weight from his spirits, and enabled him henceforward to take some of the old pleasure in the light of heaven and the occurrences of life. He saw much of Molinos, and had long conferences with him upon the solution of the greatest of all problems, that of granting religious freedom, and at the same time maintaining religious truth. Molinos thought that his system solved this problem, and although Inglesant was not altogether convinced of this, yet he associated himself heartily, if not wholly, with the Quietists, as Molinos's followers were called, in so much that he received some friendly cautions from the Jesuit College not to commit himself too far.

It must not be supposed, however, that he was altogether absorbed in such thoughts or such pursuits. To him, as to all the other inhabitants of Rome, each in his own degree and station, the twofold aspect of existence in the strange Papal city claimed his alternate regard, and divided his life and his intellect. The society of Rome, at one moment devout, the next philosophic, the next antiquarian, artistic, pleasure-seeking, imparted to all its members some tincture of its Protean character. The existence of all was coloured by the many-sided prism through which the light of every day's experience was seen. Inglesant's acquaintance with the Cardinal introduced him at once to all the different coteries, and procured him the advantage of a companion who exerted a strong and cultivated mind to exhibit each subject in its completest and most fascinating aspect. Accompanied by the Cardinal, and with one or other of the literati of Rome, each in his turn a master of the peculiar study to which the day was devoted, Inglesant wandered day after day through all the wonderful city, through the palaces, ruins, museums, and galleries. He stood among the throng of statues, that strange maze of antique life, which some enchanter's wand seems suddenly to have frozen into marble in the midst of its intricate dance, yet so frozen as to retain, by some mysterious art, the warm and breathing life. He saw the men of the old buried centuries, of the magic and romantic existence when the world was young. The beautiful gods with their white wands; the grave senators and stately kings; the fauns and satyrs that dwelt in the untrodden woods; the pastoral flute players, whose airs yet linger within the peasant's reeds; the slaves and craftsmen of old Rome, with all their postures, dress, and bearing, as they walked those inlaid pavements, buried deep beneath the soil, whose mosaic figures every now and then are opened to the faded life of to-day. Nor less entrancing were those quaint fancies upon the classic tombs, which showed in what manner the old pagan looked out into the spacious ether and confronted death,—a child playing with a comic masque, bacchanals, and wreaths of flowers, hunting parties and battles, images of life, of feasting and desire; and finally, the inverted torch, the fleeting seasons ended, and the actor's part laid down.

Still existing as a background to this phantom life was the stage on which it had walked; the ruined splendour of Rome, in its setting of blue sky and green foliage, of ivy and creeping plants, of laurels and ilex, enfolded in a soft ethereal radiance that created everywhere a garden of romance.

"Nothing delights and entertains me so much in this country," said Inglesant one day to a gentleman with whom he was walking, "as the contrasts which present themselves on every hand, the peasant's hut built in the ruins of a palace, the most exquisite carving supporting its tottering roof, cattle drinking out of an Emperor's tomb, a theatre built in a mausoleum, and pantomime airs and the "plaudite" heard amid the awful silence of the grave; here a Christ, ghastly, naked, on a cross; there a charming god, a tender harmony of form and life; triumphal arches sunk in the ruins not of their own only, but of successive ages, monuments far more of decay and death than of glory or fame; Corinthian columns canopied with briars, ivy, and wild vine, the delicate acanthus wreaths stained by noisome weeds. The thoughts that arise from the sight of these contrasts are pleasing though melancholy, such ideas, sentiments, and feelings as arise in the mind and in the heart at the foot of antique columns, before triumphal arches, in the depths of ruined tombs, and on mossy banks of fountains; but there are other contrasts which bring no such soothing thoughts with them, nothing but what may almost be called despair; profusion of magnificence and wealth side by side with the utmost wretchedness; Christ's altar blazing with jewels and marble, misery indescribable around; luxury, and enjoyment, and fine clothes almost hustled by rags, and sores, and filth. Amid the lesson of past ages, written on every ruined column and shattered wall, what a distance still exists between the poor and the rich! Should the poor man wish to overpass it, he is driven back at once into his original wretchedness, or condemned more mercifully to death, while every ruined column and obelisk cries aloud, 'Let everything that creeps console itself, for everything that is elevated falls.'"

"We Romans," said the gentleman, "preserve our ruins as beggars keep open their sores. They are preserved not always from taste; nor from a respect of antiquity, but sometimes from mere avarice, for they attract from every corner of the world that crowd of strangers whose curiosity has long furnished a maintenance to three-fourths of Italy. But you were speaking of the charming gods of the ancients. We are not inferior to them. Have you seen the Apollo of Bermini pursuing Daphne, in the Borghese Palace? His hair waves in the wind, you hear the entreaties of the god."

"Yes, I have seen it," said Inglesant; "it is another of those wonderful contrasts with which Rome abounds. We are Catholic and Pagan at the same time."

"It is true," said the other; "nevertheless, in the centre of the blood-stained Colisseo stands a crucifix. The Galilean has triumphed."

Inglesant stopped. They were standing before the Apollo in the Belvedere gardens. Inglesant took from beneath his vest a crucifix in ivory, exquisitely carved, and held it beside the statue of the god. The one the noblest product of buoyant life, the proudest perfection of harmonious form, purified from all the dross of humanity, the head worthy of the god of day and of the lyre, of healing and of help, who bore in his day the self-same name that the other bore, "the great physician;" the other, worn and emaciated, helpless, dying, apparently without power, forgotten by the world. "Has the Galilean triumphed? Do you prefer the Christ?" he said.

The gentleman smiled. "The benign god," he said, "has doubtless many votaries, even now."

It is probable that the life of Rome was working its effect upon Inglesant himself. Under its influence, and that of the Cardinal, his tone of thought became considerably modified. In a strange and unexpected way, in the midst of so much religion, his attention was diverted from the religious side of life, and his views of what was philosophically important underwent considerable change. He read Lucretius less, and Terence and Aristophanes more. Human life, as he saw it existing around him, became more interesting to him than theories and opinions. Life in all its forms, the Cardinal assured him, was the only study worthy of man; and though Inglesant saw that such a general assertion only encouraged the study of human thought, yet it seemed to him that it directed him to a truth which he had hitherto perhaps overlooked, and taught him to despise and condemn nothing in the common path of men in which he walked. If this were true, the more carefully he studied this common life, and the more narrowly he watched it, the more worthy it would appear of regard; the dull and narrow streets, the crowded dwellings, the base and vulgar life, the poverty and distress of the poorer classes, would assume an interest unknown to him before.

"This life and interest," the Cardinal would say, "finds its best exponent in the old pantomime and burlesque music of Italy. The real, every-day, commonplace, human life, which originates absolutely among the people themselves, speaks in their own music and street airs; but when these are touched by a master's hand, it becomes revealed to us in its essence, refined and idealized, with all its human features, which, from their very familiarity, escape our recognition as we walk the streets. In the peculiarity of this music, its graceful delicacy and lively frolic and grotesqueness, I think I find the most perfect presentment, to the ear and heart, of human life, especially as the slightest variation of time or setting reveals in the most lively of these airs depths of pathos and melodious sorrow, completing thus the analogy of life, beneath the gayest phases of which lie unnoticed the saddest realities."

"I have often felt," said Inglesant, "that old dance-music has an inexpressible pathos; as I listen to it I seem to be present at long past festivities, whose very haunts are swept away and forgotten; at evenings in the distant past, looked forward to as all-important, upon whose short and fleeting hours the hopes and enjoyments of a lifetime were staked, now lost in an undistinguished oblivion and dust of death. The young and the beautiful who danced to these quaint measures, in a year or two had passed away, and other forms equally graceful took their place. Fancies and figures that live in sound, and pass before the eyes only when evoked by such melodies, float down the shadowy way and pass into the future, where other gay and brilliant hours await the young, to be followed as heretofore by pale and disappointed hopes and sad realities, and the grave."

"What do you mean," said the Cardinal, "by figures that live in sound?"

"It seems to me," said Inglesant, "that the explanation of the power of music upon the mind is, that many things are elements which are not reckoned so, and that sound is one of them. As the air and fire are said to be peopled by fairy inhabitants, as the spiritual man lives in the element of faith, so I believe that there are creatures which live in sound. Every lovely fancy, every moment of delight, every thought and thrill of pleasure which music calls forth, or which, already existing, is beautified and hallowed by music, does not die. Such as these become fairy existences, spiritual creatures, shadowy but real, and of an inexpressibly delicate grace and beauty, which live in melody, and float and throng before the sense whenever the harmony that gave and maintains their life exists again in sound. They are children of the earth, and yet above it; they recall the human needs and hopes from which they sprang. They have shadowy sex and rank, and diversity of bearing, as of the different actors' parts that fill the stage of life. Poverty and want are there, but, as in an allegory or morality, purified and released from suffering. The pleasures and delights of past ages thus live again in sound, the sorrows and disappointments of other days and of other men mingle with our own, and soften and subdue our hearts. Apollo and Orpheus tamed the savage beasts; music will soften our rugged nature, and kindle in us a love of our kind and a tolerance of the petty failings and the shortcomings of men."

It was not only music that fostered and encouraged in Rome an easy tolerant philosophy. No society could be more adapted than that of the Papal city to such an end. A people whose physical wants were few and easily supplied (a single meal in such a climate, and that easily procured, sufficing for the day); a city full of strangers, festivals and shows; a conscience absolutely at rest; a community entirely set apart from politics, absolutely at one with its government by habit, by interest, and by religion;—constituted a unique state and mental atmosphere, in which such philosophy naturally flourished. The early hours of the day were spent in such business as was necessary for all classes to engage in, and were followed by the dinner of fruit, vegetables, fish, and a little meat. From dinner all went to sleep, which lasted till six o'clock in the evening. Then came an hour's trifling over the toilette, all business was at an end, and all the shops were shut. Till three o'clock in the morning the hours were devoted to enjoyment. Men, women, and children repaired to the public walks, to the corso and squares, to conversation in coteries, to assemblies in arcaded and lighted gardens, to collations in taverns. Even the gravest and most serious gave themselves up to relaxation and amusement till the next day. Every evening was a festival; every variety of character and conversation enlivened these delicious hours, these soft and starry nights.

Nothing pleased Inglesant's fancy so much, or soothed his senses so completely, as this second dawn of the day and rising to pleasure in the cool evening. Soothed and calmed by sleep, the irritated nerves were lulled into that delicious sense for which we have no name, but which we compare to flowing water, and to the moistening of a parched and dusty drought. All thoughts of trouble and of business were banished by the intervening hours of forgetfulness, from which the mind, half-aroused and fresh from dreamland, awoke to find itself in a world as strange and fantastic as the land of sleep which it had left; a land bathed in sunset light, overarched by rainbows, saluted by cool zephyrs, soothed by soft strains of music, delighted and amused by gay festivals, peopled by varied crowds of happy people, many-coloured in dress, in green walks sparkling with fairy lamps, and seated at al fresco suppers, before cosy taverns famous for delicious wines, where the gossip of Europe, upon which Rome looked out as from a Belvedere, intrigue, and the promotions of the morning, were discussed.

Inglesant had taken lodgings in an antique villa on the Aventine, surrounded by an uncultivated garden and by vineyards. The house was partly deserted and partly occupied by a family of priests, and he slept here when he was not at the Cardinal's palace, or with other of his friends. The place was quiet and remote from the throng and noise of Rome; in the gardens were fountains in the cool shade; frescos and paintings had been left on the walls and in the rooms by the owner of the villa; the tinkling of convent bells sounded from the slopes of the hills through the laurels and ilex and across the vines; every now and then the chanting of the priests might be heard from a small Chapel at the back of the house.

Inglesant awoke from his mid-day sleep one evening to the splash of the fountain, and the scent of the fresh-turned earth in the vineyard, and found his servant arranging his room for his toilette. He was to sup that evening at the Cardinal's with some of the Fathers of the Oratory, and he dressed, as was usual with him even in his most distracted moods, with scrupulous care. A sedan was waiting for him, and he set out for the Cardinal's palace.

It was a brilliant evening; upon the hill-sides the dark trees stood out against the golden sky, the domes and pinnacles of the Churches shone in the evening light. In the quiet lanes, in the neighbourhood of the Aventine, the perfume of odoriferous trees was wafted over lofty garden walls; quiet figures flitted to and fro, a distant hum of noisy streets scarcely reached the ear, mingled with the never-ceasing bells. That morning, before he went to sleep, Inglesant had been reading "The Birds" of Aristophanes, with a voluminous commentary by some old scholar, who had brought together a mass of various learning upon the subject of grotesque apologue, fable, and the fanciful representation of the facts and follies of human life under the characters of animals and of inanimate objects. A vast number of examples of curious pantomime and other stage characters were given, and the idea preserved throughout that, by such impersonations, the voices of man's existence were able to speak with clearness and pathos, and were more sure of being listened to than when they assumed the guise of a teacher or divine. Beneath a grotesque and unexpected form they conceal a gravity more sober than seriousness itself, as irony is more sincere than the solemnity which it parodies. Truth drops her stilted gait, and becomes natural and real, in the midst of ludicrous and familiar events. The broad types of life's players into which the race is divided, especially the meanest,—thieves, beggars, outcasts,—with whom life is a reality stripped of outward show, will carry a moral and a teaching more aptly than the privileged and affected classes.

Mixed with these are animals and familiar objects of household life, to which everyday use has given a character of their own. These, not in the literal repulsiveness or dulness of their monotonous existence, but abstracted, as the types or emblems of the ideas associated with each one—not a literal beggar, in his dirt and loathsomeness, but poverty, freedom, helplessness, and amusing knavery, personified in the part of a beggar—not a mere article of household use in its inanimate stupidity, but every idea and association connected with the use of such articles by generations of men and women;— these and such as these, enlivened by the sparkle of genius, set forth in gay and exquisite music, and by brilliant repartee and witty dialogue, certainly cannot be far behind the very foremost delineation of human life.

Educated in the Court of King Charles to admire Shakespeare and the Elizabethan stage, Inglesant was better able to understand these things than the Italians were, suggestive as the Italian life itself was of such reflections. The taste for music and scenery had driven dialogue and character from the stage. Magnificent operas, performed by exquisite singers, and accompanied by mechanical effects of stupendous extent, were almost the only scenic performances fashionable in Italy; but this was of less consequence where every street was a stage, and every festival an elaborate play. The Italians were pantomimic and dramatic in the highest degree without perceiving it themselves. The man who delights in regarding this life as a stage cannot attach an overwhelming importance to any incident; he observes life as a spectator, and does not engage in it as an actor; but the Italian was too impetuous to do this—he took too violent an interest in the events themselves.

The narrow streets through which Inglesant's chair passed terminated at last in a wide square. It was full of confused figures, presenting to the eye a dazzling movement of form and colour, of which last, owing to the evening light, the prevailing tint was blue. A brilliant belt of sunset radiance, like molten gold along the distant horizon, threw up the white houses into strong relief. Dark cypress trees rose against the glare of the yellow sky, tinged with blue from the fathomless azure above. The white spray of fountains flashed high over the heads of the people in the four corners of the square, and long lance-like gleams of light shot from behind the cypresses and the white houses, refracting a thousand colours in the flashing water. A murmur of gay talk filled the air, and a constant change of varied form perplexed the eye.

Inglesant alighted from his chair, and, directing his servants to proceed at once to the Cardinal's, crossed the square on foot. Following so closely on his previous dreamy thoughts, he was intensely interested and touched by this living pantomime. Human life had never before seemed to him so worthy of regard, whether looked at as a whole, inspiring noble and serious reflections, or viewed in detail when each separate atom appears pitiful and often ludicrous. The infinite distance between these two poles, between the aspirations and the exhortations of conscience, which have to do with humanity as a whole, and the actual circumstances and capacities of the individual, with which satirists and humourists have ever made free to jest,—this contrast, running through every individual life as well as through the mass of existence, seemed to him to be the true field of humour, and the real science of those "Humanities" which the schools pedantically professed to teach.

Nothing moved in the motley crowd before him but what illustrated this science,—the monk, the lover, the soldier, the improvisatore, the matron, the young girl; here the childish hand brandishing its toy, there the artisan, and the shop girl, and the maid-servant, seeking such enjoyment as their confined life afforded; the young boyish companions with interlaced arms, the benignant priest, every now and then the stately carriage slowly passing by to its place on the corso, or to the palace or garden to which its inmates were bound.

Wandering amid this brilliant fantasia of life, Inglesant's heart smote him for the luxurious sense of pleasure which he found himself taking in the present movement and aspect of things. Doubtless this human philosophy, if we may so call it, into which he was drifting, has a tendency, at least, very different from much of the teaching which is the same in every school of religious thought. Love of mankind is inculcated as a sense of duty by every such school; but by this is certainly not intended love of and acquiescence in mankind as it is. This study of human life, however, this love of human existence, is unconnected with any desire for the improvement either of the individual or of the race. It is man as he is, not man as he might be, or as he should be, which is a delightful subject of contemplation to this tolerant philosophy which human frailty finds so attractive. Man's failings, his self-inflicted miseries, his humours, the effect of his very crimes and vices, if not even those vices themselves, form a chief part in the changing drama upon which the student's eyes are so eagerly set, and without these it would lose its interest and attraction. A world of perfect beings would be to such a man of all things the most stale and unprofitable. Humour and pathos, the grotesque contrast between a man's aspirations and his actual condition, his dreams and his mean realities, would be altogether wanting in such a world.

Indignation, sorrow, satire, doubt, and restlessness, allegory, the very soul and vital salt of life, would be wanting in such a world. But if a man does not desire a perfect world, what part can he have in the Christian warfare? It is true that an intimate study of a world of sin and of misfortune throws up the sinless character of the Saviour into strong relief; but the student accepts this Saviour's character and mission as part of the phenomena of existence, not as an irreconcilable crusade and battle-cry against the powers of the world on every hand. The study of life is indeed equally possible to both schools; but the pleased acquiescence in life as it is, with all its follies and fantastic pleasures, is surely incompatible with following the footsteps of the Divine Ascetic who trod the wine-press of the wrath of God. With all their errors, they who rejected the world and all its allurements, and taught the narrow life of painful self-denial, must be more nearly right than this.

Nevertheless, even before this last thought was completely formed in his mind, the sight of the moving people, and of the streets of the wonderful city opening out on every side, full of palaces and glittering shops and stalls, and crowded with life and gaiety, turned his halting choice back again in the opposite direction, and he thought something like this:—

"How useless and even pitiful is the continued complaint of moralists and divines, to whom none lend an ear, whilst they endeavour, age after age, to check youth and pleasure, and turn the current of life and nature backward on its course. For how many ages in this old Rome, as in every other city, since Terence gossipped of the city life, has this frail faulty humanity for a few hours sunned itself on warm afternoons in sheltered walks and streets, and comforted itself into life and pleasure, amid all its cares and toils and sins. Out of this shifting phantasmagoria comes the sound of music, always pathetic and sometimes gay; amid the roofs and belfries peer the foliage of the public walks, the stage upon which, in every city, life may be studied and taken to heart; not far from these walks is, in every city, the mimic stage, the glass in which, in every age and climate, human life has seen itself reflected, and has delighted, beyond all other pleasures, in pitying its own sorrows, in learning its own story, in watching its own fantastic developments, in foreshadowing its own fate, in smiling sadly for an hour over the still more fleeting representation of its own fleeting joys. For ever, without any change, the stream flows on, spite of moralist and divine, the same as when Phaedria and Thais loved each other in old Rome. We look back on these countless ages of city life, cooped in narrow streets and alleys and paved walks, breathing itself in fountained courts and shaded arcades, where youth and manhood and old age have sought their daily sustenance not only of bread but of happiness, and have with difficulty and toil enough found the one and caught fleeting glimpses of the other, between the dark thunder clouds, and under the weird, wintry sky of many a life. Within such a little space how much life is crowded, what high hopes, how much pain! From those high windows behind the flower-pots young girls have looked out upon life, which their instincts told them was made for pleasure, but which year after year convinced them was, somehow or other, given over to pain. How can we read this endless story of humanity with any thought of blame? How can we watch this restless quivering human life, this ceaseless effort of a finite creature to attain to those things which are agreeable to its created nature, alike in all countries, under all climates and skies, and whatever change of garb or semblance the long course of years may bring, with any other thought than that of tolerance and pity—tolerance of every sort of city existence, pity for every kind of toil and evil, year after year repeated, in every one of earth's cities, full of human life and handicraft, and thought and love and pleasure, as in the streets of that old Jerusalem over which the Saviour wept."

The conversation that evening at the Cardinal's villa turned upon the antiquities of Rome. The chief delight of the Fathers of the Oratory was in music, but the Cardinal preferred conversation, especially upon Pagan literature and art. He was an enthusiast upon every subject connected with the Greeks,—art, poetry, philosophy, religion; upon all these he founded theories and deductions which showed not only an intimate acquaintance with Greek literature, but also a deep familiarity with the human heart. A lively imagination and eloquent and polished utterance enabled him to extract from the baldest and most obscure myths and fragments of antiquity much that was fascinating, and, being founded on a true insight into human nature, convincing also.

Inglesant especially sympathized with and understood the tone of thought and the line of reasoning with which the Cardinal regarded Pagan antiquity; and this appreciation pleased the Cardinal, and caused him to address much of his conversation directly to him.

The villa was full of objects by which thought and conversation were attracted to such channels. The garden was entered by a portico or door-case adorned with ancient statues, the volto or roof of which was painted with classic subjects, and the lofty doors themselves were covered with similar ones in relief. The walls of the house, towards the garden, were cased with bas-reliefs,—"antique incrustations of history" the Cardinal called them,—representing the Rape of Europa, of Leda, and other similar scenes. These antique stones and carvings were fitted into the walls between the rich pilasters and cornicing which adorned the front of the villa, and the whole was crossed with tendrils of citron and other flowering shrubs, trained with the utmost art and nicety, so as to soften and ornament without concealing the sculpture. The gardens were traversed by high hedges of myrtle, lemon, orange, and juniper, interspersed with mulberry trees and oleanders, and were planted with wide beds of brilliant flowers, according to the season, now full of anemones, ranunculuses, and crocuses. The whole was formed upon terraces, fringed with balustrades of marble, over which creeping plants were trained with the utmost skill, only leaving sufficient stone-work visible to relieve the foliage. The walks were full of statues and pieces of carving in relief. The rooms were ornamented in the same taste, and the chimney of the one in which the supper was laid was enriched with sculpture of wonderful grace and delicacy.

One of the Fathers of the Oratory asked Inglesant whether he had seen the Venus of the Medicean palace, and what he thought of it compared with the Venus of the Farnese; and when he had replied, the other turned to the Cardinal and inquired whether, in his opinion, the Greeks had any higher meaning or thought in these beautiful delineations of human form than mere admiration and pleasure.

"The higher minds among them assuredly," said the Cardinal; "but in another and more important sense every one of them, even the most unlettered peasant who gazed upon the work, and the most worldly artist buried in the mere outward conceptions of his art, were consciously or unconsciously following, and even worshipping, a divinity and a truth than which nothing can be higher or more universal. For the truth was too powerful for them, and so universal that they could not escape. Human life, in all the phases of its beauty and its deformity, is so instinct with the divine nature, that, in merely following its variety, you are learning the highest lessons, and teaching them to others."

"What may you understand by being instinct with the divine nature?" said the Priest, not unnaturally.

"I mean that general consensus and aggregate of truth in which human nature and all that is related to it is contained. That divine idea, indeed, in which all the facts of human life and experience are drawn together, and exalted to their utmost perfection and refinement, and are seen and felt to form a whole of surpassing beauty and nobleness, in which the divine image and plastic power in man is clearly discerned and intellectually received and appropriated."

The Priest did not seem altogether to understand this, and remained silent.

"But," said Inglesant, "much of this pursuit of the beautiful must have been associated, in the ideas of the majority of the people, with thoughts and actions the most unlovely and undesirable according to the intellectual reason, however delightful to the senses."

"Even in these orgies," replied the Cardinal, "in the most profligate and wild excesses of license, I see traces of this all-pervading truth; for the renouncing of all bound and limit is in itself a truth, when any particular good, though only sensual, is freed and perfected. This is, no doubt, what the higher natures saw, and it was this that reconciled them to the license of the people and of the unilluminated. In all these aberrations they saw ever fresh varieties and forms of that truth which, when it was intellectually conceived, it was their greatest enjoyment to contemplate, and which, no doubt, formed the material of the instructions which the initiated into the mysteries received. It is impossible that this could be otherwise, for there can be no philosophy if there be no human life from which to derive it. The intellectual existence and discourses of Socrates cannot be understood, except when viewed in connection with the sensual and common existence and carnal wisdom of Aristophanes, any more than the death of the one can be understood without we also understand the popular thought and feeling delineated to us by the other. And why should we be so ungrateful as to turn round on this 'beast within the man,' if you so choose to call it,— the human body and human delight to which we owe not only our own existence and all that makes life desirable, but also that very loftiness and refinement of soul, that elevated and sublime philosophy, which could not exist but for the contrast and antithesis which popular life presents? Surely it is more philosophical to take in the whole of life, in every possible form, than to shut yourself up in one doctrine, which, while you fondly dream you have created it, and that it is capable of self-existence, is dependent for its very being on that human life from which you have fled, and which you despise. This is the whole secret of the pagan doctrine, and the key to those profound views of life which were evolved in their religion. This is the worship of Priapus, of human life, in which nothing comes amiss or is to be staggered at, however voluptuous or sensual, for all things are but varied manifestations of life; of life, ruddy, delicious, full of fruits, basking in sunshine and plenty, dyed with the juice of grapes; of life in valleys cooled by snowy peaks, amid vineyards and shady fountains, among which however, 'Sæpe Faunorum voces exauditæ, sæpe visæ formæ Deorum.'"

"This, Signore Inglesant," said the Priest, passing the wine across the table, with a smile, "is somewhat even beyond the teaching of your friends of the society of the Gesu; and would make their doctrine even, excellently as it already suits that purpose, still more propitious towards the frailty of men."

Inglesant filled his glass, and drank it off before he replied. The wine was of the finest growth of the delicious Alban vineyards; and as the nectar coursed through his veins, a luxurious sense of acquiescence stole over him. The warm air, laden with perfume from the shaded windows, lulled his sense; a stray sunbeam lighted the piles of fruit and the deeply embossed gold of the service on the table before him, and the mellow paintings and decorated ceiling of the room. As he slowly drank his wine the memory of Serenus de Cressy, and of his doctrine of human life, rose before his mind, and his eyes were fixed upon the deep-coloured wine before him, as though he saw there, as in a magic goblet, the opposing powers that divide the world. It seemed to him that he had renounced his right to join in the conflict, and that he must remain as ever a mere spectator of the result; nevertheless he said,—

"Your doctrine is delightful to the philosopher and to the man of culture, who has his nature under the curb, and his glance firmly fixed upon the goal; but to the vulgar it is death; and indeed it was death until the voice of another God was heard, and the form of another God was seen, not in vineyards and rosy bowers, but in deserts and stony places, in dens and caves of the earth, and in prisons and on crosses of wood."

"It is treason to the idea of cultured life," said the Cardinal, "to evoke such gloomy images. My theory is at least free from such faults of taste."

"Do not fear me," said Inglesant; "I have no right to preach such a lofty religion. An asceticism I never practised it would ill-become me to advocate."

"You spoke of the death of Socrates," said the Priest; "does this event fall within the all-embracing tolerance of your theory?"

"The death of Socrates," said the Cardinal, "appears to have been necessary to preserve the framework of ordinary every-day society from falling to pieces. At any rate men of good judgment in that day thought so, and they must have known best. You must remember that it was Socrates that was put to death, not Plato, and we must not judge by what the latter has left us of what the former taught. The doctrine of Socrates was purely negative, and undermined the principle of belief not only in the Gods but in everything else. His dialectic was excellent and noble, his purpose pure and exalted, the clearing of men's mind's of false impressions; but to the common fabric of society his method was destruction. So he was put to death, unjustly of course, and contrary to the highest law, but according to the lower law of expediency, justly; for society must preserve itself even at the expense of its noblest thinkers. But," added the Cardinal with a smile, "we have only to look a little way for a parallel. It is not, however, a perfect one; for while the Athenians condemned Socrates to a death painless and dignified, the moderns have burnt Servetus, whose doctrine contained nothing dangerous to society, but turned on a mere point of the schools, at the stake."

"Why do they not burn you, Cardinal?" said one of the Oratorians, who had not yet spoken, a very intimate friend of the master of the house.

"They do not know whom to begin with in Rome," he replied; "if they once commenced to burn, the holocaust would be enormous before the sacrifice was complete."

"I would they would burn Donna Olympia," said the same Priest; "is it true that she has returned?"

"Have patience," said the Cardinal; "from what I hear you will not have long to wait."

"I am glad you believe in purgatory," said the Priest who had spoken first. "I did not know that your Eminence was so orthodox."

"You mistake. I do not look so far. I am satisfied with the purgatory of this life. I merely meant that I fear we shall not long have his Holiness among us."

"The moderns have burnt others besides Servetus," said one of the guests—"Vaninus, for instance."

"I did not instance Vaninus," said the Cardinal, "because his punishment was more justifiable, and nearer to that of Socrates. Vaninus taught atheism, which is dangerous to society, and he courted his death. I suppose, Mr. Inglesant, that your bishops would burn Mr. Hobbes if they dared."

"I know little of the Anglican bishops, Eminence," replied Inglesant; "but from that little I should imagine that it is not impossible."

"What does Mr. Hobbes teach?" said one of the party.

The Cardinal looked at Inglesant, who shook his head.

"What he teaches would require more skill than I possess to explain. What they would say that they burnt him for would be for teaching atheism and the universality of matter. I fancy that it is at least doubtful whether even Vaninus meant to deny the existence of God. I have been told that he was merely an enthusiastic naturalist, who could see nothing but nature, which was his god. But as for Mr. Hobbes's opinions, he seems to me to have proclaimed a third authority in addition to the two which already claimed the allegiance of the world. We had first the authority of a Church, then of a book, now Mr. Hobbes asserts the authority of reason; and the supporters of the book, even more fiercely than those of the Church, raise a clamour against him. His doctrines are very insidiously and cautiously expressed, and it proves the acuteness of the Anglican divines that they have detected, under the plausible reasoning of Mr. Hobbes, the basis of a logical argument which would, if unconfuted, destroy the authority of Holy Scripture."

The Cardinal looked at Inglesant curiously, as though uncertain whether he was speaking in good faith or not, but the subject did not seem to possess great interest to the company at table, and the conversation took another turn.

CHAPTER VI

Some few days after the conversation at the Cardinal's villa, Inglesant received his first commission as an agent of the Society of the Gesu. He was invited to sup with the Superior of the English Jesuits, Father Stafford, at the college called St. Thomasso degli Inglesi. After the meal, over which nothing was spared to render it delicious, and during the course of which the Superior exerted himself to please, the latter said,—

"I am instructed to offer you a commission, which, if I mistake not, will both prove very interesting to you, and will also be of advantage to your interests. You are probably acquainted with the story of the old Duke of Umbria. You have heard that, wearied with age, and tired of the world, he resigned the dukedom to his son, his only child, the object of all his hopes and the fruit of careful training and instruction. This son, far from realizing the brilliant hopes of his father, indulged in every kind of riot and debauchery, and finally died young, worn out before his time. The old Duke, broken-hearted by this blow, has virtually made over the succession to the Holy Father, and lives now, alone and silent in his magnificent palace, caring for no worldly thing, and devoting all his thoughts to religion and to his approaching end. He is unhappy in the prospect of his dissolution, and the only persons who are admitted to his presence are those who promise him any comfort in the anticipation, or any clearness in the vision, of the future life. Quacks and impostors of every kind, priests and monks and fanatics, are admitted freely, and trouble this miserable old man, and drive him into intolerable despair. To give to this old man, whose life of probity, of honour, of devotion to his people, of conscientious rectitude, is thus miserably rewarded—to give some comfort to this miserable victim of a jealousy which the superstitious miscall that of heaven, is a mission which the ethereal chivalry of the soul will eagerly embrace. It is one, I may say without flattery, for which I hold you singularly fitted. A passionate religious fervour, such as yours, combined in the most singular manner with the freest speculative opinions, and commended by a courteous grace, will at once soothe and strengthen this old man's shattered intellect, distracted and tormented and rapidly sinking into imbecility and dotage."

Father Stafford paused and filled his glass; then passing the wine to Inglesant, he continued, half carelessly,—

"I said that the Duke had virtually made over the succession of his State to the Papal See; but this has not been formally ratified, and there has arisen some hesitation and difficulty respecting it. Some of the unsuitable advisers to whom the Duke in his mental weakness has unfortunately lent an ear, have endeavoured to persuade him that the interests of his people will be imperilled by their country being placed under the mild and beneficent rule of the Holy Father. We hear something of a Lutheran, who, by some unexplained means, has obtained considerable influence with this unhappy old man; and we are informed that there is great danger of the Duke's hesitating so long before he completes the act of succession, that his death may occur before it is complete. You will of course exert the influence which I hope and expect that you will soon gain at the ducal Court, to hasten this consummation, so desirable for the interests of the people, of the Papacy, and of the Duke himself."

Inglesant had listened to this communication with great interest. The prospect which the earlier part of it had opened before him was in many respects an attractive one, and the flattering words of the Superior were uttered in a tone of sincerity which made them very pleasant to hear. The description of the Duke's condition offered to him opportunities of mental study of absorbing interest, and the characters of those by whom he was surrounded would no doubt present combinations and varieties of singular and unusual curiosity. It must not be denied, moreover, that there entered into his estimate of the proposal made to him somewhat of the prospect of luxurious and courtly life—of that soft clothing, both of body and spirit, which they who live in kings' houses wear. It is difficult indeed for one who has been long accustomed to refined and dainty living, where every sense is trained and strengthened by the fruition it enjoys, to regard the future altogether with indifference in respect to these things. The palace of the Duke was notorious throughout all Italy for the treasures of art which it contained, though its master in his old age was become indifferent to such delights. But though these thoughts passed through his mind as the Superior was speaking, Inglesant was too well versed in the ways of Courts and Ecclesiastics not to know that there was something more to come, and to attend carefully for its development. The latter part of the Superior's speech produced something even of a pleasurable amusement, as the skilfully executed tactics of an opponent are pleasing to a good player either at cards or chess. The part which he was now expected to play, the side which he was about to espouse, taken in connection with the difficulties and impressions which had perplexed him since he had arrived in Italy, and which had not been removed by what he had seen in Rome itself, corresponded so exactly with the scheme which, to his excited imagination, was being spiritually developed for his destruction—a morbid idea, possibly, which the lofty beneficence of Molinos's doctrine had only partially removed—that its appearance and recognition actually provoked a smile. But the smile, which the Superior noticed and entirely misunderstood, was succeeded by uneasiness and depression. There was, however, little hesitation and no apparent delay in Inglesant's manner of acceptance. The old habit of implicit obedience was far from obliterated or even weakened, and though Father St. Clare was not present the supreme motive of his influence was not unfelt. He had chosen his part when in Paris he had turned his back upon De Cressy, and accepted the Jesuit's offer of the mission to Rome. He had lived in Rome, had been received and countenanced and entertained as one who had accepted the service of those who had so courteously and hospitably treated him, and it was far too late now, when the first return was expected of him, to draw back or to refuse. To obey was not only a recognized duty, it was an instinct which not only long training but experience even served to strengthen. He assured the Superior that he was perfectly ready to set out. He assured himself indeed that it was not necessary to come to a decision at that moment, and that he should be much better able to decide upon his course of conduct when he had seen the Duke himself, and received more full instructions from Rome.

The Superior informed Inglesant that he would be expected to visit Umbria as a gentleman of station, and offered to provide the necessary means. Inglesant contented himself with declining this offer for the present. Since his arrival at Rome he had received considerable sums of money from England, the result of Lady Cardiff's bounty, and the Cardinal's purse was open to him in several indirect ways. He provided himself with the necessary number of servants, horses, and other conveniences, and some time, as would appear, after Easter, he arrived at Umbria.

On his journey, as he rode along in the wonderful clear morning light, in his "osteria" in the middle of the day, and when he resumed his journey in the cool of the evening, his thoughts had been very busy. He remembered his conversation with the Count Vespiriani, and was unable to reconcile his present mission with the pledge he had given to the Count. He was more than once inclined to turn back and refuse to undertake the duty demanded of him. Thoughts of Lauretta, and of the strange fate that had separated him from her, also occupied his mind; and with these conflicting emotions still unreconciled, he saw at last the white façade of the palace towering above the orange groves, and the houses and pinnacles of the city.

The ducal palace at Umbria is a magnificent example of the Renaissance style. It is impossible to dwell in or near this wonderful house without the life becoming affected, and even diverted from its previous course, by its imperious influence. The cold and mysterious power of the classic architecture is wedded to the rich and libertine fancy of the Renaissance, treading unrestrained and unabashed the maze of nature and of phantasy, and covering the classic purity of outline with its exquisite tracery of fairy life. Over door and window and pilaster throng and cling the arabesque carvings of foliage and fruit, of graceful figures in fantastic forms and positions,—all of infinite variety; all full of originality, of life, of motion, and of character; all of exquisite beauty both of design and workmanship. The effect of the whole is lightness and joy, while the eye is charmed and the sense filled with a luxurious satisfaction at the abounding wealth of beauty and lavish imagination. But together with this delight to eye and sense there is present to the mind a feeling, not altogether painless, of oppressive luxury, and of the mating of incongruous forms, arousing as it were an uneasy conscience, and affecting the soul somewhat as the overpowering perfume of tropical vegetation affects the senses. To dwell in this palace was to breathe an enchanted air; and as the wandering prince of story loses his valour and strength in the magic castles into which he strays, so here the indweller, whose intellect was mastered by the genius of the architecture, found his simplicity impaired, his taste becoming more sensuous and less severely chaste, and his senses lulled and charmed by the insidious and enervating spirit that pervaded the place.

At his first presentation Inglesant found the Duke seated in a small room fitted as an oratory or closet, and opening by a private door into the ducal pew in the Chapel. His person was bowed and withered by age and grief, but his eye was clear and piercing, and his intellect apparently unimpaired. He regarded his visitor with an intense and scrutinizing gaze, which lasted for several minutes, and seemed to indicate some suspicion. There was, however, about Inglesant's appearance and manner something so winning and attractive, that the old man's eyes gradually softened, and the expression of distrust that made his look almost that of a wild and hunted creature, changed to one of comparative satisfaction and repose. It is true that he regarded with pleasure and hope every new-comer, from whom he expected to derive consolation and advice.

Inglesant expected that he would inquire of the news of Rome, of the Pope's health, and such-like matters; but he seemed to have no curiosity concerning such things. After waiting for some time in silence he said,—

"Anthony Guevera tells us that we ought to address men who are under thirty with 'You are welcome,' or 'You come in a good hour,' because at that time of life they seem to be coming into the world; from thirty to fifty we ought to greet them with 'God keep you,' or 'Stand in a good hour;' and from fifty onwards, with 'God speed you,' or 'Go in a good hour,' for from thence they go taking their leave of the world. The first is easy to say, and the wish not unlikely to be fulfilled, but the last who shall ensure? You come in a good hour, graceful as an Apollo, to comfort a miserable old man; can you assure me that, when I pass out of this world, I shall depart likewise at a propitious time? I am an old man, and that unseen world which should be so familiar and near to me seems so far off and yet so terrible. A young man steps into life as into a dance, confident of his welcome, pleased himself and pleasing others; the stage to which he comes is bright with flowers, soft music sounds on every side. So ought the old man to enter into the new life, confident of his welcome, pleasing to his Maker and his God, the heavenly minstrelsy in his ears. But it is far otherwise with me. I may lay me down in the 'Angelica Vestis,' the monkish garment that ensures the prayers of holy men for the departing soul; but who will secure me the wedding garment that ensures admission to the banquet above?"

"Do you find no comfort in the Blessed Sacrament, Altezza?" said Inglesant.

"Sometimes I may fancy so; but I cannot see the figure of the Christ for the hell that lies between."

"Ah! Altezza," said Inglesant, his eyes full of pity, not only for the old Duke, but for himself and all mankind, "it is always thus. Something stands between us and the heavenly life. My temptation is other than yours. Communion after communion I find Christ, and He is gracious to me—gracious as the love of God Himself; but month after month and year after year I find not how to follow Him, and when the road is opened to me I am deaf, and refuse to answer to the heavenly call. You, Altezza, are in more hopeful case than I; for it seems to me that your Highness has but to throw off that blasphemous superstition which is found in all Christian creeds alike, which has not feared to blacken even the shining gates of heaven with the smoke of hell."

"All creeds are alike," said the Duke with a shudder, "but mostly your northern religions, harsh and bitter as your skies. I have heard from a Lutheran a system of religion that made my blood run cold, the more as it commends itself to my calmer reason."

"And that is, Altezza?" said Inglesant.

"This, that so far from the Sacrament of Absolution upon earth, or at the hour of death, availing anything, God Himself has no power to change the state of those who die without being entirely purified from every trace of earthly and sensual passion; to such as these, though otherwise sincere Christians, nothing awaits but a long course of suffering in the desolate regions of Hades, as the Lutheran calls it, until, if so may be, the earthly idea is annihilated and totally obliterated from the heart."

"This seems little different from the doctrine of the Church," said Inglesant.

"It is different in this most important part," replied the Duke, "that Holy Church purifies and pardons her penitent, though he feels the passions of earth strong within him till the last; but by this system you must eradicate these yourself. You must purify your heart, you must feel every carnal lust, every vindictive thought, every lofty and contemptuous notion, utterly dead within you before you can enjoy a moment's expectation of future peace. He that goes out of this world with an uncharitable thought against his neighbour does so with the chances against him that he is lost for ever, for his face is turned from the light, and he enters at once upon the devious and downward walks of the future life; and what ground has he to expect that he who could not keep his steps in this life will find any to turn him back, or will have power to turn himself back, from every growing evil in the world to come?"

As the Duke spoke it seemed to Inglesant that these words were addressed to him alone, and that he saw before him the snare of the Devil, bated with the murderer of his brother, stretched before his heedless feet for his eternal destruction.

The Duke took up a book that lay by him, and read,—

"The soul that cherishes the slightest animosity, and takes this feeling into eternity, cannot be happy, though in other respects pious and faithful. Bitterness is completely opposed to the nature and constitution of heaven. The blood of Christ, who on the cross, in the midst of the most excruciating torments, exercised love instead of bitterness, cleanses from this sin also, when it flows in our veins."

"I see nothing in this, Altezza," said Inglesant eagerly, "but what is in accordance with the doctrines of the Church. This is that idea of sacramental purification, that Christ's Body being assimilated to ours purifies and sanctifies. His Body, being exalted at that supreme moment and effort (the moment of His suffering death), to the highest purity of temper and of sweetness by the perfect love and holiness which pervaded His spirit, has been able ever since, in all ages, through the mystery of the Blessed Sacrament, to convert all its worthy recipients in some degree to the same pure and holy state. Many things which men consider misfortunes and painful experiences are in fact but the force of this divine influence, assimilating their hearts to His, and attempering their bodies to the lofty purity of His own. This is the master work of the Devil, that he should lure us into states of mind, as the book says, of bitterness and of violence, by which this divine sweetness is tainted, and this peace broken by suspicion, by hatred, and heat of blood."

"The book says somewhere," said the Duke, turning over the leaves, "that, as the penitent thief rose from the cross to Paradise, so we, if we long after Christ with all the powers of our souls, shall, at the hour of death, rapidly soar aloft from our mortal remains, and then all fear of returning to earth and earthly desires will be at an end."

"It must surely," said Inglesant after a pause, speaking more to himself than to the Duke, "be among the things most surprising to an angelic nature that observes mankind, that, shadows ourselves, standing upon the confines even of this shadowy land, and not knowing what, if aught, awaits us elsewhere, hatred or revenge or unkindness should be among the last passions that are overcome. When the veil is lifted, and we see things as they really are, nothing will so much amaze us as the blindness and perversity that marked our life among our fellow-men. Surely the lofty life is hard, as it seems hard to your Grace; but the very effort itself is gain."

Inglesant left the presence of the Duke after his first interview impressed and softened, but troubled in his mind more than ever at the nature of the mission on which he was sent. Now that he had seen the Duke, and had been touched by his eager questions, and by the earnest searching look in the worn face, his conscience smote him at the thought of abusing his confidence, and of persuading him to adopt a course which Inglesant's own heart warned him might not in the end be conducive either to his own peace or to the welfare of his people, whose happiness he sincerely sought. He found that, in the antechambers and reception rooms of the palace, and even at the Duke's own table, the principal subject of conversation was the expected cession of the dukedom to the Papal See; and that emissaries from Rome had preceded him, and had evidently received instructions announcing his arrival, and were prepared to welcome him as an important ally. On the other hand, there were not wanting those who openly or covertly opposed the cession, some of whom were said to be agents of the Grand Duke of Florence, who was heir to the Duchy of Umbria through his wife. These latter, whose opposition was more secret than open, sought every opportunity of winning Inglesant to their party, employing the usual arguments with which, since his coming into Italy, he had been so familiar. Many days passed in this manner, and Inglesant had repeated conferences with the Duke, during which he made great progress in his favour, and was himself won by his lofty, kindly, and trustful character.

He had resided at Umbria a little less than a month, when he received instructions by a courier from Rome, by which he was informed that at the approaching festival of the Ascension a determined effort was to be made by the agents and friends of the Pope to bring the business to a conclusion. The Duke had promised to keep this festival, which is celebrated at Venice and in other parts of Italy with great solemnity, with unusual magnificence; and it was hoped that while his feelings were influenced and his religious instincts excited by the solemn and tender thoughts and imaginations which gather round the figure of the ascending Son of man, he might be induced to sign the deed of cession. Hitherto the Duke had not mentioned the subject to Inglesant, having found his conversation upon questions of the spiritual life and practice sufficient to occupy the time; but it was not probable that this silence would continue much longer, and on the first day in Ascension week Inglesant was attending Vespers at one of the Churches in the town in considerable anxiety and trouble of mind.

The sun had hardly set, and the fête in the garden was not yet begun, when, Vespers being over, he came out upon the river-side lined with stately houses which fronted the palace gardens towering in terraced walks and trellises of green hedges on the opposite bank. The sun, setting behind the wooded slopes, flooded this green hill-side with soft and dream-like light, and bathed the carved marble façade of the palace, rising above it with a rosy glimmer, in which the statues on its roof, and the fretted work of its balustrades, rested against the darkening blue of the evening sky. A reflex light, ethereal and wonderful, coming from the sky behind him, and the marble buildings and towers on which the sun's rays rested more fully than they did upon the palace, brooded over the river and the bridge with its rows of angelic forms, and, climbing the leafy slopes, as if to contrast its softer splendour with the light above, transfigured with colour the wreaths of vapour which rose from the river and hung about its wharves.

The people were already crowding out of the city, and forcing their way across the bridge towards the palace, where the illuminations and the curious waterworks, upon which the young Duke had, during his short reign, expended much money, were to be exhibited as soon as the evening was sufficiently dark. The people were noisy and jostling, but as usual good-tempered and easily pleased. Few masques or masquerade dresses had appeared as yet, but almost every one was armed with a small trumpet, a drum, or a Samarcand cane, from which to shoot peas or comfits. At the corner of the main street that opened on to the quay, however, some disturbing cause was evidently at work. The crowd was perplexed by two contending currents, the one consisting of those who were attempting to turn into the street from the wharf, in order to learn the cause of the confusion, the other, of those who were apparently being driven forcibly out of the street, towards the wharves and the bridge, by pressure from behind. Discordant cries and exclamations of anger and contempt rose above the struggling mass. Taking advantage of the current that swept him onward, Inglesant reached the steps of the Church of St. Felix, which stood at the corner of the two streets, immediately opposite the bridge and the ducal lions which flanked the approach. On reaching this commanding situation the cause of the tumult presented itself in the form of a small group of men, who were apparently dragging a prisoner with them, and had at this moment reached the corner of the wharf, not far from the steps of the Church, surrounded and urged on by a leaping, shouting, and excited crowd. Seen from the top of the broad marble bases that flanked the steps, the whole of the wide space, formed by the confluence of the streets, and over which the shadows were rapidly darkening, presented nothing but a sea of agitated and tossing heads, while, from the windows, the bridge, and even the distant marble terraced steps that led up to the palace, the crowd appeared curious, and conscious that something unusual was in progress.

From the cries and aspect of the crowd, and of the men who dragged their prisoner along, it was evident that it was the intention of the people to throw the wretched man over the parapets of the bridge into the river below, and that to frustrate this intention not a moment was to be lost. The pressure of the crowd, greater from the opposite direction than from the one in which Inglesant had come, fortunately swept the group almost to the foot of the steps. Near to Inglesant, and clinging to the carved bases of the half-columns that supported the façade of the Church, were two or three priests who had come out of the interior, attracted by the tumult. Availing himself of their support, Inglesant shouted to the captors of the unhappy man, in the name of the Church and of the Duke, to bring their prisoner up the steps. They probably would not have obeyed him, though they hesitated for a moment; but the surrounding crowd, attracted towards the Church by Inglesant's gestures, began to press upon it from all sides, as he had indeed foreseen would be the case, and finally, by their unconscious and involuntary motion, swept the prisoner and his captors up the steps to the side of the priests and of Inglesant. It was a singular scene. The rapidly advancing night had changed the golden haze of sunset to a sombre gloom, but lights began to appear in the houses all around, and paper lanterns showed themselves among the crowd.

The cause of all this confusion was dragged by his persecutors up the steps, and placed upon the last of the flight, confronting the priests. His hair was disordered, his clothes nearly torn from his limbs, and his face and dress streaked with blood. Past the curtain across the entrance of the Church, which was partly drawn back by those inside, a flash of light shot across the marble platform, and shone upon the faces of the foremost of the crowd. This light shone full upon Inglesant, who stood, in striking contrast to the dishevelled figure that confronted him, dressed in a suit of black satin and silver, with a deep collar of Point-de-Venice lace. The priests stood a little behind, apparently desirous to learn the nature of the prisoner's offence before they interfered; and the accusers therefore addressed themselves to Inglesant, who, indeed, was recognized by many as a friend of the Duke, and whom the priests especially had received instructions from Rome to support. The confusion in the crowd meanwhile increased rather than diminished; there seemed to be causes at work other than the slight one of the seizure by the mob of an unpopular man. The town was very full of strangers, and it struck Inglesant that the arrest of the man before him was merely an excuse, and was being used by some who had an object to gain by stirring up the people. He saw, at any rate, however this might be, a means of engaging the priests to assist him, should their aid be necessary in saving the man's life.

That there was a passionate attachment among the people to a separate and independent government of their city and state, an affection towards the family of their hereditary dukes, and a dread and jealous dislike of the Pope's government and of the priests, he had reason to believe. It seemed to him that the people were about to break forth into some demonstration of this antipathy, which, if allowed to take place, and if taken advantage of, as it would be, by the neighbouring princes, would be most displeasing to the policy of Rome, if not entirely subversive of it. With these thoughts in his mind, as he stood for a moment silent on the marble platform, and saw before him, what is perhaps the most impressive of all sights, a vast assemblage of people in a state of violent and excited opposition, and reflected on the causes which he imagined agitated them,—causes which in his heart he, though enlisted on the opposite side, had difficulty in persuading himself were not justifiable,—it came into his mind more powerfully than ever, that the moment foretold to him by Serenus de Cressy was at last indeed come. Surely it behoved him to look well to his steps, lest he should be found at last absolutely and unequivocally fighting against his conscience and his God; if, indeed, this looking well to their steps on such occasions, and not boldly choosing their side, had not been for many years the prevailing vice of his family, and to some extent the cause of his own spiritual failure.

The two men who held the apparent cause of all this uproar were two mechanics of jovial aspect, who appeared to look upon the affair more in the light of a brutal practical joke (no worse in their eyes for its brutality), than as a very serious matter. To Inglesant's question what the man had done they answered that he had refused to kneel to the Blessed Sacrament, as it was being carried through the streets to some poor, dying soul, and upon being remonstrated with, had reviled not only the Sacrament itself, but the Virgin, the Holy Father, and the Italians generally, as Papistical asses, with no more sense than the Pantaleoni of their own comedies. The men gave this evidence in an insolent half-jesting manner, as though not sorry to utter such words safely in the presence of the priests.

Inglesant, who kept his eyes fixed upon the prisoner, and noticed that he was rapidly recovering from the breathless and exhausted condition the ill-treatment he had met with had reduced him to, and was assuming a determined and somewhat noble aspect, abstained from questioning him, lest he should make his own case only the more desperate; but, turning to the priests, he rapidly explained his fears to them, and urged that the man should be immediately secured from the people, that he might be examined by the Duke, and the result forwarded to Rome. The priests hesitated. Apart from the difficulty, they said, of taking the man out of the hands of his captors, such a course would be sure to exasperate the people still further, and bring on the very evil that he was desirous of averting. It would be better to let the mob work their will upon the man; it would at least occupy some time, and every moment was precious. In less than an hour the fireworks at the palace would begin, might indeed be hastened by a special messenger; and the fête once begun, they hoped all danger would be over. To this Inglesant answered that the man's arrest was evidently only an excuse for riot, and had probably already answered its purpose; that to confine the people's attention to it would be unfavourable to the intentions of those who were promoting a political tumult; and that the avowed cause of the man's seizure, and of the excitement of the mob, being disrespectful language towards the Holy Father, the tumult, if properly managed, might be made of service to the cause of Rome rather than the reverse.

Without waiting for the effect of this somewhat obscure argument on the priests, Inglesant directed the men who held their prisoner to bring him into the Church. They were unwilling to do so, but the crowd below was so confused and tumultuous, one shouting one thing and one another, that it seemed impossible that, if they descended into it again, they would be allowed to retain their prey, and would not rather be overwhelmed in a common destruction with him. On the other hand, by obeying Inglesant, they at least kept possession of their prisoner, and could therefore scarcely fail of receiving some reward from the authorities. They therefore consented, and by a sudden movement they entered the Church, the doors of which were immediately closed, after some few of the populace had managed to squeeze themselves in. A messenger was at once despatched to the palace to hasten the fireworks, and to request that a detachment of the Duke's guard should be sent into the Church by a back way.

The darkness had by this time so much increased that few of the people were aware of what had taken place, and the ignorance of the crowd as to the cause of the tumult was so general that little disturbance took place among those who were shut out of the Church. They remained howling and hooting, it is true, for some time, and some went so far as to beat against the closed doors; but a rumour being spread among the crowd that the fireworks were immediately to begin, they grew tired of this unproductive occupation, and flocked almost to a man out of the square and wharves, and crowded across the bridge into the gardens.

When the guard arrived, Inglesant claimed the man as the Duke's prisoner, to be examined before him in the morning. The curiosity of the Duke in all religious matters being well known, this seemed very reasonable to the officer of the guard, and the priests did not like to dispute it after the instructions they had received with regard to Inglesant's mission. The two artisans were propitiated by a considerable reward, and the prisoner was then transported by unfrequented ways to the palace, and shut up in a solitary apartment, whilst the rest of the world delighted itself at the palace fêtes.

The garden festivities passed away amid general rejoicing and applause. The finest effect was produced at the conclusion, when the whole mass of water at the command of the engines, being thrown into the air in thin fan-like jets, was illuminated by various coloured lights, producing the appearance of innumerable rainbows, through which the palace itself, the orangeries, the gardens, and terraces, and the crowds of delighted people, were seen illuminated and refracted in varied and ever-changing tints. Amid these sparkling colours strange birds passed to and fro, and angelic forms descended by unseen machinery and walked on the higher terraces, and as it were upon the flashing rainbows themselves. Delicious music from unseen instruments ravished the sense, and when the scene appeared complete and nothing further was expected, an orange grove in the centre of the whole apparently burst open, and displayed the stage of a theatre, upon which antic characters performed a pantomime, and one of the finest voices in Italy sang an ode in honour of the day, of the Duke, and of the Pope.

CHAPTER VII

The Duke had engaged the next morning to be present at a theatrical representation of a religious character, somewhat of the nature of a miracle play, to be given in the courtyard of the "Hospital of Death," which adjoined to the Campo Santo of the city.

Before accompanying his Highness, Inglesant had given orders to have the man, who had been the cause of so much excitement the evening before, brought into his apartment, that he might see whether or no his eccentricity made him sufficiently interesting to be presented to the Duke.

When the stranger was brought to the palace early in the morning, and having been found to be quite harmless, was entrusted by the guard to two servants to be brought into Inglesant's presence, he thought himself in a new world. Hitherto his acquaintance with Italian life had been that of a stranger and from the outside; he was now to see somewhat of the interior life of a people among whom the glories of the Renaissance still lingered, and to see it in one of the most wonderful of the Renaissance works, the ducal palace of Umbria. Born in the dull twilight of the north, and having spent most of his mature years amongst the green mezzotints of Germany, he was now transplanted into a land of light and colour, dazzling to a stranger so brought up. Reared in the sternest discipline, he found himself among a people to whom life was a fine art, and the cultivation of the present and its enjoyments the end of existence. From room to room, as he followed his guide, who pointed out from time to time such of the beauties of the place as he considered most worthy of notice, the stranger saw around what certainly might have intoxicated a less composed and determined brain.

The highest efforts of the genius of the Renaissance had been expended upon this magnificent house. The birth of a new instinct, differing in some respects from any instincts of art which had preceded it, produced in this and other similar efforts original and wonderful results. The old Greek art entered with unsurpassable intensity into sympathy with human life; but it was of necessity original and creative, looking always forward and not back, and lacked the pathos and depth of feeling that accompanied that new birth of art which sought much of its inspiration among the tombs and ruined grottoes, and most of its sympathetic power among the old well-springs of human feeling, read in the torn and faded memorials of past suffering and destruction. This new instinct of art abandoned itself without reserve to the pursuit of everything which mankind had ever beheld of the beautiful, or had felt of the pathetic or the sad, or had dreamed of the noble or the ideal. The genius of the Renaissance set itself to reproduce this enchanted world of form and colour, traversed by thoughts and spiritual existences mysterious and beautiful, and the home of beings who had found this form and colour and these mysterious thoughts blend into a human life delicious in its very sorrows, grotesque and incongruous in its beauty, alluring and attractive amid all its griefs and hardships; so much so indeed that, in the language of the old fables, the Gods themselves could not be restrained from throwing off their divine garments, and wandering up and down among the paths and the adventures of men. By grotesque and humorous delineation, by fanciful representation of human passion under strange and unexpected form, by the dumb ass speaking and grasshoppers playing upon flutes, was this world of intelligent life reproduced in the rooms and on the walls of the house through which the stranger walked for the first time.

He probably thought that he saw little of it, yet the bizarre effect was burning itself into his brain. From the overhanging chimney-pieces antique masques and figures such as he had never seen, even in dreams, leered out upon him from arabesque carvings of foliage, or skulked behind trophies of war, of music, or of the arts of peace. The door and window frames seemed bowers of fruit and flowers, and forests of carved leaves wreathed the pilasters and walls. But this was not all; with a perfection of design and an extraordinary power of fancy, this world of sylvan imagery was peopled by figures and stories of exquisite grace and sweetness, representing the most touching incidents of human life and history. Men and women; lovers and warriors in conflicts and dances and festivals, in sacrifices and games; children sporting among flowers; bereavement and death, husbandry and handicraft, hunters and beasts of chase. Again, among briony and jasmin and roses, or perched upon ears of corn and sheaves of maize, birds of every plumage confronted—so the grotesque genius willed—fish and sea monsters and shells and marine wonders of every kind.

Upon the walls, relieved by panelling of wood, were paintings of landscapes and the ruined buildings of antiquity overgrown with moss, or of modern active life in markets and theatres, of churches and cities in the course of erection with the architects and scaffold poles, of the processions and marriages of princes, of the ruin of emperors and of kings. Below and beside these were credenzas and cabinets upon which luxury and art had lavished every costly device and material which the world conceived or yielded. Inlaid with precious woods, and glittering with costly jewels and marbles, they reproduced in these differing materials all those infinite designs which the carved walls had already wearied themselves to express. Plaques and vases from Castel Durante or Faience,—some of a strange pale colour, others brilliant with a grotesque combination of blue and yellow,—crowded the shelves.

Passing through this long succession of rooms, the stranger reached at last a library, a noble apartment of great size, furnished with books in brilliant antique binding of gold and white vellum, and otherwise ornamented with as much richness as the rest of the palace. Upon reading desks were open manuscripts and printed books richly illuminated. Connected with this apartment by open arches, was an anteroom or corridor, which again opened on a loggia, beyond the shady arches of which lay the palace gardens, long vistas of green walks, and reaches of blue sky, flecked and crossed by the spray of fountains. The decorations of the anteroom and loggia were more profuse and extravagant than any that the stranger had yet seen. There was a tradition that this portion of the palace had been finished last, and that when the workmen arrived at it the time for the completion of the whole was very nearly run out. The attention of all the great artists, hitherto engaged upon different parts of the entire palace, was concentrated upon this unfinished portion, and all their workmen and assistants were called to labour upon it alone. The work went on by night and day, not ceasing even to allow of sleep. Unlimited supplies of Greek wine were furnished to the workmen; and stimulated by excitement and the love of art, emulating each other, and half-intoxicated by the delicious wine, the work exceeded all previous productions. For wild boldness and luxuriance of fancy these rooms were probably unequalled in the world.

In the anteroom facing the loggia the stranger found Inglesant conversing with an Italian who held rather a singular post in the ducal Court. He was standing before a cabinet of black oak, inlaid with representations of lutes and fifes, over which were strewn roses confined by coloured ribbons, and supporting vases of blue and yellow majolica, thrown into strong relief by the black wood. Above this cabinet was a painting representing some battle in which a former Duke had won great honour; while on a grassy knoll in the foreground the huntsmen of Ganymede were standing with their eyes turned upward towards the bird of Zeus, who is carrying the youth away to the skies, emblematical of the alleged apotheosis of the ducal hero. Richly dressed in a fantastic suit of striped silk, and leaning against the cabinet in an attitude of listless repose, Inglesant was contemplating an object which he held in his hand, and which both he and his companion appeared to regard with intense interest. This was an antique statuette of a faun, holding its tail in its left hand, and turning its head and body to look at it,—an occupation of which, if we may trust the monuments of antiquity, this singular creature appears to have been fond. The Italian was of a striking figure, and was dressed somewhat more gaily than was customary with his countrymen; and the whole group was fully in unison with the spirit of the place and with the wealth of beauty and luxury of human life that pervaded the whole.

The man who was standing by Inglesant's side, and who had the air of a connoisseur or virtuoso, was an Italian of some fifty years of age. His appearance, as has been said, was striking at first sight, but on longer acquaintance became very much more so. He was tall and had been dark, but his hair and beard were plentifully streaked with gray. His features were large and aquiline, and his face deeply furrowed and lined. His appearance would have been painfully worn, almost to ghastliness, but for a mocking and humorous expression which laughed from his eyes, his mouth, his nostrils, and every line and feature of his face. Whenever this expression subsided, and his countenance sank into repose, a look of wan sadness and even terror took its place, and the large black eyes became fixed and intense in their gaze, as though some appalling object attracted their regard.

This man had been born of a good but poor family, and had been educated by his relations with the expectation of his becoming an ecclesiastic, and he had even passed some time as a novice of some religious order. The tendency of his mind not leading him to the further pursuit of a religious life, he left his monastery, and addressed himself to live by his wits, among the families and households of princes. He had made himself very useful in arranging comedies and pageantries, and he had at one time belonged to one of those dramatic companies called "Zanni," who went about the country reciting and acting comedies. Combined with this talent he discovered great aptitude in the management of serious affairs, and was more than once, while apparently engaged entirely on theatrical performances, employed in secret State negotiations which could not so well be entrusted to an acknowledged and conspicuous agent. In this manner of life he might have continued; but having become involved in one of the contests which disturbed Italy, he received a dangerous wound in the head, and on rising from his sick bed in the Albergo in which he had been nursed, he was merely removed to another as a singular if not dangerous lunatic. The symptoms of his disease first manifested themselves in a very unpleasant familiarity with the secrets of those around him, and it was probably this feature of his complaint which led to his detention. As he improved in health, however, he ceased to indulge in any conversation which might give offence, but, assuming a sedate and agreeable manner, he conversed with all who came to him, calling them, although strangers and such as he had never before seen, by their proper names, and talking to them pleasantly concerning their parents, relations, the coats-of-arms of their families, and such other harmless and agreeable matters.

What brought him prominently into notice was the strangely prophetic spirit he manifested before, or at the moment of the occurrence of, more than one public event. He was taken from the hospital and examined by the Pope, and afterwards at several of the sovereign Courts of Italy. Thus, not long before the time when Inglesant met him in the ducal palace at Umbria, he was at Chambery assisting at the preparation of some festivals which the young Duke of Savoy was engaged in celebrating. One day, as he was seated at dinner with several of the Duke's servants, he suddenly started up from his seat, exclaiming that he saw the Duke de Nemours fall dead from his horse, killed by a pistol shot. The Duke, who was uncle to the young monarch of Savoy, was then in France, where he was one of the leaders of the party of the Fronde. Before many days were passed, however, the news reached Chambery of the fatal duel between this nobleman and the Duke of Beaufort, which occurred at the moment the Italian had thus announced it.

These and other similar circumstances caused the man to be much talked of and sought after among the courts of Italy, where a belief in manifestations of the supernatural was scarcely less universal than in the previous age, when, according to an eye-witness, "the Pope would decide no question, would take no journey, hold no sitting of the Consistory, without first consulting the stars; nay, very few cardinals would transact an affair of any kind, were it but to buy a load of wood, except after consultation duly held with some astrologer or wizard." The credit which the man gained, and the benefits he derived from this reputation, raised him many enemies, who did not scruple to assert that he was simply a clever knave, who was not even his own dupe. Setting on one side, however, the revelations of the distant and the unknown made by him, which seemed inexplicable except by supposing him possessed of some unusual spiritual faculty, there was in the man an amount of knowledge of the world and of men of all classes and ranks, combined with much learning and a humorous wit, which made his company well worth having for his conversation alone. It was not then surprising that he should be found at this juncture at the court of Umbria, where the peculiar idiosyncrasies of the aged Duke, and the interest attached to the intrigue for the session of the dukedom, had assembled a strange and heterogeneous company, and towards which at the moment all men's eyes in Italy were turned.

"Yes, doubtless, it is an antique," the Italian was saying, "though in the last age many artists produced masques and figures so admirable as to be mistaken for antiques; witness that masque which Messire Georgio Vassari says he put in a chimney-piece of his house at Arezzo, which every one took to be an antique. I have seen such myself. This little fellow, however, I saw found in a vineyard near the Miserecordia—a place which I take to have been at some time or other the scene of some terrible event, such as a conflict or struggle or massacre; for though now it is quiet and serene enough, with the sunlight and the rustling leaves, and the splash of a fountain about which there is some good carving, I think of Fra Giovanni Agnolo,—for all this, I never walk there but I feel the presence of fatal events, and a sense of dim figures engaged in conflict, and of faint and distant cries and groans."

As he spoke these last words his eye rested upon the strange figure of the man so hardly rescued from death the night before, and he stopped. His manner changed, and his eyes assumed that expression of intense expectation of which we have spoken before. The appearance of the stranger, and the contrast it presented to the objects around, was indeed such as to make him almost seem an inhabitant of another world, and one of those phantasms of past conflict of which the Italian had just spoken. His clothes, which had originally been of the plainest texture, and most uncourtly make, were worn and ragged, and stained with damp and dirt. His form and features were gaunt and uncouth, and his gesture stiff and awkward; but, with all this, there was a certain steadiness and dignity about his manner, which threw an appearance of nobility over this rugged and unpleasing form. Contrasted with the dress and manner of the other men, he looked like some enthusiastic prophet, standing in the house of mirth and luxury, and predicting ruin and woe.

At this moment a servant entered the room, bringing a sottocoppa of silver, upon which were two or three stiff necked glasses, called caraffas, containing different sorts of wine, and also water, and one or two more empty drinking-glasses, so that the visitor could please himself as to the strength and nature of his beverage. Inglesant offered this refreshment to the Italian, who filled himself a glass and drank, pledging Inglesant as he did so. The latter did not drink, but offered wine and cakes to the stranger, who refused or rather took no heed of these offers of politeness; he remained silent, keeping his eyes fixed upon the face of the man who, but a few hours before, had saved him from a violent death.

"I have had some feelings of this kind myself, in certain places," said Inglesant, in answer to the Italian's speech, "and very frequently in all places the sense of something vanishing, which in another moment I should have seen; it has seemed to me that, could I once see this thing, matters would be very different with me. Whether I ever shall or not I do not know."

"Who can say?" replied the other. "We live and move amid a crowd of flitting objects unknown or dimly seen. The beings and powers of the unseen world throng around us. We call ourselves lords of our own actions and fate, but we are in reality the slaves of every atom of matter of which the world is made and we ourselves created. Among this phantasm of struggling forms and influences (like a man forcing his way through a crowd of masques who mock at him and retard his steps) we fight our way towards the light. Many of us are born with the seeds within us of that which makes such a fight hopeless from the first—the seeds of disease, of ignorance, of adverse circumstance, of stupidity; for even a dullard has had once or twice in his life glimpses of the light. So we go on. I was at Chambery once when a man came before the Duke in the palace garden to ask an alms. He was a worker in gold, a good artist, not unworthy of Cellini himself. His sight had failed him, and he could no longer work for bread to give to his children. He stood before the Prince and those who stood with him, among whom were a Cardinal and two or three nobles, with their pages and grooms, trying with his dim eyes to make out one from the other, which was noble and which was groom, and to see whether his suit was rejected or allowed. Behind him, beyond the garden shade, the dazzling glitter stretched up to the white Alps. We are all the creatures of a day, and the puny afflictions of any man's life are not worth a serious thought; yet this man seemed to me so true an image of his kind, helpless and half-blind, yet struggling to work out some good for himself, that I felt a strange emotion of pity. They gave him alms—some more, some less. I was a fool, yet even now I think the man was no bad emblem of the life of each of us. We do not understand this enough. Will the time ever come when these things will be better known?"

As the Italian spoke the stranger took his eyes off Inglesant and fixed them on the speaker with a startled expression, as though the tone of his discourse was unexpected to him. He scarcely waited for the other to finish before he broke in upon the conversation, speaking slowly and with intense earnestness, as though above all things desirous of being understood. He spoke a strange and uncouth Italian, full of rough northern idioms, yet the earnestness and dignity of his manner ensured him an audience, especially with two such men as those who stood before him.

"Standing in a new world," he said, "and speaking as I speak, to men of another language, and of thoughts and habits distinct from mine, I see beneath the tinsel of earthly rank and splendour, and a luxury of life and of beauty, the very meaning of which is unknown to me, something of a common feeling, which assures me that the voice I utter will not be entirely strange, coming as it does from the common Father. I see around me a land given over to idolatry and sensual crime, as if the old Pagans were returned again to earth; and here around me I see the symbols of the Pagan worship and of the Pagan sin, and I hear no other talk than that which would have befitted the Pagan revels and the Pagan darkness which overhung the world to come. Standing on the brink of a violent death, and able to utter few words that can be understood, I call, in these short moments which are given me, and in these few words which I have at command—I call upon all who will listen to me, that they leave those things which are behind, with all the filthy recollections of ages steeped in sin, and that they press forward towards the light,—the light of God in Jesus Christ."

He stopped, probably for want of words to clothe his thoughts, and Inglesant replied,—

"You may be assured from the events of last night, signore, that you are in no danger of violent death in this house, and that every means will be taken to protect you, until you have been found guilty of some crime. You must, however, know that no country can allow its customs and its religion to be outraged by strangers and aliens, and you cannot be surprised if such conduct is resented both by the governors of the country and by the ignorant populace, though these act from different motives. As to what you have said respecting the ornaments and symbols of this house, and of the converse in which you have found us engaged, it would seem that to a wise man these things might serve as an allegory, or at least as an image and representation of human life, and be, therefore, not without their uses."

"I desire no representation nor image of a past world of iniquity," said the stranger, "I would I could say of a dead life, but the whole world lieth in wickedness until this day. This is why I travel through all lands, crying to all men that they repent and escape the most righteous judgment of God, if haply there be yet time. These are those latter days in which our Saviour and Redeemer Jesus Christ, the Son of God, predicted that iniquity 'should be increased;' wherein, instead of serving God, all serve their own humours and affections, being rocked to sleep with the false and deceitful lullaby of effeminate pleasures and delights of the flesh, and know not that an horrible mischief and overthrow is awaiting them, that the pit of Hell yawns beneath them, and that for them is reserved the inevitable rigour of the eternal fire. Is it a time for chambering and wantonness, for soft raiment and dainty living, for reading of old play-books such as the one I see on the table, for building houses of cedar, painted with vermilion, and decked with all the loose and fantastic devices which a disordered and debauched intellect could itself conceive, or could borrow from Pagan tombs and haunts of devils, full of uncleanness and dead sins?"

"You speak too harshly of these things," said Inglesant. "I see nothing in them but the instinct of humanity, differing in its outward aspect in different ages, but alike in its meaning and audible voice. This house is in itself a representation of the world of fancy and reality combined, of the material life of the animal mingled with those half-seen and fitful glimpses of the unknown life upon the verge of which we stand. This little fellow which I hold in my hand, speaks to me, in an indistinct and yet forcible voice, of that common sympathy—magical and hidden though it may be— by which the whole creation is linked together, and in which, as is taught in many an allegory and quaint device upon these walls, the Creator of us all has a kindly feeling for the basest and most inanimate. My imagination follows humanity through all the paths by which it has reached the present moment, and the more memorials I can gather of its devious footsteps the more enlarged my view becomes of what its trials, its struggles, and its virtues were. All things that ever delighted it were in themselves the good blessings of God—the painter's and the player's art—action, apparel, agility, music. Without these life would be a desert; and as it seems to me, these things softened manners so as to allow Religion to be heard, who otherwise would not have been listened to in a savage world, and among a brutal people destitute of civility. As I trace these things backward for centuries, I live far beyond my natural term, and my mind is delighted with the pleasures of nations who were dust ages before I was born."

"I am not concerned to dispute the vain pleasures of the children of this world," exclaimed the stranger with more warmth than he had hitherto shown. "Do you suppose that I myself am without the lusts and desires of life? Have I no eyes like other men, that I cannot take a carnal pleasure in that which is cunningly formed by the enemy to please the eye? Am not I warmed like other men? And is not soft clothing and dainty fare pleasing to me as to them? But I call on all men to rise above these things, which are transitory and visionary as a dream, and which you yourself have spoken of as magical and hidden, of which only fitful glimpses are obtained. You are pleasing yourself with fond and idle imaginations, the product of delicate living and unrestrained fancies; but in this the net of the devil is about your feet, and before you are aware you will find yourself ensnared for ever. These things are slowly but surely poisoning your spiritual life. I call upon you to leave these delusions, and come out into the clear atmosphere of God's truth; to tread the life of painful self-denial, leaving that of the powerful and great of this world, and following a despised Saviour, who knew none of these things, and spent His time not in kings' houses gorgeously tricked out, but knew not where to lay His head. You speak to me of pleasures of the mind, of music, of the painter's art; do you think that last night, when beaten, crushed, and almost breathless, in the midst of a blood-thirsty and howling crowd, I was dimly conscious of help, and looking up I saw you in the glare of the lanterns, in your courtier's dress of lace and silver, calm, beneficent, powerful for good, you did not seem to my weak human nature, and my low needs and instincts, beautiful as an angel of light? Truly you did; yet I tell you, speaking by a nature and in a voice that is more unerring than mine, that, to the divine vision, of us two at that moment you were the one to be pitied,—you were the outcast, the tortured of demons, the bound hand and foot, whose portion is in this life, who, if this fleeting hour is left unheeded, will be tormented in the life to come."

The Italian turned away his head to conceal a smile, and even to Inglesant, who was much better able to understand the man's meaning, this result of his interference to save his life appeared somewhat ludicrous. The Italian, however, probably thinking that Inglesant would be glad to be relieved from his strange visitor, seemed desirous of terminating the interview.

"His Grace expects me," he said to Inglesant, "at the Casa di Morte this morning, and it is near the time for him to be there. I will therefore take my leave."

"Ah! the Casa di Morte; yes, he will expect me there also," said Inglesant, with some slight appearance of reluctance. "I will follow you anon."

He moved from the indolent attitude he had kept till this moment before the sideboard, and exchanged with the Italian those formal gestures of leave-taking and politeness in which his nation were precise. When the Italian was gone Inglesant summoned a servant, and directed him to provide the stranger with an apartment, and to see that he wanted for nothing. He then turned to the fanatic, and requested him as a favour not to attempt to leave the palace until he had returned from the Duke. The stranger hesitated, but finally consented.

"I owe you my life," he said,—"a life I value not at a straw's weight, but for which my Master may perchance have some use even yet. I am therefore in your debt, and I will give my word to remain quiet until you return; but this promise only extends to nightfall; should you be prevented by any chance from returning this day, I am free from my parole."

Inglesant bowed.

"I would," continued the man, looking upon his companion with a softened and even compassionate regard, "I would I could say more. I hear a secret voice, which tells me that you are even now walking in slippery places, and that your heart is not at ease."

He stopped, and seemed to seek earnestly for some phrases or arguments which he might suppose likely to influence a courtier placed as he imagined Inglesant to be; but before he resumed, the latter excused himself on the ground of his attendance on the Duke, and, promising to see him again on his return, left the room.

Inglesant found a carriage waiting to convey him to the "Hospital of Death," as the monastic house adjoining the public Campo Santo was called. The religious performance had already begun. Passing through several sombre corridors and across a courtyard, he was ushered into the Duke's presence, who sat, surrounded by his Court and by the principal ecclesiastics of the city, in an open balcony or loggia. As Inglesant entered by a small door in the back of the gallery a most extraordinary sight met his eyes. Beyond the loggia was a small yard or burial-ground, and beyond this the Campo Santo stretching out into the far country. The whole of the yard immediately before the spectators was thronged by a multitude of persons, of all ages and ranks, apparently just risen from the tomb. Many were utterly without clothing, others were attired as kings, bishops, and even popes. Their attitudes and conduct corresponded with the characters in which they appeared, the ecclesiastics collecting in calm and sedate attitudes, while many of the rest, among whom kings and great men were not wanting, appeared in an extremity of anguish and fear. Beyond the sheltering walls which enclosed the court the dazzling heat brooded over the Campo Santo to the distant hills, and the funereal trees stood, black and sombre, against the glare of the yellow sky. At the moment of Inglesant's entrance it appeared that something had taken place of the nature of an excommunication, and the ecclesiastics in the gallery were, according to custom, casting candles and flaming torches, which the crowd of nude figures below were struggling and fighting to obtain. A wild yet solemn strain of music, that came apparently from the open graves, ascended through the fitful and half-stifled cries.

The first sight that struck upon Inglesant's sense, as he entered the gallery from the dark corridors, was the lurid yellow light beyond. The second was the wild confused crowd of leaping and struggling figures, in a strange and ghastly disarray, naked or decked as in mockery with the torn and disordered symbols of rank and wealth, rising as from the tomb, distracted and terror-stricken as at the last great assize. The third was the figure of the Duke turning to him, and the eyes of the priests and clergy fixed upon his face. The words that the fanatic had uttered had fallen upon a mind prepared to receive them, and upon a conscience already awakened to acknowledge their truth. A mysterious conviction laid hold upon his imagination that the moment had arrived in which he was bound to declare himself, and by every tie which the past had knotted round him to influence the Duke to pursue a line of conduct from which his conscience and his better judgment revolted. On the one hand, a half-aroused and uncertain conscience, on the other, circumstance, habit, interest, inclination, perplexed his thoughts. The conflict was uneven, the result hardly doubtful. The eyes of friends and enemies, of agents of the Holy See, of courtiers and priests, were upon him; the inquiring glance of the aged Duke seemed to penetrate into his soul. He advanced to the ducal chair, the solemn music that streamed up as from the grave, wavered and faltered as if consciousness and idea were nearly lost. Something of the old confusion overpowered his senses, the figures that surrounded him became shadowy and unreal, and the power of decision seemed no longer his own.

Out of the haze of confused imagery and distracting thought which surrounded him, he heard with unspeakable amazement the Duke's words,—

"I have waited your coming, Mr. Inglesant, impatiently, for I have a commission to entrust you with, or rather my daughter, the Grand Duchess, has written urgently to me from Florence to request me to send you to her without a moment's delay. Family matters relating to some in whom she takes the greatest interest, and who are well known, she says, to yourself, are the causes which lead to this request."

Inglesant was too bewildered to speak. He had believed himself quite unknown to the Grand Duchess, whom he had never seen, but as he had passed before her in the ducal receptions at Florence. Who could these be in whom she took so great an interest, and who were known to him?

But the Duke went on, speaking with a certain melancholy in his tone.

"I have wished, Mr. Inglesant," he said, "to mark in some way the regard I have conceived for you, and the obligation under which I conceive myself to remain. It may be that, in the course that events are taking, it will no longer in a few weeks be in my power to bestow favours upon any man. I desire, therefore, to do what I have purposed before you leave the presence. I have caused the necessary deeds to be prepared which bestow upon you a small fief in the Apennines, consisting of some farms and of the Villa-Castle of San Georgio, where I myself in former days have passed many happy hours." He stopped, and in a moment or two resumed abruptly, without finishing the sentence.

"The revenue of the fief is not large, but its possession gives the title of Cavaliere to its owner, and its situation and the character of its neighbourhood make it a desirable and delightful abode. The letters of naturalization which are necessary to enable you to hold this property have been made out, and nothing is wanting but your acceptance of the gift. I offer it you with no conditions and no request save that, as far as in you lies, you will be a faithful servant to the Grand Duchess when I am gone."

The Duke paused for a moment, and then, turning slightly to his chaplain, he said, "The reverend fathers will tell you that this affair has not been decided upon without their knowledge, and that it has their full approval."

These last words convinced Inglesant of the fact that had occurred. Although the Duke had said nothing on the subject, he felt certain that the deed of cession had been signed, and that for some reason or other he himself was considered by the clerical party to have been instrumental in obtaining this result, and to be deserving of reward accordingly. He had never, as we have seen, spoken to the Duke concerning the succession, and his position at the moment was certainly a peculiar one. Nothing was expected of him but that he should express his grateful thanks for the Duke's favour, and leave the presence. Surely, at that moment, no law of heaven or earth could require him to break through the observances of civility and usage, to enter upon a subject upon which he was not addressed, and to refuse acts of favour offered to him with every grace and delicacy of manner. Whatever might be the case with other men, he certainly was not one to whom such a course was possible. He expressed his gratitude with all the grace of manner of which he was capable, he assured the Duke of his readiness to start immediately for Florence, and he left the ducal presence before many minutes had passed away.

He found before long that all his conjectures were correct. The Duke had signed the deed of cession, and the report which was sent to Rome by the Papal agents stated that, in the opinion of the most competent judges, this result was due to Inglesant's influence. Before his arrival the Duke had leaned strongly towards the secular and anti-Papal interest, and had even encouraged heretical and Protestant emissaries. "Avoiding with great skill all positive allusion to the subject," the report went on to state, "Il Cavaliere

Inglesant had thrown all his influence into the Catholic and religious scale, and had by the loftiness of his sentiment and the attraction of his manner entirely won over the vacillating nature of the Duke." Too much satisfaction, the Cardinal of Umbria and the heads of the Church in that city assured the Papal Court, could not be expressed at the manner in which the agent of the Society had fulfilled his mission.

Inglesant's departure from Umbria was so sudden that he had no opportunity of again seeing the stranger whom he had left in the palace, and he was afterwards at some trouble in obtaining any information respecting him. As far as could be ascertained he waited in the palace, according to his promise, until the evening, when, finding that Inglesant did not return, he walked quietly forth, no man hindering him. What his subsequent fate was is involved in some obscurity; but it would appear that, having publicly insulted the Host in some cathedral in the south of Italy, he was arrested by the Holy Office, and thrown into prison, from which there is reason to believe he never emerged.

CHAPTER VIII

Not very long after Inglesant had left for Umbria, his friend, Don Agostino di Chigi, suddenly came to Rome. The Pope's health was rapidly failing, and the excitement concerning his successor was becoming intense. The choice was generally considered to lie between the Cardinals Barbarini and di Chigi, though Cardinal Sacchetti was spoken of by some, probably however merely as a substitute, should both the other parties fail in electing their candidate.

It was the policy of the Chigi family to conduct their matters with great caution; none of the family, with the exception of the Cardinal, were openly in Rome; and when Don Agostino arrived he resided in one of the deserted villas hidden among vineyards and the gardens of solitary convents, which covered the Palatine and the Aventine in the southern portion of Rome within the walls. He remained within or with the Cardinal during the day, but at night he ventured out into the streets, and visited the adherents of his family and those who were working to secure his uncle's elevation.

One night the fathers of the Oratory gave a concert at which one of the best voices in Rome was to sing. It happened that Don Agostino passed the gate as the company were assembling, and as he did so the street was blocked by the train of some great personage who arrived in a sedan of blue velvet embroidered with silver, accompanied by several gentlemen and servants. Among the former, Agostino recognized the Cavaliere di Guardino, the brother of Lauretta, of whose acquaintance with Inglesant at Florence it may be remembered he was aware, and with him another man whose appearance seemed to recall some distant reminiscence to his mind. He could, however, see him but imperfectly in the flickering torchlight.

Apart from his desire to remain unrecognized in Rome, Agostino had no desire to associate with the Cavaliere, of whose character he had a very bad opinion. To his annoyance, therefore, as the sedan entered the courtyard, the two persons he had noticed, instead of following their patron, turned round, and in leaving the doorway met Agostino face to face. The Cavaliere recognized him immediately, and appeared to grasp eagerly the opportunity to accost him. He began by complimenting him on the near prospect of his uncle's elevation to the Papacy, professing to consider the chances of his election very good indeed, and added that he presumed business connected with these matters had brought him to Rome. To this Agostino replied that, so far as he knew, his uncle had no expectation of such an honour being at all likely to be offered him, and that private affairs of his own, of a very delicate nature,—of a kind indeed which a gentleman of the Cavaliere's known gallantry could well understand,—had brought him to Rome, as indeed he might see from the secrecy he maintained, and by his not being present at any of the entertainments which were going forward. He then inquired in his turn why the Cavaliere had not entered the college. The other made some evasive answer, but it appeared to Agostino that both the Cavaliere and his companion were not on the most familiar terms with the nobleman they had accompanied, although it might suit their purpose to appear in his train. Guardino indeed changed the subject hastily, and spoke of Inglesant, praising him highly. He inquired whether the Cardinal di Chigi was acquainted with him, and whether it was likely that either as an attendant upon him or upon Cardinal Rinuccini, Inglesant would be admitted into the conclave.

Don Agostino replied vaguely that Inglesant was then at Umbria, and that he could offer no opinion as to the probability of the latter part of his inquiry.

He thought that he could see from the expression on the other's face that the Cavaliere thought that he was deceiving him, and that he jumped at once to the conclusion that, as the attendant of one or other of the Cardinals, Inglesant would be present at the conclave.

Guardino went on to speak of Inglesant's character, regretting the craze of mind, as he called it, which his ill health had produced, and which rendered him, as he said, unfit for business or for taking his part in the affairs of life. He went on to speak with unconcealed contempt of Inglesant's religious ideas and scruples, and of his association with Molinos; intimating, however, his opinion that it would not be impossible to overcome these scruples, could a suitable temptation be found. These fancies once removed, he continued, Inglesant's value as a trusted and secret agent would be greatly increased.

He seemed to be talking abstractedly, and as a perfectly disinterested person, who was discussing an interesting topic of morals or mental peculiarity.

Agostino could not understand his drift. He answered him that the Jesuits did not need unscrupulous bravoes. If they did, they could be found in every street corner by the score. He added that he imagined that the services which Inglesant had already performed, and might perform again, were of a special and delicate character, for which his temperament and habit of mind, which were chiefly the result of the Society's training, especially fitted him.

They had by this time reached the Corso, and Agostino took the opportunity of parting with his companions, excusing himself on the ground of his pretended assignation.

He was no sooner gone than the Cavaliere, according to the narrative which was afterwards related by Malvolti, began to explain more clearly than he had hitherto done what his expectations and intentions were. He was forced to confide in Malvolti more than he otherwise would have done, to prevent his ridding himself of Inglesant's presence by violent means.

When the Italian first saw Inglesant, whom he had never met in England, in the theatre in Florence, he was startled and terrified by his close resemblance to his murdered brother; and his first thought was that his victim had returned to earth, and, invisible to others, was permitted to avenge himself upon his murderer by haunting and terrifying his paths. When he discovered, however, that the Cavaliere not only saw the appearance which had so alarmed him, but could tell him who Inglesant was, and to a certain extent what the motives were which had brought him to Italy, his superstitious fears gave place to more material apprehensions and expedients. He at once resolved to assassinate Inglesant on leaving the theatre, in the first street through which he might pass—a purpose which he might easily have accomplished during Inglesant's careless and unguarded wanderings round the house of Lauretta's father that night. From this intention he was with difficulty diverted by the reasoning of the Cavaliere, who represented to him the rashness of such an action, protected as Inglesant was by the most powerful of Societies, which would not fail to punish any act which deprived it of a useful agent; the unnecessary character of the attempt, Inglesant being at present in complete ignorance that his enemy was near him; and above all, the folly of destroying a person who might otherwise be made the medium of great personal profit and advantage. He explained to Malvolti Inglesant's connection with the Chigi family, and the position of influence he would occupy should the Cardinal be elected to the Popedom; finally, he went so far as to hint at the possibility of an alliance between Malvolti and his sister, should Inglesant remain uninjured.

Malvolti had only arrived in Florence on the previous day, and the Cavaliere met him accidentally in the theatre; but Guardino's plans with relation to Inglesant and his sister were already so far matured, that he had arranged for the abrupt departure of his father and Lauretta from Florence. His object was to keep in his own hands a powerful magnet of attraction, which would bind, as he supposed, Inglesant to his interests; but he was by no means desirous that he should marry his sister immediately, if at all. The election for the Papacy was of very uncertain issue, and if the di Chigi faction failed, Inglesant's alliance would be of little value. He had two strings to his bow. Malvolti, between whom and the Cavaliere association in vice and even crime had riveted many a bond of interest and dependence, was closely connected with the Barbarini faction, as an unscrupulous and useful tool. Should the Cardinal Barbarini be elected Pope, or should Cardinal Sacchetti, who was in his interest, be chosen, his own connection with Malvolti might be of great value to the Cavaliere, and the greater service the latter could render to the Barbarini faction in the approaching crisis the better. The weak point of his position on this side was the character of Malvolti, and the subordinate position he occupied among the adherents of the Barbarini. On the other hand, if Cardinal Chigi were the future Pontiff, the prospects of any one connected with Inglesant would be most brilliant, as the latter, from his connection with the Jesuits, and as the favourite of the Pope's nephew, would at once become one of the most powerful men in Italy. The weak point on this side was that his hold on Inglesant was very slight, and that, even supposing it to be strengthened by marriage with Lauretta, Inglesant's character and temper were such as would probably make him useless and impracticable in the attempt to secure the glittering and often illicit advantages which would be within his reach. Between this perplexing choice the only wise course appeared to be to temporize with both parties, and to attempt, in the meantime, to secure an influence with either. The fortunes both of the Cavaliere and of Malvolti were at this moment pretty nearly desperate, and their means of influencing any one very small; indeed, having wasted what had once been considerable wealth and talent, there remained nothing to the Cavaliere but his sister, and of that last possession he was prepared to make unscrupulous use. It would be of small advantage to him to give his sister's hand to Inglesant unless he could first, by her means, corrupt and debase his conscience and that lofty standard of conduct which he appeared, to the Cavaliere at least, unswervingly to follow; and the Italian devil at his side suggested a means to this end as wild in conception as the result proved it impotent and badly planned.

This Italian devil was not Malvolti, though that person was one of his most successful followers and imitators. When the inspired writer has described the princes and angels which rule the different nations of the earth, he does not go on to enumerate the distinct powers of evil which, in different countries, pursue their divers malific courses; yet it would seem that those existences are no less real than the others. That the character of the inhabitants of any country has much to do in forming a distinct devil for that country no man can doubt; or that in consequence the temptations which beset mankind in certain countries are of a distinct and peculiar kind. This fact is sometimes of considerable advantage to the object of the tempter's art, for if, acting upon his knowledge of the character of any people, this merely local devil lays snares in the path of a stranger, it is not impossible that the bait may fail. This was very much what happened to John Inglesant. Of the sins which were really his temptations the Cavaliere knew nothing; but he could conceive of certain acts which he concluded Inglesant would consider to be sins. These acts were of a gross and sensual nature; for the Italian devil, born of the fleshly lusts of the people, was unable to form temptations for the higher natures, and of course his pupils were equally impotent. The result was singular. Acting upon the design of ruining Inglesant's moral sense, of debasing the ideal of conduct at which he aimed, and of shattering and defiling what the Cavaliere considered the fantastic purity of his conscience, he formed a scheme which had the effect of removing Inglesant from a place where he was under the strongest temptation and in the greatest danger of violating his conscience, and of placing him in circumstances of trial which, though dangerous, he was still, from the peculiarity of his character, much better able to resist.

A marriage connection with Inglesant would at this juncture be of little avail; but a wild and illicit passion, which would involve him in a course of licentious and confused action, in which the barriers of morality and the scruples of conscience would be alike annihilated, and the whole previous nature of the victim of lawless desire altered, would, if any agent could produce so great a change, transform Inglesant into the worldly-minded and unscrupulous accomplice that the Cavaliere wished him to become. How great the fall would be he could of course in no way estimate; but he had sufficient insight to perceive that the shock of it would probably be sufficient (acting upon a consciousness so refined and delicate as that of Inglesant) to render recovery, if ever attained, very difficult and remote.

Upon this wild scheme he acted. He had removed his sister when he had thought that Inglesant had been sufficiently ensnared to make his after course certain and precipitate. Inglesant's character, which was so very imperfectly known to the Cavaliere, and circumstances, such as his confinement in the pest-house, had delayed the consummation of the plot. But the Cavaliere conceived that the time had now arrived for its completion. He brought his sister back to Florence, and placed her with the Grand Duchess, in some subordinate situation which his family and his sister's character enabled him to obtain. Having had some previous knowledge of her, the Duchess soon became attached to Lauretta, and obtained her confidence. From her she learnt Inglesant's story and character, and wished to see him at the Court. While the two ladies were planning schemes for future pleasure, the Cavaliere suddenly appeared at Florence, and informed his sister that he had concluded, with the approbation of his father, a marriage contract between herself and Malvolti.

Terrified by this threatened connection with a man whose person she loathed and whose character she detested, Lauretta flew to the Duchess, and entreated her to send at once for Inglesant, who, they were both aware, was at that moment with the Duke of Umbria, the Grand Duchess's aged father. With the result we are acquainted.

CHAPTER IX

On his arrival at Florence Inglesant found himself at once fêted and caressed, though the nature of his mission to Umbria, antagonistic as his supposed influence had been to the interests of the ducal party, might naturally have procured for him a far different reception. Trained as he had been in courts, the caprices of princes' favour did not seem strange to him, and were taken at their true worth. Unsuspicious, therefore, of any special danger, relieved from the intolerable strain which the position at Umbria had exerted upon his conscience, delighted with the society of his recovered mistress, and flattered by the attentions of the Duchess and of the whole Court, he gave himself up freely to the enjoyments of the hour. Plentifully supplied with money from his own resources, from the kindness of the aged Duke, and from the subsidies of his patrons at Rome, he engaged freely in the parties formed for the performance of masques and interludes, in which the Court delighted, and became conspicuous for the excellence of his acting and invention.

But it was not the purpose of the demon that followed on his footsteps to give him longer repose than might lull his senses, and weaken his powers of resisting evil. Day after day devoted to pleasure paved the way for the final catastrophe, until the night arrived when the plot was fully ripe. Supper was over, and the Court sat down again to play. Inglesant remembered afterwards, though at the time it did not attract his attention, that several gentlemen, all of them friends of Guardino, paid him particular attention, and insisted on drinking with him, calling for different kinds of wine, and recommending them to his notice. The saloons were crowded and very hot, and when Inglesant left the supper room and came into the brilliant marble hall lighted with great lustres, where the Court was at play, he was more excited than was his wont. The Court was gathered at different tables,—a very large one in the centre of the hall, and other smaller ones around. The brilliant dresses, the jewels, the beautiful women, the reflections in the numberless mirrors, made a dazzling and mystifying impression on his brain. The play was very high, and at the table to which Inglesant sat down especially so. He lost heavily, and this did not tend to calm his nerves; he doubled his stake, with all the money he had with him, and lost again. As he rose from the table a page touched his elbow and handed him a small note carefully sealed and delicately perfumed. It was addressed to him by his new title, "Il Cavaliere di San Georgio," and scarcely knowing what he did, he opened it. It was from Lauretta.

"Cavaliere,

Will you come to me in the Duchess's lodgings before the Court rises from play? I need your help. L."

Inglesant turned to look for the boy, who, he expected, was waiting for him. He was not far off, and Inglesant followed him without a word. They passed through many corridors and rooms richly furnished until they reached the lodgings of the Grand Duchess. The night was sultry, and through the open windows above the gardens the strange odours that are born of darkness and of night entered the palace. In the dark arcades the nightingales were singing, preferring gloom and mystery to the light in which all other creatures rejoice; and in the stillness the murmur of brooks and the splash of the fountains oppressed the ear with an unearthly and unaccustomed sound. Around the casements festoons of harmless and familiar flowers and leaves assumed wild and repulsive shapes, as if transformed into malicious demons who made men their sport. Inglesant thought involuntarily of those plants that are at enmity with man, which are used for enchantments and for poisoning, and whose very scent is death; such saturnine and fatal flowers seemed more at home in the lovely Italian night than the innocent plants which witness to lovers' vows, and upon which divines moralize and preach. The rooms of the Duchess were full of perfume of the kind that enervates and lulls the sense. It seemed to Inglesant as though he were treading the intricate pathways of a dream, careless as to what befell him, yet with a passionate longing which urged him forward, heedless of a restraining voice which he was even then half-conscious that at other times he should have heard. The part of the palace where he was seemed deserted, and the page led him through more than one anteroom without meeting any one, until they reached a curtained door, which the boy opened, and directed Inglesant to enter. He did so, and found himself at once in the presence of Lauretta, who was lying upon a low seat at the open window. The room was lighted by several small lamps in different positions, giving an ample, yet at the same time a soft and dreamy light. Lauretta was carelessly dressed, yet, in the soft light, and in her negligent attitude, there was something that made her beauty the more attractive, and her manner to Inglesant was unrestrained and clinging. Her growing affection, the urgency of her need, and the circumstances of the hour, caused her innocently to speak and act in a way the most fitted to promote her brother's atrocious purposes.

"Cavaliere," she said, "I have sent for you because I have no friend but you. I have sent for you to help me against my own family—my own brother—my father even, whom I love—whom I loved—more than all the world beside. They are determined to marry me to a man whom I hate; to the man whom you hate; to that Signor Malvolti, who, though they deny it, is, I am fully persuaded, the murderer of your brother; to that wretch whom Italy even refuses to receive; who, but for his useful crimes, would be condemned to a death of torment. My brother tells me that he will be here to-morrow to see me and demand my consent. He brings an authorization from my father, and insists upon the contract being made without delay. I would die rather than submit to such a fate, but it is not necessary to die. I must, however, leave the Court and escape from my brother's wardship. If I can reach some place of safety, where I can gain time to see my father, I am certain that I shall be able to move him. It cannot be that he will condemn me to such a fate,—me! the pride and pleasure of his life. He must be deceived and misled by some of these wicked intrigues and manoeuvres which ruin the happiness and peace of men."

"I am wholly yours," said Inglesant; "whatever you desire shall be done. Have you spoken to the Duchess?"

"The Duchess advises me to fly," replied Lauretta; "she says the Duke will not interfere between a father and his child; especially now, when all Italy hangs in suspense concerning the Papacy, and men are careful whom they offend. She advises me to go to the convent of St. Catherine of Pistoia, where I lodged not many years ago while my father was in France. The Abbess is a cousin of my father's; she is a kind woman, and I can persuade her to keep me for a short time at least. I wish to go to-night. Will you take me?"

She had never looked so lovely in Inglesant's eyes as she did while she spoke. The pleading look of her dark eyes, and the excitement of her manner, usually so reserved and calm, added charms to her person of which he had previously been unconscious. In that country of formal restraint and suspicion, of hurried, furtive interviews, a zest was given to accidental freedom of intercourse such as the more unrestricted life of France and England knew little of. In spite of a suspicion of treachery, which in that country was never absent, Inglesant felt his frame aglow with devotion to this lovely creature, who thus threw herself unreservedly into his keeping. He threw himself upon a cushion at Lauretta's feet, and encircled her with his arms. She spoke of youth and life and pleasure,—of youth that was passing away so rapidly; of life that had been to her dreary and dull enough; of her jealously-guarded Italian home, of her convent cell, of her weak and helpless father, of her tyrannous brother; of pleasure, of which she had dreamed as a girl, but which seemed to fly before her as she advanced; finally of himself, whom, from the first day she had seen him in her father's room, she had loved, whom absence had only endeared, her first and only friend.

He spoke of love, of protection, of help and succour for the rest of life; of happy days to come at San Georgio, when all these troubles should have passed away, when at last he should escape from intrigue and State policy, and they could make their home as joyous and free from care as that house of a Cardinal, on a little hilly bank near Veletri, whence you can see the sea, and which is called Monte Joiosa. He spoke of an Idyllic dream which could not long have satisfied either of them,—himself especially, but which pleased them at that moment, with an innocent and delicate fancy which calmed and purified their excited thoughts. Then, as the hour passed by, he rose from her embrace, promising to provide horses, and when the palace was quiet, to meet her at the end of one of the long avenues that crossed the park; for the Court was not at the Pitti Palace, but at the Poggia Imperiale without the walls of Florence.

The soft night air played upon Inglesant's forehead as he led his horses to the end of a long avenue, and waited for the lady to join him. He did not wait long; she came gliding past the fountains, by the long rows of orange and cypress hedges, and across the streaks of moonlight among the trees that closed the gardens and the park. As he lifted her into the saddle, her glance was partly scared and partly trustful; he felt as though he were moving in a delicious dream.

As they rode out of the park she told him that she had received a message from the Duchess, recommending her to stop at a pavilion on the borders of the great chase, beyond the Achaiano Palace, half-way to Pistoia, which the Duchess used sometimes when the Duke was diverting himself in the chase. She had sent a messenger to prepare the people who kept the pavilion for their coming. There was something strange in this message, Lauretta said, which was brought, not by one of the Duchess's usual pages, but by a boy who had not been long at the palace, and who scarcely waited to give his message, so great was his hurry. It seemed of little moment to Inglesant who brought the message, or whether any treachery were at work or no; he was only conscious of a delicious sense of coming pleasure which made him reckless of all beside. Along the first few miles of their road they passed nothing but the long lines of elms, planted between ridges of corn, upon which the vines were climbing in already luxuriant wreaths. Presently, however, after they had passed the Achaiano Palace, the country changed, and they came within the confines of the Duke's chase, thirty miles in compass, planted with cork trees and ilex, with underwood of myrtle thickets. Through these shades, lovely indeed by day, but weird and unhealthy by night, they rode silently, startled every now and then by strange sounds that issued from the forest depths. The ground was fenny and uneven, and moist exhalations rose out of the soil and floated across the path.

"The Duchess never sleeps at the pavilion," said Lauretta at last suddenly; "it is dangerous to sleep in the forest."

"It will be as well to stop an hour or so, however," said Inglesant, "else we shall be at Pistoia before they open the gates."

Presently, in the brilliant moonlight, they saw the pointed roofs of the pavilion on a little rising-ground, with the forest trees coming up closely to the walls. The moon was now high in the heavens, and it was as light as day. The upper windows of the pavilion were open, and within it lights were burning. The door was opened to them before they knocked, and the keeper of the pavilion came to meet them, accompanied by a boy who took the horses. The man showed no surprise at their coming, only saying some servants of the Duchess had been there a few hours previously, and had prepared a repast in the dining-room, forewarning him that he should expect visitors. He accompanied them upstairs, for they saw nothing of the other inmates of the place. The rooms were arranged with a sort of rustic luxury, and were evidently intended for repose during the heat of the day. A plentiful and delicate collation was spread on one of the tables, with abundance of fruit and wine. The place looked like the magic creation of an enchanter's wand, raised for purposes of evil from the unhealthy marsh, and ready to sink again, when that malific purpose was fulfilled, into the weird depths from which it rose.

The old man showed them the other rooms of the apartment and left them. At the door he turned back and said,—

"I should not advise the lady to sleep here; the miasma from the forest is very fatal to such as are not used to it."

Inglesant looked at him, but could not perceive that he intended his word to have any deeper meaning than the obvious one. He said,—

"We shall stay only an hour or two; let the horses be ready to go on."

The man left them, and they sat down at the table.

The repast was served in Faience ware of a strange delicate blue, and consisted of most of the delicacies of the season with a profusion of wine.

"This was not ordered by the Duchess," said Lauretta.

"We are safe from poison, Mignone," said Inglesant; "to destroy you as well as me would defeat all purposes. Not that I believe the Cavaliere would wish me dead. He rather hopes that I may be of use to him. Let us drink to him."

And he filled a glass for Lauretta of the Monte-pulciano, the "King of Wines," and drank himself.

Lauretta was evidently frightened, yet she followed his example and drank. The night air was heavy and close, not a breath of wind stirred the lights, though every window was thrown open, and the shutters that closed the loggia outside were drawn back. In the brilliant moonlight every leaf of the great forest shone with an unnatural distinctness, which, set in a perfect silence, became terrible to see. The sylvan arcades seemed like a painted scene-piece upon a Satanic stage, supernaturally alight to further deeds of sin, and silent and unpeopled, lest the wrong should be interrupted or checked. To Inglesant's excited fancy evil beings thronged its shadowy paths, present to the spiritual sense, though concealed of set purpose from the feeble human sight. The two found their eyes drawn with a kind of fascination to this strange sight, and Inglesant arose and closed the shutters before the nearest casement.

They felt more at ease when the mysterious forest was shut out. But Lauretta was silent and troubled, and Inglesant's efforts to cheer and enliven her were not successful. The delicious wines to which he resorted to remove his own uneasiness and to cure his companion's melancholy, failed of their effect. At last she refused to drink, and rising up suddenly, she exclaimed, —

"Oh, it is terribly hot. I cannot bear it. I wish we had not come!"

She wandered from the room in which they sat, through the curtained doorway into the next, which was furnished with couches, and sank down on one of them. Inglesant followed her, and, as if the heat felt stifling also to him, went out upon the open verandah, and looked upon the forest once more.

Excited by the revels of the past few days, heated with wine, with the night ride, and with the overpowering closeness of the air, the temptation came upon him with a force which he had neither power nor desire to resist. He listened, but no sound met his ear, no breath stirred, no living being moved, no disturbance need be dreaded from any side. From the people in the pavilion he looked for no interference, from the object of his desires he had probably no need to anticipate any disinclination but what might easily be soothed away. The universal custom of the country in which he was now almost naturalized sanctioned such acts. The hour was admirably chosen, the place perfectly adapted in every way, as if the result not of happy chance but deeply concerted plan.

Why then did he hesitate? Did he still partly hope that some miracle would happen? or some equally miraculous change take place in his mind and will to save him from himself? It is true the place and the temptation were not of his own seeking, so far he was free from blame; but he had not come wholly unharmed out of the fiery trial at Umbria, and, by a careless walk since he came to Florence, he had prepared the way for the tempter, and this night even he had disregarded the warning voice and drifted recklessly onward. We walk of our own free will, heated and inflamed by wine, down the flowery path which we have ourselves decorated with garlands, and we murmur because we reach the fatal goal.

He gazed another moment over the illumined forest, which seemed transfigured in the moonlight and the stillness into an unreal landscape of the dead. The poisonous mists crept over the tops of the cork trees, and flitted across the long vistas in spectral forms, cowled and shrouded for the grave. Beneath the gloom indistinct figures seemed to glide,—the personation of the miasma that made the place so fatal to human life.

He turned to enter the room, but even as he turned a sudden change came over the scene. The deadly glamour of the moonlight faded suddenly, a calm pale solemn light settled over the forest, the distant line of hills shone out distinct and clear, the evil mystery of the place departed whence it came, a fresh and cooling breeze sprang up and passed through the rustling wood, breathing pureness and life. The dayspring was at hand in the eastern sky.

The rustling breeze was like a whisper from heaven that reminded him of his better self. It would seem that hell overdid it; the very stillness for miles around, the almost concerted plan, sent flashing through his brain the remembrance of another house, equally guarded for a like purpose—a house at Newnham near Oxford, into which years ago he had himself forced his way to render help in such a case as this. Here was the same thing happening over again with the actors changed; was it possible that such a change had been wrought in him? The long past life of those days rushed into his mind; the sacramental Sundays, the repeated vows, the light of heaven in the soul, the kneeling forms in Little Gidding Chapel, the face of Mary Collet, the loveliness that blessed the earth where she walked, her deathbed, and her dying words. What so rarely happens happened here. The revulsion of feeling, the rush of recollection and association, was too powerful for the flesh. The reason and the affections rallied together, and, trained into efficiency by past discipline, regained the mastery by a supreme effort, even at the very moment of unsatisfied desire. But the struggle was fierce; he was torn like the demon-haunted child in the gospel story; but, as in that story, the demon was expelled.

He came back into the room. Lauretta lay upon a couch with rich drapery and cushions, her face buried in her hands. The cloak and hood in which she had ridden were removed, and the graceful outline of her figure was rendered more alluring by the attitude in which she lay. As he entered she raised her head from her hands, and looked at him with a strange, apprehensive, expectant gaze. He remained for a moment silent, his face very pale; then he said, slowly and uncertainly, like a man speaking in a dream,—

"The fatal miasma is rising from the plain. Lauretta, this place is safe for neither of us, we had better go on."

The morning was cloudy and chill. They had not ridden far before a splash of thunder-rain fell, and the trees dripped dismally. A sense of discomfort and disappointment took possession of Inglesant, and so far from deriving consolation from his conquest, he seemed torn by the demon of discontent. He was half-conscious that his companion was regretting the evil and luxurious house they had left. The ride to Pistoia was silent and depressed. As they passed through the streets, early as it was, they were watched by two figures half concealed by projecting walls. One of them was the Cavaliere, the other was tall and dark. Whether it was the devil in the person of Malvolti, or Malvolti himself, is not of much consequence, nor would the difference be great. In either case the issue was the same,—the devil's plot had failed. It is not so easy to ruin him with whom the pressure of Christ's hand yet lingers in the palm.

When Inglesant presented himself again at the Convent grate, after a few hours' sleepless unrest at an inn, he was refused admittance; nor did repeated applications during that day and the next meet with a more favourable response. He became the prey of mortification and disgust that, having had the prize in his hand, he had of his own free will passed it into the keeping of another. On the evening of the third day, however, he received a note from Lauretta informing him that her brother had consented to postpone her betrothal to Malvolti indefinitely, and that she, on her part, had promised not to see Inglesant again until the Papal election had been decided. She entreated her lover not to attempt to disturb this compromise, as by so doing he would only injure her whom he had promised to help. She promised to be true, and did not doubt but that, having obtained the delay she sought, she should be able to gain her father's consent to their marriage, especially if the Papal election took the course they hoped it would.

There was something cold and formal about the wording of this note, which, however, might be explained by its contents having been dictated to the writer; but, unsatisfactory as it was, Inglesant was compelled to acquiesce in the request it contained. He was angry and disappointed, and it must be admitted that he had some cause. His mistress and his pleasant life at the ducal Court had vanished in the morning mist and rain, like the delusive pleasures of a dream, and the regret which a temptation yielded to would leave behind is not always counterbalanced by a corresponding elation when the trial is overcome. He departed for Rome, having sent orders to Florence for his servants and baggage to meet him on the road, and the same night on which he entered the city Pope Innocent the Tenth expired.

CHAPTER X

The portion of the Vatican Palace set apart for the election of the Pope, and called the Conclave, consisted of five halls or large marble rooms, two chapels, and a gallery seventy feet long. Each of these halls was divided temporarily into small apartments, running up both sides, with a broad alley between them, formed of wood, and covered with green or violet cloth. One of these apartments was assigned to each Cardinal with his attendants. The entrance to the whole of these rooms, halls, chapels, and gallery was by a single door fastened by four locks and as many keys. As soon as the Cardinals had entered the Conclave this door was made fast, and the four keys were given to the four different orders of the city,—one to the Bishop of Rome, one to the Cardinals themselves, a third to the Roman Nobility, and the fourth to the Officer, a great noble, who kept the door. A wicket in the door, of which this Officer also kept the key, permitted the daily meals and other necessaries to be handed to the Cardinals' servants, every dish being carefully examined before it was allowed to pass in. Within the Conclave light and air were only obtained by sky-lights or windows opening upon interior courts, precluding communication from without. The gloom of the interior was so great, that candles were burnt throughout the Conclave at noon-day.

From the moment the Conclave was closed a silence of expectation and anxiety fell upon all Rome. The daily life of the city was hushed. The principal thoroughfares and fortresses were kept by strong detachments of armed troops, and the approaches to the mysterious door were jealously watched. Men spoke everywhere in whispers, and nothing but vague rumours of the proceedings within were listened to in the places of public resort, and in the coteries and gatherings of all ranks and conditions of the people.

In the interior of the Conclave, for those who were confined within its singular seclusion, the day passed with a wearisome monotony marked only by intrigue not less wearisome. Early in the morning a tolled bell called the whole of its inmates to mass in one of the small Chapels darkened with stained glass, and lighted dimly by the tapers of the altar, and by a few wax candles fixed in brass sockets suspended from the roof. The Cardinals sat in stalls down either side of the Chapel, and at the lower end was a bar, kept by the master of the ceremonies and his assistants, behind which the attendants and servants were allowed to stand. Mass being over, a table was placed in front of the altar, upon which was a chalice and a silver bell. Upon six stools near the table are seated two Cardinal-Bishops, two Cardinal-Priests, and two Cardinal-Deacons. Every Cardinal in his turn, upon the ringing of the bell, leaves his seat, and having knelt before the altar in silent prayer for the guidance of heaven in his choice, goes round to the front of the table and drops a paper, upon which he has written the name of a Cardinal, into the chalice, and returns in silence to his stall.

A solemn and awful stillness pervades the scene, broken only by the tinkling of the silver bell. The Cardinals, one by one, some of them stalwart and haughty men with a firm step and imperious glance, others old and decrepit, scarcely able to totter from their places to the altar, or to rise from their knees without help, advance to their mysterious choice. To the eye alone it was in truth a solemn and impressive scene, and by a heart instructed by the sense of sight only, the awful presence of God the Paraclete might, in accordance with the popular belief, be felt to hover above the Sacred Host; but in the entire assembly to whom alone the sight was given there was probably not one single heart to which such an idea was present. The assembly was divided into different parties, each day by day intriguing and manoeuvring, by every art of policy and every inducement of worldly interest, to add to the number of its adherents. "If perchance," says one well qualified to speak, "there entered into this Conclave any old Cardinal, worn by conflict with the Church's enemies 'in partibus infidelium,' amid constant danger of prison or of death, or perchance coming from amongst harmless peasants in country places, and by long absence from the centre of the Church's polity, ignorant of the manner in which her Princes trod the footsteps of the Apostles of old, and by the memory of such conflict and of such innocence, and because of such ignorance, was led to entertain dreams of Divine guidance, two or three days' experience caused such an one to renounce all such delusion, and to return to his distant battlefield, and so to see Rome no more."

When every Cardinal has deposited his paper, the Cardinal-Bishop takes them out of the chalice one by one, and hands them to the Cardinal-Deacon, who reads out the name of the elected, but not of the Cardinal who had placed the paper in the chalice (which is written on part of the paper so folded that even the reader does not see it); and as he reads the name, every Cardinal makes a mark upon the scroll of names he has before him. When all the names have been read, the Cardinal-Priest, from a paper which he has prepared, reads the name of him who has had the most voices and the number of the votes. If the number be more than two-thirds of the whole, the

Cardinal who has received the votes is thereby elected Pope; but if not, the Cardinal-Priest rings the silver bell once more, and at the signal the master of the ceremonies, Monsignor Fabei, advances up the Chapel, followed by a groom carrying a brazier of lighted coals, into which, in the face of the whole assembly, the papers are dropped one by one till all are consumed.

At the beginning of the Conclave the Cardinals were always divided into two, if not more parties, of such relative strength as to make the attainment of such a majority by either of them impossible for many days. It was not until the persistent intrigues of a fortnight had increased the majority of any one Cardinal so much as to give a probability of his being ultimately elected, that the waverers of all sides, not willing to be known as the opponents of a new Pope, recorded their voices in his favour, and thus raised the majority to its necessary proportion. For this very delicate matter occurred at this period of the election, that, should the requisite majority of voices be obtained, the master of the ceremonies and his brazier were no longer called for, but the whole of the papers were opened to their full extent, and the names of the voters given to the world, whereby, as one conversant in these matters observes, "Many mysteries and infidelities are brought to light." It is evident, therefore, that, as the majority of any one Cardinal increased or showed signs of increasing, morning and evening, as the suffrages were taken, the voting became a very exciting and delicate matter. No one could be certain but that at the next voting the majority from the cause mentioned would suddenly swell to the necessary size, and every man's name be made clear and plain on whose side he had been.

Upon entering the Conclave the friends of Cardinal Chigi adopted a quiet policy, and waited for the progress of events to work for them. The abuses of the late Pontificate, and the excitement and indignation of popular opinion, had made it clear to all parties that it was necessary to elect a Pope whose character and reputation would restore confidence. In these respects no one seemed more qualified than Cardinal Chigi, who was supposed to possess all the qualifications necessary to ensure the Romans from the apprehension of a revival of the past disorders, and to inspire the whole Christian world with the hopes of witnessing a worthy successor of St. Peter displaying the Christian virtues from the Papal Chair. The great reputation he had gained at Münster, the determination he was said to have manifested to reform all abuses, the authority and influence he derived from his post of Secretary of State, his attractive and gracious manner, the recommendation of the late Pope upon his death-bed,—all tended to bring his name prominently forward. He was supported by the Spanish Cardinals, chiefly on account of the enmity of the French Court and of his professed opposition to Cardinal Mazarin.

But, in spite of these advantages, the enmity of the French Court, and the opposition of the Barbarini family, the relations and supporters of the late Pope, made it necessary for his friends to observe extreme caution. The French Cardinals were ordered to vote for Sachetti, and Cardinal Barbarini for the present supported him, also, with all his party, chiefly because he had not yet made terms with the Spanish Court, which opposed Sachetti; but also, as was supposed, because he himself had aspirations towards the Papal Chair, should he find the electors favourable to such a scheme.

Upon the entrance into the Conclave, therefore, Cardinal Sachetti immediately obtained thirty-two or thirty-three votes. These were not quite so many as the Barbarini expected, and indeed had a right to count upon, after the professions which the Cardinals of the party had made. This was owing to the defection of some members of what was called the Flying Squadron, composed chiefly of young Cardinals, who were supposed to be devoted to the Barbarini, but of whom several were secretly favourable to Cardinal Chigi.

The Spanish faction, which was numerous enough to have secured the election of any Cardinal had it been united, but the members of which were agreed upon nothing but their determined opposition to Sachetti, contented itself with voting negatively at every scrutiny, making use of the form "accedo nemini." This course was pursued for two entire months, during which time the scrutinies were taken regularly morning and evening, always with a slightly varying but indecisive result.

It would be difficult to realize the wearisomeness which reigned in the Conclave during so protracted a period. The crowding together of so large a number of persons in a few apartments, the closeness of the air, and the unbroken monotony of the hours that passed so slowly, made the confinement almost intolerable. One Cardinal was taken ill, and was obliged to be removed. The great gallery was generally used by the Cardinals themselves, for exercise and conversation, while their attendants were compelled to content themselves with their masters' apartments, or the corridors and passages. Those which opened on the interior courts, and thereby afforded some fresh air, were especially resorted to. Communication from without, though in theory absolutely prevented, was really frequent, all the chief among the Cardinals receiving advices from foreign Courts, and conveying intelligence thither themselves.

At intervals the whole of the inmates were assembled to listen to Father Quaechi, preacher to the Conclave, a Jesuit, and secretly in favour of Cardinal Chigi, as was the Society in general. The sermon was so contrived as to influence its hearers considerably by its evident application to the manners and conduct of the Cardinal.

The famous De Retz, then an exile from France and a supporter of Chigi, by whom he always sat in the Chapel, was the principal intriguer in his favour. He was in communication with the nominal supporters of Barbarini, who sent him intelligence by Monsignor Fabei when to vote for Sachetti, on occasions when it would be of no real service to him, and when to refrain. On one of these latter occasions Fabei entrusted his message to Inglesant, with whom he was intimate, and it afterwards appeared that Sachetti, on that scrutiny, wanted but very few votes to have secured his election. This circumstance made a deep impression on De Retz, and he never recognized Inglesant afterwards without alluding to it.

The day after this scrutiny Cardinal Barbarini appears to have thought that the time was come for his friends to make a demonstration in his behalf, and to the astonishment of the Conclave thirty-one votes appeared in his favour in the next scrutiny. This caused the friends of Cardinal Chigi to pay more attention to his conduct, and to the discourses of his Conclavists and other partizans, who neglected no opportunity of exalting his good qualities.

The exhaustion of the Conclave became extreme. Cardinal Caraffa, who, next to Sachetti and Chigi, stood the greatest chance of election, became ill and died. Twelve other Cardinals were balloted for, one after another, without result. Cardinal San Clemente was then brought forward, and, but for the hostility of the Jesuits, might have been elected; but the Spanish Cardinals who supported him did not dare openly to offend the Society, and the election failed.

The Barbarini began to despair of electing their candidate, and having received favourable advices from the Court of Spain, were willing, either with or without the concurrence of their leader, to negotiate with the friends of Cardinal Chigi. Sachetti, finding his own chances hopeless, was not averse to be treated with. There remained only the Court of France.

The MSS. are here defective.

Be this as it may, Cardinal Sachetti's letter had the desired effect upon Mazarin, who immediately sent the necessary letters to the French Cardinals, withdrawing the veto upon Chigi. Nothing remained now but to gain the concurrence of Cardinal Barbarini. For a long time he refused to accede, but, the members of his party who had from the first secretly supported Chigi having now openly declared in his favour, Barbarini at last consented to hold a conference. It took place immediately after the morning scrutiny, and lasted but a short time. But it sat long enough to arrange that the next morning Cardinal Chigi should be elected Pope.

This determination was so suddenly arrived at, and was concealed so carefully, that nothing certainly was known during the rest of the day, outside the number of those who had taken part in the conference. There were vague rumours, and many discontents, but the time was so short that many who would have declared in favour of Sachetti, had longer time been given them, were not able to recover from their surprise.

Inglesant was of course informed by Cardinal Chigi of what had occurred immediately after the conference, and about mid-day he received a message from De Retz warning him to be upon his guard. During the afternoon, however, some further intelligence of the feeling within the Conclave came to the knowledge of that astute intriguer, and he sent Monsignor Fabei to Inglesant about five o'clock.

This man was a favourable specimen of the Italian servant of an Ecclesiastical Court. Belonging to a family which had been trained for generations in the service of the Curia, he was a man to whom the difficulties which perplexed others, and the anomalies which appeared to some men to exist between Christian polity as it might be conceived to be and Christian polity as it was practised in Rome, did not exist;—a man to whom the Divine, so far as it was manifested to him at all, took the form, without doubt or scruple, of that gorgeous though unwieldy, and, as it seemed to some, slightly questionable, economy of which he was the faithful servant. He was honest, yet he appeared—such was the peculiarity of his training and circumstances—to have solved the, on good authority, insoluble problem of serving two masters at the same time; for two opposing Cardinals, or two factions of Cardinals, alike commanded his reverence and service at the same moment. Much of this service was no doubt unthinking and unconscious, else the memoirs of such a man, composed by himself without reserve, would be perhaps as interesting a book as could be written.

"Something is going on within the Conclave, Cavaliere," he said, "of which I am not entirely cognizant. Of course I am aware of the communications which have been made from outside during this most protracted Conclave. The Princes of the Church must have every opportunity given them of arriving at a just conclusion in this most important matter, and I have never been backward in affording every assistance to their Eminences; but what we have to deal with to-night is of a very different kind. You have nothing to dread from the chiefs of the opposite party; they have accepted the situation, and will loyally carry out their engagements. But they have altered their policy without consulting or remembering their supporters, and among these, especially the inferior ones outside the Conclave, the disappointment is severe. They have not time, nor are they in a position to make terms with the successful party, and their expectations of advancement are annihilated. They are, many of them, absolutely unscrupulous, and would hazard everything to gain time. They have some means of communication between the outside world of Rome and their partizans within the Conclave, which they have not used till now, and with which, therefore, I am unacquainted. They are employing it now. What the exact effort will be I do not know, but should your Padrone, Cardinal Chigi, fall ill before to-morrow's scrutiny, it would delay his election, and delay is all they want. There are sufficient malcontents to prevent his election if they had only time; two or three days would give them all they want. I should advise you not to sleep to-night, but to watch with a wakefulness which starts at every sound."

The apartment assigned to Cardinal Chigi was subdivided into three smaller ones, the largest of which was appropriated to the bedchamber of the Cardinal, the two others to his attendants. These apartments communicated with each other, and only one opened upon the centre corridor running down the Hall. The Cardinal retired early to his own chamber, and most of the other Cardinals did the same. A profound silence reigned in the Conclave; if any of the attendants still stirred they were velvet-shod, and the floors and walls, lined with velvet, prevented the least sound from being heard.

Inglesant remained alone in the outermost of the three apartments, and determined to keep his faculties on the alert. For some reason, however, either the fatigue of the long confinement, or the deathlike stillness of the night, a profound drowsiness overpowered him, and he continually sank into a doze. He tried to read, but the page floated before his eyes, and it was only by continually rising and pacing the small chamber that he kept himself from sinking into a deep sleep.

A profound peace and repose seemed to reign in a place where so many scheming and excited brains, versed in every art of policy, were really at work.

Inglesant had sat down again, and had fallen once more into a slight doze, when suddenly, from no apparent cause, his drowsiness left him, and he became intensely and almost painfully awake. The silence around him was the same as before, but a violent agitation and excitement disturbed his mind, and an overpowering apprehension of some approaching existence, inimical to himself, aroused his faculties to an acute perception, and braced his nerves to a supreme effort. In another moment, this apprehension, at first merely mental, became perceptible to the sense, and he could hear a sound. It was, as it were, the echo of a low faint creeping movement, the very ghost of a sound. Whence it came Inglesant could not determine, but it was from without the apartment in which he sat. No longer able to remain passive, he rose, drew back the velvet curtain that screened the entrance from the corridor, opened the door silently, and went out.

The corridor was lighted here and there along its great length by oil lamps suspended before every third door of the Cardinals' rooms; but the dark and massive hangings, the loftiness of the hall overhead, and the dimness of the lamps themselves, caused the light to be misty and uncertain, as in a confused and troubled dream. One of these lamps was suspended immediately above the door at which Inglesant had appeared, and he stood in its full light, being himself much more distinctly seen than he was himself able to see anything. He was richly dressed in dark velvet, after the French fashion, and in the uncertain light his resemblance to his murdered brother was, in this dress, very great. He held a slight and jewelled dagger in his hand.

As he paused under the suspended lamp the sound he had before heard developed itself into low stealthy footsteps approaching down the corridor, apparently on the opposite side, and the next moment a figure, more like a phantom thrown on the opposite wall than a substantial being, glided into sight. It was shrouded in dark and flowing drapery, and kept so close to the heavy hangings that it seemed almost the waving of their folds stirred by some unknown breeze. Though it passed down the opposite side, it kept its attention turned in Inglesant's direction, and almost at the same moment at which he appeared through the opening door it saw him and instantly stopped. It lost its stealthy motion and assumed an attitude of intense and speechless terror, such as Inglesant had never seen depicted in a human being, and by this attitude revealed itself more completely to his gaze. The hood which shaded its face fell partly back, and displayed features pale as death, and lustrous eyes dilated with horror, and Inglesant could see that it held some nameless weapon in its hand. As it stood, arrested in its purpose, breathless and uncertain, it seemed to Inglesant a phantom murderer, or rather the phantom of murder itself, as though nothing short of the murderous principle sufficed any longer to dog his steps.

This strange figure confronted Inglesant for some seconds, during which neither stirred, each with his eyes riveted upon the other, each with his weapon in his hand. Then the phantom murmured in an articulate and broken voice, that faltered upon the air as though tremulous with horror, "It is himself! He has taken the dagger from his bleeding wound."

Then, as it had come, it glided backwards along the heavy drapery, becoming more and more lost in its folds, till, at first apparently but the shadow of a shade, it faded more and more into the hanging darkness, and vanished out of sight.

The next morning, at the scrutiny after early mass, Fabitis Chigi, Cardinal and Secretary of State, was, by more than two-thirds of the whole Conclave, elected Pope.

CHAPTER XI

There is, perhaps, no comparison so apposite, though it be a homely one, to the condition of affairs in Italy at this time—upon the election of a new Pope—as that of a change of trumps at a game of cards. All persons and matters remain the same as they were before, yet their values and relationships are all changed; the aspect of the entire scene is altered; those who before were in little esteem are exalted, and those who were in great power and estimation are abased. All the persons with whom Inglesant had been connected were more or less affected by it, except Cardinal Rinuccini, to whom it made little difference. To the Cavaliere and to Malvolti it was ruin. The former was so deeply involved in debt, in private feuds, and entanglements with the authorities, his character was so utterly lost with all parties, and his means of usefulness to any so small, that it is probable that even the elevation to power of the Barbarini faction would not have been of much use to him. But, whatever might have been his prospects had the election resulted otherwise, his only chance now of safety from prison and even death was in Inglesant's connection with his sister, and in the protection he might hope to experience upon that account; his only hope depended upon the force of Inglesant's affection. The fear of private assassination kept him almost confined to his chamber. Malvolti's circumstances were still more hopeless; notorious for every species of vice and crime, and hateful even to the very bravoes and dregs of the Italian populace, he had now lost all hope of alliance or even assistance from his friend the Cavaliere, who discarded him the moment that he was of no further use. Maddened by this treatment and by despair, no way seemed open to him except that of desperate revenge. Towards Inglesant his hatred was peculiarly intense, being mixed with a certain kind of superstitious dread. He regarded him almost as the shade of his murdered brother, returned from the grave to dog his steps. It was his presence which had thwarted his last desperate attempt within the Conclave, his last hope of earning protection and rewards. He expected nothing but punishment and severe retribution at Inglesant's hands. Surrounded as he was by perils and enemies on every side, this peril and this dreaded enemy stood most prominently in his path; a blow struck here would be not only a measure of self-defence, but a sweet gratification of revenge, and a relief from an appalling supernatural terror. This terrible semblance of his murdered victim once out of his path, he might hope that the vision of a bloody hearthstone in England might not be so constantly before his eyes.

To Inglesant himself the bright prospects which seemed opening before him gave little satisfaction. He was exhausted in body by his long detention within the Conclave, and the tone of his spirit was impaired by the intrigue and hypocrisy of which he had been a witness and a partaker. It is impossible to kneel morning after morning before the Sacrament, in a spirit of worldliness and chicane, without being soiled and polluted in the secret places of the soul. The circumstances of his visit to Umbria and to Florence, howbeit in both he had been preserved almost by a miracle from actual sin, had left an evil mark upon his conscience. He felt little of the sweet calm and peace he had enjoyed for a season in the company of Molinos, during his first visit to Rome. Something of his old misery returned upon him, and he felt himself again the sport of the fiend, who was working out his destruction by some terrible crime, of which he was the agent, and the Italian murderer the cause.

"This man is at large in Rome," said Don Agostino to him one day; "I should advise you to have him assassinated. It is time the earth was rid of such a villain, and the Roman law is useless in such a case. All protection is withdrawn from him, and every man, high and low, within the city will rejoice at his death."

Inglesant shook his head.

"I do not value my life, God knows, at a straw's worth," he said. "Because he murdered my brother, foully and treacherously, he and I shall too surely meet some day; but the time is not yet come. Surely if the devil can afford to wait, much more can I."

He spoke more to himself than to the other, and there is reason to suppose that Don Agostino made arrangements to have Malvolti assassinated on his own responsibility; but the Italian avoided his bravoes for a time.

Some short time after the Pope's election, in the height of the Carnival,[#] a masked ball was given in the Palace Doria, at which Don Agostino had arranged a set composed entirely of his own friends. It was composed in imitation of the old comedies of the Atellanas, upon which the Punchinello and Harlequinade of all nations has been formed, and which, being domestic dramas performed in masques by the Roman youth with an old-fashioned elegance and simplicity, were peculiarly fitted for performance at a modern masquerade. A primitive and rude form of pantomime, founded on caricature and burlesque, with a few characters boldly drawn, has none of the charm of the later comedy, which is a picture of real life with its variety of character and incident, and possesses that excellent art of showing men as they are, while representing them as they seem to be. But, though it fell short of this higher perfection, the broad farce and few characters of the older form of comedy are not wanting in much lively and yet serious painting of human life, which is all the more serious and pathetic from its broad and unconscious farce. The jester, the knave, the old man, the girl, the lover,—these types that are eternal and yet never old,—with the endless complication in which, both on the stage and real life, they are perpetually involved, are susceptible of infinite application and interest to the imagination. As the rehearsal progressed Inglesant was struck and interested with these ideas, and as the night came on there seemed to him to be in the world nothing but play within play, scene within scene. Between the most incidental acts of an excited and boisterous crowd and the most solemn realities of life and death it seemed to him impossible to distinguish otherwise than in degree; all appeared part of that strange interlude which, between the Dramas of Eternity, is performed continually upon the stage of life.

> [#] It is generally stated by historians that the election of Cardinal Chigi took place on April 7th, 1655, and as Easter that year fell on April 15th, there appears some discrepancy in this part of the narrative. The reader must decide between these contending authorities.

The set was a large one, consisting of the ordinary pantomime types, supplemented by duplicates, peasants, priests, sbirri (always a favourite subject of satire and practical jokes), country girls, and others. Don Agostino, whose wit was ready and brilliant, took the part of clown or jester, and Inglesant that of the stage lover, a *rôle* requiring no great effort to sustain. The part of Columbine was sustained by a young girl, a mistress of Don Agostino, of considerable beauty and wit, and as yet unspoiled by the wicked life of Rome. She was dressed as a Contadina, or peasant girl, in holiday costume. Harlequin was played by a young Count, a boy of weak intellect, involved in every species of dissipation, and consigned to ruin by designing foes, of whom some were of his own family.

As the ball progressed the party attracted great notice by the clever interludes and acts they performed between the dances. In these the usual tricks and practical jokes were introduced sparingly, relieved by a higher style of wit, and by allusions to the topics of the day and to the foibles of the society of Rome. The parts were all well sustained, and Don Agostino exerted himself successfully to give brilliancy and life to the whole party. The young Harlequin-Count, who had at first seemed only to excel in lofty capers and somersaults, was the first who showed tokens of fatigue. He became gradually listless and careless, so that he changed his part, and became the butt of the rest, instead of their tormentor.

A dance in sets had just begun, and Inglesant could not help being struck with his disconsolate manner, which showed itself plainly, even through his masque and disguise. It seemed that others noticed it as well, for as Inglesant met the Contadina in one of the combinations of the figure, she said in the pause of the dance,—

"Do you see the Count, Cavaliere? He is on the brink of ruin, body and soul. His cousin, and one or two more who are in the set, are engaged with him in some desperate complication, and are working upon his feeble mind and his terror. Cannot you help him at all?"

When the dance ceased Inglesant went over to the Count, intending to speak to him, but his cousin and others of the set were talking earnestly to him, and Inglesant stepped back. He saw that the longer his treacherous friends spoke to him the more broken down and crushed in spirit did the poor Harlequin-Count become; and it was evident to Inglesant that here a play was being enacted within the play, and that, as often is the case, one of the deep tragedies of life was appearing in the fantastic dress of farce. As he stood dreamily watching what occurred, Don Agostino called him off to commence another comic act, and when at the first pause he turned to look for the Count, he could no longer see him. His cousin and the others were present, however, and soon after the set was again formed for another dance.

The stifling air of the crowded rooms, and the fatigue of the part he had to perform, wrought upon Inglesant's brain; the confused figures of the dance dazzled his sight, and the music sounded strange and grotesque. As the partners crossed each other, and he came again to the Contadina in his turn, she grasped his hand in hers, and said, hurriedly,—

"Do you see who is standing in the Count's place?"

Inglesant looked, and certainly, in the place of the dance which should have been occupied by the Count, was a tall figure in the dress of a white friar, over which was carelessly thrown a black domino, which allowed the dark fiery eyes of the wearer to be seen.

"The Count has gone," whispered the girl, trembling all over as she spoke, "no one knows whither; no one knows who this man is who has come in his place. He is gone to drown himself in the river; this is the devil who supports his part."

In spite of the girl's visible agitation and his own excitement, Inglesant laughed, and, taking her words as a jest, turned again to look at the strange masque, intending to make some ludicrous comment to reassure his friend. To his astonishment the words died upon his lips, and an icy chill seemed to strike through his blood and cause his heart to beat violently. A sensation of dread overpowered him, the dance-music sounded wild and despairing in his ears, and the ever-varying throng of figures, waving with a thousand colours, swam before his eyes. In the appearance of the stranger, which was simply that of a tall man, there was nothing to account for this; and except that he kept his piercing eyes steadily fixed upon Inglesant, there was nothing in his manner to attract attention. Inglesant went through the rest of the dance mechanically, and suddenly, as it seemed to him, the music stopped.

The dance being over, most of Don Agostino's party, tired with their exertions, withdrew to the buffet of an adjoining apartment for refreshment. Inglesant had taken off his masque, and standing by the buffet, a little apart from the rest, was fanning himself with it, and cooling his parched throat with iced wine, when he was aware that the strange figure had followed him. It was standing before him with a glass in its hand, which it seemed to fill from a bottle of peculiar shape, which Inglesant recognized as one only used to contain a rare Italian wine.

"Cavaliere," the strange masque said in a soft and polite voice, "this wine will do you more good than that which you are drinking; it cools and rests the brain. Will you drink with me?"

As he spoke he offered Inglesant the glass he held, and filled another, and at the same instant, the Contadina came up to Inglesant and hung upon his arm.

Inglesant, who was unmasked, stood with the glass in his hand, waiting for the other to remove his domino before he bowed and drank; but the stranger did not do so.

After a moment's pause, amid the breathless silence of the whole group, who were looking on, the stranger said, speaking with a courteous speech and gesture, which if acted were perfectly well assumed,—

"Pardon me that I do not remove my masque; it is my misfortune that I am not able to do so."

Impressed by the other's manner, it struck Inglesant in a moment that this must be some great noble, perhaps a Prince of the Church, for whom it would be injudicious to appear unmasked, and bowing courteously, he raised the glass to his lips.

As he did so the black eyes of the disguised friar were fixed steadily upon him, and the Contadina said in his ear, in an eager, frightened whisper,—

"Do not drink."

The tremor of her voice, and of her figure on his arm, brought back in a moment the terror and distrust which the bearing and manner of the other had dispelled, and raising the cup, he let his lip rest for a moment in the liquor, but did not drink. Then replacing the glass upon the buffet, he said coolly,—

"It is a good wine, but my English habit has spoiled my taste. I do not like the Italian Volcanic wines."

"I regret it," said the other, turning away; "they are a quietus for the fever of life."

The party breathed more freely as he left the room, and the Contadina, taking the glass which Inglesant had put down, emptied its contents upon the floor.

They followed the domino into the ball-room, where they saw him speaking to the Count's cousin, and to two or three others of the group, who had remained there or sought refreshment elsewhere.

As the last dance began, in the early daybreak which made the lamps burn faintly, and cast a pale and melancholy light over the gay dresses and the moving figures, over the gilding and marble, and the dim lovely paintings on the walls, Inglesant was conscious of a strange and death-like feeling that benumbed his frame. He was bitterly cold, and his sight became dim and uncertain. The music seemed to grow wilder and more fantastic, and the crowded dancers, grotesque and goblin-like to any eyes, became unreal as a dream to his.

Suddenly, as before, the music ceased, and not knowing what he did, Inglesant became separated from his friends, and was borne by the throng to the doors and down the staircase into the courtyard and the street.

The Piazza and the Corso beyond were crowded with carriages, and with servants carrying dim torches, and the morning air was rent with confused noise.

Nearly unconscious, Inglesant allowed himself to be carried onward by the crowd of persons leaving the palace on foot—a motley throng in every variety of costume, and he was soon borne out of the square into the Corso and down the street.

Suddenly he heard a voice behind, clear and distinct to his ears, at least, amid the confused noise,—

"There he is—now strike!"

Turning round quickly, he saw the masque within two yards of him, with something in the folds of his gown which shone in the light. In another moment he would have been close to him, when they were swept apart by a sudden movement of the crowd, and Don Agostino's carriage, surrounded by servants, passed close by the spot to which Inglesant had drifted. He was recognized, and Agostino welcomed him eagerly, saying,—

"I have been looking for you everywhere."

They proceeded along the Corso, Inglesant still like a man in a dream, and turned down towards the bridge of St. Angelo. At the corner of a street leading to the river, another pause occurred. The carriage of a great French noble and Prince of the Church—which had followed the Corso farther on—was passing when they turned into the street, and according to the formal etiquette of the day, even at that hour and in the crowded street, Don Agostino's coachman stopped his horses before the carriage of his master's superior, and the servants opened the door that one of the gentlemen at least might alight. At the same moment, there seemed to be some confusion in the crowd at the top of the short street leading to the river; and Inglesant, still hardly knowing what he did, alighted, with the double purpose of seeing what was the matter, and of saluting his patron. As he did so, one of the servants said to him,—

"They are bringing up a dead body, sir."

It was true. A body had just been drawn out of the river, and, placed on nets and benches of a boat, was being carried on the shoulders of fishermen up the street. As it passed, Inglesant could see the face, which hung drooping towards him over the edge of the nets. It was the face of the Harlequin-Count.

It had scarcely passed, when Inglesant heard—as a man hears over and over again repeated in a ghastly dream—the same voice that spoke before, saying,—

"There he is again. If you let him get back to the coach you will lose him. Go round by the horses' heads."

The restlessness of the impatient horses had made a little space clear of the crowd, and the same had happened in front of the horses of the Cardinal-Duke, so that the street between them was comparatively clear. Strangely frightened and distressed, Inglesant struggled back to Agostino's carriage, and had just reached the door when the masque, passing round the horses' heads, sprang upon him, and struck a violent blow with the glancing steel. The state of his victim's brain saved him. The moment he reached the door he reeled against it, and the weapon glanced off his person, the hilt striking him a violent blow on the chest. He fell backwards into the coach, and Agostino caught a second blow in his sleeve. The startled servants threw themselves upon the murderer, but he slipped through their hands and escaped.

Two days after the ball, when the morning of Ash Wednesday broke with the lovely Italian dawn, a strange and sudden transformation had passed over Rome. Instead of a people wild with pleasure, laughing, screaming, joking like children, feasting, dancing, running about, from mere lightness of heart; in the place of fairs, theatres, and booths in the open streets, instead of the public gardens and walks crowded with parti-coloured masquers, full of sportive pranks, and decked out with every vagary and grotesque freak of costume, you saw a city quiet and silent as the grave, yet full of human forms; you heard nothing but the tolling of bells and the faint echo of solemn chants. The houses and churches were hung with black; the gay tapestries and silks, the theatres, the play-actors, and the gay dresses, had all vanished, and in their place the streets were full of cowled and silent penitents. They walked with downcast and pallid faces; if you spoke to them they did not answer, but gazed upon you with wondering eyes. Men and women alike wore the black gown and hood of penance, and from the proudest noble to the poorest peasant, thronged into the Churches and received alike the emblem of their common fate—the ashes and dust from whence they came, and to which they would return.

Before the masked ball, exhausted in health by the long confinement in the Conclave, and tormented in mind by disappointed desire and by accusing conscience, Inglesant had been sinking into almost as great misery as that which he had endured before he came to Rome. The perils and terror that had entered unbidden among the guests during that night of revelry had worked a marvellous change upon him, and he awoke from a species of trance, which had lasted two days, with his spirits cleared and strengthened. He was, in fact, like a man whom a violent fever has just left, languid in body, but with a mind at rest and in peace, with the wild dreams and visions of delirium gone. The earth seems, at least to him, calm and peaceful, full of voices of prayer and strains of penitential song. He looks out upon life languidly, it is true, but with a friendly, pleased countenance, as upon a well-known landscape recalling happy days. So it was with Inglesant, that the wild riot of the Carnival being over, the peace of Lent began within his soul. The blow that had been struck at his life restored him to life, and took away the superstitious dread that was gradually consuming his reason. He had met his brother's murderer, not alone in some solitary place and picked time, planned before with diabolic purpose by the enemy of mankind, but in a crowd, and as it seemed by chance. He had himself been passive, and urged by no demoniac prompting to some terrible act of vengeance; still more, his enemy had failed, miraculously, as it seemed to him. Surely, then, his fears had been in vain; he was not delivered over to Satan, nay, probably the Lord Himself still regarded him with compassion, still watched over and defended his life. Some work was doubtless reserved for him to do; for him, living always on the verge of delirium, whom a little extra pressure upon the brain-nerve might at any moment estrange altogether from reason, and deprive of intellect and of intercourse with men. For such as he, nevertheless, under such protection, what might not yet be possible? The dews of the Divine Grace cool the fevered brain more surely than any cordial, and soften and water the parched and thirsty heart. The pleasant Italian March day was soft and balmy as the loveliest day of June in England. The scent of jasmin and Daphne flowers filled the air; soft showers fell at intervals over the garden slopes of that part of Rome; the breath of Zephyr swept sweetness into the weary sense. Let him join the hooded throng of penitents; let him, dust and ashes, snatched it may be "è flamma" from the very flames, yet still by the grace of God in his right mind, take his ashes with a grateful heart.

For the appearance, amid the chaos of his life, of a guiding Divine Hand, delightful as it is to any man, must be unspeakably so to him who, to the difficulties, sufficiently great, which ordinarily beset a man in his path through life, adds this overwhelming one—the imminent chance at any moment of losing consciousness altogether, with the power of thought and choice of seeing objects rightly, and of self-control and self-command. How eagerly one to whom life is complicated in such sort as this must welcome a Divine guidance may easily be seen—one who otherwise is wandering among a phantasmagoria of objects, among which he must, so far as his wavering consciousness allows him, and for the moment that consciousness may remain his own, shape his course so as to avoid ruin.

In the fresh morning air, full of delicious warmth and sweetness, and with this angelic messenger leading his soul, Inglesant went out. He had no sufficient motive to take him to any particular Church; but chance or some nobler power directed that he should turn his steps to the right in passing into the Via di S. Giovanni, and following the crowd of penitents, should arrive at the portico of the Church of the Lateran.

The space in front of the magnificent façade was crowded with draped forms, and the wail of the rare organ music reached the outer perfumed air. The marble pavement of the interior, precious beyond calculation, was thronged with the dark crowd, and the costly marble of the walls and tombs was streaked and veiled by the wreaths of incense which lingered in the building. The low chanting and the monotonous accompaniment of the organs filled the Church, and high over the altar, brilliant with a thousand lights, flashed the countless gems of the wonderful tabernacle, and the Cœna of plate of inestimable cost. On either side the gilded brass of the four columns of the Emperor Titus, brought from Jerusalem itself, reflected back the altar lights; and beset with precious stones where the body of the Lord once had hung, was evident to all beholders the very wood of the Holy Cross.

As Inglesant entered, the ashes had been sprinkled three times with holy water, and the clouds of incense gradually rose over the kneeling crowd, as the people began to receive the ashes upon their foreheads, thronging up in silence and order. At the same time the choir began to sing the Antiphons, accompanied by the heavenly music of the matchless organs, and penetrating by their distinct articulation the remotest corners of the Church.

"Immutemur habitu," they began, "let us change our garments; in ashes and sackcloth let us fast and lament before the Lord. Because," and the pealing anthem rose in ecstatic triumph to the emblazoned roof, "plenteous in mercy to forgive our sins is this God of ours."

"Ah! yes," thought Inglesant, "let us change our garments; these dark robes that seem ashes and sackcloth, may they not be the chosen garment of the marriage supper of the King? Clothed and in one's right mind, by the heavenly mercy we already walk the celestial pavement, and hear the pealing anthems of the angelic choir."

"Emendemus in melius," the anthem went on, "let us amend for the better in that in which we have ignorantly sinned—ne subito præoccupati die mortis, quæramus spatium poenitentiæ, et invenire non possimus."

The mighty voice, as of God Himself, seemed to single out and speak to Inglesant alone, "Lest suddenly overtaken by the day of death." Ah! who so well as he knew what that meant, who so lately as he had stood face to face with the destroyer?

He covered his face with his hands.

As the chanting of the Antiphon continued; he reached the steps of the high altar, and in his turn knelt to receive the ashes upon his brow.

In a pause of the anthem the chanting ceased, and the organs played a slow movement in the interval. Nothing was heard but the monotonous undertone of the priests.

As Inglesant knelt upon the marble an overpowering sense of helplessness filled his soul, so worthless and fragile he seemed to himself before the eternal existence, that the idea of punishment and penitence was lost in the sense of utter nothingness.

"Ah! Lord God," he thought, "shattered in mind and brain I throw myself on Thee; without Thee I am lost in the vortex of the Universe; my intellect is lost except it steadies itself upon the idea of Thee. Without Thee it has no existence. How canst Thou be angry with that which is not?"

He bowed his head in utter prostration of spirit to receive the ashes.

"Memento, homo," the priest began—ah! surely it must be easy to remember that, "quia pulvis es——"

Inglesant heard no more. A sudden thrill of earth, like the familiar scent of flowers to a dying man, passed through him, and he lifted up his eyes. Opposite to him across the corner of the altar steps knelt Lauretta, her lustrous eyes full of tears fixed upon him with an inexpressible tenderness and interest. His eyes met hers for an instant, then he dropped his head again before the priest; but the thought and presence of heaven was gone from him, and nothing but the roses and loves of earth remained.

He rose from his knees. The throng of penitents surrounded him, and he suffered himself to be swept onward, down the long nave, till he reached the door through which the crowd was pouring out. There, however, he stopped.

CHAPTER XII

The old Duke of Umbria was dying. He lay clothed, as he had once said to Inglesant, in the "Angelica Vestis," the sacred wafer in his mouth. Below in the Palace Chapel, in the great Duomo, in Rome itself, masses were being said day by day, and the ineffable Host raised to heaven, in intercessory prayer for this man's soul. If any deserved an unruffled passage over the dark river, he did. He had sought long and earnestly to find a more excellent way, and had shrunk from no effort nor painful mortification if he might at last walk in it when found. He had resigned himself and all that he possessed in implicit obedience to the doctrine and the See of Rome. He had crowned a blameless and beneficent life by acts of unparalleled devotion and piety; nevertheless, an unruffled passage he did not have. The future was dark and full of dread, and he suffered all the terrors of the grave with a troubled mind. Lying thus in dull misery of body, and in mental apprehension and unrest, he bethought himself of Inglesant. Having surrendered himself, soul and body, into the hands of those who stood about his bed, he knew that it was useless to let his mind wander after any of those unauthorized teachers from whom in past days he had sought instruction; but in Inglesant he had, for the first time, met a man who, walking to all appearance in the straitest paths of the Catholic Church, seemed to possess a freedom of spirit greater than the Sectaries themselves could boast. Even when suffering the rebukes of an accusing conscience, and the bewilderment of a disordered brain, there was in Inglesant an unfettered possession of the things of this life, and even of the life to come, which had astonished the old man, who, unaccused by his own conscience, was yet so confined and hampered in this world, and in such continual dread of that other which was shortly to be revealed to him.

He expressed to his director a wish that Inglesant might be sent for. It was impossible to deny him this request, even had it been thought desirable. Inglesant was a trusted confidant of the dominant Society of Rome, a favourite of the new Pope, and had, besides, been influential, as was believed, in obtaining that crowning triumph—the cession of the Duchy to the Papal See. A messenger was therefore despatched to Rome requesting his immediate presence. The summons found him with Lauretta and her father, engaged in preparations for his speedy marriage.

This connection was regarded with great favour by Don Agostino and most of his friends; but was looked upon, as far as they condescended to notice it at all, with suspicion by the heads of the Jesuit Society.

They were beginning to dread the influence of Molinos, and Inglesant had already incurred some suspicion by his intimacy with the Spaniard. The Pope was supposed to be not altogether opposed to the new doctrine, and the Jesuits were unwilling to lose an obedient servant, who might be useful to them. There was, however, no sufficient reason in this why he should be forbidden to visit the old Duke, who was certainly dying, and therefore beyond the reach of dangerous influence; and Inglesant, remembering the interest he had felt in the Duke, and the favours which he had lavished upon him, hastened to set out.

When he arrived in Umbria he found the Duke had rallied a little, and he received him with the warmest expressions of delight. He was never content save when he was in the room, and his very presence seemed to restore strength and life to the exhausted old man. Those who watched about his bed in the interests of Rome, if they had felt any apprehensions of the result of Inglesant's visit, were speedily reassured, for the Duke did not seem desirous of conversing upon religious matters with him, and, indeed, rather avoided them. He seemed to cling to Inglesant as to the only remaining link to that world which he was so soon to leave, and to take a strange pleasure in furnishing him with those appliances of earthly enjoyment which had until now long ceased to be of interest to himself. Among other gifts he insisted on his accepting a suit of superb armour which had been made expressly for his idolized son. In this suit, in which he caused Inglesant to be arrayed, he declared that he well represented the patron saint of his nation, St. George of England, and pleased himself with the reflection that the fief with which he had endowed Inglesant bore the name of the same saint.

"You are il Cavaliere di San Georgio," he said to his favourite, as he stood by his couch, sheathed in the superb but useless and fantastic armour of the seventeenth century, with cuirass, greaves, and cuisses of polished and jewelled metal, worn over the ordinary dress, and combined with the lace and velvet which ornamented the whole. It is true that the steel plates were covered with silver and gold chasing of arabesques not of the most Christian type, and the perfect sword-blade was engraved with hieroglyphics not of the most saintly kind; nevertheless Inglesant, as he stood, did certainly resemble somewhat closely a splendid renaissance St. George.

"You are il Cavaliere di San Georgio," said the Duke, "and you must wear that armour when you go to meet your bride. I have arranged a train worthy of so illustrious a bridegroom."

Inglesant's marriage had taken a great hold in the imagination of the dying man, and his mind, to the surprise of those who had known him longest, seemed to dwell entirely upon nuptials and festivals. The strain and terror which his spirit had suffered for so long had probably done their work, and, like as on a harpsichord with a snapped string, the set purpose and composure was lost, and nothing but fragments of fantasias could be played. That magic influence of the wonderful ducal palace which Inglesant had been conscious of at his first visit, and of which the Duke had seemed hitherto altogether regardless, at the last moments of his life appeared to assert its power and force; and what to others seemed mere dotage appeared to Inglesant like a wintry gleam of mysterious light that might be the earnest of a happier time,—a return from the dark regions of superstitious fear to the simple delights of common human life. The sway of this strange house was as powerful over Inglesant himself as it had been before; but he now stood upon higher ground than he had done formerly. The events which had occurred in the meantime had not been entirely without effect. His triumph over the temptation of the flesh in the forest pavilion had secured to him a higher place in the spiritual walk, and the escape from the assassin's dagger had sobered his spirit and indescribably touched his heart. The "Kings' Courts," of which this house was but a type,—the Italian world in which he had lived so long,—had, therefore, now less power than ever to crush Inglesant's religious instinct; but it gave it a certain colour, a sort of renaissance Christianity, which bore a likeness to the character of the art-world in which it had grown up,—a Christianity of florid ornament and of somewhat fantastic issues.

As the Duke gradually became weaker, and seemed every day to be on the point of death, he became the more anxious that Inglesant's marriage should be completed, and at last insisted upon his delaying his return to Rome no longer. Inglesant, who expected almost hour by hour the Duke's decease, would have been content to wait; but the dying man would take no denial. He pleased himself with giving orders for Inglesant's train, and ordered his favourite page, an Austrian boy, to accompany him, and to return immediately when the marriage was celebrated, that he might receive the fullest description of the particulars of the event.

It was long before sunrise that Inglesant set out, accompanied by his train, hoping to cross the mountains before the heat began. His company consisted of several men-at-arms, with their grooms and horse boys, and the Austrian page. They ascended the mountains in the earlier part of the night, and towards dawn they reached a flat plain. The night had been too dark to allow them to see the steep and narrow defiles, full of oaks and beech; and as they passed over the dreary plain in the white mist, their figures seemed vast and indistinct in the dim light; but now, as the streaks of the dawn grew brighter in the east behind them, they could see the fir trees clothing the distant slopes, and here and there one of the higher summits still covered with white snow. The scene was cold and dead and dreary as the grave. A heavy mist hung over the mountain plain, and an icy lake lay black and cold beneath the morning sky. As they reached the crest of the hill the mist rose, stirred by a little breeze at sunrise, and the gorges of the descent lay clear before them. The sun arose behind them, gilding the mountain tops, and tracing streaks and shades of colour on the rising mist sparkling with glittering dew-drops; while dark and solemn beneath them lay the pine-clothed ravines and sloping valleys, with here and there a rocky peak; and farther down still the woods and hills gave place at last to the plain of the Tiber, at present dark and indistinguishable in the night.

As the sun arose behind them one by one the pine ravines became lighted, and the snowy summits, soft and pink with radiant light, stood out against the sky, which became every instant of a deeper blue. The sunlight, stealing down the defiles and calling forth into distinct shape and vision tree and rock and flashing stream, spread itself over the oak woods in the valleys, and shone at last upon the plain, embossed and radiant with wood and green meadow, and marble towers and glistering water—the waters of the Tiber running onwards towards Rome. Mysterious forms and waves of light, the creatures of the morning and of the mist, floated before the sight, and from the dark fir trees murmurs and mutterings of ethereal life fell upon the ear. Sudden and passionate flushes of colour tinted the pine woods and were gone, and beneath the branches and across the paths fairy lights played for a moment and passed away.

The party halted more than once, but it was necessary to make the long descent before the heat began, and they commenced carefully to pick their way down the stony mountain road, which wound down the ravines in wild unequal paths. The track now precipitous, now almost level, took them round corners and masses of rock sometimes hanging above their heads, revealing continually new reaches of valley, and new defiles clothed with fir and oak. Mountain flowers and trailing ivy and creeping plants hung in festoons on every side, lizards ran across the path, birds fluttered above them or darted into the dark recesses where the mountain brooks were heard; everything sang the morning psalm of life, with which, from field and mountain solitudes, the free children of nature salute the day.

The Austrian boy felt the beauty of the scene, and broke out into singing.

"When the northern gods," he said to Inglesant, "rode on their chevisance they went down into the deep valleys singing magic songs. Let us into this dark valley, singing magic songs, also go down; who knows what strange and hidden deity, since the old pagan times lost and forgotten, we may find among the dark fir dingles and the laurel shades?"

And he began to sing some love ditty.

Inglesant did not hear him. The beauty of the scene, ethereal and unreal in its loveliness, following upon the long dark mountain ride, his sleepless nights and strange familiarity with approaching death by the couch of the old Duke, confused his senses, and a presentiment of impending fate filled his mind. The recollection of his brother rose again in his remembrance, distinct and present as in life; and more than once he fancied that he heard his voice, as the cry of some mountain beast or sound of moaning trees came up the pass. No other foreshadowing than this very imperfect one warned him of the approaching crisis of his life.

The sun was fully up, and the light already brilliant and intense, when they approached a projecting point where the slope of wood ended in a tower of rock jutting upon the road. The path by which they approached it was narrow and ragged, but beyond the rock the ground spread itself out, and the path was carried inward towards the right, having the sloping hillside on the one hand, covered with scattered oaks, while, on the other, a slip of ground separated it from the ravine. At the turning of the road, where the opening valley lay before them as they reached the corner, face to face with Inglesant as he checked his horse, was the Italian, the inquisitive stranger of the theatre at Florence, the intruder into the Conclave, the masque of the Carnival ball, the assassin of the Corso—that Malvolti who had treacherously murdered his brother and sought his own life. Alone and weary, his clothes worn and threadbare, he came toiling up the pass. Inglesant reined in his horse suddenly, a strange and fierce light in his eyes and face. The Italian started back like some wild creature of the forest brought suddenly to bay, a terrified cry broke from him, and he looked wildly round as if intending flight. The nature of the ground caught him as in a trap; on the one hand the sloping hillside steep and open, on the other tangled rugged ground, slightly rising between the road and the precipice, cut off all hope of sudden flight. He looked wildly round for a moment, then, when the horsemen came round the rocky wall and halted behind their leader, his eyes came back to Inglesant's face, and he marked the smile upon his lips and in his eyes, and saw his hand steal downwards to the hunting piece he carried at the saddle; then with a terrible cry, he threw himself on his knees before the horse's head, and begged for pity,—pity and life.

Inglesant took his hand from his weapon, and turning slightly to the page and to the others behind him, he said,—

"This man, messeri, is a murderer and a villain, steeped in every crime; a cruel secret midnight cut-throat and assassin; a lurker in secret corners to murder the innocent. He took my brother, a noble gentleman whom I was proud to follow, treacherously at an advantage, and slew him. I see him now before me lying in his blood. He tried to take my life,—I, who scarcely even knew him,—in the streets of Rome. Now he begs for mercy, what say you, gentleman? what is his due?"

"Shoot the dog through the head. Hang him on the nearest tree. Carry him into Rome and torture him to death."

The Italian still continued on his knees, his hands clasped before him, his face working with terror and agony that could not be disguised.

"Mercy, monsignore," he cried. "Mercy. I cannot, I dare not, I am not fit to die. For the blessed Host, monsignore, have mercy—for the love of Jesu—for the sake of Jesu."

As he said these last words Inglesant's attitude altered, and the cruel light faded out of his eyes. His hand ceased to finger the carabine at his saddle, and he sat still upon his horse, looking down upon the abject wretch before him, while a man might count fifty. The Italian saw, or thought he saw, that his judge was inclining to mercy, and he renewed his appeals for pity.

"For the love of the crucifix, monsignore; for the blessed Virgin's sake."

But Inglesant did not seem to hear him. He turned to the horsemen behind him, and said,—

"Take him up, one of you, on the crupper. Search him first for arms. Another keep his eye on him, and if he moves or attempts to escape, shoot him dead. You had better come quietly;" he continued, "it is your only chance for life."

Two of the men-at-arms dismounted and searched the prisoner, but found no arms upon him. He seemed indeed to be in the greatest distress from hunger and want, and his clothes were ragged and thin. He was mounted behind one of the soldiers and closely watched, but he made no attempt to escape, and indeed appeared to have no strength or energy for such an effort.

They went on down the pass for about an Italian league. The country became more thickly wooded, and here and there on the hillsides patches of corn appeared, and once or twice in a sheltered spot a few vines. At length, on the broad shoulder of the hill round which the path wound, they saw before them a few cottages, and above them, on the hillside, in a position that commanded the distant pass till it opened on the plain, was a Chapel, the bell of which had just ceased ringing for mass.

Inglesant turned his horse's head up the narrow stony path, and when the gate was reached, he dismounted and entered the Chapel, followed by his train. The Capella had apparently been built of the remains of some temple or old Roman house, for many of the stones of the front were carved in bold relief. It was a small narrow building, and possessed no furniture save the altar and a rude pulpit built of stones; but behind the altar, painted on the plaster of the wall, was the rood or crucifix, the size of life. Who the artist had been cannot now be told; it might have been the pupil of some great master, who had caught something of the master's skill, or, perhaps, in the old time, some artist had come up the pass from Borgo san Sepolcro, and had painted it for the love of his art and of the Blessed Virgin; but, whoever had done it, it was well done, and it gave a sanctity to the little Chapel, and possessed an influence of which the villagers were not unconscious, and of which they were even proud.

The mass had commenced some short time as the train entered, and such few women and peasants as were present turned in surprise.

Inglesant knelt upon the steps before the altar, and the men-at-arms upon the floor of the Chapel, the two who guarded the prisoner keeping close behind their leader.

The priest, who was an old and simple-looking countryman, continued his office without stopping; but when he had received the sacred elements himself, he turned, and, influenced probably by his appearance and by his position at the altar, he offered Inglesant the Sacrament. He took it, and the priest, turning again to the altar, finished the mass.

Then Inglesant rose, and when the priest turned again he was standing before the altar with his drawn sword held lengthwise across his hands.

"My Father," he said, "I am the Cavaliere di San Georgio, and as I came across the mountains this morning on my way to Rome, I met my mortal foe, the murderer of my brother, a wretch whose life is forfeit by every law, either of earth or heaven, a guilty monster steeped in every crime. Him, as soon as I had met him,—sent by this lonely and untrodden way as it seems to me by the Lord's hand,—I thought to crush at once, as I would a venomous beast, though he is worse than any beast. But, my Father, he has appealed from me to the adorable Name of Jesus, and I cannot touch him. But he will not escape. I give him over to the Lord. I give up my sword into the Lord's hands, that He may work my vengeance upon him as it seems to Him good. Henceforth he is safe from earthly retribution, but the Divine Powers are just. Take this sword, reverend Father, and let it lie upon the altar beneath the Christ Himself; and I will make an offering for daily masses for my brother's soul."

The priest took the sword, and kneeling before the altar, placed it thereon like a man acting in a dream.

He was one of those child-like peasant-priests to whom the great world was unknown, and to whom his mountain solitudes were peopled as much by the saints and angels of his breviary as by the peasants who shared with him the solitudes and the legends that gave to these mountain fastnesses a mysterious awe. To such a man as this it seemed nothing strange that the blessed St. George himself, in jewelled armour, should stand before the altar in the mystic morning light, his shining sword in his hand.

He turned again to Inglesant, who had knelt down once more.

"It is well done, monsignore," he said, "as all that thou doest doubtless is most well. The sword shall remain here as thou sayest, and the Lord doubtless will work His blessed will. But I entreat, monsignore, thy intercession for me, a poor sinful man; and when thou returnest to thy place, and seest again the Lord Jesus, that thou wilt remind Him of His unworthy priest. Amen."

Inglesant scarcely heard what he said, and certainly did not understand it. His sense was confused by what had happened, and by the sudden overmastering impulse upon which he had acted. He moved as in a dream; nothing seemed to come strange to him, nothing startled him, and he took slight heed of what passed. He placed his embroidered purse, heavy with gold, in the priest's hand, and in his excitement totally forgot to name his brother, for whose repose masses were to be said.

He signed to his men to release the prisoner, and, his trumpets sounding to horse before the Chapel gate, he mounted and rode on down the pass.

But his visit was not forgotten, and long afterwards, perhaps even to the present day, popular tradition took the story up, and related that once, when the priest of the mountain Chapel was a very holy man, the blessed St. George himself, in shining armour, came across the mountains one morning very early, and himself partook of the Sacrament and all his train; and appealed triumphantly to the magic sword—set with gold and precious stones—that lay upon the altar from that morning, by virtue of which no harm can befall the village, no storm strike it, and, above all, no pillage of armed men or any violence can occur.

The Austrian boy returned to Umbria with his story of the marriage; but the old Duke never heard it. No sooner had Inglesant left him than his depression and despair returned; he loathed the sight of the day, and of the costly palace in which he lived; the gay arts and the devised fancies by which men have sought to lure happiness became intolerable to him; and, ill as he was, he caused himself to be removed to the Castel Durante, amid the lonely mountain ravines, to abide his end. As Inglesant bowed beneath the care-cloth—the fine linen cloth laid over the newly-married in the Church,—kneeling till mass was ended, with his heart full of love and brightness and peace, the last of the house of Revere—"worn out," says the chronicler, with a burst of unusual candour, "by priestly torments"—breathed his last, and went to another world, where, it may be hoped, sacrifice and devotion are better rewarded than they are here, and superstitious terrors are unknown.

CHAPTER XIII

The Castello di San Georgio, or, as it might more properly have been called, the "Casa" or Villa di San Georgio, was built upon the summit of a small conical hill, amid the sloping bases of the Apennines, at a part of their long range where the summits were low and green. In that delightful region, the cultivation and richness of the plain is united to the wildness and beauty of the hills. The heat is tempered in the shady valleys and under the thick woods. A delicious moisture and soft haze hangs about these dewy, grassy places, which the sun has power to warm and gladden, but not to parch. Flowers of every hue cover the ground beneath the oaks and elms. Nightingales sing in the thickets of wild rose and clematis, and the groves of laurel and of the long-leaved olives are crowded with small creatures in the full enjoyment of life and warmth. Little brooks and rippling streams, half hidden by the tangled thickets, and turned from their courses by the mossy rocks, flow down from the hill ravines, as joyful and clear as in that old time when each was the care of some protecting nymph or rural god. In the waters of the placid lake are reflected the shadows of the hills and the tremulous shimmer of waving woods.

In this favoured region, the Villa di San Georgio stood upon its leafy hill-top, set in the background of the mountains. The steep slope was terraced here and there in patches of ground planted with fruit-trees, and at the foot, towards the south, a large lake slept beneath the blue sky, its shores lined with brushwood, interspersed here and there with grassy slopes, where the orchis and hyacinth and narcissus sprang up from the green rich turf.

Through this pastoral land, at all seasons of the year, wandering shepherds with their flocks, peasants with their cattle and dogs, ladies and cavaliers from the neighbouring villas, woodmen, vine-dressers, fishermen from the lake, traversed the leafy stage, and diversified the scene; but when the grape was fully ripe, and the long year was crowned at last with the fatness of the vintage, a joyous age of rural wealth and jollity seemed for a time to fill the mellow, golden-tinted land. Then, indeed, wandering amid the woods and rocks interspersed with vineyards and patches of yellow wheat, as you met the loaded wain, or came upon the wine-press, trodden by laughing girls and boys, you seemed to understand the stories of the rural wanderings of the gods, for you met with many a scene to which it might well be fancied that they might still be allured, as to that garden at the foot of Mount Bermion where the roses grew. The gracious gods of plenty still filled the luscious vats; rustling Zephyr still whispered love among the flowers, still came laden with the ripening odours of the fruit. The little cherub Loves peeped out from behind oak stems and ruined plinth and sculptured frieze, half hidden among roots and leaves.

The Castello was a modern building, although there were ruins in one of the courtyards of a very antique date. It consisted of three or four lofty blocks of buildings, at right angles to each other, covered with low, red-tiled roofs. The principal windows were in the upper stories, and gave light to large and handsome rooms, from which on all sides the most enchanting landscapes satisfied the eye.

The weeks that succeeded Inglesant's marriage grew into months, and the months into years, in this delightful scene. The old Count spent some months in peaceful satisfaction with his daughter and her husband, delighted with the company of his one grandchild, a little boy. In the spacious dining-saloon, with its cool polished floor, it was a pretty sight to see the old, courteous nobleman tempting the child with the ripest fruit. The shaded light fell upon the plate and yellow ware on the table, and upon the old cabinets of Italian marqueterie against the walls; whilst by the carved mantel-piece sat the pleased parents, of whom it is recorded that in Rome they passed for the handsomest pair in Italy. In this way, the days of some three sunny summers passed away, while the winters were spent in the Papal city.

But this Arcadian life was not lasting. The old Count was not long content if absent from city life, and the time at the Castello hung somewhat heavily upon the spirits of both Inglesant and his wife. They were neither of them fitted by previous habits and education for a retired country life; but the circumstance which outwardly appeared to weigh upon Lauretta's mind was uncertainty concerning her brother's fate. From the time of the marriage the Cavaliere had disappeared, and from that day no word of tidings had been received respecting him. It was known that his circumstances were desperate, and the danger he lay under from secret enemies imminent. The account which her husband had given her of the condition in which he had seen Malvolti dwelt in her imagination, and she brooded over the idea of her brother in a similar state of destitution and misery. It seemed probable that, had he been assassinated, tidings of the event would have reached his family; and if alive, it was strange that he had made no application for assistance to those who were so well able and so willing to render it. This suspense and mystery were more insupportable than certainty of evil would have been.

The characters of Inglesant and his wife were of such a nature as most effectively to produce and aggravate this sleepless uneasiness. Upon Lauretta's lenient and gracious, if somewhat pleasure-loving disposition, the impression of the unkindness she had experienced from her brother faded without leaving a trace, and she thought only of some pleasant, long-past incidents, when she had been a pretty, engaging child; whilst the life of romance and excitement, combined with a certain spiritual Quixotism, which Inglesant had so long followed, had rendered any other uncongenial to him, and it required little persuasion to induce him to re-enter upon it.

But there were other causes at work which led to the same result. For many weeks a sultry wind had, without variation, passed over the south of Italy, laden with putrid exhalations from the earth, and by its sullen steadiness causing stagnation in the air. It would be difficult to describe the terrible effect upon the mind and system of the long continuance of such a state of the atmosphere. A restless fear and depression of spirits prepared the body for the seeds of disease, and the contagion, which was not perhaps generated in the atmosphere, was carried by it with fearful rapidity. The plague struck down its victims at once in city and in country, and spared no rank nor condition of life. Then all bond of fellowship and of society was loosened, strange crimes and suspicions,—strange even to that land of crime and treachery,—influenced the lives and thoughts of all men. Innocent persons were hunted to death, as poisoners and spreaders of infection; the terrors of the grave broke through the forms of artificial life, and the depravity of the heart was exposed in ghastly nakedness, as the bodies of the dead lay unburied by the waysides.

The Castello di San Georgio, standing on the summit of a breezy hill, in a thinly-peopled district, was as safe a refuge as could perhaps be found, and, if uneasiness of mind could have been banished, might have been a happy one. Three hundred years before, in the child-like unconsciousness of spiritual conflict which the unquestioned rule of Rome for so long produced, it had been possible, in the days of Boccacio, for cultivated and refined society to shut itself up in some earthly paradise, and, surrounded by horrors and by death, to spend its days in light wit and anecdote, undisturbed in mind, and kept in bodily health by cheerful enjoyment; but the time for such possibilities as these had long gone by. A mental trouble and uneasiness, which pervaded the whole of human life at the most quiet times, gave place, at such periods of dread and fear, to an intolerable restlessness, which altogether precluded the placid enjoyment of the present, however guarded and apparently secure.

The apprehension which most weighed upon Lauretta's mind, was that her brother, flying from some city where the pestilence raged, might be refused succour and assistance, and might even be murdered in the village to which he might flee. Such incidents were of daily occurrence, nor can it be wondered at that human precaution and terror became cruel and merciless, when it is an authenticated fact that the very birds themselves forsook the country places, and disappeared from their native groves at the approach of the plague. Nor were inanimate things, even, indifferent to the scourge; patches and blotches of infection broke out upon the walls and houses, and when scraped off would reappear until the house itself was burnt down.

It was in the midst of this ghastly existence, this life in death, that a wandering mendicant, driven from Rome by the pestilence and craving alms at the Castello, asserted that he knew the Cavaliere di Guardino, and that he was ill in Rome, doubtless by this time dead. The man probably lied, or, if it were true that he had known the Cavaliere, as he had passed him on the steps of the Trinita, the latter part of his story was certainly imaginary. It caused Lauretta, however, so much distress, that her husband, to comfort her, proposed to ride to Rome, and endeavour to discover the truth. The plague was not so virulent in Rome as it was in the south of Italy, and especially in Naples, and to a man using proper precautions the danger might not be very great. Lauretta was distracted. The restless anxiety, which gave her no peace until her brother's fate was known, urged her to let her husband go. How, then, should she be more at ease when, in addition to one vision of dread and apprehension, she would be haunted by another? The new anxiety seemed a relief from the old; anyhow the old was intolerable,— any change offered hope.

Upon his arrival at Rome Inglesant went hither and thither, from place to place, as one false report and another led him. Every beggar in the city seemed to have known the Cavaliere. The contagion was sufficiently virulent to stop all amusements, and to drive every one from the city who was not compelled to remain. The streets were almost deserted, and those who passed along them walked apart, avoiding each other, and seldom spoke. The most frequented places were the churches, and even there, the services were short and hurried, and divested of everything that could attract the eye. In the unusual silence the incessant tolling of the bells was more marked than ever. White processions carrying the Host glided over the hushed pavements.

Once Inglesant thought he had discovered the man of whom he was in search. The Cavaliere, the story now ran, had arrived in Rome a few days ago from Naples, where the plague had the mastery, so that the living could not bury the dead. He had come, flying towards the healthy north before the pestilence, which had overtaken him as he entered the Giovanni gate, and had taken refuge in a pest-house, which had been established in the courtyard of a little church, "S. Salvatoris in Laterano ad scalas sanctas." Thither Inglesant repaired, in the full glare of an afternoon in the late summer. In a sort of cloister, round a little courtyard, the beds were laid out side by side, on which lay the dying and the dead. Between the worn stones of the courtyard, sprinkled with water, bright flowers were springing up. The monks were flitting about; two or three of these also were dead already. Inglesant inquired for the stranger who had arrived from Naples. He was dead, the monks told him, but not yet taken away for burial; he lay there still upon his couch. They took Inglesant to a corner of the courtyard, where, looking down upon the dead body, he saw at once it was not that of the Cavaliere. It was the body of a man in the very prime of life, of a singularly noble and lofty look. He lay with his hand clasped over a little bit of crossed wood the monks had made, his eyes closed, something like a smile upon his lips.

"The Cavaliere will not look like that," thought Inglesant to himself.

Who was he? In some part of Italy, doubtless, there were at that moment those who waited for him, and wondered, just as he and Lauretta were doing. Perhaps in some distant lazaretto some one might be standing over the body of the Cavaliere, at just such a loss for a name and clue. It did not seem strange to Inglesant; he had wandered through these cross ways and tangled paths of life from a child.

He went out into the hot sunshine and down the long straight street, by the great church of the Sancta Maria, into the Via Felix, scarcely knowing where he went. Across the whole breadth of Rome the few persons he met regarded him with suspicion, and crossed over to the other side. He himself carried a pomander of silver in the shape of an apple, stuffed with spices, which sent out a curious faint perfume through small holes. He wandered down the steps of the Trinita, where even the beggars were few and quiet, and seeking unconsciously the cooler air of the river, passed the desolate Corso, and came down to the Ripetta, to the steps.

The sun was sinking now, and the western sky was all ablaze with a strange light. All through the streets the image of the dead man had haunted Inglesant, and the silent city seemed full of such pale and mystic forms. The great dome of St. Peter's stood out dark and clear against the yellow light, which shone through the casements below the dome till the whole seemed faint and ethereal as the air itself. In the foreground, across the river, were low meadows, and the bare branches of trees the leaves of which had already withered and fallen. In the distance the pollard firs upon the ramparts stood out distinctly in fantastic forms; to the left the spires and domes of the city shone in the light; in front flowed the dark river, still and slow. The large steps by the water's edge, usually so crowded and heaped with market produce, were bare and deserted; a wild superstitious terror took possession of Inglesant's mind.

In this solitude and loneliness, amid the busiest haunts of life, with the image of death on every hand, he felt as though the unseen world might at any moment manifest itself; the lurid sky seemed ready to part asunder, and amid the silent courts and pavements the dead would scarcely seem strangers were they to appear. He stood waiting, as though expecting a message from beyond the grave.

And indeed it seemed to come. As he stood upon the steps a gray form came along the pathway on the further side beneath the leafless trees and down the sloping bank. It entered the small boat that lay moored beneath the alders and guided itself across the stream. It stood erect and motionless, propelling the skiff doubtless by an oar at the stern, but from the place where Inglesant stood the boat seemed to move of its own accord, like the magic bark in some romance of chivalry. In its left hand the figure held something which shone in the light; the yellow glamour of the sunset, dazzling to Inglesant's eyes, fluttered upon its vestment of whitish grey, and clothed in transparent radiance this shadowy revenant from the tomb. It made no stay at the landing-place, but, as though on an errand of life and death, it came straight up the wide curved steps, holding forward in its left hand a crucifix of brass. It passed within a step of Inglesant, who was standing, wonderstruck, at the summit of the steps, his silver pomander in his hand. As it passed him he could see the face, pale and steadfast, with a bright lustre in the eyes, and looking full upon him without pausing, the friar, if it were a friar, said,—

"He is in Naples. In that city, or near it, you will find the man you seek. Ay! and far more than you seek. Let there be no delay on your part."

Then, still holding the crucifix forward at arm's length, as though to cleave the poisoned air before him as he went, the figure passed up the street, turning neither to the right nor to the left, and, taking no notice of any of the few loiterers in his way, passed quickly out of sight.

Inglesant turned to two fishermen who were coming slowly down towards the ferry.

"Did you see that Servite friar?" he said.

The men gazed at him uneasily. "He is light-headed," one of them muttered; "he has the plague upon him, and does not know what he says."

Though he said this, they might have seen the friar all the same, for Inglesant's manner was excited, and those were perilous times in which to speak to strangers in the streets. The two men got into the boat, and passed over hastily to the other side.

Naples! It was walking straight into the jaws of death. The dead were lying in the streets in heaps, sprinkled hastily with lime; and lavish gifts of freedom and of gold could scarcely keep the galley slaves from breaking out of the city, though they knew that poverty and probably destruction awaited them elsewhere. But this strange message from another world, which bore such an impress of a higher knowledge, how could he disobey it? "Far more than he sought." These words haunted him. He made inquiries at the monastery of the Jesuits in the Corso, but could hear nothing of such a man. Most of those to whom he spoke were of opinion that he had seen a vision. He himself sometimes thought it an illusion of the brain, conjured up by the story of the man who came from Naples, by the afternoon heat, and by the sight of the dead; but in all this the divine wisdom might be working; by these strange means the divine hand might guide. "Let there be no delay on your part." These words sounded like a far-off echo of Father St. Clare's voice; once again the old habit of obedience stirred within him. Wife and child and home stood in the path, but the training which first love had been powerless to oppose was not likely to fail now. Once again his station seemed to be given him. Before—upon the scaffold, at the traitor's dock, in prison,—he had been found at the appointed post; would it be worth while now, when life was so much farther run out, to falter and turn back? The higher walks of the holy life had indeed proved too difficult and steep, but to this running-footman's sort of business he had before proved himself equal;—should he now be found untrustworthy even in this?

He resolved to go. If he returned at all, he would be back at the Castello before any increased apprehension would be felt; if it were the will of God that he should never return, the Jesuit fathers would undertake the care of Lauretta and his child.

He confessed and received the Sacrament at the Church of the Gesu, in the Chapel of St. Ignatio, in the clear morning light, kneeling upon the cold brilliant marble floor. It was the last day of July, very early, and the Church was swept and garnished for the great festival of the Saint. Inglesant did not wait for the saddened festival, but left Rome immediately that the early mass was done.

CHAPTER XIV

When Inglesant had passed the Pontine Marshes, and had come into the flowery and wooded country about Mola, where the traveller begins to rejoice and to delight his eyes, he found this beautiful land little less oppressive than the dreary marshes he had left. The vineyards covered the slopes, and hung their festoons on every side. The citron and jasmin and orange bloomed around him; and in the cooler and more shady walks flowers yet covered the ground, in spite of the heat. The sober tints of the oaks and beeches contrasted with the brilliant orange groves and vineyards, and, with the palms and aloes, offered that variety which usually charms the traveller; and the distant sea, calm and blue, with the long headlands covered with battlements and gay villas, with plantations and terraces, carried the eye onward into the dim unknown distance, with what is usually a sense of delightful desire.

But as Inglesant rode along, an overpowering sense of oppression and heaviness hung over this beautiful land. The heat was intense; no rain nor dew had fallen for many weeks. The ground in most places was scored and hard, and the leaves were withered. The brooks were nearly dry, and the plantations near the roads were white with dust. An overpowering perfume, sickly and penetrating, filled the air, and seemed to choke the breath; a deadly stillness pervaded the land; and scarcely a human form, either of wayfarer or peasant, was to be seen.

At the small towns near to Naples every form of life was silent and inert. Inglesant was received without difficulty, as he was going towards Naples; but he was regarded with wonder, and remonstrated with as courting certain death. He halted at Aversa, and waited till the mid-day heat was passed. Here, at last, there seemed some little activity and life. A sort of market even appeared to be held, and Inglesant asked the host what it meant.

"When the plague first began in Naples, signore," he said, "a market was established here to supply the city with bread, fresh meat, and other provisions. Officers appointed by the city came out hither, and conveyed it back. But, as the plague became more deadly, most of those thus sent out never returned to the city, in spite of the penalties to which such conduct exposed them. Since the plague spread into the country places, the peasants have mostly ceased to bring their produce; but what little is brought you see here, and one of the magistrates is generally obliged to come out from Naples to receive it."

"Is the city suffering from famine, then?" asked Inglesant.

"The city is like hell itself, Signore il Cavaliere," replied the host. "They tell me that he who looks upon it will never be able to sleep peacefully again. They lie heaped together in the streets, the dying and the dead. The hospitals are choked with dead bodies, so that none dare go in. They are blowing up masses of houses, so as to bury the bodies under the ruins with lime and water and earth. Twenty thousand persons have died in a single day. Those who have been induced to touch the dead to cart them away never live more than two days."

"The religious, and the physicians, and the magistrates, then, remain at their posts?" said Inglesant.

The host shrugged his shoulders.

"There is not more to be said of one class than another," he said; "there are cowards in all. Many of the physicians fled; but, on the other hand, two strange physicians came forward of their own accord, and offered to be shut up in the Sancta Casa Hospital. They never came out alive. Many of the religious fled; but the Capuchins and the Jesuits, they say, are all dead. Most of the Franciscan Friars are dead, and all the great Carmelites. They run to all houses that are most infected, and to those streets that are the most thronged with putrefied bodies, and into those hospitals where the plague is hottest; and confess the sick and attend them to their last gasp; and receive their poisonous breath as though it were the scent of a rose."

"But is no attempt made to bury the dead?"

"They are letting out the galley slaves by a hundred at a time," replied the host; "they offer freedom and a pension for life to the survivors, but none do survive. Fathers and mothers desert their own children; children their parents; nay, they throw them out into the streets to die. What would you have?"

The host paused, and looked at Inglesant curiously, as he sat drinking some wine.

"Have you a lady-love in Naples, signore?" he said at last; "or are you heir to a rich man, and wish to save his gold?"

"I am leaving wife and child," replied Inglesant, bitterly, "to seek a man whom I hate, whom I shall never find under the heaps of dead. You had better say at once that I am mad. That is nearest to the truth."

The host looked at him compassionately, and left the room.

In the cool of the evening Inglesant rode through the deserted vineyards, and approached the barriers. On the way he met some few foot-passengers, pale and emaciated, trudging doggedly onwards. They were leaving death behind them, but they saw nothing but misery and death elsewhere. They took no notice of Inglesant as they passed. Many of them, exhausted and smitten with the disease, sank down and died by the wayside. When he arrived at the barriers, he found them deserted, and no guard whatever kept. He left his horse at a little osteria without the gate, which also seemed deserted. There was hay in the stable, and the animal might shift for himself if so inclined. Inglesant left him loose. As he entered the city, and passed through the Largo into the Strada Toledo, the sight that met his eyes was one never to be forgotten.

The streets were full of people,—more so, indeed, than is usual even in Naples; for business was at a stand, the houses were full of infection, and a terrible restlessness drove every one here and there. The stately rows of houses and palaces, and the lofty churches, looked down on a changing, fleeting, restless crowd,—unoccupied, speaking little, walking hither and thither with no aim, every few minutes turning back and retracing their steps. Every quarter of an hour or thereabouts a confused procession of priests and laymen, singing doleful and despairing misereres, and bearing the sacred Host with canopy and crosses, came from one of the side streets, or out of one of the churches, and proceeded along the Strada. As these processions passed, every one prostrated themselves, with an excess and desperate earnestness of devotion, and many followed the host; but in a moment or two those who knelt or those who followed rose or turned away with gestures of despair or distraction, as though incapable of sustained action, or of confidence in any remedy. And at this there could be no wonder, since this crowd of people were picking their way amid a mass of dead corruption on every side of them under their feet. On the stone pavement of the stately Strada, on the palace stairs, on the steps before the churches, lay corpses in every variety of contortion at which death can arrive. Sick people upon beds and heaps of linen—some delicate and costly, some filthy and decayed—lay mingled with the dead; they had been turned out of the houses, or had deserted them to avoid being left to die alone; and every now and then some one of those who walked apparently in health would lie down, stricken by the heat or by the plague, and join this prostrate throng, for whom there was no longer in this world any hope of revival.

This sight, which would have been terrible anywhere, was unutterably distressing and ghastly in Naples, the city of thoughtless pleasure and of reckless mirth,—a city lying under a blue and cloudless sky, by an azure sea, glowing in the unsurpassable brilliancy and splendour of the sun. As this dazzling blue and gold, before which all colours pale, made the scene the most ghastly that could have been chosen as the theatre for such an appalling spectacle, so, among a people child-like and grotesque, seducing the stranger into sympathy with its delight—a people crowned with flowers, and clothed in colours of every shade, full of high and gay spirits, and possessed of a conscience that gives no pain—this masque and dance of death assumed an aspect of intolerable horror. Naples was given over to pantomime and festival, leading dances and processions with Thyrsis and garlands, and trailing branches of fruit. The old Fabulag and farce lingered yet beneath the delicious sky and in the lovely spots of earth that lured the Pagan to dream that earth was heaven. The poles and scaffolds and dead flowers of the last festival still lingered in the streets.

In this city, turned at once into a charnel-house,—nay, into a hell and place of torment,—the mighty, unseen hand suddenly struck down its prey, and without warning seized upon the wretched conscience, all unprepared for such a blow. The cast of a pantomime is a strange sight beneath the glare and light of mid-day; but here were quacks and nobles, jugglers and soldiers, comic actors and "filosofi," pleasure seekers and monks, gentry and beggars, all surprised as it were, suddenly, by the light and glare of the death angel's torch, and crowded upon one level stage of misery and despair.

Sick and dizzy with horror, and choked with the deadly smell and malaria, Inglesant turned into several osteria, but could find no host in any. In several he saw sights which chilled his blood. At last he gave up the search, and, weary as he was, sought the hospitals. The approaches to some of these were so blocked up by the dead and the dying who had vainly sought admission, that entrance was impossible. In others the galley slaves were at work. In every open spot of ground where the earth could be disturbed without cutting off the water pipes which ran through the city, trenches had been dug, and the bodies which were collected from the streets and hospitals were thrown hastily into them, and covered with lime and earth. Inglesant strayed into the "Monte della Misericordia," which had recently been cleared of the dead. A few sick persons lay in the beds; but the house seemed wonderfully clean and sweet, and the rooms cool and fresh. The floors were soaked with vinegar, and the place was full of the scent of juniper, bay berries, and rosemary, which were burning in every room. It seemed to Inglesant like a little heaven and he sank exhausted upon one of the beds. They brought him some wine, and presently the Signore di Mauro, one of the physicians appointed by the city, who still remained bravely at his post, came and spoke to him.

"I perceive that you are a stranger in Naples, and untouched by the disease," he said. "I am at a loss to account for your presence here. This house is indeed cleared for a moment, but it is the last time that we can expect help. The supply of galley slaves is failing, and when it stops entirely, which it must in a few days, I see nothing in the future but the general extirpation of all the inhabitants of this fated city, and that its vast circumference, filled with putrefaction and venom, will afterwards be uninhabitable to the rest of mankind."

This doleful foreboding made little impression upon Inglesant, who was, indeed, too much exhausted both in mind and body to pay much attention to anything.

"I am come to Naples," he said faintly, "in search of another; will you let me stay in this house to-night? I can find no one in the inns."

"I will do better for you than that," said the good physician; "you shall come to my own house, which is free from infection. I have but one inmate, an old servant, who, I think, is too dry and withered a morsel even for the plague. I am going at once."

Something in Inglesant's manner probably attracted him, otherwise it is difficult to account for his kindness to a stranger under such circumstances.

They went out together. Inglesant by chance seemed to be about to turn into another and smaller street—the physician pulled him back hurriedly with a shudder.

"Whatever you do," he said in a whisper, "keep to the principal thoroughfares. I dare not recollect—the most heated imagination would shrink from conceiving—the unutterable horrors of the bye-streets."

Picking their way among the dead bodies, which the slaves, with handkerchiefs steeped in vinegar over their faces, were piling into carts, the two proceeded down the Strada.

Inglesant asked the physician how the plague first began in Naples.

"It is the terrible enemy of mankind," replied the other—he was rather a pompous man, with all his kindness and devotion, and used long words—"that walks stained with slaughter by night. We know not whence it comes. Before it are beautiful gardens, crowded habitations, and populous cities; behind it unfruitful emptiness and howling desolation. Before it the guards and armies of mighty princes are as dead men, and physicians are no protection either to the sick or to themselves. Some imagine that it comes from the cities of the East; some that it arises from poverty and famine, and from the tainted and perishing flesh, and unripe fruits and hurtful herbs, which, in times of scarcity and dearth, the starving people greedily devour to satisfy their craving hunger. Others contend that it is inflicted immediately by the hand of God. These are mostly the priests. When we have puzzled our reason, and are at our wit's end through ignorance, we come to that. I have read something in a play, written by one of your countrymen—for I perceive you are an Englishman—where all mistakes are laid upon the King."

They were arrived by this time at the physician's house, and were received by an old woman whose appearance fully justified her master's description. She provided for Inglesant's wants, and prepared a bed for him, and he sank into an uneasy and restless sleep. The night was stiflingly hot, suppressed cries and groans broke the stillness, and the distant chanting of monks was heard at intervals. Soon after midnight the churches were again crowded; mass was said, and thousands received the Sacrament with despairing faith. The physician came into Inglesant's room early in the morning.

"I am going out," he said; "keep as much as possible out of the churches; they spread the contagion. The magistrates wished to close them, but the superstitious people would not hear of it. I will make inquiries, and if any of the religious, or any one else, has heard your friend's name, I will send you word. I may not return."

Shortly after he was gone, the crowd thronging in one direction before Inglesant's window caused him to rise and follow. He came to one of the slopes of the hill of Santo Martino, above the city. Here a crowd, composed of every class from a noble down to the lowest lazzaroni, were engaged, in the clear morning light, in building a small house. Some were making bricks, some drawing along stones, some carrying timber. A nun had dreamed that were a hermitage erected for her order the plague would cease, and the people set to work, with desperate earnestness, to finish the building. By the wayside up the ascent were set empty barrels, into which the wealthier citizens dropped gold and jewels to assist the work. As Inglesant was standing by, watching the work, he was accosted by a dignified, highly bred old gentleman, in a velvet coat and Venice lace, who seemed less absorbed in the general panic than the rest.

"This is a strange sight," he said; "what the tyranny of the Spaniards was not able to do, the plague has done. When the Spaniard was storming the gates the gentlemen of the Borgo Santa Maria and the lazzaroni fought each other in the streets, and the gentlemen avowed that they preferred any degree of foreign tyranny to acknowledging or associating with the common people. With this deadly enemy not only at the gates but in the very midst of us, gentlemen and lazzaroni toil together without a thought of suspicion or contempt. The plague has made us all equal. I perceive that you are a stranger. May I ask what has brought you into this ill-fated city at such a time?"

"I am in search of my relation, il Cavaliere di Guardino," replied Inglesant; "do you know such a name?"

"It seems familiar to me," replied the old gentleman. "Have you reason to suppose that he is in Naples?"

Inglesant said that he had.

"The persons most likely to give you information would be the Signori, the officers of the galleys. They would doubtless be acquainted with the Cavaliere before the plague became so violent, and would know, at any rate, whether it was his intention to leave Naples or not. The galleys lie, as you know, moored together there in the bay, and many other ships lie near them, upon which persons have taken refuge who believe that the plague cannot touch them on the water—an expectation in which, I believe, many have been fatally deceived."

Inglesant thanked the gentleman, and inquired how it was that he remained so calm and unconcerned amidst the general consternation.

"I am too old for the plague," he replied; "nothing can touch me but death itself. I am also," he continued with a peculiar smile, "the fortunate possessor of a true piece of the holy Cross; so that you see I am doubly safe."

Inglesant went at once to the harbour, musing on the way on these last words, and wondering whether they were spoken in good faith or irony.

The scenes in the streets seemed more terrible even than on the preceding day. The slaves were engaged here and there in removing the bodies, but the task was far beyond their strength. Cries of pain and terror were heard on all sides, and every now and then a maddened wretch would throw himself from a window, or would rush, naked perhaps, from a house, and, stumbling and leaping over the corpses and the dying, like the demoniac among the tombs, would fling himself in desperation into the water of the harbour, or over the walls into the moats. One of these maniacs, passing close to Inglesant, attempted to embrace a passer-by, who coolly ran him through the body with his sword, the bystanders applauding the act.

In the harbour corpses were floating, which a few slaves in boats were feebly attempting to drag together with hooks. They escaped their efforts, and rose and sank with a ghastly resemblance to life. Upon the quay Inglesant fortunately found the physician, Signore Mauro, who was himself going on board the galleys to endeavour to procure the loan of more slaves. He offered to take Inglesant with him.

As they went the physician told him he had not discovered any trace of the Cavaliere; but what was very curious, he said, many other persons appeared to be engaged in the same search. It might be that all these people were in fact but one, multiplied by the forgetfulness, and by the excited imaginations, of those from whom Signore Mauro had obtained his information; but, if these persons were to be believed, monks, friars, physicians, soldiers, and even ladies, were engaged in this singular search in a city where all ties of friendship were forgotten, for a man whom no one knew.

As they shot over the silent water, and by the shadowy hulks of ships lying idle and untended, with the cry of the city of the dead behind them and the floating corpses around, Inglesant listened to the physician as a man listens in a dream. Long shadows stretched across the harbour, which sparkled beneath the rays of the newly-risen sun; a sudden swoon stole over Inglesant's spirits, through which the voice of the physician sounded distant and faint. He gave himself up for lost, yet he felt a kind of dim expectation that something was about to happen which these unknown inquirers foretold.

The galleys lay moored near together, with several other ships of large size in company. Signore Mauro climbed to the quarter-deck of the largest galley, on which the commodore was, and Inglesant followed him, still hardly knowing what he did. The oars were shipped, but the slaves were chained to their benches, as though the galleys were at sea. They were singing and playing at cards. Upon the quarterdeck, pointing to the long files of slaves, were two loaded howitzers, behind each of which stood a gunner with a lighted match. Soldiers, heavily armed and with long whips, paraded the raised gangway or passage, which ran the whole length of the ship between the rows of benches upon which the slaves were placed. The officers were mostly on the quarter-deck; they looked pale and excited, though it was singular that few or no cases of the plague had occurred among the slaves who remained on board. The decks were washed with vinegar, and the galleys and slaves were much cleaner than usual.

The physician stated his request to the commander, who ordered ten slaves from every galley to be sent on shore. Some were wanted to act as bakers, some as butchers, most of the artizans in the city having fled or perished. A boatswain was ordered to make the selection. He chose one or two, and then called upon the rest to volunteer. Inglesant was standing by him on the gangway, looking down the files of slaves. There were men of every age, of every rank, and almost of every country. As the boatswain gave the word, every hand was held up; to all these men death was welcome at the end of two or three days' change of life, abundance of food, and comparative freedom. The boatswain selected ten by chance.

Signore Mauro inquired among the officers concerning the Cavaliere, but could obtain no positive information. Most had heard the name, some professed to have known him intimately; all united in saying he had left Naples. Inglesant and the physician visited two or three other galleys, but with no greater success. They returned on shore as the heat was becoming intense; the churches were crowded, and the Holy Sacrament was exhibited every few moments. The physician refused to enter any of them.

Then Inglesant determined to try the hospitals again. He went to the "Santa Casa degli Incurabile," which the day before he had not been able to approach for the dying and the dead. The slaves had worked hard all night, and hundreds of corpses had been removed and buried in a vast trench without the wall of the hospital. Inglesant passed through many of the rooms, and spoke to several of the religious persons who were tending the sick, but could learn nothing of the object of his search. At last one of the monks conducted him into the strange room called the "Anticamera di Morte," to which, in more orderly times, the patients whose cases were hopeless were removed.

There, at the last extremity of life, before they were hurried into the great pit outside the walls, lay the plague-stricken. Some unconscious, yet with fearful throes and gasps awaiting their release; some in an agony of pain and death, crying upon God and the Saints. Kneeling by the bedsides were several monks; but at the farther end of the room, bending over a sick man, was a figure in a friar's gown that made Inglesant stop suddenly, and his heart beat quicker as he caught his companion's arm.

"Who is that friar, Father?" he said, "the one at the end, bending over the bed?"

"Ah! that," said the priest, "that is Father Grazia of the Capuchins; a very holy man, and devoted to mortification and good works. He is blind, though he moves about so cleverly. He says that, to within the last few years, his life was passed in every species of sin; and he relates that he was solemnly given over to the vengeance of the blessed Gesu by his mortal enemy, the minion of a Cardinal, and that the Lord has afflicted him with untold sorrows and sufferings to bring him to Himself, and to a life of holy mortification and charity, which he leads unceasingly—night and day. He is but now come in hither, knowing that the sick man by whose bed he is, is dying of the plague in its most fearful form,—a man whom none willingly will approach. Mostly he is in the vilest dens of the city, reeking with pestilence, where to go, to all save him, is certain death. His holiness and the Lord's will keep him, so that the plague cannot touch him. Ah! he is coming this way."

It was true. The friar had suddenly started from his recumbent position, conscious that the man before him was no more. At the same moment, his mind, released from the attention which had riveted it before, seemed to become aware of a presence in the chamber of death which was of the intensest interest. He came down the passage in the centre of the room with an eager unfaltering step, as though able to see, and coming to within a few feet of the two men, he stopped, and looked towards them with an excited glance, as though he saw their faces. Inglesant was embarrassed, and hesitated whether to recognize him or not. At last, pitying the look in the blind man's face, he said,—

"This holy Father is not unknown to me, though I know not that he would desire to meet me again. I am 'the minion of a Cardinal' of whom you spoke."

The friar stretched out his hands before him, with an eager, delighted gesture.

"I knew it," he said; "I felt your presence long before you spoke. It signifies little whether I am glad to find you or no. It is part of the Lord's purpose that we should meet."

"This is a strange and sanctified meeting," said the priest, "in the room of death, and by the beds of the dead. Doubtless you have much to say that can only be said to yourselves alone."

"I cannot stay," said the friar, wildly. "I came in here but for a moment; for this wretched man who is gone to his account needed one as wretched and as wicked as himself. But they are dying now in the streets and alleys, calling upon the God whom they know not; they need the vilest sinner to whom the Lord has been gracious to kneel by their side; they need the vilest sinner; therefore I must go."

He stopped for a moment, then he said more calmly,—"Meet me in the Santa Chiara, behind the altar, by the tomb of the wise King, this evening at sunset. By that time, though the need will be as pressing, yet the frail body will need a little rest, and I will speak with you for an hour. Fail not to come. You will learn how your sword was the sword, and your breath was the breath of the Lord."

"I will surely be there," said Inglesant.

The friar departed, leaving the priest and Inglesant alone. They went out into the garden of the hospital, a plot of ground planted with fruit-trees, and with vines trailing over the high stone walls. Walking up and down in the shade, with the intense blue of the sky overhead, one might for a time forget the carnival of death that was crowding every street and lane around. Inglesant inquired of his companion more particularly concerning the friar.

"He is a very holy man," said the priest, with a significant gesture; "but he is not right in his head. His sufferings have touched his brain. He believes that he has seen the Lord in a vision, and not only so, but that all Rome was likewise a witness of the miracle. It is a wonderful story, which doubtless he wishes to relate to you this evening."

CHAPTER XV

In the vast Church of the Santa Chiara, with its open nave which spread itself on every side like a magic hall of romance, the wide floor and the altars of the side Chapels had been crowded all day by prostrate worshippers; but when Inglesant entered it about sunset, it was comparatively empty. A strange unearthly perfume filled the Church, and clouds of incense yet hovered beneath the painted ceiling, and obscured the figure of the Saint chasing his enemies. Streaks of light, transfigured through the coloured prism of the prophets and martyrs that stood in the painted glass, lighted up the wreaths of smoke, and coloured the marbles and frescoes of the walls and altars. The mystic glimmer of the sacred tapers in the shaded chapels, and the concluding strains of the chanting before the side altars, which had followed the vesper service and benediction, filled the Church with half light and half shadow, half silence and half sound, very pleasing and soothing to the sense.

Inglesant passed up the Church towards the high altar, before which he knelt; and as he did so, a procession, carrying the Sacrament, entered by another door, and advanced to the altar, upon which it was again deposited. The low, melancholy miserere—half entreating, half desponding—spoke to the heart of man a language like its own; and as the theme was taken up by one of the organs, the builder's art and the musician's melted into one— in tier after tier of carved imagery, wave after wave of mystic sound. All conscious thought and striving seemed to fade from the heart, and before the altar and amid the swell of sound the soul lost itself, and lay silent and passive on the Eternal Love.

Behind the high altar Inglesant found the friar by the grave of the wise King. Upon the slabs of the Gothic tomb, covered with carving and bas-relief, the King is seated and dressed in royal robes; but upon the sarcophagus he lies in death bereft of all his state, and clothed in no garment but a Franciscan's gown. Beside him lies his son in his royal robes, covered with fleurs-de-lis; and other tombs of the kingly race of Anjou surround him, all emblazoned with coat armour and device of rank.

Between the tombs of the two kings stood the friar, his head bowed upon his hands. The light grew every moment less and less bright, and the shadows stretched ever longer and longer across the marble floor. The lamps before the shrines, and the altar tapers in the funeral chapels, shone out clearer and more distinct. The organs had ceased, but the dolorous chanting of the miserere from beyond the high altar still came to them with a remote and wailing tone.

Inglesant advanced towards the friar, who appeared to be aware of his presence by instinct, and raised his head as he drew near. He returned no answer to Inglesant's greeting, but seated himself upon a bench near one of the tombs, and began at once, like a man who has little time to spend.

"I am desirous," he said, "of telling you at once of what has occurred to me. Who can tell what may happen at any moment to hinder unless I do? It is a strange and wonderful story, in which you and I and all men would be but puppets in the Divine Hand were not the Divine Love such that we are rather children led onward by their Father's hand—welcomed home by their Mother's smile."

It was indeed a strange story that the friar told Inglesant in the darkening Church. In places it was incoherent and obscure. The first part of his narrative, as it relates to others besides himself, is told here in a different form, so that, if possible, what really happened might be known. The latter part, being untranslatable into any other language and inexplicable upon any basis of fact, must be told in his own words.

"When you left me at the mountain chapel," said the friar, "I thought of nothing but that I had escaped with life. I thought I had met with a Fantastic, whose brain was turned with monkish fancies, and I blessed my fortunate stars that such had been the case. I thought little of the Divine vengeance that dogged my steps."

When Inglesant met Malvolti upon the mountain pass (as he gathered from the friar's narrative) the latter, utterly penniless and undone, having exhausted every shift and art of policy, and being so well-known in all the cities of Italy that he was safe in none of them, had bethought himself of his native place. It was, indeed, almost the only place where his character was unknown, and his person comparatively safe. But it had other attractions for the hunted and desperate man. Malvolti's father had died when his son was a boy, and his mother in a year or two married again. His step-father was harsh and unkind to the fatherless child, and the seeds of evil were sown in the boy's heart by the treatment he received; but a year after this marriage a little girl was born, who won her way at once into the heart of the forlorn and unhappy lad. He was her constant playmate, protector, and instructor. For several years the only happy moments of his life were passed when he could steal away with her to the woods and hills, wandering for hours together alone or with the wood-cutters and charcoal-burners; and when, after a few years, the unkindness of his parents and his own restless and passionate nature sent him out into the world in which he played so evil a part, the image of the innocent child followed him into scenes of vice, and was never obliterated from his memory. The murmur of the leaves above the fowling-floor where they lay together during the mid-day heat, the splash of the fountains where they watched the flocks of sheep drinking, followed him into strange places and foreign countries, and arose to his recollection in moments of danger, and even of passion and crime.

The home of Malvolti's parents had been in the suburb, of a small town of the Bolognese. Here, at some little height above the town on the slope of the wooded hills, a monastery and chapel had been erected, and in course of time some few houses had grouped themselves around, among which that of Malvolti's father had been the most considerable. The sun was setting behind the hills when Malvolti, weary, dispirited, and dying of hunger, came along the winding road from the south, which skirted the projecting spurs of the mountains. The slanting rays penetrated the woods, and shone between the openings of the hills, lighting up the grass-grown buildings of the monastery, and the belfry of the little Chapel, where the bell was ringing for vespers. Below, the plain stretched itself peacefully; a murmur of running water blended with the tolling of the bell. A waft of peace and calm, like a breeze from paradise, fell upon Malvolti's heart, and he seemed to hear soft voices welcoming him home. He pictured to himself his mother's kind greeting, his sister's delight; even his stern step-father's figure was softened in the universal evening glow. It was a fairy vision, in which the passing years had found no place, where the avenging footsteps that follow sin did not come, and which had no reality in actual existence. He turned the angle of the wood, and stood before his home. It lay in ruins and desolate.

The sun sank below the hills, the bell went on tolling monotonously through the deepening gloom. Dazed and faint, Malvolti followed its tones into the Chapel, where the vesper service began. When it was ended the miserable man spoke to one of the monks, and craved some food. Deprived of his last hope, his senses faint and dull with weariness and hunger, and lulled by the soft strains of devout sound—his life confessed at last to have been completely a failure, and the wages of sin to have turned to withered leaves in his hand—his heart was more disposed than perhaps it had ever been to listen to the soft accents of penitence, and to hear the whispering murmur that haunts the shadowy walks of mortified repentance. Comforted by food, the kindly words of pity and exhortation stole upon his senses, and he almost fancied that he might find a home and peace without further wandering and punishment. He was much deceived.

He inquired concerning the fate of those whom, debased and selfish as he was, he still loved, especially now, when the sight of long-forgotten but still familiar places recalled the past, and seemed to obliterate the intervening years. The monks told him a story of sorrow and of sin, such as he himself often had participated in, and would have heard at another time with a smile of indifference. His step-father was dead, killed in a feud which his own insolent temper had provoked. His mother and sister had continued for some time to live in the same house, and there perhaps he might have found them, had not a gentleman, whose convenience had led him to claim the hospitality of the monastery for a night's rest, chanced to see his sister in the morning as he mounted his horse. The sight of a face, whose beauty combined a haughty clearness of outline with a certain coy softness of expression, and a figure of perfect form, detained him from his intended journey, and he obtained admittance into the widow's house. What wizard arts he practised the monks did not know, but when he departed he left anxiety and remorse where he had found content and a certain peace. In due time the two women, despairing of his return, had followed him, and the younger, the monks had heard (and they believed the report)—ill-treated and spurned—was now living in Florence a life of sin. The softened expression of rest and penitence which had begun to show itself in Malvolti's face left it, and the more habitual one of cruel and hungry sin returned as he inquired,—

"Did the Reverend Fathers remember the name of this man?"

The good monks hesitated as they saw the look in the inquirer's face; but it was not their duty to conceal the truth from one who undoubtedly had a right to be informed of it.

"It is our duty to practise forgiveness, even of the greatest injuries, my son," one of them replied; "our blessed Lord has enjoined it, and left us this as an example, that He has forgiven us. The man was called il Cavaliere di Guardino."

The monks were relieved when they saw that their guest showed no emotion upon hearing this name; only he said that he must go to Florence and endeavour to find his sister.

But in truth there was in the man's mind, under a calm exterior, a crisis of feeling not easy to describe. That the Cavaliere, his familiar accomplice, in whose company and by whose aid he had himself so often committed ravages upon the innocent, should, in the chance medley of life, be selected to inflict this blow, affected him in a strange and unaccustomed way, with the sense of a hitherto unrecognized justice at work among the affairs of men. He was so utterly at the end of all his hopes, life was so completely closed to him, and his soul was so sorely stricken, in return for all his sins, in the only holy and sacred spot that remained in his fallen nature,—his love and remembrance of his sister,—that it seemed as if a revulsion of feeling might take place, and that, in this depth and slough, there might appear, though dimly, the possibility of an entrance into a higher life. He was better known in Florence than in any city of Italy, except Rome; and if he went there his violent death was almost certain, yet he determined to go. He assured Inglesant afterwards, in relating the story, that his object was not revenge, but that his desire was to seek out and rescue his sister. Revenge doubtless brooded in his mind; but it was not the motive which urged him onward.

He told Inglesant a strange story of his weary journey to Florence, subsisting on charity from convent to convent; of his wandering up and down in the beautiful city, worn out with hunger and fatigue, unknown, and hiding himself from recognition. Amid the grim forms of vice that haunted the shadowy recesses of the older parts of the city, in the vaulted halls of deserted palaces and the massive fastnesses of patrician strife, he flitted like a ghost, pale and despairing, urged on by a restless desire that knew no respite. In these dens of a reckless life, which had thrown off all restraint and decorum, he recognized many whom he had known in other days, and in far different places. In these gloomy halls, which had once been bright with youth and gaiety, but were now hideous with poverty and crime,—in which the windows were darkened, and the coloured ceilings and frescoed walls were blurred with smoke and damp, and which were surrounded by narrow alleys which shut out the light, and cut them off from all connection with the outer world,—he at last heard of the Cavaliere. He was told that, flying from Rome after his sister's marriage, he had been arrested for some offence in the south of Italy, and those into whose hands he fell being old enemies, and bearing him some grudge, he was thrown into prison, and even condemned to the galleys; for, since the Papal election, he was no longer able to claim even a shadow of protection from any of the great families who had once been his patrons. After a short imprisonment he was deputed, among others, to perform some such office as Inglesant had seen undertaken by the slaves in Naples; for the plague had raged for some summers past, with more or less intensity, in southern Italy. While engaged in this work he had managed to make his escape, and had not long since arrived in Florence, where he had kept himself closely concealed. Malvolti was told the secret lurking-place where he might probably be found.

"It was a brilliantly hot afternoon," continued Malvolti, speaking very slowly; "you will wonder that I tell you this; but it was the last time that I ever saw the sun. I remember the bright and burning pavements even in the narrow alleys out of which I turned into the long and dark entries and vaulted rooms. I followed some persons who entered before me, and some voices which led me onward, into a long and lofty room in the upper stories, at the farther end of which, before a high window partially boarded up, some men were at play. As I came up the room, all the other parts of which lay in deep shadow, the light fell strongly upon a corner of the table, and upon the man who was casting the dice. He had just thrown his chance, and he turned his head as I came up. He appeared to be naked except his slippers and a cloak or blanket of white cloth, with pale yellow stripes. His hair was closely cropped; his face, which was pale and aquiline, was scarred and seamed with deep lines of guilt and misery, especially around the eyes, from which flashed a lurid light, and his lips were parted with a mocking and Satanic laugh. His dark and massive throat and chest and his long and sinewy arms forced their way out of the cloth with which he was wrapped, and the lean fingers of both hands, which crossed each other convulsively, were pointed exultantly to the deuce of ace which he had thrown. The last sight I ever saw, the last sight my eyes will ever behold until they open before the throne of God, was this demon-like figure, standing out clear and distinct against the shadowy gloom in which dim figures seemed to move, and the dice upon the table by his side.

"He burst out into a wild and mocking laugh. 'Ah, Malvolti,' he said, 'you were ever unlucky at the dice. Come and take your chances in the next main.'

"I know not what fury possessed me, nor why, at that moment especially, this man's mocking villany inspired me with such headlong rage. I remembered nothing but the crimes and wrongs which he had perpetrated. I drew the dagger I carried beneath my clothes, and sprang upon him with a cry as wild as his own. What happened I cannot tell. I seemed to hear the laughter of fiends, and to feel the tortures of hell on every side. Then all was darkness and the grave."

Overpowered as it seemed by the recollection of his sufferings, the friar paused and sank upon his knees upon the pavement. The miserere had died away, and a profound gloom, broken only by the flicker of tapers, filled the Church. Inglesant was deeply moved,—less, however, by sympathy with the man's story than by the consciousness of the emotions which he himself experienced. It was scarcely possible to believe that he was the same man who, some short years before, had longed for this meeting with a bloodthirsty desire that he might take some terrible vengeance upon his brother's murderer. Now he stood before the same murderer, who not so long before had attempted to take his life also with perhaps the very dagger of which he now spoke; and as he looked down upon him, no feeling but that of pity was in his heart. In the presence of the awful visitant who at that moment was filling the city which lay around them with death and corruption, and before whose eternal power the strife and enmity of man shrank away appalled and silenced, it was not wonderful that inordinate hate should cease; but, as he gazed upon the prostrate man before him, an awe-inspiring feeling took possession of Inglesant's mind, which still more effectually crushed every sentiment of anger or revenge. The significance of his own half-conceived action was revealed to him, and he recognized, with something approaching to terror, that the cause was no longer his, that another hand had interposed to strike, and that his sword had spared the murderer of his brother only that he might become the victim of that divine vengeance which has said, "I will repay."

The friar rose from his knees. "I found myself in the monastery of the Cappucines on the bank of the river, blind, and holding life by the faintest thread. That I lived was a miracle. I had been struck with some twenty wounds, and in mere wantonness my eyes had been pierced as I lay apparently dead. I was thrown into the river which flowed by gloomy vaults beneath the houses, and had been carried down by the stream to the garden of a monastery where I was found. As I recovered strength the monks thought that my reason would not survive. For days and nights I lay bound, a raving madman. At last, when my pains subsided, and my mind was a little calmed and subdued, I was sent out into the world and begged my way from village to village, not caring where I went, my mind an utter blank, filled only now and then with horrible sights and dreams. I had no sense of God or Christ; no feeling but a blind senseless despair and confusion. Thus I wandered on. I got at last a boy to lead me and buy me food. I know not why I did not rather lie down and die. Sometimes I did fling myself down, resolving not to move again; but some love of life or some divine prompting caused me to rise and wander on in my miserable path. At last, towards the end of the year, I came to Rome, and wandered about the city seeking alms. The boy who led me, and who had attached himself to me, God knows why, told me all he saw and all that passed; and I, who knew every phase and incident of Roman life, explained to him such things in a languid and indifferent way; for I found no pleasure nor relief in anything. I grew more and more miserable; our life was hard, and we were ill-fed, and the terrors of my memory haunted my spirits, weakened and depressed for want of food. The forms of those whom I had wronged, nay, murdered, lay before me. They rose and looked upon me from every side. My misery was greater than I could bear. I desired death, and tried to accomplish it, but my hand always failed. I bought poison, but my boy watched me and changed the drink. I did not know this, and expected death. It did not come. Then suddenly, as I lay in a kind of trance, that morning in the mountain pass came into my remembrance, and it flashed suddenly into my mind that I was not my own; that no poison could hurt me, no sword slay me; that the sword of vengeance was in the Lord's hand, and would work His will alone. What greater punishment could be in store for me I knew not, but stunned by this idea I ceased to strive and cry any more. I waited in silence for the final blow; it came. The year had come nearly to an end, and it was Christmas Eve. All day long, in the Churches in Rome, had the services, the processions, the religious shows, gone on. My boy and I had followed them one by one, and he had, in his boyish way, told me all that he saw. The new Pope went in procession to St. John di Laterano, with all the Cardinals, Patriarchs, Archbishops, and Bishops, all the nobility and courtiers, and an interminable length of attendants, Switzers, soldiers, led horses, servants, pages, rich coaches, litters, and people of every class, under triumphal arches, with all excess of joy and triumph. As midnight drew on the streets were as light as day. Every pageant became more gorgeous, every service more sweet and ravishing, every sermon more passionate. I saw it all in my mind's eye,—all, and much beside. I saw in every Church, lighted by sacred tapers before the crucifix, the pageants and ceremonies that, in every form and to every sense, present the story of the mystic birth, of that divine fact that alone can stay the longing which, since men walked the earth, they have uttered in every tongue, that the Deity would come down and dwell with man. We had wandered through all the Churches, and at last, wearied out, we reached the Capitol, and sank down beneath the balusters at the top of the marble stairs. Close by, in the Ara Cœli, the simple country people and the faithful whose hearts were as those of little children, kneeling as the shepherds knelt upon the plains of Bethlehem, saw the Christ-Child lying in a manger, marked out from common childhood by a mystic light which shone from His face and form; while the organ harmonies which filled the Church resigned their wonted splendours, and bent for once to pastoral melodies, which, born amid the rustling of sedges by the river brink, have wandered down through the reed-music and festivals of the country people, till they grew to be the most fitting tones of a religion which takes its aptest similes from the vineyard and the flock. All over Rome the flicker of the bonfires mingled with the starlight. I was blind, yet I saw much that would have been hidden from me had I been able to see. I saw across the roofs before me, the dome of the Pantheon and St. Peter's, and the long line of the Vatican, and the round outline of St. Angelo in the light of the waning moon. This I should have seen had I had my sight; but I saw behind me now what otherwise I should not have seen—the Forum, and the lines of arches and ruins, and beyond these the walks of the Aventine and of the Cœlian, with their vineyards and white convents, and tall poplar and cypress trees.

I saw beyond them the great Churches of the Lateran and Santa Croce in Gerusalemme, standing out from the green country, pale and spectral in the light. To the left I saw Santa Maria Maggiore, stately and gorgeous, facing the long streets of palaces and courts, and the gardens and terraces of the Quirinale, all distinct and clear in the mystic light. The white light covered the earth like a shroud, and over the vault of the sky were traced, by the pale stars, strange and obscure forms, as over the dome of St. Peter's at evening when the Church is dim. A confused sound filled my ears, a sound of chanting and of praise for that advent that brought peace to men, a sound of innumerable passing feet, and in all the Churches and basilicas I saw the dead Christs over the altars and the kneeling crowds around. Suddenly it seemed to me that I was conscious of a general movement and rush of feet, and that a strange and wild excitement prevailed in every region of Rome. The Churches became emptied, the people pouring out into the streets; the dead Christs above the altars faded from their crosses, and the sacred tapers went out of their own accord; for it spread through Rome, as in a moment, that a miracle had happened at the Ara Cœli, and that the living Christ was come. From where I stood I could see the throngs of people pouring through every street and lane, and thronging up to the' Campadoglio and the stairs; and from the distance and the pale Campagna, and San Paolo without the walls, and from subterranean Rome, where the martyrs and confessors lie, I could see strange and mystic shapes come sweeping in through the brilliant light.

"He came down the steps of the Ara Cœli, and the sky was full of starlike forms, wonderful and gracious; and all the steps of the Capitol were full of people down to the square of the Ara Cœli, and up to the statue of Aurelius on horseback above; and the summit of the Capitol among the statues, and the leads of the palace Caffarelli, were full of eager forms; for the starlight was so clear that all might see; and the dead gods, and the fauns, and the satyrs, and the old pagans, that lurked in the secret hiding-places of the ruins of the Cæsars, crowded up the steps out of the Forum, and came round the outskirts of the crowd, and stood on the fallen pillars that they might see. And Castor and Pollux, that stood by their unsaddled horses at the top of the stairs, left them unheeded and came to see; and the Marsyas who stood bound broke his bonds and came to see; and spectral forms swept in from the distance in the light, and the air was full of Powers and Existences, and the earth rocked as at the Judgment Day.

"He came down the steps into the Campadoglio, and He came to me. He was not at all like the pictures of the saints; for He was pale, and worn, and thin, as though the fight was not yet half over—ah no!—but through this pale and worn look shone infinite power, and undying love, and unquenchable resolve. The crowd fell back on every side, but when He came to me He stopped. 'Ah!' He said, 'is it thou? What doest thou here? Knowest thou not that thou art mine? Thrice mine—mine centuries ago when I hung upon the cross on Calvary for such as thou—mine years ago, when thou camest a little child to the font—mine once again, when, forfeit by every law, thou wast given over to me by one who is a servant and friend of mine. Surely, I will repay.' As He spoke, a shudder and a trembling ran through the crowd, as if stirred by the breath of His voice. Nature seemed to rally and to grow beneath Him, and heaven to bend down to touch the earth. A healing sense of help and comfort, like the gentle dew, visited the weary heart. A great cry and shout rose from the crowd, and He passed on; but among ten thousand times ten thousand I should know Him, and amid the tumult of a universe I should hear the faintest whisper of His voice."

The friar stopped and looked at Inglesant with his darkened eyeballs, as though he could read his looks. Inglesant gazed at him in silence. That the man was crazed he had no doubt; but that his madness should have taken this particular form appeared to his listener scarcely less miraculous than if every word of his wonderful story had been true.

"Heard you nothing else?" he said at last.

An expression of something like trouble passed over the other's face.

"No," he said in a quieter voice; "by this time it was morning. The artillery of St. Angelo went off. His Holiness sang mass, and all day long was exposed the cradle of the Lord."

There was another pause which Inglesant scarcely knew how to break. Then he said,—

"And have you heard nothing since of the Cavaliere?"

"He is in this neighbourhood," said Malvolti, "but I have not found him. I wondered and was impatient, ignorant and foolish as I am; now I know the reason. The Lord waited till you came. How could he be found except by us both? We must lose no time, or it will be too late. How did you know that he was here?"

Inglesant told him.

"It was the Lord's doing," said the friar, a light breaking over his darkened face. "It was Capace. You remember, at Florence, the leader of that extravagant frolic of the Carnival, who was dressed as a corpse?"

"I remember," said Inglesant, "and the poor English lad who was killed."

"He is one of the Lord's servants," continued the friar, "whom He called very late. I do not know that he was guilty of any particular sins, but he was the heir of a poor family, and lived for many years in luxury and excess. He was brought under the influence of Molinos's party, and shortly after I had seen the Lord, he came to me to know whether he should become a religious. I told him I thought there was a time of trial and of sifting for the Lord's people at hand, and that I thought the strongholds were the safest spots. He joined the order de Servi. Not three weeks ago I was with him at Frescati, at the house of the Cappucines, when I heard that the Cavaliere was here. You must have seen him three or four days afterwards."

CHAPTER XVI

The night after Inglesant had met the friar in Naples there was "the sound of abundance of rain," and the "plague was stayed." As constantly happened in the cities desolated by this mysterious pestilence, no adequate reason could be perceived for its cessation. Some change in the state of the atmosphere took place, and the sick did not die, at least in the same proportion as formerly. This was the only indication that the most acute observer could detect; but the change was marvellously rapid. The moment that contact with the dead bodies became less fatally infectious, help offered on all sides, tempted by the large rewards. The dead rapidly disappeared from sight, and the city began to resume something of its ordinary appearance. The terrors of the grave vanished into air, and gloomy resolutions faded from the mind. The few survivors of the devoted men who, throughout the heat of the conflict, had remained at their posts were, many of them at least, forgotten and overlooked; for their presence was an unpleasing reminder to those whose conduct had been of a far more prudent and selfish sort. Those who had fled returned into the city to look after their deserted homes, and to re-open their shops. The streets and markets were once more gay with wares. The friar was now as eager to leave Naples as he had before been determined to remain. His sole object was to find the Cavaliere, and he constantly insisted that no time was to be lost if they wished to see him alive. They left Naples together; the friar mounted upon a mule which Inglesant purchased for him.

Notwithstanding the friar's eagerness, their journey was slow, for he was not able to resist the impulse to turn aside to help when any appearance of distress or poverty called upon them for aid. Inglesant was not impatient at this delay, nor at the erratic and apparently meaningless course of their singular journey. The country was delightful after the heavy rains, and seemed to rejoice, together with its inhabitants, at the abatement of the plague. People who had remained shut up in their houses in fear now appeared freely in the once deserted roads. Doors were thrown open, and the voice of the lute and of singing was heard again in the land. As for those who had passed away, it was wonderful how soon their name was forgotten, as of "a dead man out of mind;" and those who had come into comfortable inheritance of fruit-closes, and olive-grounds and vineyards, and of houses of pleasure in the fields, which, but for the pestilence, had never been theirs, soon found it possible to reconcile themselves to the absence of the dead.

For some time after leaving Naples the road lay through a richly cultivated land, with long straight ditches on either side. Rows of forest trees crossed the country, and shaded the small closes of fruit-trees and vines. Here and there a wine tavern, or a few cottages, or a village church, stopped them. At all of these the friar alighted from his mule, and made inquiries for any who were ill or in distress. In this way they came across a number of people of the peasant class, and heard the story of their lives; and now and then a religious, or a country signore, riding by on his mule or palfrey, stopped to speak with them.

They had proceeded for many days through this cultivated country, and had at last, after many turnings, reached that part of the road which approaches the slopes of the Apennines about Frosinone. The path wound among the hills, the slopes covered with chestnut trees, and the crags crowned with the remains of Gothic castles. Fields of maize filled the valleys, and lines of lofty poplars crossed the yellow corn. As the road ascended, distant reaches of forest and campagna lay in bright sunlight between the craggy rocks, and down the wooded glens cascades fell into rapid streams spanned here and there by a half-ruined bridge. At last they entered a deep ravine of volcanic tufa, much of which cropped out from the surface, cold and bare. Between these sterile rocks laurels forced their way, and spread out their broad and brilliant leaves. Creeping plants hung in long and waving festoons, and pines and forest trees of great size crowned the summits. Here and there sepulchral excavations were cut in the rock, and more than one sarcophagus, carved with figures in relief, stood by the wayside.

The air in these ravines was close and hot, and sulphurous streams emitted an unpleasant odour as they rode along. Inglesant felt oppressed and ill. The valley of the Shadow of Death, out of which he had come into the cool pastures and olive-yards, had left upon the mind an exaltation of feeling rather than terror; and in the history of the friar, through the course of which traces of a devised plan penetrated the confusion of a disordered brain, the gracious prediction of Molinos seemed to promise fulfilment. The supreme effort of Divine mercy surely is that which shapes the faltering and unconscious actions of man into a beneficent and everlasting work.

But the very clearness and calm of this transcendental air produced a wavering of the spiritual sense; and the companionship of a blind enthusiast, who, from the lowest depth of reckless sin, had suddenly attained a height of religious fervour, did not tend to reduce the fever of his thoughts. The scenes and forms of death with which he had been familiar in Naples returned again and again before his eyes, and his old disease again tormented him; so that once more he saw strange figures and shapes walking by the wayside. These images of a disordered fancy jostled and confused his spiritual perceptions. He felt wearied by those thoughts and desires which had formerly been dear to him, and the ceaseless reiteration of the friar's enthusiastic conceptions jarred and irritated him more than he liked to confess. The brain of the blind man, unoccupied by the sights of this world, was full of visions of a mystic existence, blended and confused with such incidents and stories of earth as he had heard along the way. With such phantasmal imaginations, he filled Inglesant's ears.

Proceeding in this manner, they came to a place where the ravine, opening out a little, exposed a distant view of the Campagna, with its aqueducts and ruined tombs. At the opening of the valley stood one of those isolated rocks so strange to English eyes, yet so frequently seen in the paintings of the old masters, crowned with the ruins of a Temple, and fringed with trees of delicate foliage, poplars and pines. At the foot of the rock an arch of ruined brickwork, covered with waving grass and creepers, spanned the road with a wide sweep, and on the opposite side a black sulphurous pool exhaled a constant vapour. Masses of strange, nameless masonry, of an antiquity dateless and undefined, bedded themselves in the rocks, or overhung the clefts of the hills; and out of a great tomb by the wayside, near the arch, a forest of laurel forced its way, amid delicate and graceful frieze-work, moss-covered and stained with age.

In this strangely desolate and ruinous spot, where the fantastic shapes of nature seem to mourn in weird fellowship with the shattered strength and beauty of the old Pagan art-life, there appeared unexpectedly signs of modern dwelling. The base of the precipitous rock for some distance above the road, was concealed by a steep bank of earth, the crumbling ruin and dust of man and of his work. At the top of this bank was one of those squalid erections, so common in Italy, where, upon a massive wall of old brickwork, embedded in the soil, a roof of straw affords some kind of miserable shelter. Some attempt had been made to wall in the space covered by this roof, and a small cross, reared from the gable, and a bell beneath a penthouse of wood, seemed to show that the shed had been used for some ecclesiastical purpose. At the bottom of the slope upon which this structure was placed, and on the other side of the ruined arch and of the road, there stood, near to the tomb, a very small hut, also thatched, and declared to be a tavern by its wine-bush. At the door of this hut, as Inglesant and the friar rode up, stood a man in a peasant's dress, in an attitude of perplexity and nervous dread. A long streak of light from the western sun penetrated the ruined arch, and shone upon the winding road, and against the blaze of light, rock and arch and hanging woods stood out dark and lowering in the delicate air.

The dazzling light, the close atmosphere of the valley, and the fumes of the sulphurous lake, affected Inglesant's brain so much that he could scarcely see; but they did not appear to disturb the friar. He addressed the man as they came up, and understanding more from his own instinct than from the few words that Inglesant spoke that the man was in trouble, he said,—

"You seem in some perplexity, my son. Confide in me, that I may help you."

As the man hesitated to reply, Inglesant said, "What is that building on the hill?"

"It is a house for lepers," said the peasant.

"Are you the master of this tavern?" said Inglesant.

"No, Santa Madre," replied the man. "The mistress of the inn has fled. This is the case, Padre," he continued, turning to the friar. "I was hired a week or so ago at Ariano to bring a diseased man here, who was a leper; but I did not know that he was a leper who was stricken with the plague. I brought him in my cart, and a terrible journey I had with him. When I had brought him here, and the plague manifestly appeared upon him, all the lepers fled, and forsook the place. The Padrona, who kept this tavern upon such custom as the peasants who brought food to sell to the lepers brought her, also fled. I stayed a day or two to help the wretched man—they told me that he was a gentleman—till I could stay no longer, such was his condition, and I fled. But, my Father, I have a tender heart, and I came back to-day, thinking that the holy Virgin would never help me if I left a wretched man to die alone—I, who only know where and in what state he is. I spoke to one or two friars to come and help me, but they excused themselves. I came alone. But when I arrived here my courage failed me, and I dared not go up. I know the state he was in two days ago; he must be much more terrible to look at now. Signore," concluded the man, turning to Inglesant with an imploring gesture, "I dare not go up."

"Do you know this man's name?" said Inglesant.

"Yes; they told me his name."

"What is it?"

"Il Cavaliere di Guardino."

At the name of his wife's brother, Inglesant started, and would have dismounted, but checked himself in the stirrup, struck by the action of the friar. He had thrown his arms above his head with a gesture of violent excitement, his sightless eyeballs extended, his face lighted with an expression of rapturous astonishment and delight.

"Who?" he exclaimed. "Who sayest thou? Guardino a leper, and stricken with the plague! Deserted and helpless, is he? too terribly disfigured to be looked upon? The lepers flee him, sayest thou? Holy and blessed Lord Jesus, this is Thy work! He is my mortal foe—the ravisher of my sister—the destroyer of my own sight! Let me go to him! I will minister to him—I will tend him! Let me go!"

He dismounted from his mule, and, with the wonderful instinct he seemed to possess, turned towards the rock, and began to scramble up the hill, blindly and with difficulty, it is true, but still with sufficient correctness to have reached the ruin without help. There was, to Inglesant, something inexpressibly touching and pitiful in his hurried and excited action, and his struggling determination to accomplish the ascent.

The peasant would have overtaken him to prevent his going up, probably misdoubting his intention. Inglesant checked him.

"Do not stop him," he said. "He is a holy man, and will do what he says. I will go with him. Stay here with my horse."

"You do not know to what you are going, signore," said the peasant, looking at Inglesant with a shudder; "let him go alone. *He cannot see.*"

Inglesant shook his head, and, his brain still slightly dizzy and confused, hastened after the friar, and assisted him to climb the rocky bank. When they had reached the entrance to the hut the friar went hastily in, Inglesant following him to the doorway.

It was a miserable place, and nearly empty, the lepers having carried off most of their possessions with them. On a bed of straw on the farther side, beneath the rock, lay what Inglesant *felt* to be the man of whom he was in search. What he saw it is impossible to describe here. The leprosy and the plague combined had produced a spectacle of inexpressible loathing and horror, such as nothing but absolute duty would justify the description of. The corruption of disease made it scarcely possible to recognize even the human form. The poisoned air of the shed was such that a man could scarcely breathe it and live.

The wretched man was rolling on his couch, crying out at intervals, groaning and uttering oaths and curses. Without the slightest faltering the friar crossed the room (it is true he could not see), and kneeling by the bedside, which he found at once, he began, in low and hurried accents, to pour into the ear of the dying man the consoling sound of that Name, which alone, uttered under heaven, has power to reach the departing soul, distracted to all beside. Startled by the sound of a voice close to his ear, for his sight also was gone, the sick man ceased his outcries and lay still.

Never ceasing for a moment, the friar continued, in a rapid and fervent whisper, to pour into his ear the tenderness of Jesus to the vilest sinner, the eternal love that will reign hereafter, the sweetness and peace of the heavenly life. The wretched man lay perfectly still, probably not knowing whether this wonderful voice was of earth or heaven; and Inglesant, his senses confused by the horrors of the room, knelt in prayer in the entrance of the hut.

The fatal atmosphere of the room became more and more dense. The voice of the friar died slowly away; his form, bending lower over the bed, faded out of sight; and there passed across Inglesant's bewildered brain the vision of Another who stood beside the dying man. The halo round His head lighted all the hovel, so that the seamless coat He wore, and the marks upon His hands and feet, were plainly seen, and the pale alluring face was turned not so much upon the bed and upon the monk as upon Inglesant himself, and the unspeakable glance of the Divine eyes met his.

A thrill of ecstasy, terrible to the weakened system as the sharpest pain, together with the fatal miasma of the place, made a final rush and grasp upon his already reeling faculties, and he lost all consciousness, and fell senseless within the threshold of the room.

When he came to himself he had been dragged out of the hut by the peasant, who had ventured at last to ascend the hill. The place was silent; the Cavaliere was dead, and the friar lay across the body in a sort of trance. They brought him out and laid him on the grass, thinking for some time that he was dead also. By and by he opened his sightless eyes, and asked where he was; but he still moved as in a trance. He seemed to have forgotten what had happened; and, with the death of the Cavaliere, the great motive which had influenced him, and which, while it lasted, seemed to have kept his reason from utterly losing its balance, appeared to be taken away. He had lived only to meet and bless his enemy, and this having been accomplished, all reason for living was gone.

Inglesant and the peasant dug a grave with some implements they found in the tavern, and hastily buried the body, the friar pronouncing a benediction. The latter performed this office mechanically, and seemed almost unconscious as to what was passing. His very figure and shape appeared changed, and presented but the shadow of his former self; his speech was broken and unintelligible. Inglesant gave the peasant money, which seemed to him to be wealth, and they mounted and rode silently away.

At Venafro, where they found a monastery of the Cappucines, they stayed some days, Inglesant expecting that his companion would recover something of his former state of health. But it soon became apparent that this would not be the case; the friar sank rapidly into a condition of mental unconsciousness, and the physicians told Inglesant that, although he might linger for weeks, they believed that a disease of the brain was hastening him towards the grave. Inglesant was impatient to return to the Castello; and, leaving the friar to the care of the brothers of his own order, he resumed his journey.

Was it a strange coincidence, or the omniscient rule and will of God, that, at the moment Inglesant lay insensible before the hut, the plague had done its work in the home that he had left? The old Count died first, then some half of the servants, finally, in the deserted house, a little child lay dead upon its couch, and beside it, on the marble floor, lay Lauretta—dead—uncared for.

It was the opinion of Martin Luther that visions of the Saviour, which he himself had seen, were delusions of Satan for the bewildering of the Papists; and there is a story of a monk who left the Beatific Vision that he might take his service in the choir.

Malvolti died at Venafro a short time after Inglesant had left him.

CHAPTER XVII

After the narration of the events just detailed the papers from which the life of Mr. Inglesant has hitherto been compiled become much less minute and personal in character; and when the narrative is resumed, a considerable period of time has evidently elapsed. It is stated that some time after the death of his wife Mr. Inglesant returned to Rome, and assumed a novice's gown in some religious order, but to which of the religious bodies he attached himself is doubtful. It might be thought that he would naturally become a member of the Society of Jesus; but there is reason to conclude that the rule which he intended to embrace was either that of the Benedictines or the Carmelites. As will soon appear, he proceeded no farther than the noviciate, and this uncertainty therefore is of little consequence.

It must be supposed that the distress caused by the death of his wife and child, and by his absence from them at the last, was one motive which caused Inglesant to seek in Rome spiritual comfort and companionship from the Spanish priest Molinos, in whose society he had before found so much support and relief. It was thought, indeed, by many beside Inglesant, amid the excitement which the spread of the method of devotion taught by this man had caused, that a dawn of purer light was breaking over spiritual Rome. God seemed to have revealed Himself to thousands in such a fashion as to make their past lives and worship seem profitless and unfruitful before the brightness and peace that was revealed; and the lords of His heritage seemed for a time to be willing that this light should shine. It appeared for a moment as if Christendom were about to throw off its shackles, its infant swaddling clothes, in which it had been so long wrapped, and, acknowledging that the childhood of the Church was past, stand forth before God with her children around her, no longer distrusted and enslaved, but each individually complete, fellow-citizens with their mother of the household of God. The unsatisfactory rotation of formal penitence and sinful lapse, of wearisome devotion and stale pleasures, had given place to an enthusiasm which believed that, instead of ceremonies and bowing in outer courts, the soul was introduced into heavenly places, and saw God face to face. A wonderful experience, in exchange for lifeless formality and rule, of communion with the Lord, with nothing before the believer, as he knelt at the altar, save the Lord Himself, day by day, unshackled by penance and confession as heretofore. Thousands of the best natures in Rome attached themselves to this method; it was approved by a Jesuit Father, the Pope was known to countenance it, and his nephews were among its followers. The bishops were mostly in favour of it, and in the nunneries of Rome the directors and confessors were preaching it; and the nuns, instead of passing their time over their beads and "Hours," were much alone, engaged in the exercise of mental prayer.

It would indeed be difficult to estimate the change that would have passed over Europe if this one rule of necessary confession before every communion had been relaxed; and in the hope that some increased freedom of religious thought would be secured, many adopted the new method who had no great attachment to the doctrine, nor to the undoubted extravagances which the Quietists, in common with other mystics, were occasionally guilty of, both in word and deed. It cannot be denied, and it is the plea that will be urged in defence of the action of the Jesuits, that freedom of thought as well as of devotion was the motive of numbers who followed the teaching of Molinos. That free speculation and individual growth could be combined with loyalty to acts and ceremonies, hallowed by centuries of recollection and of past devotion, was a prospect sufficiently attractive to many select natures. Some, no doubt, entered into this cause from less exalted motives—a love of fame and a desire to form a party, and to be at the head of a number of followers; but even among those whose intentions were not so lofty and spiritual as those of Molinos probably were, by far the greater number were actuated by a desire to promote freedom of thought and of worship among Churchmen.

But it was only for a moment that this bright prospect opened to the Church.

The Jesuits and Benedictines began to be alarmed. Molinos had endeavoured to allay the suspicion attached to his teaching, and diminish the aversion that the Jesuits felt towards him, by calling his book "The Spiritual Guide," and by constantly enjoining the necessity of being in all things under the direction of a religious person; but this was felt to point more at the submission to general council than to coming always to the priest, as to the minister of the sacrament of penance, before every communion; especially as Molinos taught that the only necessary qualification for receiving was the being free from mortal sin.

Suddenly, when the reputation of this new society appeared to be at its height, Molinos was arrested, and Father Esparsa, the Jesuit whose approbation had appeared before "The Spiritual Guide," disappeared. What became of the latter was not known, but it was generally supposed that he was "shut up between four walls;" and at any rate he appeared no more in Rome. In the midst of the excitement consequent on these events seventy more persons, all of the highest rank,—Count Vespiniani and his lady, the Confessor of Prince Borghese, Father Appiani of the Jesuits, and others equally well-known,—were arrested in one day, and before the month was over more than two hundred persons crowded the prisons of the Inquisition.

The consternation was excessive, when a method of devotion which had been extolled throughout Italy for the highest sanctity to which mortals could aspire was suddenly found to be heretical, and the chief promoters of it hurried from their homes and from their friends, shut up in prison, and in peril of perpetual confinement, if not death. The arrest of Father Appiani was the most surprising. He was accounted the most learned priest in the Roman College, and was arrested on a Sunday in April as he came from preaching. After this no one could guess on whom the blow would fall next. The Pope himself, it was reported, had been examined by the Jesuits. The imminence of the peril brought strength with it. The prisoners, it was whispered, were steady and resolute, and showed more learning than their examiners. Their friends who were still at large, recovering from their first panic, assumed a bold front. Many letters were written to the Inquisitors, advising them to consider well what they did to their prisoners, and assuring them that their interests would be maintained even at the cost of life. Nor did these protests end here. As soon as possible after the arrests a meeting was held at Don Agostino's palace in the Piazza Colonna, to which ladies were summoned as well as men. There, in a magnificent saloon, amid gilding and painting and tapestry, whose splendour was subdued by softened colour and shaded light, were met the elite of Rome. There were ladies in rich attire, yet in whose countenances was seen that refinement of beauty which only religion and a holy life can give—ladies, who, while appearing in public in the rank which belonged to them, were capable in private of every self-denial, trained in the practice of devotion and acts of mercy. There were nuns of the Conception and of the Palestrina, distressed and mortified at being compelled to return to their beads and to their other abandoned forms. There were present Cereri, Cardinal-Bishop of Como; Cardinals Carpegna and Cigolini, and Cardinal Howard of England (the noblest and most spiritually-minded of the Sacred College), Absolini and Coloredi, Cardinals and Fathers of the Oratory, and Cardinal D'Estrées. Petrucci himself, the most prominent advocate of the Quietist doctrine, was in the room, though incognito, it not being generally known that he was in Rome. There were present many Fathers of the Oratory, men of intellect, refinement, and blameless lives; Don Livio, Duke di Ceri, the Pope's nephew was there, and the Prince Savelli, many of the highest nobility, and above a hundred gentlemen, all of whom, by their presence, might be supposed to prove their attachment to the teaching of Molinos, their superiority to the sordid motives of worldly prudence and pleasure, and their devotion to spiritual instincts and desires. It would be difficult to imagine scenes more unlike each other; yet, strange as it may appear, it was nevertheless true that this brilliant company, attired in the height of the existing mode, sparkling with jewels and enriched with chastened colour, might not unfitly be considered the successor of those hidden meetings of a few slaves in Nero's household, who first, in that wonderful city, believed in the crucified Nazarene.

The addresses were commenced by the Duke di Ceri, who spoke of the grief caused by the arrest of their friends, and of the exertions that had been made on their behalf. He was followed by other of the great nobles and cardinals, who all spoke in the same strain. All these speeches were delivered in somewhat vague and guarded terms, and as one after another of the speakers sat down, a sense of incompleteness and dissatisfaction seemed to steal over the assembly, as though it were disappointed of something it most longed to hear. The meeting was assured, over and over again, that extreme measures would not be taken against those in prison; that their high rank and powerful connections would save them; the Duke di Ceri had expressly said that he believed his relation and servant, Count Vespiniani, and his lady would soon be released. The fact was, though the Duke did not choose, to state it publicly, that they had been proscribed solely from information gained at the confessional; and this having been much talked of, the Jesuits had resolved, rather than bring any further odium on the sacrament of confession, to discharge both the lady and her husband at once. But, though all this might be true, there was something that remained unsaid—something that was filling all hearts.

What was to be the spiritual future of those assembled? Was this gate of Paradise and the Divine Life to be for ever closed, and was earth and all its littleness once more to be pressed upon them without denial, and hypocrisy and the petty details of a formal service once more to be the only spiritual food of their souls? Must they, if they resolved to escape this spiritual death, quit this land and this glorious Church, and seek, in cold and distant lands, and alien Churches, the freedom denied by the tyranny of the leaders of their own? These thoughts filled all minds, and yet none had given them utterance, nor was it surprising that it should be so. Select and splendid as that assembly was, no one knew for certain that his neighbour was not a spy. As was known soon after, Cardinal D'Estrées, who sat there so calm and lofty-looking, furnished the principal evidence against Molinos, swearing that, being his intimate friend, he knew that the real meaning of his friend's printed words was that heretical one of which, in fact, Molinos had never dreamt. It was no wonder that the speeches were cautious and vague.

At last Don Agostino rose, and in a quiet and unaffected tone, requested a hearing for his very dear friend, the Cavaliere di San Georgio, one well known to most of them, whose character was known to all.

A murmur of satisfaction ran through the room, and the audience settled itself down to listen, as though they knew that the real business of the day was about to begin. Inglesant rose in his seat immediately behind his host. He was evidently dressed carefully, with a view to the effect to be produced upon a fastidious and ultra-refined assembly. He wore a cassock of silk, and the gown of a Benedictine made of the finest cloth. His head was tonsured, and his hair cut short. He had round his neck a band of fine cambric, and at his wrists ruffles of rich lace; and he wore on his hand a diamond of great value. He had, indeed, to one who saw his dress and not his face, entirely the look of a petit-maître, and even—what is more contemptible still—of a petit-maître priest; yet, as he rose in his seat, there was not a man in all that assembly who would have given a silver scudo for the chances of his life.

His romantic and melancholy story, the death of his wife and child, his assumption of the religious life, and, above all, his friendship with Molinos, were known to all; it seemed to many a fitting close to a life of such vicissitude, that at this crisis he should sacrifice himself in the spiritual cause that was dear to all.

He had his speech written before him, every word carefully considered and arranged by himself and some of the first masters of style then in Rome. He began deliberately and distinctly, so that every word was heard, though he spoke in a low voice.

After deprecating the judgment of the assembly upon the artless and unpolished words he was about to address to it, and excusing his rashness in consenting to speak in such an assembly at all, he said,—

"The words of the noble and august personages who have already spoken have left me little to say. Nothing is necessary to be added to their wise and reverend advice. All that remains for us to do is to attempt to carry out in action what they have so well counselled. Our first object, our first duty, is the safety of our friends. But, when this is happily accomplished—as, under such leaders and protected by such names, how can we doubt that it will be?—there are many among us who, with sinking hearts and hushed voices, are inquiring, 'What will come next?'"

He paused, and looked up for a moment, and a murmur of encouragement ran through the room.

"I am not mistaken when I say that in this room, and also in Rome, are many hearts which, within the last few years, and by the teaching of him for whom night and day the prayers of the Church ascend to heaven, have found a peace and a blessedness before unknown; many who have breathed celestial air, and walked the streets of God. Nor am I mistaken—my heart and your presence tell me I am not mistaken—when I say that many are asking themselves, 'How can they renounce this heavenly birthright? How can they live without this Divine intercourse, which they have found so sweet—which the purest saints have hallowed with their approval? How can they live without God who have seen Him face to face?' And many are asking themselves, 'Must we leave the walks of men, and the Churches where the saints repose, and wander into the wilderness—into byways among the wild places of heresy, since the Church seems to close the gates upon this way which is their life?' I risk the deserved censure of this august assembly when I venture to advise—yet even this I am willing to do, if I may serve any—and I venture to advise, No. I myself was born in another country, amid contending forms of faith. I believe that, in the sacrificial worship of our most Holy Church, room is amply given for the perfection of the Contemplative State; and that such lofty devotion can find no fitter scene than the altar of the Lord. As we may hope that, at some future time, the whole Church may come to this holy state, and be raised above many things which, though now perhaps necessary, may in a higher condition fall away; so, if by our continuing in this posture we may hasten such a happy time, this doubtless will be the path Heaven wishes us to walk in. But"—he paused, and the whole assembly listened with breathless attention—"if such is to be our course, it is evident that an understanding is necessary of adjustment between ourselves and the Fathers of the Holy Office and of the Society of Jesus—an adjustment by which a silence must be allowed our Faith—a silence which, for the sake of those amongst us whose consciences are the most refined and heaven-taught, must be understood to imply dissent to much that has lately been acted and taught. We must understand that this exertion of authority is aimed only at the open teaching of doctrines in which we still believe, and which are still dear to us; and that liberty is allowed our faith so long as we observe a discreet silence—a liberty which shall extend as far as to admission to the Sacrament without previous confession. On this point surely it is necessary that we have a clearer understanding."

Inglesant stopped, and applause, sufficiently loud and unmistakably sincere, showed that a large proportion of the assembly approved of what had been said.

He spoke a word to Don Agostino, and then went on, —

"I am willing to confess, and this august assembly will be willing to confess, that to the rulers of Christ's ark—those who have to answer for the guidance of the peoples of the world, and who know far better than we can the difficulties and dangers which environ such a task—this allowance to the lower masses of the people, so prone to run to extremes and to err in excess, would seem unwise; and I am not unwilling also to admit that we may have erred in making this way too public, before the world was sufficiently prepared for it. Both for this, and for any other fault, we are willing to suffer penance, and to submit to the Holy Church in silence; but, this acknowledged and performed, we must be allowed, within certain limits, to retain the freedom we have enjoyed, and some manifest token must be given us that such will be the case."

A singular murmur again filled the room—a murmur compounded of intense sympathy and of admiration at the boldness of the speaker.

Inglesant went on.

"But you will ask me, how is this to be obtained? I am allowed to say that I have not undertaken the mission save at the request of others whom it well becomes to direct my service in all things. They consider that for some reason I am fitted for the task. I am—and I speak with all gratitude—a pupil of the reverend and holy Society of Jesus, and whatever I possess I owe to its nursing care. I am besides, though I have never acted in such capacity, still an accredited agent of the Queen Mother of England, that most faithful daughter—I had almost said Martyr—of the Church. I will see the General of the Order, and if this assembly will allow me to speak in its name, I will offer to him our dutiful submission if he, on his part, will give us some public sign that we are allowed our private interpretation upon the late events, and our liberty upon the point which I have named."

When Inglesant sat down Cardinal Howard spoke. He was followed by several others, all of whom complimented the Cavaliere upon his devotion to so good a cause; but abstained from expressing any decided opinion on the expediency of his proposal. But when two or three speeches had been made, the mixed character of the assembly began to show itself. It is true that it had been carefully selected, yet, in order to give it importance and influence, it had been necessary to include in the invitations as many as possible, and the result was soon apparent. There were many present who had joined the ranks of the Quietists more from a weariness of the existing order than from sincere devotion. There were many present who had joined them sincerely, but who, from timidity and caution, were desirous to escape the anger of the Inquisition by submission and silence, and who deprecated any risk of exciting a still more harsh exertion of authority. Both these parties, increased by waverers from the more devoted portion of the company, united in advising that no action should be taken, farther than that which had been already used, and which, it might be hoped, had secured the principal object of their wishes, the release of their friends.

They argued that confession before each communion could not be burdensome to those who were in a state of grace, and therefore had nothing to confess; and even if it were, as the Fathers of the Church judged it necessary for the suppression of error, and for the good of the ignorant and unenlightened, it ought to be submitted to most willingly by those farthest advanced in the spiritual life. These speakers also argued that many things which were held by the Quietists harmlessly to themselves were liable to be misunderstood, and that anything which tended to draw off the mind from the mystery of the Sacrifice of the Mass, or from the examples of the saints, tended to divert the vulgar from devotion to the Saviour, and savoured of Deism.

They argued that although perhaps many things were unnecessary to those whose religious life was far advanced, such as the breviary, beads, images, many prayers, etc., yet it was not so to others, and that no doubt, where it was suitable, relaxation would be easily obtained from one's director. No one had insisted more upon the necessity of a spiritual guide than had Molinos, and it was now the time to prove the reality of our obedience to the voice of the Church.

It was argued that many things in Molinos's writings seemed to tend towards Calvinism, and the doctrine of Efficacious Grace, which no one present—no true child of the Church—could defend,—a doctrine which limited the Grace of God, and turned the free and wide pastures of Catholicism into the narrow bounds of a restricted sect; and it was finally hinted that there was some reason to believe that the promoters of the meeting were acting with a farther intention than at first appeared, and that they desired to introduce changes into the Catholic faith and discipline, under cover of this discussion.

This last insinuation was a home thrust, and was so felt by the meeting. The subject of Efficacious Grace had also been introduced very skilfully by a young priest, a pupil of the Jesuits himself.

After a brief consultation with his party Inglesant replied that a great deal of what had been advanced was unanswerable; that he himself, a pupil of the Jesuits, was as much opposed to the doctrine of Efficacious Grace as any one could be; that it was the intention of no one present to urge any course of action unless the meeting unanimously approved of it; and that, as it appeared that the majority of those present were prepared to submit to the Holy Office, and did not desire any negotiation, nothing farther would be attempted.

There weighed, in truth, upon the hearts of all, and had probably oppressed Inglesant as he spoke, a sense of hopelessness and of contention with an irresistible power. In spite of this feeling, however, the decision of the chiefs drew forth expressions of impatience and regret from the more enthusiastic partisans; but as these were mostly women, who could not address the assembly, or such as were not prepared to make themselves prominent in face of almost certain arrest, the discussion became desultory and ineffectual, and the meeting finally broke up without any decision having been arrived at.

The Piazza was full of carriages and servants, and the Duke di Ceri had an enormous train of equipages following his carriage to escort him beyond the gate, on the way to his villa near Civita Vecchia, whither he returned immediately, not choosing to stay in Rome.

The meeting being over, Don Agostino urged Inglesant to leave Rome; indeed, the Duke had already pressed him to accompany him to Civita Vecchia, but Inglesant declined.

The motives which influenced him were of a mixed nature. He was prompted by the most sincere desire to find out a way, both for himself and for others, in which the highest spiritual walk, and the purest condition of spiritual worship, might be possible within the Church of Rome. There was probably nothing in this world which he desired more than this, for in this was included that still more important freedom, the liberty of the reason; for if it were possible for the spirit to be free, while fulfilling the outward observances, and participating in the outward ordinances of the Church, so also it must be possible for the reason to be free too.

It had been this very desire, singular as it may seem, which had attached him to the Society of the Jesuits. Not only were their tenets—notably that of sufficient grace given to all men—of wider and more catholic nature than the Augustinian doctrines held by most bodies both of Churchmen and

Protestants, but the Society had always, in all its dealings with men, shown a notable leaning to tolerance, even, so its enemies asserted, of sin and vice.

But besides these motives which had something of a refined and noble character, Inglesant had others. A life of intrigue and policy had, from training and severe practice, become a passion and necessity of his life. To leave the field where such a fight was going on, to remain in Rome, even, an inactive spectator, allowed to pursue his own path merely from the ignoble fact that he was not worth arrest,—both these courses of action were intolerable to him. He had promised Molinos that he would not be wanting in the hour of trial, and he would keep his word. He was utterly powerless, as the events of the last few moments would have shown him had he not known it before. The most powerful, the noblest confederacy fell away impotently before an invisible yet well-understood power, and a sense of vague irresistible force oppressed him, and showed him the uselessness of resistance.

Nevertheless he requested the loan of Don Agostino's carriage that he might go at once to the General of the Society. He was shown at once into a small cabinet, where he was kept waiting a few moments, the General in fact being engaged at that moment in listening to a detailed account of the meeting, and of the speeches delivered at it. He however entered the room in a few minutes, and the two men saluted each other with the appearance of cordial friendship. Inglesant had not changed his dress, and the General ran his eyes over it with somewhat of an amused expression, doubtless comparing the account he had just received with the appearance of his visitor, the purpose of which he was fully alive to.

Inglesant began the conversation.

"Your reverence is probably acquainted already with the meeting in the Piazza Colonna, and with its objects and results. I, however, have come to relate what passed as far as you may be disposed to listen, and to give any information, in a perfectly open and sincere manner, which you may wish to receive. In return for this I wish to ask your reverence two or three questions which I hope will not be unpleasant, and which you will of course answer or not as it pleases you."

"As I understand the meeting, Signore Cavaliere," said the General with a slight smile, "it rejected your mediation, in spite of the elaborate care with which the proposal was brought before it, a care extending to the minutest particulars, and the chastened eloquence and perfect style in which it was offered."

This sarcasm fell comparatively harmlessly upon Inglesant, preoccupied as his thoughts were. He therefore bowed, saying,—

"The meeting rejected my mediation, or rather it thought that no mediation was necessary, and trusted itself implicitly to the fatherly care of the Society of Jesus."

"What does the meeting representing this new heresy demand?"

"It demands nothing but the deliverance of its friends now in prison."

"And nothing else?"

"Nothing else from the meeting. I am here to demand something else."

"On your own behalf alone?"

"On my own responsibility solely; but if my request is granted, many will be benefited by my work."

"Have you no abettors? You came here in Don Agostino's coach."

"I am Don Agostino's dear and intimate friend, and it is not much that he should lend me his coach. I have many friends in Rome."

"I know it," said the Jesuit cordially, "and among them the Order of Jesus is not the least sincere."

Inglesant bowed, and there was a slight pause. Then the General said,—

"What do you demand?"

"I demand spiritual freedom—the freedom of silence."

"Freedom will be abused."

"Not by me nor by my friends. We pledge ourselves to unbroken silence. All we demand is freedom to worship God in private as He Himself shall lead us. We ask for no change in public doctrine. We seek no proselytes. In fact, we confine ourselves to one desire, the sacrament without confession."

The Jesuit made no reply, but continued to look fixedly into Inglesant's face.

"It seems to me, Father," Inglesant went on, with a touch of bitterness in his tone, "that the Society is changing its policy, or rather that it has a different policy for different classes of men. So far as I have known it, it has pursued a course of compromise with all men, and especially with the weak and frail. It has always appeared to me a trait much to be admired, that in which it is likest to the divine charity itself; but the world has been very severe upon it. And when the world says, 'You have pandered to vice in every form; you have rendered the confessional easy of approach, and the path of penitence smooth to the impenitent; you have been lenient, nay more than lenient, to the loose liver, to the adulterers and menslayers,—surely you might be mild to the devout; surely you might extend a little of this infinite pity to the submissive and obedient, to the pure in life and soul who seek after God; 'Difficile est satiram non scribere. Nam quis iniquae tam patiens urbis, tam ferreus, ut teneat se.' If the world says this, what am I to answer?' For, if it be so necessary to confine the soul to narrow dogmas lest she go astray, it must be also necessary to deal freely and sharply with these sins of the flesh, lest they bring men to sensuality and to hell. By thus acting, as it seems to me, and not by making the righteous sad, you would follow the teaching of those beautiful words of one of your Fathers, who says, 'that the main design of our Society is to endeavour the establishment of virtue, to carry on the war against vice, and to cultivate an infinite number of souls.'"

"You are a bold man, Signore Cavaliere. For far less words than you have spoken men have grown old in the dungeons of Saint Angelo, where the light of day never comes."

Inglesant, who rather wished to be imprisoned, and flattered himself that he should soon be released, was not alarmed at this menace, and remained silent.

A pause ensued, during which something like this ran through the Jesuit's mind:—

"Shall I have this man arrested at once, or wait? He came to us well recommended—the favourite pupil of an important member of the Society, who assured us that he was an instrument perfectly trained, ready at all points for use, and of a temper and spirit far above the average, not to be lost to the Order on any account. He has proved all that was said of him, and much more. The Papal throne itself is under obligation to him. But do we want such a man so much? I have scores of agents, of instruments ready to my hand, with whom I need use no caution—no finesse; why waste any on one, however highly finished and trained? But, on the other hand, I speak this in Rome, where everything is our own, and where the sense of power may have unfitted me from properly understanding this man's value. In the rough regions *in partibus* such a tool as this, fine and true as steel, tried in the fire as steel, doubtless is not lightly to be thrown away; at all events, nothing is to be done hastily. So long as he is in Rome he is safe, and may be clapped up at any moment. I almost wish he would leave, and go back to his teacher."

All this occupied but a few seconds, and, as the Jesuit made no answer, Inglesant, who scarcely expected any definite reply, took his leave. To his surprise, however, the General insisted on accompanying him to his coach. They crossed the courtyard to where the equipage of Don Agostino stood in the street. In the excited imagination of Rome at that moment, the sight of Don Agostino's carriage before the Jesuits' College had attracted a crowd. When Inglesant appeared, accompanied by the General, the excitement became intense. As they reached the carriage door, Inglesant knelt upon the pavement, and requested the Jesuit's blessing; the foremost of the crowd, impressed by this action, knelt too. Inglesant rose, entered the carriage, and was driven off; and two different rumours spread through Rome—one, that the Society had come to terms with the Quietists through the mediation of the Cavaliere; the other, that the Cavaliere di San Georgio had betrayed the Quietists, and made his peace with the Order; and this last report received the greatest amount of credit.

CHAPTER XVIII

The Inquisitors and the Jesuits continued to adopt a policy of great leniency to those who were in prison. The majority, after one examination, were released, merely going through the form of abjuring heresies and errors of which they had never dreamed. Owing to this politic course of action, assisted by the dislike and contempt which the people felt towards the then Pope, who was supposed to be a favourer of Molinos, and of whose dull reign the Romans were weary, a great change took place in the opinions of the populace. The credit of the Jesuits rose exceedingly, and they became celebrated for their excessive mildness, who before had been blamed for their rigour. To such an extent did they gain in popular estimation, that the chiefs of the defeated party were unable to keep back great numbers of the followers of Molinos from coming in to the Inquisitors every day, to accuse themselves of heresy, and to offer themselves to penance. These being very gently treated, and dismissed in peace, testified everywhere to the clemency of the Holy Office and of the Jesuits. The excitement, which before had set in one direction, was now turned with equal impetuosity in another; and many who had before, doubtless in perfect sincerity, found—or fancied they found—spiritual satisfaction in the "method of contemplation," now discovered an equal benefit in an excessive orthodoxy. The Quietist party was utterly crushed, and put to ignominious silence; and Molinos himself became an object of hatred and contempt; while, all the time, with extraordinary inconsistency, it was publicly reported that the reason of this surprising clemency was the great support which his doctrine received from the mystical Divinity, which had been authorized by so many canonizations, and approved by so many Councils and Fathers of the Church. The leaders of the defeated party lived as in a desert. Their saloons, which only a few days before had been crowded, were now empty, and Cardinal Petrucci himself was visited by no one; while the Jesuits were everywhere received with enthusiasm, so true to the character that the Satirist gave a thousand years before did the Roman populace remain—

"Sequitur fortunam, ut semper, et odit

"Damnatos."

Some slight portion of this popular applause fell to Inglesant's lot, whichever report was believed—whether, as the agent of the Society he had betrayed his friends, or had used his influence to procure this unexpected policy of mercy—either supposition procured him notoriety and even approbation. It now only remained to watch the fate of Molinos, and the inmates of Don Agostino's palace waited in silence the policy of their triumphant opponents. The Jesuits began by circulating reports of his hypocrisy and lewd course of life—facts of which they said they had convincing evidence. They said that these scandals had been proved before the Pope, who then, and not till then, had renounced his cause. The Romans replied to this story that they believed it, for the Pope was a good judge of such matters, but none at all of the questions of theology on which the quarrel had previously turned. There was not at the time, and there never has been since, the slightest evidence offered publicly that these stories had the least foundation; but they amply served their turn, insomuch that when Molinos was brought out to the Minerva on the day of his condemnation, he was saluted by the people with cries of "Fire! Fire!" and, but that his coach was resolutely defended by the Sbirri and guards, he would have been massacred by the furious mob.

When the morning rose upon the day on which his condemnation was to take place, the tribunal of the Minerva, and all the avenues and corridors leading to it, were thronged with an excited crowd. For days before, all the efforts both of money and favour had been exerted to procure good places in the court itself, and those who were unable to gain these coveted seats lined the corridors and staircases, while the populace outside thronged the streets leading from the prison of the Inquisition. The windows and house tops were crowded; scarcely an inhabitant of Rome but was to be found somewhere on the line of route; the rest of the city was a desert.

The vine-clad wastes of the Aventine, the green expanse of the Campo Vacchino, and the leafy walls of the Colosseum and of the arches, were lying under the morning sunlight, calm and quiet as in the midst of a happy and peaceful world. As Inglesant came across from the lonely convent where he still occasionally lodged, and turned out of the square of the Ara Cœli, the silent tenantless houses and palaces looked down with dim eyes like a city of the dead; and as he came into the Via del Gesu the distant hum and murmur of the crowd first broke upon his ear. Here and there a belated spectator like himself turned out of some bye-street or doorway, and hastened towards the Piazza della Minerva.

Inglesant turned off by a side street, and, following the narrow winding lanes with which he was well acquainted, came out into the Via di Coronari at some midway distance between the prison of the Inquisition and the Minerva. He was just in time. As he stationed himself against the wall of the Church of St. Maria de Anima and the German Hospital, he knew, by the excitement and frantic cries of the crowd, that Molinos was not far off. He was brought along the street in a large coach with glass windows, a Dominican friar seated at his side. On each side of the carriage and at the horses' heads the Sbirri and Swiss guards exerted themselves manfully to keep back the people and to clear the way. A deafening shout and cry rose unceasingly, and every few moments the crowd, pressing upon the carriage and the guards, caused them to come to a dead stop. Clinging to the horses' heads, to the carriage itself, to the halberds of the Swiss, climbing on the steps and on the back of the coach, had the crowd desired a rescue, Inglesant thought one bold and decided leader might have accomplished it in a few desperate moments. But the mob desired nothing less. This man—who but a few weeks ago had been followed by admiring crowds, who had been idolized in courtly saloons, whose steps and walks had been watched with the tender and holy devotion with which a people watches the man whose life it takes to be hid in God; whom loving modest women had pointed out to their children as the holy monk whom they must love and remember all their lives; whom passionate women, on whose souls the light of God had broken, had followed trembling, that they might throw themselves at his feet, and clinging to his gown, hear the words of gospel from his lips; to whom desperate men had listened whom no other voice had ever moved;— this man was now the execration of the mob of Rome. Amidst the roar and din around no word was distinguishable but that terrible one of "Fire!" that pointed to a heretic's death at the stake; and, but for the determined resistance of the guards, Molinos would have been dragged from the coach and butchered in the streets.

When the carriage arrived opposite the spot upon which Inglesant had posted himself, he could see Molinos's face as he sat in the coach. He was carefully dressed in his priestly habit, and looked about him with a cheerful serene countenance. "He looks well," said a man, not far from Inglesant, who had been very bitter against the prisoner; "the secret of his success is not far to seek, for his face possesses all the charms that are able to captivate, especially the fair sex."

When the coach was close to Inglesant the crowd made another and most determined attack, and the horses came to a stand. The cries of "Fire! Fire!" rose louder and more fiercely, and the guards were for a moment beaten from one of the doors. It seemed that nothing could prevent the people from dragging their victim into the street; Inglesant felt his blood turn cold, fully expecting to see the massacre performed before his eyes; but before the people could open the door, which seemed fastened on the inside, the guard rallied, and by the free use of their halberds and short swords recovered the coach, and drove back the mob.

Through all this scene Molinos had preserved his perfectly unconcerned expression, and his eyes, wandering calmly over the people, at last rested upon the spot where Inglesant stood. Whether he recognized him or not Inglesant did not know, for he involuntarily drew back and shrank from his eye. He learnt afterwards that Molinos did recognize him, and also noticed his recoil. "He fears I should compromise him with the furious crowd," he thought; "he need not fear."

Inglesant's movement was caused, however, by a thought very different from this one, which indeed never occurred to him. He was ashamed to meet Molinos's eye. In the daylight and sunshine they had walked together, but when the trial came, the one was taken, and all the rest escaped. It was impossible but that some at least of the fortunate many should feel some pangs of uneasiness and doubt. Inglesant especially, the agent and confidant of the Jesuits, was open to such thoughts, and before the single-hearted uncompromising priest and confessor could not but feel in some sort condemned. The carriage passed on amid the unabated fury of the people, and, turning aside down a narrow winding lane, he entered the Dominicans' Church, to the reserved part of which he had a ticket of admission, to be ready for the final scene.

Molinos was taken to one of the corridors of the Minerva, where he stood for some time looking about him very calmly, and returning all the salutes which were made him by those who had formerly been of his acquaintance. To all inquiries he returned but one answer; that they saw a man who was defamed, but who was penitent (infamato ma penitente). After he had stood here some time he was conducted into a small apartment, where a sumptuous repast was spread before him, and he was invited to partake as of his last luxurious indulgence before being shut up in a little cell for life. A strange banquet! and a strange taste such delicacies must have to a man at such a time.

After dinner he was carried into the Church, as in a triumph, in an open chair upon the shoulders of the Sbirri. The tapers upon the altar shrines showed more clearly than did the dim and sober daylight that penetrated beneath the darkened roofs the three mystic aisles of the strange Church, which were filled with a brilliant company of cardinals, nobles, innumerable ladies, gentlemen of every rank, ecclesiastics without end. The dark marble walls, the sumptuous crowd, the rich colours of the stained glass, gave a kind of lurid splendour to the scene; while on every side the sculptured forms upon the monuments, with stolid changeless features, stood out pale amidst the surrounding gloom; and here and there, where free space was kept, the polished marble floor reflected the sombre brilliancy of the whole.

As Molinos was brought up to his place he made a low and devout reverence to the Cardinals, and his manner was perfectly possessed and without a show of fear or shame. He was made to stand up before the altar, a chain was bound round him and fastened to his wrists, and a wax taper was placed in his hands. Then with a loud voice a friar read his Process, so as to be heard by all in the Church: and as some of the articles were read, there were loud cries from the reverend and polite assembly of "Fire! Fire!"

In a few moments the sight was over, and Molinos was led back to the street, to be placed this time in a close carriage, and taken back to the prison, where his cell was prepared. As Inglesant stepped back into the aisle of the Church he felt some one pull him by his Benedictine gown, and turning round, he saw a lady in a velvet masque. She appeared excited, and, as far as he could see, was weeping, and her voice, which he thought he recognized, was broken and indistinct.

"Cavaliere," she said, "he will stop a moment in the vestibule before they put him in the coach. I want him to have this—he must have it—it will be a relief and consolation to him unspeakable. They will stop all of us, and will let no one come to him; but they will let you. You are a Jesuit, and their friend. For the love of Gesu, Cavaliere, do him and me, and all of us, this favour. He will bless you and pray for you. He will intercede for you. For the love of God, Cavaliere!"

She was pleading with such eager tearfulness and such hurried speech and gesture, that he could not doubt her truth, yet he paused a moment.

"Surely I know your voice?" he said.

"Ah! you know me," replied the masque, "but that is of no consequence. Another moment, and it will be too late. Cavaliere! for the love of Gesu!"

Inglesant took the small paper packet, which seemed to contain a casket, and went down the fast emptying Church. As he reached the entrance he turned and looked back for the velvet masque, but she was nowhere to be seen. His mind was full of suspicion, yet he was not unwilling to fulfil his mission. He should, at any rate, speak to Molinos, and perhaps grasp his hand.

In the vestibule Molinos stood alone, a circle being kept at some distance round him by the guard. His manner was unchanged and calm. The select crowd stood around gazing at him with eager curiosity; outside might be heard again the shouting of the mob, and the cry of "Fire!" Inglesant advanced towards the Captain of the Sbirri; but, to his surprise, before he could speak, the latter made a sign, and the guards fell back to let him pass. A murmur ran through the crowd, and every one pressed forward with intense eagerness. Molinos looked up, and an expression of grateful pleasure lighted up his face as he extended his hand. Inglesant grasped it with emotion, and looking him in the face, said,—

"Adieu, Father, you are more to be envied than we. You are clothed in the heavenly garment and sit down at the supper of the King; we wander in the outer darkness, with an aching conscience that cannot rest."

The expression of the other's face was compassionate and beautiful, and he said,—

"Adieu, Cavaliere, we shall meet again one day, when the veil shall be taken from the face of God, and we shall see Him as He is."

As Inglesant grasped his hand he slipped the casket into it, and as he did so dropped on one knee. The hand of the monk rested on his head for a moment, and in the next he had risen and stepped back, and the guards closed in for the last time round Molinos, and the crowd pressed after, following them to the coach.

When the carriage had driven off, and the crowd somewhat dispersed, Inglesant came down the steps, and was turning to the right into the Corso when he was surprised to see that the Captain of the Sbirri had not followed his prisoner, but was standing on the causeway with two or three of his men, near a plain carriage which was waiting. As Inglesant came up he turned to him, and said politely,—

"Pardon, Signore Cavaliere, I must ask you to come with me. You have conveyed a packet to a condemned prisoner—a grave offence—a packet which contains poison. You will come quietly, no doubt."

"I will come quietly, certainly," said Inglesant. "Where are we going? to the Inquisition?"

"No, no," said the other, as he followed the new prisoner into the coach, "yours is a civil offence; we are going to the St. Angelo."

"The General must have a taste for theatricals," thought Inglesant as the coach rolled off, "or he never could have planned such a melodrama."

On their arrival at the castle he was conducted into a good room, not in the tower, which commanded an extensive view of St. Peter's. Great liberty was allowed him, everything he liked to pay for was procured for him, and at certain hours he was allowed to walk on the glacis and fortifications.

The second day of his confinement was drawing to a close when he was visited by the Dominican who had attended Molinos. This monk, who seemed a superior person, had evidently been impressed by the conversation and character of his prisoner. After the first greeting he said,—

"That unhappy man requested me to bring you a message. It was to the effect that he had done you wrong. He saw you among the crowd as he was being brought to the Minerva, and noticed that you shrank back. He accused you in his mind of fearing to be compromised; he knows now that, on the contrary, you were watching for an opportunity to do him a service. It was but the thought of a moment, but he could not rest until he had acknowledged it, and begged your forgiveness. He bade me also to tell you that 'the bruised reed is not broken, nor the smoking flax quenched.'"

"Where did you leave him?" said Inglesant.

"At the door of his cell, which he calls his cabinet."

"'The smoking flax is not quenched,'" said Inglesant; "I hear that one of his followers, a day or two ago, before the tribunal told the examiners to their faces that they 'were a company of unjust, cruel, and heretical men, and that the measure which they dealt to others was the same that Christ Himself had received from His persecutors.'"

"It is true," said the Dominican, "and it is true also that he is released; such, on the contrary, is the clemency of the Church."

After an imprisonment of about a fortnight, as Inglesant was one day taking his usual walk upon the fortifications, he was informed that the General of the Order was in his room, and desired to see him. He went to him immediately, and was received with great appearance of friendliness.

"You will pardon my little plot, Cavaliere," said the General, "especially as I gave orders that you should be made very comfortable here. I wished to see in what manner and how far you were our servant, and I have succeeded admirably. I find, as I imagined, that you are invaluable; but it must be on your own terms, and at your own time. You are faithful and unflinching when you have undertaken anything, but each mission must be entered upon or renounced at your own pleasure. I hope you have not been nourishing bitter thoughts of me during your incarceration here."

"Far from it," replied Inglesant; "I have nothing to complain of. I have all I want, and the view from these windows is, as you see, unrivalled in Rome. If it consists with your policy I should take it as a great favour were you to inform me whether the velvet masque was a mere tool or not. I could have sworn that her accent and manner were those of a person speaking the truth; still, when the Captain of the Sbirri made way for me I thought I was in the toils."

"Your penetration did not err. The lady was the Countess of ——. She conceived the idea of communicating with Molinos herself, and confided it to her director—not in confession, observe. He consulted me, and we advised what took place; and what may console you still farther, we did the lady no wrong. We have reason to know that, besides the poison, some writing was conveyed to Molinos together with the casket, by which he obtained information which he was very desirous of receiving. You will forgive me now, since your 'amour propre' is not touched, and your friend's purpose is served."

There was a pause, after which the General said,—

"You have deserved well of the Order—few better; and whatever their enemies may say, the Companions of Jesus are not unmindful of their children, nor ungrateful, unless the highest necessities of the general good require it. You look upon the prosecution of Molinos as an act of intolerable tyranny, and you are yourself eager to enter upon a crusade on behalf of religious freedom and of the rights of private devotion and judgment. You are ready to engage almost single-handed against the whole strength of the Society of Jesus, of the Curia, and of the existing powers. I say nothing of the Quixotic nature of the enterprise; that would not deter you. Nor of its utter hopelessness; how hopeless you may judge from the sudden collapse of the party of Molinos—a party so favoured in high places, so fashionable, patronized, as has been said, even by the Pope himself. You may also judge of this from the fact, of which you are probably aware, that every detail of your late meeting was communicated to us by the President of that meeting, and by many of those who attended it. But in speaking of these matters to you, whose welfare I sincerely seek, I address myself to another argument which I imagine will have more weight. You have only considered this coveted spiritual freedom as the right of the favoured few, of the educated and refined. You have no desire and no intention that it should be extended to the populace. But you do not consider, as those who have the guidance of the Church polity are bound to consider, that to grant it to the one and deny it to the other is impossible; that these principles are sure to spread; that in England and in other countries where they have spread they have been the occasion of incalculable mischiefs. You are standing, at this moment, thanks chiefly to the nurture and clemency of the much-abused Society of Jesus, at a point where you may choose one of two roads, which, joining here, will never meet again. The question is between individual license and obedience to authority; and upon the choice, though you may not think it, depends the very existence of Christianity in the world. Between unquestioning obedience to authority and absolute unbelief there is not a single permanent resting-place, though many temporary halts may be made. You will scarcely dispute this when you remember that every heretical sect admits it. They only differ as to what the authority is to which obedience is due. We, in Rome at least, cannot be expected to allow any authority save that of the

Catholic Church, and indeed what other can you place instead of it—a Book? Do you think that those who have entered upon the path of inquiry will long submit to be fettered by the pages of dead languages? You know more of this probably than I do from your acquaintance with the sceptics of other lands."

He paused as if waiting for a reply, but Inglesant did not speak; perhaps the logic of the Jesuit seemed to him unanswerable—especially in the St Angelo at Rome.

After a few seconds the latter went on,—

"Ah! I fear you still bear me some malice. If so, I regret it very much. As I said before, you have no truer friend in Rome than the Order and its unworthy General. I am convinced, both by my own experience and by the reports of others, that you are an invaluable friend and agent of the Society in countries where men like you, gentlemen of honour, bold, unflinching, and of spotless name, are wanted at every turn,—men who have the confidence of both parties, of enemies as well as friends. But long ere this you will have seen that here in Rome we do things differently; here we strike openly and at once, and we require agents of a far lower type, not so much agents, indeed, as hammers ready to our hand. Your refined nature is altogether out of place. As a friend I recommend your return to England. Father St. Clare is there, and no doubt requires you, and I am very certain that the climate of Rome will not suit your health. You have passed some years very pleasantly in Italy, as I believe, in spite of your share in those great sorrows to which we all are heir; and though I am grieved to separate you from your friends, the noblest in Rome, yet it is better that you should be parted in this manner than by sharper and more sudden means. Every facility shall be given you for transferring your property to England, and I hope you will take with you no unpleasant recollections of this city, and of the poor Fathers of Jesus, who wish you well."

He pronounced these last words with so much feeling that Inglesant could only reply,—

"I have nothing to say of the Society but what is good. It has ever been most tender and parental to me. I shall go away with nothing but sadness and affection in my heart; with nothing but gratitude towards you, Father, with nothing but reverence towards this city—the Mother of the World."

CHAPTER XIX

For a long time nothing was found among the papers from which these memoirs have been compiled relative to Mr. Inglesant's life subsequent to his return to England; but at last the following imperfect letter was found, which is here given as containing all the information on the subject which at present is known to exist.

The date, with the first part of the letter, is torn off. The first perfect line is given. The spelling has been modernized throughout. The superscription is as follows:—

    Mr. Anthony Paschall,

    Physician,

    London,

    from his friend,

    Mr. Valentine Lee,

    Chirurgeon,

    Of Reading.

From a certain tone in parts of the letter it would seem that the writer was one of those who gave cause for the accusation of scepticism brought in those days against the medical profession generally.

that vine, laden with grapes worked in gold and precious stones, after the manner of Phrygian work, which, according to Josephus, Tacitus, and other writers, adorned the Temple at Jerusalem, and was seen of many when that Temple was destroyed; a manifest continuance of the old Eastern worship of Bacchus, so dear to the human fraility. As says the poet Anacreon, "Make me, good Vulcan, a deep bowl and carve on it neither Charles's wain, nor the sad Orion, but carve me out a vine with its swelling grapes, and Cupid, Bacchus, and Bathillus pressing them together." For it is a gallant philosophy, and the deepest wisdom, which, under the shadow of talismans and austere emblems, wears the colours of enjoyment and of life.

Methinks if the Puritans of the last age had known that the same word in Latin means both worship and the culture of polite life, they would not have condemned both themselves and us to so many years of shadowy gloom and of a morose antipathy to all delight. And though they will perchance retort upon me that the same word in the Greek meaneth both worship and bondage, yet I shall reply that it was a service of love and pleasure—a service in which all the beauties of earth were called upon to aid, and in which the Deity was best pleased by the happiness of His creatures, whose every faculty of delight had been fully husbanded and trained. In these last happy days, since his gracious Majesty's return, we have seen a restoration of a cheerful gaiety, and adorning of men's lives, when painting and poetry, and, beyond all, music, have smoothed the rough ways and softened the hard manners of men.

I came to Oxford, travelling in the Flying Coach with a Quaker who inveighed greatly against the iniquity of the age. At Oxford I saw more than I have space to tell you of; amongst others, Francis Tatton, who, you will recollect, left his religion since the King's return, and sheltered himself amongst the Jesuits. He was but lately come to Oxford, and lodged at Francis Alder's against the Fleur-de-lis. I dined with him there along with some others, and it being a Friday, they had a good fish dinner with white wine. Among the guests was one Father Lovel, a Jesuit. He has lived in Oxford many years to supply service for the Catholics, so bold and free are the Papists now.

I conversed with another of the guests, a physician, who after dinner took me to his house in Bear Lane, and showed me his study, in a pleasant room to the south, overlooking some of Christ Church gardens. Here he began to complain of the Royal Society, and the Virtuosi, and I soon saw that he was a follower of Dr. Gideon Harvey and Mr. Stubbes. "The country owes much," he said, "to such men as Burleigh, Walsingham, Jewel, Abbot, Usher, Casaubon; but if this new-fangled philosophy and mechanical education is to bear the bell, I foresee that we shall look in vain in England for such men again. In these deep and subtle inquiries into natural philosophy and the intricate mechanisms by which this world is said to be governed, neither physic will be unconcerned nor will religion remain unshaken amidst the writings of these Virtuosi. That art of reasoning by which the prudent are discriminated from fools, which methodizes and facilitates our discourse, which informs us of the validity of consequences and the probability of arguments—that art which gives life to solid eloquence, and which renders statesmen, divines, physicians, and lawyers accomplished—how is this cried down and vilified by the ignoramuses of these days!"

I pleased myself with inspecting this man's books, with which his study was well stored, and with the view from his window; but I let his tongue run on uncontradicted, seeing that he was of the old Protestant and scholastic learning, which is never open to let in new light. He entertained me, besides, with a long discourse to prove that Geber the chemist was not an Indian King, and informed me with great glee that the Royal Society, among other new-fangled propositions, had conceived the idea of working silk into hats, which project, though the hatters laughed at it, yet to satisfy them trial was made, and for twenty shillings they had a hat made, but it proved so bad that any one might have bought a better one for eighteenpence.

He was entering upon a long argument against Descartes, to refute whom he was obliged to contradict much that he had said before, but at this time I excused myself and left him.

When I came out from this man's house the college bells were going for Chapel, as they used to do in the old time; methought it was the prettiest music I had heard for many a day. I went to see an old man I remembered in Jesus Lane. I found him in the same little house, dressed in his gown tied round the middle, the sleeves pinned behind, and his dudgeon with a knife and bodkin; it was the fashion for grave people to wear such gowns in the latter end of Queen Elizabeth's days. He says he is 104. When I was a boy at Oxon I used to be always inquiring of him of the old time, the rood lofts, the ceremonies in the College Chapels; and his talk is still of Queen Bess her days, and of the old people who remembered the host and the wafer bread and the roods in the Churches. In my time, at Oxford, crucifixes were common in the glass in the study windows, and in the chamber windows pictures of saints. This was "before the wars." What a different world it was before the wars! What strange old-world customs and thoughts and stories vanished like phantoms when the war trumpets sounded, and great houses and proud names, and dominions and manors, and stately woods, crumbled into dust, and every man did as seemed good to himself, and thought as he liked.

On the Sunday I went to St. Mary's, and heard a preacher and herbalist, who spoke of the virtues of plants and of the Christian life in one breath. He told us that Homer writ sublimely and called them [Greek: cheires theon], the hands of the Gods, and that we ought to reach to them religiously with praise and thanksgiving. "God Almighty," he said, "hath furnished us with plants to cure us within a few miles of our own abodes, and we know it not."

The next day I came to Worcester by the post, to the house of my old friend Nathaniel Tomkins, who is now one of the Prebends and Receptor. He lives in the close, or college green, as they call it here. He comes of a family of musicians. His grandfather was chanter of the choir of Gloucester; his father organist to this same Cathedral of Worcester, and one of his uncles organist of St. Paul's and gentleman of the Chapel Royal, and another, of whom more anon, gentleman of the Privy Chamber to His Majesty Charles the First, and well skilled in the practical part of music, and was happily translated to the celestial choir of angels before the troubles.

I was pleased to see the faithful city recovered from the ashes in which she sat when I was here last, and the daily service of song again restored to the Cathedral Church, though the latter is much out of repair and dimmed as to its splendour. I like that religion the best which gives us sweet anthems and solemn organ music and lively parts of melody.

I had not been here long when my friend the Receptor told me that if I should stay two or three days longer, I should hear as good a concert of violins as any in England, and also hear a gentleman lately come from Italy, whose skill as a lutinist and player on the violin had preceded him. When I asked for the name of this gentleman, he told me it was that Mr. John Inglesant who was servant to the late King, and of whom so much was spoken in the time of the Irish Rebellion. When I heard this I resolved to stay, as you may suppose, considering that we have more than once spoken together of this person and desired to see him, especially since it had been reported that he was returned to England.

I therefore willingly promised to remain, and spent my time in practising on the violin, and in the city and cathedral. I walked upon the river bank, and up and down the fine broad streets leading from the bridge to the cathedral. From the gates of the chancel down the stone steps the strange light streamed on to the paved floor of the nave, chill and silent as the grave until the strains of the organs awoke. Mr. Tomkins told me that the loyal gentry of the surrounding counties had, during the usurpation, made it a point of honour to purchase and trade in Worcester, for the relief and encouragement of the citizens, who were reduced to so low an ebb by the battle and taking of the city.

Thursday was the day appointed for the music meeting, and on that day I accompanied Mr. Tomkins to the house of Mr. Barnabas Oley, another of the Prebends, who, you may remember, wrote a preface, a year or two ago, to Mr. Herbert's "Country Parson." He also lives in the College Green, and we found the company assembling in an oak parlour, which looked upon an orchard where the trees were in full blossom. There were present several of the clergy, and two or three physicians and other gentlemen, who practised upon the violin.

As we entered the room, Mr. Oley was speaking of Mr. Inglesant, who was expected to come presently with the Dean. "I remember him well," he was saying, "when I was in poverty and sequestration in the late troubles. He was supposed to be in all the King's secrets, and was constantly employed in private messages and errands. Some said that he was a concealed Papist, but I have known him to attend the Church service very devoutly. I recollect when I was in the garrison at Pontefract Castle, and used to preach there as long as it held out for His Majesty, that this Mr. Inglesant suddenly appeared amongst us, though the leaguer was very close, and I know he attended service there once or twice. I was often at that time in want of bread, during my hidings and wanderings, and obliged to change my habit, and did constantly appear in a cloak and grey clothes. On one of these occasions, when I was in great distress and was diligently and particularly sought for by the rebels, who would willingly have gratified those that would have discovered me, I fell in with this Mr. Inglesant at an inn in Buckinghamshire. He was then in company with one whom I knew to be a Popish priest, but they both exerted themselves very kindly in my behalf, and conducted me to the house of a Catholic gentleman in those parts by whom I was entertained several days. Before this, I now recollect, at the beginning of the wars, I met Mr. Inglesant at Oxford. I was in the shop of a bookseller named Forrest, against All Soul's College. I remember that I took up Plato's select dialogues 'De rebus divinis,' in Greek and Latin, and excepted against some things as superfluous and cabalistical, and that Mr. Inglesant, who was then a very young man, defended the author in a way that showed his scholarship. It was summer weather and very warm, and the enemy's cannon were playing upon the city as we could hear as we talked in the shop."

While Mr. Oley was thus recollecting his past troubles, Mr. Dean was announced, and entered the room accompanied by Mr. Inglesant and by a servant who carried their violins. You are, I know, acquainted with the Dean, who is also Bishop of St. David's, and who, they say, will be Bishop of Worcester also before long, so I need not describe him. The first sight of Mr. Inglesant pleased me very much. He wore his own hair long, after the fashion of the last age, but in other respects he was dressed in the mode, in a French suit of black satin, with cravat and ruffles of Mechlin lace. His expression was lofty and abstracted, his features pale and somewhat thin and his carriage gave me the idea of a man who had seen the world, and in whom few things were capable of exciting any extreme interest or attention. His eyes were light blue, of that peculiar shade which gives a dreamy and indifferent expression to the face. His manner was courteous and polite, almost to excess, yet he seemed to me to be a man who was habitually superior to his company, and I felt in his presence almost as I should do in that of a prince. Something of this doubtless was due to the sense I had of the part he had played in the great events of the late troubles, and of the nearness of intercourse and of the confidence he had enjoyed with his late Majesty of blessed memory. It was impossible not to look with interest upon a man who had been so familiar with the secret history of those times, and who had been taken into the confidence both of Papists and Churchmen.

When he had been introduced to the company, Mr. Oley reminded him of the incidents he had been relating before his arrival. When he mentioned the meeting in the inn in Buckinghamshire, Mr. Inglesant seemed affected.

"I remember it well," he said. "I was with Father St. Clare, whose deathbed I attended not two months after my return to England. Do you remember, Mr. Oley," he went on to say, "the sermons at St. Martin's in Oxford, where Mr. Giles Widdowes preached? I remember seeing you there, sir, and indeed his high and loyal sermons were much frequented by the royal party and soldiers of the garrison; and I have heard that he was most benevolent to many of the most needy in their distress. I remember that poor Whitford played the organs there often, before he was killed in the trenches."

"Ah," said Mr. Oley, "we have heard strange music in our day. I was in York when it was besieged by three very notable and great armies—the Scotch, the Northern under Lord Fairfax, and the Southern under the Earl of Manchester and Oliver. At that time the service at the Cathedral every Sunday morning was attended by more than a thousand ladies, knights, and gentlemen, besides soldiers and citizens; when the booming of cannon broke in upon the singing of the psalms, and more than once a cannon bullet burst into the Minster amongst the people, like a furious fiend or evil spirit, yet no one hurt."

After some talk of this nature we settled ourselves to our music and to tune our instruments. Mr. Inglesant's violin was inscribed "Jacobus Stainer in Absam prope Œnipontem 1647;" Œnipons is the Latin name of Inspruck in Germany, the chief city of the Tyrol, where this maker lived. As soon as

Mr. Inglesant drew his bow across the strings I was astonished at the full and piercing tone, which seemed to me to exceed even that of the Cremonas.

We played a concert or two, with a double bass part for the violone, which had a noble effect; and Mr. Inglesant being pressed to oblige the company, played a descant upon a ground bass in the Italian manner. I should fail were I to attempt to describe to you what I felt during the performance of this piece. It seemed to me as though thoughts, which I had long sought and seemed ever and anon on the point of realizing, were at last given me, as I listened to chords of plaintive sweetness broken now and again by cruel and bitter discords—a theme into which were wrought street and tavern music and people's songs, which lively airs and catches, upon the mere pressure of the string, trembled into pathetic and melancholy cadences. In these dying falls and closes all the several parts were gathered up and brought together, yet so that what before was joy was now translated into sorrow, and the sorrowful transfigured to peace, as indeed the many shifting scenes of life vary upon the stage of men's affairs.

The concert being over, Mr. Dean informed us that it was his intention to attend the afternoon service in the Cathedral, and Mr. Inglesant accompanying him, the physicians departed to visit their patients, and my host and some of the clergy and myself went to the Cathedral also, entering rather late.

After the service, in which was sung an anthem by Dr. Nathaniel Giles, Mr. Dean retired to the vestry, and Mr. Inglesant coming down the Church, I found myself close to him at the west door. We stopped opposite to the monument of Bishop Gauden, who is depicted in his effigy holding a book, presumably the "Icôn Basilikè" in his hand. I inquired of Mr. Inglesant what his opinions were concerning the authorship of that work, and finding that he was disposed to converse, we went down to the river side, the evening being remarkably fine, and, crossing by the ferry, walked for some time in the chapter meadows upon the farther bank. The evening sun was setting towards the range of the Malvern Hills, and the towers and spires of the city were shining in its glow, and were reflected in the water at our feet.

I said to Mr. Inglesant that I was greatly interested in the events of the last age, in which he had been so trusted and prominent an actor, and that I hoped to learn from him many interesting particulars, but he informed me that he knew but little except what the world was already possessed of. He said that he very deeply regretted that, during the last two years of the life of the late King, he himself was a close prisoner in the Tower;

and was therefore prevented from assisting in any way, or being useful to His Majesty. He said that there was something peculiarly affecting in the position of the King in those days, as he was isolated from his friends, and entirely dependant upon three or four faithful and subordinate servants. He said that, since his return to England, he had made it his business to seek out several of these, and had received much interesting information from them, which, as he hoped it would soon be made public, he was not at present at liberty to communicate. Mr. Inglesant, however, told me one incident relating to the last days of the King of so affecting a character that, as it is too long to be repeated here, I shall hope to inform you of when we meet together. He said, moreover, that the fatal mistake the King made was consenting to the death of Lord Strafford; that on many occasions he had yielded when he should have been firm; but that most of his misfortunes, such as reverses and indecisions in the field, were caused by circumstances entirely beyond his control. There is nothing new in these opinions, but I give them just as Mr. Inglesant stated them, lest you should think I had not taken advantage of the opportunity presented to me. It appeared to me that he was not very willing to discourse upon these bygone matters of State intrigue.

Seeing this I changed the topic, and said that as Mr. Inglesant had had much experience in the working of the Romish system, I should be glad to know his opinion of it, and whether he preferred it to that of the English Church. Here I found I was on different ground. I saw at once beneath the veil of polite manner, which was this man's second nature, that his whole life and being was in this question.

"This is the supreme quarrel of all," he said. "This is not a dispute between sects and kingdoms; it is a conflict within a man's own nature— nay, between the noblest parts of man's nature arrayed against each other. On the one side obedience and faith, on the other, freedom and the reason. What can come of such a conflict as this but throes and agony? I was not brought up by the Papists in England, nor, indeed, did I receive my book learning from them. I was trained for a special purpose by one of the Jesuits, but the course he took with me was different from that which he would have taken with other pupils whom he did not design for such work. I derived my training from various sources, and especially, instead of Aristotle, and the school-men, I was fed upon Plato. The difference is immense. I was trained to obedience and devotion; but the reason in my mind for this conduct was that obedience and devotion and gratitude were ideal virtues, not that they benefited the order to which I belonged, nor the world in which I lived. This take to be the difference between the Papists and myself. The Jesuits do not like Plato, as lately they do not like Lord Bacon. Aristotle, as interpreted by the school-men, is more to their mind. According to their reading of Aristotle, all his Ethics are subordinated to an end, and in such a system they see a weapon which they can turn to their own purpose of maintaining dogma, no matter at what sacrifice of the individual conscience or reason. This is what the Church of Rome has ever done. She has traded upon the highest instincts of humanity, upon its faith and love, its passionate remorse, its self-abnegation and denial, its imagination and yearning after the unseen. It has based its system upon the profoundest truths, and upon this platform it has raised a power which has, whether foreseen by its authors or not, played the part of human tyranny, greed, and cruelty. To support this system it has habitually set itself to suppress knowledge and freedom of thought, before thought had taught itself to grapple with religious subjects, because it foresaw that this would follow. It has, therefore, for the sake of preserving intact its dogma, risked the growth and welfare of humanity, and has, in the eyes of all except those who value this dogma above all other things, constituted itself the enemy of the human race. I have perhaps occupied a position which enables me to judge somewhat advantageously between the Churches, and my earnest advice is this. You will do wrong—mankind will do wrong—if it allows to drop out of existence, merely because the position on which it stands seems to be illogical, an agency by which the devotional instincts of human nature are enabled to exist side by side with the rational. The English Church, as established by the law of England, offers the supernatural to all who choose to come. It is like the Divine Being Himself, whose sun shines alike on the evil and on the good. Upon the altars of the Church the divine presence hovers as surely, to those who believe it, as it does upon the splendid altars of Rome. Thanks to circumstances which the founders of our Church did not contemplate, the way is open; it is barred by no confession, no human priest. Shall we throw this aside? It has been won for us by the death and torture of men like ourselves in bodily frame, infinitely superior to some of us in self-denial and endurance. God knows— those who know my life know too well—that I am not worthy to be named with such men; nevertheless, though we cannot endure as they did, at least do not let us needlessly throw away what they have won. It is not even a question of religious freedom only; it is a question of learning and culture in every form. I am not blind to the peculiar dangers that beset the English Church. I fear that its position, standing, as it does, a mean between two extremes, will engender indifference and sloth; and that its freedom will prevent its preserving a discipline and organizing power, without which any community will suffer grievous damage; nevertheless, as a Church it is unique: if suffered to drop out of existence, nothing like it can ever take its place."

"The Church of England," I said, seeing that Mr. Inglesant paused, "is no doubt a compromise, and is powerless to exert its discipline, as the events of the late troubles have shown. It speaks with bated assurance, while the Church of Rome never falters in its utterance, and I confess seems to me to have a logical position. If there be absolute truth revealed, there must be an inspired exponent of it, else from age to age it could not get itself revealed to mankind."

"This is the Papist argument," said Mr. Inglesant; "there is only one answer to it—Absolute truth is not revealed. There were certain dangers which Christianity could not, as it would seem, escape. As it brought down the sublimest teaching of Platonism to the humblest understanding, so it was compelled, by this very action, to reduce spiritual and abstract truth to hard and inadequate dogma. As it inculcated a sublime indifference to the things of this life, and a steadfast gaze upon the future; so, by this very means, it encouraged the growth of a wild unreasoning superstition. It is easy to draw pictures of martyrs suffering the torture unmoved in the face of a glorious hereafter; but we must acknowledge, unless we choose to call these men absolute fiends, that it was these selfsame ideas of the future, and its relation to this life, that actuated their tormentors. If these things are true,—if the future of mankind is parcelled out between happiness and eternal torture,—then, to ensure the safety of mankind at large, the death and torment for a few moments of comparatively few need excite but little regret. From the instant that the founder of Christianity left the earth, perhaps even before, this ghastly spectre of superstition ranged itself side by side with the advancing faith. It is confined to no Church or sect; it exists in all. Faith in the noble, the unseen, the unselfish, by its very nature encourages this fatal growth; and it is nourished even by those who have sufficient strength to live above it; because, forsooth, its removal may be dangerous to the well-being of society at large, as though anything could be more fatal than falsehood against the Divine Truth."

"But if absolute truth is not revealed," I said, "how can we know the truth at all?"

"We cannot say how we know it," replied Mr. Inglesant, "but this very ignorance proves that we can know. We are the creatures of this ignorance gainst which we rebel. From the earliest dawn of existence we have known nothing. How then could we question for a moment? What thought should we have other than this ignorance which we had imbibed from our growth, but for the existence of some divine principle, 'Fons veri lucidus' within us? The Founder of Christianity said, 'The kingdom of God is within you.' We may not only know the truth, but we may live even in this life in the very household and court of God. We are the creatures of birth, of ancestry, of circumstance; we are surrounded by law, physical and psychical, and the physical very often dominates and rules the soul. As the chemist, the navigator, the naturalist, attain their ends by means of law, which is beyond their power to alter, which they cannot change, but with which they can work in harmony, and by so doing produce definite results, so may we. We find ourselves immersed in physical and psychical laws, in accordance with which we act, or from which we diverge. Whether we are free to act or not we can at least fancy that we resolve. Let us cheat ourselves, if it be a cheat, with this fancy, for we shall find that by so doing we actually attain the end we seek. Virtue, truth, love, are not mere names; they stand for actual qualities which are well known and recognized among men. These qualities are the elements of an ideal life, of that absolute and perfect life of which our highest culture can catch but a glimpse. As Mr. Hobbes has traced the individual man up to the perfect state, or Civitas, let us work still lower, and trace the individual man from small origins to the position he at present fills. We shall find that he has attained any position of vantage he may occupy by following the laws which our instinct and conscience tell us are Divine. Terror and superstition are the invariable enemies of culture and progress. They are used as rods and bogies to frighten the ignorant and the base, but they depress all mankind to the same level of abject slavery. The ways are dark and foul, and the grey years bring a mysterious future which we cannot see. We are like children, or men in a tennis court, and before our conquest is half won the dim twilight comes and stops the game; nevertheless, let us keep our places, and above all things hold fast by the law of life we feel within. This was the method which Christ followed, and He won the world by placing Himself in harmony with that law of gradual development which the Divine Wisdom has planned. Let us follow in His steps and we shall attain to the ideal life; and, without waiting for our 'mortal passage,' tread the free and spacious streets of that Jerusalem which is above."

He spoke more to himself than to me. The sun, which was just setting behind the distant hills, shone with dazzling splendour for a moment upon the towers and spires of the city across the placid water. Behind this fair vision were dark rain clouds, before which gloomy background it stood in fairy radiance and light. For a moment it seemed a glorious city, bathed in life and hope, full of happy people who thronged its streets and bridge, and the margin of its gentle stream. But it was "breve gaudium." Then the sunset faded, and the ethereal vision vanished, and the landscape lay dark and chill.

"The sun is set," Mr. Inglesant said cheerfully, "but it will rise again. Let us go home."

I have writ much more largely in this letter than I intended, but I have been led onward by the interest which I deny not I feel in this man. When we meet I will tell you more.

Your ever true friend,

VALENTINE LEE.